THE NOAH OPTION

MICHAEL MCCARTHY

30 CUBITS PRESS

The Noah Option
Copyright 2009 by Michael McCarthy

ISBN-13: 978-0-615-48659-8
ISBN-10: 0615486592

30 CUBITS PRESS

www.TheNoahOption.com

To purchase additional copies, and to learn about upcoming books, go to:
www.TheNoahOption.com
Or email info@TheNoahOption.com

Cover design by Kathy Peterson / Advertising PLUS. adplus@mac.com

THE NOAH OPTION

"Dr. Washington, I have a warrant for your arrest and a message for you." He flashed an FBI badge in one hand and handed her a cell phone with the other.

Speechless, she put the phone to her ear. "Dr. Washington, you will now regret that you released your so-called super-seeds to feed the people of the third world . . ."

Seeds that can end world hunger . . . An extremist group and their government cronies try to destroy the new super-seeds. Brilliant and beautiful botanist Dr. Grace Washington struggles to get the seeds into the hands of hard-working farmers in the third world.

An agonizing decision . . . When Grace is arrested on false charges, she faces an impossible choice: go to jail or destroy her life's work, the seeds that could save millions of lives.

An economic tsunami of political corruption and control engulfs the entire nation, choking the daily lives and livelihoods of friends in her small home town. Grace and her ally, software genius Isaiah Mercury, realize they have to do something drastic, something their opponents don't expect, something radical . . .

They begin a countdown to a daring plan . . . *The Noah Option*

Reach for the stars. Although you will never touch them, you may get a
little stardust on your hands.

Norman Borlaug 1914 – 2009
Father of the Green Revolution in Africa, India, and Asia.

For Norman Borlaug and all inventors and entrepreneurs who help
mankind by offering the fruits of their minds.
Let us learn to emulate them, not envy and punish them.
When we do, our reward will be so much
prosperity that we can scarce hold it all.

Michael McCarthy
May 2011

 **Chapter One**

Time: The Near Future

With AK-47 rifles slung over their shoulders, two young drivers dressed in military camouflage put their farm tractors in gear. They dragged a heavy chain between them like a scythe through the maize stalks, destroying the livelihood of a farmer they had never met.

Bending as a field of wheat bends before the wind, the healthy maize stalks bowed down and snapped under the weight of the chain. A swath of stubble emerged in the wake of the two tractors. Birds began to hover and dive for the exposed ears of corn, like seagulls following a fishing trawler dragging nets full of fish.

Sweat trickled down their faces from under their hats, baking in the strong mid-day sun of Botswana. Nearby, two more uniformed teenagers armed with AK-47s sat in the back of a lorry, practicing their frowns of intimidation. The white driver and a taller black man stepped out of the cab. Like the young mercenaries, they were also in camouflage.

The white man gestured toward the two young soldiers and turned to his companion. "Tell them to stop anyone who tries to stop us." The tall man translated this into Tswana for the two recruits. They nodded and fingered the triggers of their automatic weapons.

The white man looked at the growing swath of maize stubble and nodded in satisfaction. "These new strains of maize must be destroyed." He scratched his armpit.

His companion grunted, "As you say. My men expect to be paid in cash and ammunition." He looked at the tractors destroying the crops, then added, "And food."

*   *   *   *   *   *

Three miles away, the same fierce Botswanan sun beat down on Mantate Kubabupe as he tilled his field. He patiently and rhythmically chopped at weeds with his hoe. At the edge of his field, a secretary bird peered at him from her perch in a marula tree. The leaves were just beginning to turn yellow as they did every fall in this dry land. Mantate paused and leaned on the handle of his hoe. He looked around at his crop of maize and smiled. He would do well this year. More than enough to feed his family and much left over to sell.

"Papa!" He turned to see his eight-year-old son Moroka running down the row of maize toward him. Moroka carried a small water bottle in his hand.

"Moroka, my son. What is it?" The boy stopped, panting with the effort of his run.

"Papa, a woman from America is here with Mr. Phewai the seed man. Here is water for you, my father." Mantate looked into his son's eager face as he took the water bottle. His son's eyes shone with excitement. A visitor from America! This was indeed an unusual day. He raised the bottle to his lips and and let the cool water wash the dust from his throat. It was good.

As he tilted his head back down, he could see a trail of dust rising at the edge of his field. That would be William Phewai's truck. "Moroka, let us go and meet our visitor from America." He put his hand on his son's shoulder, and they began walking toward the marula tree, where the truck now came to a halt. The secretary bird flew away, lazily flapping its wings. A man emerged from the driver's door, and a tall black woman in Western clothing got out on the passenger side.

"Dumela [hello], Mantate Kubabupe. May I introduce Doctor Grace Washington, a botanist from the great Tuskegee University in America?" Mr. Phewai spoke and gestured toward the tall woman in khaki pants and blouse. Her clothing fit trimly, revealing a slim athletic figure.

She extended her hand, and Mantate shook it. He said gravely, "Dumela. I am pleased to meet a visitor who has traveled far."

She smiled at him, revealing dazzling white teeth. "Dumela. I am pleased to meet you as well. And who might this handsome gentleman be?" she asked, extending her hand to Moroka. The boy looked down shyly, rubbing his big toe in the dust.

"This is my son, Moroka. Shake her hand, Moroka." The boy looked up and extended his hand tentatively. Grace Washington gravely shook the proffered hand, then smiled again, revealing a dimple. Moroka's smile deepened into a dimple of his own. She laughed. Moroka laughed. Mantate and Mr. Phewai threw their heads back and laughed deep belly laughs that boomed across the clearing.

"I am pleased to meet you, Moroka. In America, we always ask the children, where do you go to school?"

2

Moroka spoke up eagerly, "My mother is teaching me to read, and Papa says that if our crops do well I may go to the school in the town. I have read three books already."

Grace replied, "Three books. You've done well. I will send you another book when I return home."

Moroka took her hand excitedly with both his hands, "What book? What book will you send?"

Looking at his shining eyes, Grace remembered when she was a small girl and was as eager about reading and learning new things. As a child, Grace loved to walk in the woods and in gardens, examining leaves and flowers. After reading a book about how the famous botanist George Washington Carver loved to walk and collect plant specimens, she began her own collection of leaves, flowers, and stems. He became her hero and role model. She still loved to take hikes, collect samples, and sketch plant life as Carver had done.

Grace said, "It is a book about one of my heroes, George Washington Carver. He was a famous botanist in America, and he developed better ways to grow food crops. Like you, he was eager to learn to read, and studied and worked hard. His work helped many farmers. Maybe when you are older, you will come to study at the Tuskegee University, where he taught and researched crops, and where I now teach and research. You could learn to help many good farmers like your father."

Mantate looked at his son proudly. "My son, let your elders talk business now."

Grace looked at Mantate with a smile. "Mr. Kubabupe, as a favor to me, will you allow him to stay with us? Young ones can learn by listening to their elders. My hero George Washington Carver often took his students for walks through farm fields. He said 'A large part of a child's education must be gotten outside of the four walls designated as a classroom.'"

Mantate looked down at Moroka, "Moroka, you may stay, if you will be silent and listen. You may indeed learn something."

Grace looked at the field of maize appraisingly. "Mr. Kubabupe, I developed the strain of maize seeds that you planted here. Mr. Phewai's employer, Nutritional Abundance Industries, paid me to do the research for this high yield strain. May we walk your field with you and ask some questions?"

3

Mantate nodded, "Of course."

They walked between stalks of maize. Grace stopped and felt a cob of maize, then asked, "When did you plant this maize?"

Mantate replied, "About eight weeks ago. See how it is nearly ripe already. I have used only one-tenth the irrigation water, as instructed by Mr. Phewai. This is a blessing, as using the foot pedal pump is hard work for me. Moroka is too small to operate it just yet."

Mr. Phewai looked closely at several stalks. "It seems that you are getting more cobs of maize on each stalk. Last year with the other seeds we got less. This looks to be nearly a fourfold increase!"

"Yes," agreed Mantate, "I will have extra maize to sell. There are markets for maize in Kenya, I hear, that will pay a good price. I don't know how to contact those Kenyan markets, but I hope to make enough money to pay for Moroka to attend the school in the town. He is a smart boy." Here he looked down at Moroka and smiled. Moroka proudly grinned back.

Grace Washington squatted at the base of a stalk and fingered the soil. "Tell me about the fertilizer you use?"

"The same fertilizer as last year," explained Mantate, "but only a tenth as much, again, as instructed by Mr. Phewai. Again, a blessing, since I did not have to spend as much money on fertilizer this year." He smiled at his small son, "I bought a book for Moroka. He read it to me in the evenings."

Grace looked at the man and his small son standing alert and full of curiosity. She thought, *Dear Lord, what industriousness and initiative and promise! Thank You for your blessings on this family.*

She said, "I am happy, Mr. Mantate Kubabupe, that my seeds have grown well for you and are a blessing for your family. I am happy, Mr. Moroka Kubabupe, that you have read a book to your father. You are a blessing to your family." She turned to Mr. Phewai, "And you, Mr. Phewai, have done well in instructing this region's farmers how to use the new seed. You are a blessing to this region." Mr. Phewai gave her a small bow of his head in acknowledgement.

"Thank you, Mr. Kubabupe, and Moroka, for showing us your maize crop. We will go now," said Grace.

Mantate raised his hand in farewell, "*Tsamaya sentle* — Go well."

When Grace and William Phewai began driving back to his office in the town of Maun, they discussed what they had seen on their field visits.

"Dr. Washington, you and I have visited six farmers in two days. I tell you, all of the farmers in this region report the same good results that you heard today from Mantate Kubabupe. I believe you can call your new seed strains a success. Those farmers will prosper this year."

Just then they heard the distinctive *bratatatat* of automatic weapons fire in the distance. William pulled over and turned off the engine. They both climbed onto the bed of his truck in order to see farther over the fields.

They saw smoke rising about a mile away, in the direction of the next farm. Then they heard more gunfire. Grace's knuckles turned white as she tightened her grip on the roll bar. She felt fear stab through her.

Controlling her breathing, Grace said, "There is trouble. We should help. Are you willing?"

William nodded, and they got back into the cab of the truck. They drove on. Grace unconsciously reached up and began twisting a strand of her hair. When they pulled up at the farmstead, the farmhouse and storage sheds were on fire. The farmer and his wife lay on the ground, bleeding.

"I'll get the first aid kit," said William. Grace knelt beside the woman. She was bleeding from two bullet wounds in her chest. Grace tore a strip from the woman's dress and pressed it hard against the wounds, trying to stop the bleeding. William rose from the man and looked at Grace, shaking his head. He took gauze from the first aid box and gave it to Grace. She replaced the strips of cloth from the dress.

"Who did this to you?" asked Grace softly.

The woman coughed up blood and said, "Young men dressed like soldiers with tractors and chains were pulling down our maize stalks. Without our crops, we will starve!" She coughed again, and Phewai gave her a sip of water from a bottle.

"My husband and I tried to stop them. The young men shot us and set our home on fire. Why do they do this to us? We till our fields and mind our own business. Why?" The woman's eyes looked imploringly at Grace. Then the young body sagged under Grace's hands, and the head lolled sideways.

William felt her neck for a pulse. "She's gone," he murmured.

Grace gently closed the woman's eyes and whispered a prayer, "Lord, welcome this good woman and her husband home to you." She stood up and looked at the field of stubble where the chains had passed. She could see dust and birds hovering on the horizon.

"William, the direction they've taken leads towards Mantate Kubabupe's farm. Let's go." They drove back at breakneck speed, scattering dust and gravel. William said, "That was Winnie and Felix Reentse. I knew them well. They were good people. Hard working farmers. This killing makes no sense."

Grace saw a puff of diesel exhaust smoke in the maize field ahead. "Stop. There they are." She pointed to a trail of dust and circling birds.

William Phewai looked. "How can we stop them?" he asked.

Grace thought for a moment. "Look over there. There's a truck with a trailer. That's how they transported the tractors out here. Let's sneak up to it and see what they're doing. Have you had any military training?"

William nodded, "I served in the army. I can disarm someone if we can get close enough. And you?"

"Tae-kwon-do and self defense." They took cord and a roll of duct tape from the truck, then made their way slowly and quietly between the stalks of maize, listening for movement. They heard voices. Slowly they inched forward.

The two teenage mercenaries had put down their Kalashnikov rifles and were faced away from them, urinating. Softly, Grace and William advanced and took the rifles. With the butt ends of the rifles, they struck behind the boys' knees. Both boys fell to the ground. William spoke in Tswana, "Keep silent, put your hands behind you, and you will not be harmed." He tied their wrists and taped their mouths while Grace covered them with one of the confiscated AK-47s. "Now, walk back to your truck. Be silent," William commanded.

As they walked toward the truck, the taller mercenary saw them, bared his teeth in a snarl and swung his rifle up. William fired from the hip, instinctively. The mercenary went down. William ran forward and kicked the rifle away. A white man came around the truck from the other side, "What the . . . ?!" William covered him with the rifle. "I'm unarmed!" shouted the white man, raising his hands.

"Help these two into the truck," said William. The white man helped the teenagers up, and all three sat on the bed of the truck. William covered them while Grace examined the wounded mercenary.

She tore off strips of his shirt and bound his wounds. "They are flesh wounds. He's unconscious, but he'll live. You!" she said to the white man. "Help me lift him into the truck." Together they lifted the limp man into the back of the truck. Suddenly the white man grabbed Grace and held her in front of him as a shield from William's rifle.

Grace raised her right foot and stomped down on the man's instep with her boot. When he flinched, she shot her left elbow into his rib cage, twisted around in his locked arms to face him and gouged out his left eyeball with her thumb. He screamed and released her, clutching at his face. She took two steps away, pivoted, and shot out a side kick to his kneecap. He crumpled to his knees. Grace quickly stepped behind him and applied a choke hold until he lost consciousness. As he slumped, she pulled him onto his back. Retrieving her rifle, she smashed the butt on his right arm, breaking it. Then she knelt down and popped the eyeball back into place.

"This one will live too, but he won't be grabbing me again with a broken arm and a dislocated kneecap," she drily observed.

She and William lifted and swung him onto the truck bed beside the other wounded mercenary. Then they unhitched the trailer and drove the truck toward Mantate Kubabupe's farmhouse.

When they drove up, Moroka ran to the truck. "Mr. Phewai! Help us! My father has gone to stop the men with the tractors, but they have guns!"

Grace looked over at William. "William, I'm a good shot. My father took me deer hunting with him. Those men will feel less threatened by a woman and may hold their fire when I approach. Let me go, while you guard these others."

William smiled at her, "And if they lay a hand on you, they lose their kneecaps! He chuckled. "Agreed. Be careful, my friend."

Moroka led Grace in the direction his father had gone. They heard shots and began to run. They saw Mantate ahead, holding a harvesting scythe and hiding behind the marula tree. The boy drivers were standing on the tractors in the adjacent field and firing their AK-47s at the tree. Grace reached out and grabbed Moroka and crouched down in the maize.

"Moroka," she whispered, "keep quiet and stay down. They must not know we're here." She took a kneeling position and aimed carefully. Her first burst shredded a tractor tire and ricocheted off the metal fender. The thirteen-year-old soldier was startled and dropped his rifle. He had never been under fire before. He jumped down and ran away. Her second burst hit the other tractor's fuel tank. It burst into flame. The driver screamed and dropped his rifle too. Then he jumped and fled.

Mantate ran out and confiscated the rifle left behind by the first driver. He turned toward the burning tractor just as the heat caused the ammo from the second rifle to begin popping off. He retreated behind the marula tree, where Grace and Moroka joined him.

"Are you all right?" Grace asked.

"Yes," said Mantate. He hugged Moroka. "Let us go back to your mother."

"Yes, my father."

As the three of them walked up, Mrs. Kubabupe ran out of the house to hug her son and husband. "You are safe, thanks be to God!"

William gestured to the back of the truck where the white man was now conscious. "This one is British. Claims to be acting on behalf of mother earth. Wants to destroy all hybridized or genetically modified crops. Claims they are unnatural."

Grace looked at him and said, "These crops can end the food shortage in Africa."

He snarled, "These crops are unnatural. We won't allow them!"

"Who is we?" asked Grace.

The man looked down sullenly. "I'm not saying. These crops are forbidden!"

Grace looked at his paunchy stomach. "Easy for you to say. You seem to be eating enough for three people. By the way, who made you ruler of Africa?"

Grace covered the prisoners with her AK-47 while William called the authorities on his cell phone. "The constable will be here with reinforcements in an hour. These men will face jail time for their murders and destruction."

The white man snapped, "We haven't murdered anyone! That's a lie!"

William fixed him with a harsh stare. "Two good people, Winnie and Felix Reentse, were shot and killed by your tractor drivers. That makes you an accomplice to murder. When you hired thirteen-year-olds and gave them AK-47s, what did you think would happen?" William started to turn away, then paused. "Just one more thing. Winnie and

8

Felix were not using hybrid seeds on their farm. You destroyed the wrong crop and murdered the wrong people."

*   *   *   *   *   *

From a ridgeline overlooking the Kubabupe farmhouse, a short squat man in a floppy hat watched Grace and her companions through powerful binoculars. He put down the binoculars and turned to reach into his Land-Rover. When he did, the sunshine revealed his broken nose and the scars on his knuckles.

He straightened up, holding a satellite phone. Dialing a Chicago area code, he waited for the uplink to make the connection.

"Director? Our operatives were arrested before they could finish the job."

The voice replied with the crackle of static on the satellite link.

"Unfortunate. Well, get more mercenaries and finish the job."

"Director, our men killed some people, a farmer and his wife. We'll have to lay low for a while."

"Did they know who financed them? Can we be linked to them?"

The man snorted, "No, of course not. I didn't get in this business yesterday. I used a cut-out as a go between. All arrangements were by phone and cash. Nobody met anybody. Nobody can identify anybody, and nobody has links to anybody."

"Good. Well, a few lives are necessary casualties for the greater good. The earth must be restored to its pristine condition. Keep me informed."

*   *   *   *   *   *

Later that afternoon in William's office in the town of Maun, he and Grace were on speakerphone to his employer, Minerva Stone, President of Nutritional Abundance Industries.

"I'm just grateful that you both are safe. How dreadful that two innocent people were killed by these eco-terrorists. Are the other farmers in our test program at risk? Should we cancel the hybrid trials?"

William spoke up, "Ms. Stone, Constable Motalaete told me that this British subject will be in jail here for the next twelve or more years. His associates are known to Interpol, and our Customs and Immigration

Authorities are alerted to stop them at the borders. The mercenary was from Angola, although he hired local boys to do the dirty work. He will also be in jail a long time. These outsiders are easy to spot, and we will tell all villagers and farmers to be on the lookout for them. I have spoken to five of the farmers in our test program, and they wish to continue. They are not afraid. I'll speak to the others tomorrow."

He sat up straighter. "All sixteen farmers in our hybrid seed test report a fourfold increase in crop yield. They expect to feed their families and sell their surpluses to buy things to help their families." William turned and looked at Grace Washington, "Like one small boy who will go to school this fall. These seeds are helping to feed hungry people and lift small farmers out of poverty. This is a good thing for our country, and no foreign eco-terrorists will dictate their wishes to us."

"Mr. Phewai, with that vote of confidence, we shall continue," said Minerva. "Any idea who's behind this?"

William spoke slowly, "The British man would not tell what group financed this operation, but they overlooked one link. Constable Motalaete told me they searched the British man's hotel room. They found his plane ticket and traced payment for it to an organization in America called the Pristine Influence on Society Foundation. Ever heard of them?"

"Oh, yes. We've run into their staged protests and lawsuits before. But never violence like this. They are a radical environmental activist group that claims we upset the ecological balance of the planet by feeding more people."

William grunted. "They claim the right to tell the people of Botswana who we may or may not feed? And what seeds we may or may not use? They are arrogant, these people. They should take care of their own land and leave us alone."

"Yes, they are arrogant, Mr. Phewai," Minerva continued. "They have many ties to our government, so they have protections and power that the rest of us do not have. They have persuaded my government to tell other governments to outlaw these seeds."

"I thought the US economy was in trouble? They have plenty of work to do at home. Yet your government still has time to reach across the sea and try to control what farmers do in other lands? More arrogance from busybodies with too much power."

10

He reached up and removed a book from a shelf over his desk. He began thumbing through the pages. "I'm reminded of a line from this novel about Botswana, *The No. 1 Ladies' Detective Agency.* In it, the father reflects on his long life, and describes government under the British Protectorate."

He stopped at a page. "Here it is: 'So for many years, nothing at all happened. It was a good system of government, because most people want nothing to happen. That is the problem with governments these days. They want to do things all the time; they are always very busy thinking of what things they can do next. That is not what people want. People want to be left alone to look after their cattle.' I have heard many people in Botswana say the same thing."

Minerva laughed and replied, "I agree. Would that people in my country were so wise! Grace, we will prepare a press release on this attack. Any comment from you, as our star scientist and Nobel Prize winning botanist?"

Grace's face was drawn from the stress and fatigue. "This is probably futile, but how about quoting that BBC article by their science and environment reporter James Morgan in October of 2008. You could post it on your web site, too, Minerva. Remember the one?"

"Yes," said Minerva, "I just Googled it. October 8, 2008, on the BBC news web site. **'Seeking Africa's green revolution'** is the headline. The best part is the quote from Norman Borlaug. Let me read it to you."

"Yes, please," said Grace, "I need to hear some sanity right now."

Minerva read from the web site article:

BBC science and environment reporter James Morgan has gone into the field to meet the families who are sowing the seeds of what is being hailed as "a uniquely African green revolution."

"If [environmentalists] lived for just one month among the misery of the developing world, as I have for 50 years, they'd be crying out for tractors and fertiliser and irrigation canals."

So said Norman Borlaug, one of the founding fathers of the original Green Revolution - credited with wiping out starvation in Asia.

11

But can technology really be the saviour of Africa's struggling farmers? It has become a terribly unfashionable opinion in the UK, where "green" campaigners are no longer content to denounce GM* [*Genetically Modified] *crop trials. They simply rip them up.*

"Responsible biotechnology is not the enemy," said Borlaug. "Starvation is."

Grace sighed into the phone, "Amen, sister, amen." She remembered her first trip to Africa, when she had seen plenty of bulging bellies on starving children, not to mention the adults. Starvation was indeed the enemy. She knew her enhanced seeds would win the fight against that ancient enemy, if only these eco-crazies would let them.

Minerva could hear the discouragement in Grace's voice and spoke up, "Fight the good fight, girlfriend. They stage protests and destroy food crops; we fill empty bellies. You and I can hold our heads up when we stand before our Maker."

Grace lifted her chin, her voice suddenly stronger, "Amen, sister, amen."

 **Chapter Two**

The CBC Evening News with Kathy Coeur-Saignant: "Tonight, public fear and outrage over the so-called "Franken-fruit" surfaced at the American Sociological Society for Ethical Science in Society (ASSESS) conference in Philadelphia. For the story, we go to our Philadelphia correspondent, Abby Trammel. Abby?"

"Kathy, several spokespersons for ASSESS have expressed concern about the privately funded research being conducted by Dr. Grace Washington at Tuskegee University in Alabama. Dr. Washington traces her family heritage back to Booker T. Washington, founder of the original Tuskegee Institute and advocate of self-improvement for African Americans. Some say her achievements rival that of George Washington Carver, the famous scientist and botanist. She won the Nobel Prize two years ago for her groundbreaking research in plant genetics. She is researching genetic improvements for vegetables, grains, and fruit trees that would improve their resistance to insects and blight, thereby reducing the use of pesticides and other chemicals by farmers. Critics, however, call such genetically engineered crop seeds 'Franken-fruit' and vigorously oppose it.

"Dr. Aaron Smith, this year's President of ASSESS and author of the widely used middle school textbook *Science and Society, Threats and Concerns*, has issued a press release on behalf of the society that charges *'grave dangers to the sustainability of our world if Dr. Washington's research is ever released for use by farmers anywhere in the world. She claims that her genetically altered crops will yield four times more food on just one-tenth of the land and with only one-tenth of the water currently used for irrigating similar crops. While this sounds attractive, the consensus of ethical sociologists around the world is that this will lower the infant mortality rate in sub-Saharan Africa, and the increased food supply will increase life spans on the rest of the globe. Our planet simply cannot sustain more people. We need fewer people on the planet, not more. This research is irresponsible and is a threat to the ecology of the planet. It must be outlawed.*

"We could not reach Dr. Washington for comment before our deadline for videotaping this segment, and so there is no response to these serious charges at this time. Kathy?"

"Thanks, Abby. That certainly is cause for concern for Americans and their fellow citizens of the planet. I wonder if other nations will allow it. Next up, some greedy private businessmen claim that the high wages they pay their workers above the union pay scale is nobody's business but theirs. Stay tuned."

Dr. Grace Washington turned off the small TV in her office with a curse. "So, they ignored my press release response that I e-mailed to Ms. Trammel two days ago! Pretended that they could not reach me for comment when my office phone number was on the press release, is in the phone book, and posted on the university's web site. What dishonesty! Intellectual dishonesty in not examining the data, and journalistic dishonesty in not reporting the other side of the story. How can anyone say this is not sustainable if you can produce more food with fewer resources? You can't win with these propagandists!" She sat at her desk absently twisting a lock of her hair.

Sitting across the desk from her was a handsome man with a clipped moustache and salt and pepper hair, close-cropped, military style. His conservative grey pinstriped suit showed an understated good taste and a style that proclaimed, "I have nothing to prove to anyone." He leaned back and took another sip of his scotch before replying.

"Grace, you should be used to it by now. When your last strain of improved maize reduced child malnutrition in Africa by nearly sixty percent, did they give you credit then? No. These so-called humanitarians could not find any positive words for your achievement. Who do you think you are, to go and achieve what the US, the UN, and the EU could not? Colossal conceit!" He snorted sarcastically.

"Well, they put you and Nutritional Abundance Industries in your place. The United Nations and the Associated African States slapped a forty percent tariff on your seed corn. That showed you! The African farmers couldn't afford it then, and the next year the infant mortality rate went back up. More dead babies. That'll teach you to feed hungry children without government permission."

His mouth was set in a tight line on his mahogany face. Dr. George T'Chaka Wright was the President of Tuskegee University. He supported solid research and teaching backed by data instead of political correctness. He supported faculty scientists like Grace who produced tangible research results and set a serious example of hard work and achievement for the students. He did not suffer fools gladly. Like his

14

namesake, the great Zulu chieftain and warrior T'Chaka (sometimes spelled Shaka in the history books), he was fearless and innovative.

"Now George, you know that sarcasm doesn't become you," Grace replied lightly.

"Well, you sound like you're ready to let it go already," George replied.

"I just needed to sound off. If you focus on those rectums, it leads you into an agenda of revenge, or worse, thinking that you can actually convince them of the merits of your case based on data. That's a real black hole for your energy, with no return on the investment of your time whatsoever. So, I've learned to let it go. *After*, of course, one good outburst, which is good for my mental health."

"Well! You are being big about this. You yourself were threatened by those Green mercenaries who were willing to kill innocent African farmers to enforce their agenda."

"Yes. And they're now facing hard time in an African jail. Done."

With that, she gestured to his glass, "Ready for a refill?"

"No thanks. One's my limit. Just enough to take the edge off my outrage about this foolishness on TV. Actually, this is a notch above your everyday foolishness. This is *durned* foolishness, and that's the worst kind."

"I wish I had a nickel for every time you've said that," she smiled sadly.

"The fault, dear Horatio, is not in the stars, but in ourselves. Or, more accurately, *themselves*. With apologies to Hamlet and Master Shakespeare."

"That's one of the things I like about you. A good scientist who can also quote Shakespeare." Her smile went from sad to bright.

Dr. Wright had a string of research publications as long as his arm, plus assorted patents on his discoveries in biotechnology. Several of his patents helped support the university budget in a big way.

He continued, "Nowadays, I think, *Who owns my mind? And the fruits thereof?* These sociologists act like all scientific work belongs to them, and that they can decide what to do with it, even when they didn't perform or pay for the research. Anybody who thinks he can just take the fruit of my mental labor is worse than a slave owner. At least slave owners could only take the fruits of the physical labor of our ancestors. These guys think they can control the fruits of my mind too. Well, let

15

them try it. I'll just 'dummy up' and do exactly what I'm told to do. No mind, no fruit. They can force the body, but not the mind."

"Amen, brother!" She rose from her desk and reached for his glass. She was a tall, graceful woman. Her clothes draped well on her trim frame. She placed the glass on a tray.

"Say, George, why don't you and Estelle come to my house for supper tonight? Isaiah Mercury is back in town with a beta copy of his latest software for researchers. Should be interesting to hear what digital magic he's cooked up this time around." Her eyes twinkled.

"Oh, I don't know . . ." Dr. Wright began.

"Isaiah promised to barbecue some ribs."

"Sold! Estelle loves that man's barbeque, and so do I. See you at seven?"

"Seven it is. You'll smell the mesquite smoke when you drive up."

*   *   *   *   *   *

Isaiah Mercury gracefully and efficiently turned ribs over in the big Weber grill on Grace Washington's patio. Dipping his basting brush into a bowl, he painted each rib lovingly with a coating of his secret sauce. Like his software code, no one had yet winkled out of him the secret recipe for his "Mercury's Barbecue Sauce." He had won a regional barbecue cook-off in Memphis, and was contemplating licensing the sauce for his favorite charity, his alma mater Tuskegee University.

Isaiah Mercury was a tall man with big hands - most would say a basketball player's hands, although he had never played professionally. In his sophomore year he led the Tuskegee University varsity to the Southern Intercollegiate Athletic Conference championship. Like his namesake, Mercury, the winged messenger of the gods, he was quick on the court. Deceptively quick for a big man. He still had the slimness and muscles of an athlete.

While he had been quick on the court, he was even quicker with computer code. He turned down an NBA draft offer from the Cavaliers, choosing instead to start a doctorate in computer science at Stanford, working his way through with a Navy ROTC scholarship. After earning his Ph.D., he served his tour of duty in the Navy working on electronic warfare. To him, effective software code had a rhythm and a cadence, like good poetry or song. His fingers would gracefully play over a keyboard tapping out code like a jazz pianist playing syncopated rhythm. He had a talent, and he used it well.

Now, with a van Dyke goatee, most would say he resembled the actor Samuel L. Jackson. Like Jackson, his smile it lit up the room, but when he scowled, people took notice and responded cautiously. His handsome face could go from smile to scowl in an instant, but his default expression was a small wry grin that made people wonder what he found so amusing. Needless to say, he was feared by his weekly poker buddies, who found him inscrutable when he looked at the cards in his hand.

After his discharge from the Navy, Isaiah used his contacts in the world of software venture capitalists to gain investors for a new software company. His reputation among defense contractors in the software world was such that he was able to launch his start-up within six months of his discharge. Within eighteen months he had a positive cash flow and projected second-year revenues of fifteen million dollars.

Again, like Mercury, his secret was speed. His spartan software code was quicker to execute than the "fat" code of his competitors. His combination antivirus software and firewall for universities and the Department of Defense seemed to play a zone defense and man-to-man at the same time. Nobody knew how it worked, and even the patent did not reveal his exact approach — safer that way, like the formula for Coca Cola. Easier to keep it secret than to sue those who stole the code concept from the patent filings. His own proprietary software locks kept it that way. Those who had tried to reverse engineer it discovered that it self-destructed whenever they tried. The firewall "zone defense" kept out ninety-nine percent of hackers. The remaining few invaders that managed to wiggle through the firewall were immediately identified and covered by a "man-to-man" software defense that smothered, isolated, and deleted them before they could do any damage.

Isaiah hummed to himself as he turned the ribs again and began to paint on another glistening coat of his secret recipe barbecue sauce.

Grace came up beside him. "Umm, don't those smell good? Let me have a taste?"

He cut off a small piece and offered it to her.

A smile came to her face as she chewed, "Mmm, tastes as good as it smells."

He glanced appreciatively at her, "Umm, don't you look good. How about a sweet barbecue kiss?"

17

She looked coquettishly at him with a dimpled smile. "OK, but quick before George and Estelle get here." She lifted her face, closed her eyes, and puckered. He leaned down and kissed her tenderly. He had tongs in one hand, and a knife in the other, so he didn't attempt a hug.

"Umm, you taste as good as you look, girl."

She sighed and opened her eyes. "Umm, you look and taste good your own self, brother man." She stepped back and looked him up and down. "How do you stay so slim? I swear you haven't gained a pound since you played varsity."

"Nervous energy, girl. I have a stand-up desk in my office. Mark Twain and Ernest Hemingway used stand-up desks to write. I like to stand while I talk on the phone or work on my computer. Like the baseball great Satchel Page said, I just gently 'jangle' myself, moving from one foot to the other. Keeps the blood flowing to my brain. I think better that way."

She looked him up and down again. "Yes, I've seen you do it. I'm glad it works for you. I have to be very still and not 'jangle' when looking at an electron microscope screen or a DNA sequencer read-out."

"Woo-hoo! I smell mesquite smoke, I smell ribs cooking, and I smell the secret Mercury Barbecue Sauce!" This enthusiastic shout came in a deep baritone from the direction of the driveway.

"Estelle! And George T'Chaka his own self! Did my secret sauce lure you out of that big president's house again? Good to see you both!" Isaiah boomed out in his own resonant voice to his friends walking around the gravel path to the back patio.

President George T'Chaka Wright of Tuskegee University wore a green polo shirt and khaki slacks. Although now in his late fifties, he kept himself in shape with trips to the school gym, swimming in the school pool, teaching martial arts, and long walks with Estelle. He was stocky, but not fat. No bulge hung over his belt. Estelle was perhaps five years younger than George, and approximately three inches shorter. As they exchanged hugs, Isaiah and Grace towered a head taller than Estelle.

Estelle was fuller figured than the tall and willowy Grace, voluptuous but discreetly draped in stylish white twill slacks and a crisp linen shirt. She reminded Isaiah of the full-figured Vanessa Williams on a once popular TV show: *Ugly Betty*.

He openly looked her up and down, still holding his barbecue tongs and knife. "Whew, girl, you are looking *good*. Tell Mr. T'Chaka he is one lucky man."

George smiled and said, "Remember that T'Chaka was a warrior who protected what was *his*. He invented the short spear for close-in combat, too."

Isaiah threw his head back and laughed heartily. "I'll remember! I've got the only woman I want right here," he said as he put his arm around Grace's waist, "and she knows how to concoct deadly toxins, too. My mama didn't raise no fool. I know when I've got it good."

He squeezed Grace's waist and she giggled a little. "You hush! You two are carrying on like thirteen-year-olds at the eighth grade dance, strutting your stuff. Let's eat."

Isaiah loaded up a platter with ribs and carried it to the picnic table. "Everybody dig in. Extra barbecue sauce in the bowl." For the next five minutes conversation stopped while everyone enjoyed their hot food. It was a pleasant spring evening, and the dogwoods were in bloom. Birdsong was the only accompaniment to their meal.

Finally Estelle said, "Mmm. Isaiah, there's one thing I like about you, and that is your barbeque. Grace, did you know you were dating an award-winning barbeque sauce man?"

"No! I know his home-made barbeque sauce is good, but award winning? Do tell!"

Isaiah grinned, "Like the man says, it ain't bragging if it's true, and it's true. Last May, at the Memphis National Barbeque Competition. First place in sauce, tomato category. I have the blue ribbon to prove it!"

"He's been obsessed with barbeque ever since I've known him, going back to his freshman year," said George. "He can't hardly see a barbeque joint without stopping. A psychologist would call him obsessive-compulsive."

"I could have worse habits!" exclaimed Isaish with a toothy smile.

"And we're the beneficiaries of your obsession!" laughed Estelle. "George, don't you dare try to cure him. I'd waste away to nothing for want of good 'ole Mercury barbeque!" Everyone laughed again.

Estelle turned to Grace, "Grace, I am so sorry about that snotty TV newscaster's report about your research. Those reporters can't find anything good to say unless it's about themselves or some silly government program."

"What TV report?" asked Isaiah. "I was concocting my secret sauce and didn't see any TV tonight."

"Oh, it was the usual pompous green slash sustainable party line," said George. "Grace went off and did something worthwhile that might feed hungry children without kissing the ring of the powers that be, so of course she has to be in the wrong."

"Wrong?" said Isaiah quizzically, "Wrong about what?"

"Oh," replied George, "it's not good enough that her new strains of grain, fruit, and vegetable seeds will yield four times as much food. Oh sure, it might end world hunger, but if there is more food, people might live instead of dying of starvation, you see. We might have more people on the planet. Not sustainable, you see. We have to let them die off sooner with less food. That's the humanitarian thing to do, the sustainable thing to do. They'll have to invent a new term, *planetarian* instead of humanitarian. Can't do anything to benefit humans, for God's sake! It has to benefit the planet, not people." George snorted and took another bite of rib. "Now this deserves a Nobel prize. This barbecue sauce benefits humans, the planet, and the entire universe!"

They all laughed.

Then Isaiah's face went from smile to scowl. "I thought producing more food with fewer resources fits the definition of sustainability."

Grace smiled sweetly at him. "Now there you go making sense again. The sooner you stop that, the happier you'll be, Isaiah."

He sighed. "You're right. Trying to get these people even to *try* to act like they've got good sense is a losing battle. The hell we go through, trying to be decent!" Everybody laughed and ate more barbecue. Isaiah sneaked a look at Grace. She looked serene.

After a light dessert of strawberries and cream, everyone leaned back in their chairs, enjoying a fresh cup of coffee.

"So Isaiah, tell us about your new magic software," said George.

"Well, it helps researchers like Grace crunch the numbers more easily. They can tell if their results are statistically significant with fewer input hassles. Depending on the parameters of the research, my new algorithms can derive conclusions you can be confident in, with smaller sample sizes."

"How can that be?" asked Grace. "Everybody knows that the bigger the sample size, the more accurate the calculations."

"That's true," said Isaiah, "but what my algorithm does is factor in the variability of the data from your initial samples with the standard sample size, and this allows you to reduce the sample size from later sampling with the same accuracy. As long as the process and the sample collecting procedure remain the same, of course. Our project name for it is Shewhart, after the father of Statistical Process Control."

"Wow, some algorithm." said Estelle. "If that is true, then couldn't clinical drug trials be concluded more quickly? Then the people in the placebo group could benefit from the drug, if it is efficacious, while there is still time for it to do them some good. Thousands of lives could be saved."

"Yes, that's one of the immediate benefits. Except that it would upset our *planetarianism* friends, who object to more lives on the planet," said Isaiah with a straight face.

"Too true," sighed Grace. "There you go making sense again."

"Say," said Isaiah, "my company has sold more copies of the DNA sequencing software that Grace and I collaborated on. George, the university will be getting a nice check for your royalties."

George rubbed his hands together. "Excellent! I have some lab upgrades in mind."

Grace spoke up, "Don't forget about my new DNA sequencer. It's expensive."

"Aye, there's the rub," quoted George with a glum face.

"Hamlet again?" laughed Grace. "How can you think so fast so late in the evening? And you are not even jangling at a stand-up desk!"

"Jangling?" George looked puzzled.

"It's a non-Shakespearean quote. Another story for another time." With that Grace stood up and began to collect dishes.

Estelle looked at George. "Say goodnight, Gracie."

George stood up. "Good night, Gracie. We had a good time, and as the philosopher says, there ain't nothing like a good time. Ready, Estelle?"

Grace and Isaiah walked them to their car and waved as they drove off. The stars were clear and brilliant in the spring sky of Alabama. Grace leaned against Isaiah's shoulder and put her arms around his waist. "Mmmm. I'm sleepy."

"I'd better go," he said, glancing at his car parked in her driveway.

Grace yawned. "Tell you what. You can sleep on the couch. And make breakfast for us. Deal?"

"The couch?" he said plaintively.

"The couch," she responded firmly. "Deal or no deal?"

"Deal," he smiled.

The stars twinkled brightly as the two geniuses held hands and kissed.

*   *   *   *   *   *

It had been a chance meeting the previous December at a Tuskegee University home basketball game. Like many loyal alums, Grace was there to cheer for her team. Two of her undergraduate students were on the team. Besides, she had played varsity herself. Going to the women's and men's games was her relaxation. It was the one time it was acceptable for the normally quiet and reserved Dr. Grace Washington to yell and get emotional. And it was fun!

"Woo-hoo! Three pointer! That's what I'm talking about! Go Shawn!" Grace shouted from the bleachers. Shawn Mitchell was one of her students, and a star on the Tuskegee team.

"Yeah!" shouted George Wright. Seated in the row in front of Grace, he had stood up to cheer. He turned to Grace and his wife Estelle to exchange high fives.

"That's right! That's right! Whooo! Good head-fake! Golden Tigers!" Grace was having a good time yelling and not worrying about how loud she was.

"You call that a good head-fake?" a deep voice spoke behind her. A tall handsome black man in a windbreaker jacket looked at her with a twinkle in his eye. "Any ten-year-old can head-fake better than that!"

"And who might you be, some loser Kentucky State fan?" Grace gave it right back to him.

"Whoa! She's beautiful and she can trash talk! I think I'm in love." Now there were twinkles in both eyes.

George, hearing the exchange, looked around, and jumped up with delight. "Well, bless my soul! Estelle, look what the cat dragged in!" He hugged the newcomer and enthusiastically pounded him on the back.

Estelle stepped up and was engulfed in a big hug herself. "Isaiah Mercury, you tall good looking thing!" Estelle exclaimed. "What are

22

you doing in town, trolling for Tuskegee cheerleaders? It's illegal to turn on that much masculine charm around any female under the age of twenty-five, you know!" Estelle loved to tease Isaiah.

"Then I guess this one's off limits?" Isaiah nodded his head at Grace.

"Oh, I'm sorry," said Estelle, "Grace, this trash-talking too-tall excuse for a TU graduate is Isaiah Mercury. Isaiah, this is Dr. Grace Washington, ace botany professor and winner of the Nobel Prize for her revolutionary discoveries in bio-engineering for food crops."

They shook hands. "Pleased to meet you," said Isaiah. "My first Nobel Prize winner." She blushed.

"And before you try any more trash-talking," announced George, "Isaiah, I will warn you that Grace was the star center on the TU women's team in 1992. She had a mean turnaround jump shot."

"I still do, I'll have you know! And I played on the team with Vanessa White, who, the year after I graduated, led the nation in rebounding, 17.3 rebounds per game. She learned it all by watching me, you know!" Grace added.

George turned to Grace, "And to keep a level playing field for any more trash-talking tournaments between the two of you, I will inform you that Isaiah was star forward on the 1988 TU team."

"And," injected Isaiah, "played in the first Tuskegee basketball game in the James Center, in 1987, I'll have you know!"

"Oh," said Grace, "so, George, you're saying there is some suspicion that this big talker might actually know what he's talking about?"

"Ouch!" Isaiah made a wounded face. "1992, huh? No wonder I didn't recognize her. She missed my glory years at TU."

"The only glory I see is a glorious opinion of yourself!" Grace snorted.

"Ouch again!" Isaiah clutched at his chest and ripped back the snaps of his windbreaker to reveal a TU Golden Tigers jersey. "I need medical attention from a doctor. Doctor Washington, you better put your ear to my chest. You'll hear my heart breaking!"

Grinning, she gave him a playful shove. "You big show off!" she said with her trademark dimple appearing above her big smile. A refreshments vendor came down the bleacher steps.

"And may I buy you a hot dog?" asked Isaiah with an equally big smile.

"Lots of mustard," she said, eyes down coquettishly.

George leaned over to Estelle and whispered, "Ten will get you twenty those two are married inside of six months!"

Estelle looked at Isaiah's face again and leaned back, "My ten bucks says five months," she whispered back.

 **Chapter Three**

They met for lunch the very next day after the game. Isaiah had offered some ideas about how software could help Grace in her research. He suggested a lunch meeting to discuss it. Grace had explained that they would have to start a little late because she had a faculty committee meeting.

"May I sit in on part of the meeting if I come early?" Isaiah asked with an impish smile.

Grace raised her eyebrows. "Do you know what you're asking for? Death by boredom."

"Can't be any worse than a software code peer review," countered Isaiah, still smiling. "Besides, I might learn something."

"O.K. You were warned."

The Committee For Textbook Approval Review began their meeting at 9:30 a.m. in the conference room next to Dr. Grace Washington's office. Isaiah slipped into the room at 11:30 and sat next to Grace. They had just tabled their third agenda item (out of thirteen) without a conclusion or recommendation.

"Excuse me, Dr. Statutes," Grace spoke up to the chairperson. "I would like to introduce a Tuskegee graduate, Mr. Isaiah Mercury. He founded Promethean Software International, recently profiled in the *Forbes 100 Fastest Growing Companies in America*. As I mentioned earlier, we're meeting over lunch to discuss new software for research in botanical hybrid strains. He asked if he could sit in on a portion of our meeting."

"Of course, of course," rumbled Dr. Statutes, glad for the interruption. "I remember when young Isaiah played forward for the Golden Tigers. His free throw record still stands."

He looked benignly at Isaiah over the rim of reading glasses perched on the tip of his nose.

"Thank you, sir. You are kind. I'm just proud to be here."

Isaiah flashed his big smile at the people around the table. They proceeded to introduce themselves.

Dr. Cromwell of the Philosophy Department summoned up his practiced wry half-smile of ironic amusement when the introductions came to him. His shoulder length blond hair framed his pale face.

"So, Mr. Mercury, I read where you now have fifty employees. How does it feel to get rich by exploiting lowly software code writers?" He glanced around the room make sure everyone noticed his dig.

Isaiah looked calmly at him with his own relaxed smile. "I take it you are the obligatory Green Marxist in this committee? I created fifty jobs that support thirty families and twenty single people in an upper middle class lifestyle. Twenty of my employees pay the college tuitions of two children simultaneously, and still drive a Lexus or equivalent to work. How many people are on your personal payroll, as opposed to the university payroll?"

Cromwell squirmed a little in his seat and looked down.

"Well, if you must know, I support one domestic worker and my lawn man."

Isaiah kept up his calm stare. "And if I checked with the IRS, that domestic worker would have had FICA and other payroll taxes taken out and filed? What kind of car does your domestic worker drive?"

"She rides the bus, as anyone would who loves the earth."

"Uh-huh. And what is that vehicle in the parking lot with the global warming bumper stickers? Isn't that your ride? And what is the make and model?"

"Well, it's a GMC SUV, but my wife and I need a big car for the safety of our children!"

"Uh-huh. And has your housekeeper had Alabama's list of employer responsibilities for worker safety and sexual harassment read to her? Does she know that she can sue for sexual harassment?"

Isaiah had quickly sized up Cromwell's type. Self important and practiced at bullying those around him with rehearsed righteous indignation about "oppression of the powerless." Cromwell prided himself that he was "showing solidarity with the working class" when he pressured the illegal immigrant maid into having sex with him when his wife was out. He had deluded himself that she wanted him because of his intellectual virility. In fact, she had been afraid of losing her job. Isaiah was fluent in Spanish and had just overheard the female Hispanic janitors gossiping about Cromwell and his maid out in the hall as they mopped. Word had gotten around in the Hispanic community.

Startled, Dr. Cromwell looked up at Isaiah with a panicked look.

"Why? Has she said something? Has she . . . ," catching himself, he realized what he had just blurted out. Embarrassed, he quickly looked around at his colleagues. "I only meant . . . " he stopped again, confused.

"Not to me, but I'll be sure to let the local inspector for the State Department of Workplace Safety, Dignity, and Entitlements know to be sure to ask her what she has to say about sexual harassment."

Cromwell stood up. "Excuse me. I have an appointment." He quickly packed his briefcase and left.

There was a buzz of gossip after he closed the door behind him. Isaiah was busy with the keypad of his cell phone for a minute. Then he leaned over to Grace and whispered in her ear.

"Just texted the State Inspector to add Cromwell to her inspection schedule this week. I overheard Louisa, your department's Hispanic janitor, gossiping about it in the hall just now. It's time for him to live with his answers. That is, live by the same standards he preaches and tries to impose on everyone else."

Grace nodded solemnly and turned away to hide a little smile of her own. *I've been trying to think of a way to put that pompous, self-righteous windbag in his place for over a year now. And Isaiah waltzes in here and does it in three minutes flat. The man gets points in my book.* She shivered a little.

It was 12 noon. Dr. Statutes cleared his throat and said, "Well, I doubt we'll get much else done. It's a question of whether we still have a quorum anyway. Master at Arms, do you make a motion to dismiss for lack of a quorum?"

Statutes insisted on adhering to every element of Robert's Rules of Order, whether they applied or not, including having a Master at Arms to "keep order" in these genteel faculty committee meetings.

Dr. Quail, the Master at Arms, quickly said, "I so move."

Dr. Statutes looked around the table. "I second the motion," Grace said quickly.

Statutes said, "All in favor signify by saying aye." A chorus of ayes rose.

"All opposed signify by saying nay." Silence. Statutes banged his gavel. "This meeting is adjourned."

On the way out, two faculty members whispered to Isaiah, "Well done!" and "About time that windbag got his comeuppance." Six others shook his hand warmly and winked.

Isaiah looked at Dr. Statutes and shook his hand. "Thank you for a most informative meeting! I learned some things today."

"Think nothing of it. Glad you could come." Statutes smiled benignly.

Isaiah wondered, *was that a twinkle in his eye?* "Good day, sir."

      *   *   *   *   *   *

As Isaiah held the chair for her at the restaurant, Grace thought, *what a gentleman! He can outwit intellectual poseurs like Cromwell and treat a lady like a lady. More points in my book.* She looked up and flashed a smile at him.

That smile! So bright! And the dimple that comes with it, thought Isaiah. *I'm starting to fall for this classy lady scientist.*

"So, I assume there are a lot more in the faculty just like Cromwell?" Isaiah said as he opened the menu.

"Not really. We have the usual assortment of liberal slash progressive poseurs who like to strike a self-righteous pose about the sins of society, but Cromwell is only our second avowed Marxist. Tuskegee is still very much in the tradition of the hard sciences: show me the data. Marxists, of course, know all too well that the data on Marxist-run countries shows starvation, shortages, and rationing of everyday basic commodities, from toilet paper to medical care. They don't say too much around here, because they know their colleagues will ask for actual data to back up what they are asserting. And they don't have any."

"I'm glad to hear it. How's the barbeque here?"

"So-so. You told Dr. Statutes that you learned some things. What, pray tell?"

"I learned two things: one, that the default mode of academics is still pomposity (present company excluded!), and two, more proof that when experts in one field, like philosophy, try to act authoritative about other fields, like economics, they are incredible asses."

"Amen, brother!" She flashed another dazzling smile at him. He broke into a laugh. "What's so funny?" she asked.

"Nothing. I'm just happy to be here seated across from a beautiful woman who is not only brilliant in her field, but still has common sense about other subjects. I'm so happy I had to laugh out loud." He grinned

28

back at her. Her dimple deepened. She looked down, suddenly shy at his compliments.

Their waiter arrived. Isaiah looked up. "The lady first." He looked at Grace.

Grace had recovered her composure. "I'll have the chicken Caesar salad. Iced tea to drink."

"Grace, any suggestions?"

"The mahi-mahi is good here." Isaiah nodded at the waiter, who wrote it down, took their menus and left.

Grace held up her glass of ice water. "Here's to a successful collaboration on software for computer aided design of food crop DNA sequencing." She smiled at her own long and technical toast.

Isaiah clinked his glass with hers. "Amen, sister!"

She took out a pad of paper and her pen. "Now, what were you hoping your software could do for me?"

Isaiah whistled. "Man, you don't wait around, do you? OK, what's the biggest bottleneck or wait time in your research for new hybrid strains of crops?"

Grace brightened. "That's easy. Waiting for the seeds to grow to maturity to see if the predicted characteristics really are present. For example, waiting for corn to bear fruit with less water and fertilizer, as we theorized."

Isaiah leaned toward her, interested in the theoretical problem. "Have you isolated the DNA sequences that control water absorption and other desirable characteristics?"

"Yes. We have a library of DNA sequences associated with various plant characteristics." Unconsciously, she leaned forward too, focused on what he was saying.

"And you have the research results of combining various sequences?"

"Yes, we do, but it's only about five percent of all possible mix and matching of DNA sequences. The number of permutations is enormous." She shrugged.

He took out a pad and began jotting down notes. "That's where we can use the power of the computer to perform 'virtual crop maturation.' My team and I can derive algorithms from the results of your previous research. You can let the computer algorithms predict the best

29

combinations. Then you can pick out the most promising combinations for your actual growing tests to confirm the theory."

Grace frowned. "But this doesn't speed up the time for a seed to grow to maturity and bear crops."

Isaiah looked up from his page of notes. "No it doesn't. But you can only grow so many test crop combinations at a time. If one growing season doesn't yield the results you want, you have to start again with a new set of DNA sequence combinations for test crops, adding the time for another growing season. My algorithms will "pre-test" the combinations, so that you are growing only the most promising combinations. You'll save time in the long run."

She leaned back and looked up and to her left, visualizing what he was saying. "So this is similar to computer aided design for manu-facturing, where the computer tells the engineers whether the dimensions on hundreds of parts will allow them all to fit together correctly, before they even build a physical prototype to test for fit."

"Wow! You catch on quickly, for a non-computer scientist. That's it, exactly."

She calmly looked him in the eye. "I do read about other fields, looking for analogous processes that can help me in my field. That is part of the TRIZ methodology created by the Russians, you know."

"Whew! A fabled turnaround jump shot, familiarity with CAD, and talking TRIZ trash too! What can't you do, girl?" His smile seemed to expand.

The waiter placed their entrees in front of them.

"I can't talk and eat at the same time. Let's say grace." She reached over and held his hand. "Dear Lord, we thank you for this bounteous meal, and we thank you for the bounty of your natural world. Help us to be good stewards of your plants to feed a hungry world. Amen." She took a bite of her Caesar salad.

"Amen." Isaiah watched her eat. *I want her to hold my hand again*, he thought. He sampled his fish. "Delicious. You were right. Again."

As they were leaving the restaurant, she turned to him and paused. "There is a concert of gospel music at my church tonight. Percy Gray and my own church choir. I sing soprano. Will you come as my date?"

"When a beautiful woman asks me on a date, she doesn't have to ask me twice. Yes! May I take you to dinner first at my favorite barbeque restaurant?"

"Not before. I can't sing well when I'm full of barbeque. After?" She smiled hopefully.

"Deal. When shall I pick you up?" He held her car door open for her.

Still the gentleman, she thought. After he got in on the passenger side, she said, "Six o'clock. The concert is at seven, but I need to be early to get into my choir robe and prepare. Here's my address and phone number." She wrote them on a pad, tore off the sheet, and handed it to him.

"I'll be there at six." *I do like a woman confident enough to ask a man on a date. Thank you, Lord.*

*   *   *   *   *   *

The trial for the murder of the farmers was being held in Gaborone, the capital city of Botswana. The undercover agent for the Pristine Influence on Society Foundation put in a phone call to their headquarters from a cafe one block from the courthouse.

"Director? The trial is over. We lost. Our British operative was sentenced to fifteen years in prison as an accomplice to murder. Our anonymously paid local lawyer tried to argue that he was just a soldier fighting a war of liberation from the oppression of genetically modified seeds, but the judge here didn't buy it. The two young boys who actually pulled the triggers got twenty-five years each. Their boss got twenty. The other two got eighteen months for armed vandalism."

The Director's voice sounded tinny over the long-distance connection. "Unfortunate, but they are expendable."

The man with the broken nose shifted his feet uncomfortably. "There was one bad thing. The police traced payment of the airline ticket from Great Britain to PRIS."

The voice grew more shrill. "You told me there were no links to us!"

"Well, instead of using my cut-out, a clerk in your London office used her own credit card because she wanted the frequent flyer points. Then she turned in a request for reimbursement. It left a paper trail."

"I'll have her sacked at once!"

"The good news is that there's no criminal liability, but some ambulance-chasing lawyer might file a civil suit against PRIS on behalf of the relatives of the dead farmers."

He could hear the Director draw a deep breath.

"Well, we have plenty of judges in our pockets and plenty of legal help. We can beat any lawsuits filed in this country. It's just that I don't want the bad publicity."

The agent drew a deep breath of his own. "What next?"

"We'll fight our next battle against these seeds in the United States court system, where there's a more flexible interpretation of the law, and a more *Pristine* influence on the judiciary, if you take my meaning."

"Got it. See you back in the office." He hung up and looked around, assessing his surroundings. His hard eyes, broken nose and stubby physique marked him as an 'enforcer' type typically employed by bookies to collect gambling debts and intimidate rivals. In his pocket was a plane ticket back to the foundation headquarters in Chicago.

*   *   *   *   *   *

At the church that night, Isaiah listened in the congregation as Percy Gray and the choir sang "God Is My Everything." It took him back to his childhood and the rhythmic gospel singing at his family's church. "He's my shelter, a shelter in the time of storm," Percy sang, and the congregation sang along with him and the choir. Percy Gray finished singing and everyone applauded wildly. Isaiah joined in.

Now the church choir began their first hymn, a slow chanting song called "Faithful Is Our God." Isaiah felt himself swaying to the music. Midway through, the choir fell silent as Grace sang a solo verse, a capella. "I'm reaping the harvest God promised me," her clear soprano floated out over the congregation. Then the altos took up the same verse, followed by the sopranos, then the tenors.

Is this the harvest God promised me? wondered Isaiah as he kept his eyes on Grace in her shimmering blue choir robe. He thought of all the years spent building his company, the years of loneliness as he attempted to find a *simpatico* woman who would appreciate who he was and what he was trying to build.

He closed his eyes when he suddenly remembered his short and acrimonious first marriage that lasted nine months.   Annabelle had expected that she would be the one and only priority in his life. She resented the time and energy he put into his software projects, even though he was attentive to her at home.

He finally had an epiphany: Either do what I love; and be who I am, or do just enough to get by at work in order to meet this woman's expectations. He had realized that it would be an act of self-murder, the murder of his better self, if he began just going through the motions at work. That marriage had ended four years ago.

After that, he had despaired of finding someone who would understand him and love him for who he was. One lonely night, alone in his condo, he wrote a zen-like epigram as advice for himself: *Learn loneliness. Embrace it.*

Now, he had a flicker of hope about a possible relationship with Grace Washington. *Could she be the one I've been hoping for?* The choir began the next song:

"What shall I do? What steps should I take? What move should I make? Oh Lord, what shall I do? I'm going to wait, for an answer from you . . . I know He'll come through, with a blessing for me . . ."

Lord, Isaiah prayed silently, *what shall I do? I think you sent me this hymn to tell me to wait, not to push, to enjoy each moment as it comes. I think you are asking me to trust that there will be a blessing for me. Lord, help me to trust you, help me to wait and to let it happen in Your own good time. Amen.*

He opened his eyes as the choir finished. He stood up and began clapping. "Amen!" he spoke out in his clear resonant baritone. Grace looked straight at him and smiled. He felt warm and good. *Thank you, Lord,* he prayed as he had in childhood, in gratitude.

After their supper, Isaiah drove Grace home. He walked her to the door.

After unlocking the door, Grace turned to him.

"Would you like to come in for a cup of coffee and some pecan pie? We didn't have dessert at the restaurant."

"Sold!"

They walked into the living room. He noticed that one wall was lined with bookshelves and books.

Isaiah exclaimed, "O boy! A book lover. A woman after my own heart."

"If you love books, let me show you my study." Grace led the way. Her study was lined on three sides by custom-built bookshelves of a beautifully grained red oak. The fourth side had tall windows to let sunlight in over the shoulder of the person sitting at the desk. On the desk were several upright volumes between heavy, brass book ends.

Isaiah looked around appreciatively.

"Grace, the craftsmanship of these wooden shelves is fine."

"Thank you. Jeremy at my church made these for me. He's an excellent cabinet maker. Make yourself at home here and browse the books while I make the coffee and slice the pie."

Ten minutes later she returned with a tray and placed it on her desk. It held a carafe, two substantial mugs, and two slices of pecan pie on blue plates. When she poured the coffee, a fragrant aroma steamed up from the mugs.

"Pull your chair up." She seated herself behind the desk and took a sip of the coffee.

Isaiah savored a forkful of sweet, flaky-crusted pie.

"Mmm. Grace, this is delicious."

"Thank you. My neighbor baked it. When she heard I had a date, she said I needed something for a man's stomach. You know, the way to his heart?"

"Books and pecan pie. You're on the highway to my heart. Say, what's this?" He pulled out one of the books from between the brass bookends on the desk before him.

"*The Story of George Washington Carver.* This was one of my favorite books when I was in the fourth grade. Carver inspired me to go tinker and make things." He began thumbing through the pages. Grace was silent. He looked up.

Grace's eyes were shining. She spoke in a low voice. "It was my favorite book too. I've treasured this book ever since I got it as a gift in the third grade. Carver became my hero. He's the reason I went into botany and agricultural science. That and having Booker T. Washington as one of my ancestors. I loved how they both believed in building your family's prosperity by working hard and making things and inventing things and using your own two hands. And their faith in God."

"And their faith in God. Thank you for inviting me to your church, Grace. I've decided not to be ashamed of my Christian faith, or hide it, even though that's the politically correct thing to do nowadays."

34

He stood up. "Thank you for a great evening. I'll see you tomorrow at your office."

She walked him to the door. "Isaiah?" He turned. "I want to kiss you."

"And I want to kiss you too." He took her in his arms. She kissed him, lightly at first, then more firmly. She tilted her head back and looked at his eyes.

"Any man who loves George Washington Carver and can put that poseur Cromwell in his place like you did today, deserves a second kiss." She pulled his head down to hers. "Goodnight."

He found himself sitting in his car in the driveway, dazed. *What just happened?* Isaiah thought back to the hymn line, *I know He'll come through, with a blessing for me.* He leaned his head on the steering wheel for a moment. *Lord, You came through with a blessing fast! Thank You, Lord.*

*   *   *   *   *   *

Carlos Hernandez was the regular janitor for Promethean Software International. He was employed by Seito Shine Services, the cleaning service contractor. The previous morning, he had stopped for coffee at a local cafe after his shift ended at 6 a.m., just as he always did. A man with a broken nose sat beside him at the counter. When Carlos opened his newspaper, the man slipped some powder into his coffee. When he woke up at home that afternoon, his head was pounding. He called in sick.

That evening at ten, a substitute came to clean at PSI.

"Where's Carlos?" asked the security guard in the lobby.

"Called in sick," said the substitute. He was dressed in the overalls of Seito Shine Services, and carried a photo I.D. His broken nose was visible in the ID photo.

He followed the standard cleaning route in Carlos' neat diagram of the offices. When he got to the office where the new software project on buying and selling was located, it was one a.m. A hand-lettered sign taped to the door read "Project Adam Smith." One of the software engineers was just leaving.

"Late night, huh?" said the substitute janitor.

"Yeah. Good night." The engineer glanced at the ID badge and photo, then left.

After ten minutes, the substitute took a thumb drive out of his pocket and sat down at one of the computers. Logging on with a stolen password, he found the file he was looking for: *Project Adam Smith Alpha Copy.* He tried to copy it to his thumb drive. The firewall within the firewall and the PSI encryption stopped him three times. He looked at his watch. Fifteen minutes had elapsed. He had to complete the cleaning routine to avoid suspicion. *What else would be useful?*

He scrolled through the folder for Project Adam Smith, looking at the names of files. Draft marketing brochure for AdamSmith.doc. *Maybe.* He scanned the file names: Specifications, Performance Characteristics, Features and Benefits, and Comparison to other selling software. *This is valuable to know.* It was unencrypted, and outside the firewall. He copied it to the thumb drive, logged off, looked around, and continued his cleaning rounds.

When he left PSI at six a.m. he went to an internet coffee shop near the university. He sent the stolen marketing brochure off to a rival software firm that had hired him for industrial espionage. As a freelance intelligence operative, his services were available to corporations as well as groups like PRIS. By 10:15 that morning, an R&D team at the rival firm was studying the specifications for Isaiah's latest software project.

*   *   *   *   *   *

That evening, Grace attended a viewing at the funeral home for an acquaintance who had died. It was Lou Ellen Parker, cousin to Regina Bell, head of campus security at Tuskegee University. After signing the guest registry, Grace saw Regina and her husband Bill walking away from the casket. She walked over and took Regina's hand in both of hers.

"Regina, Bill, I am so sorry about Lou Ellen."

Bill looked grim. "We're sad and mad at the same time."

Surprised, Grace looked back to Regina. "Mad? Regina, what is it? Tell me."

Her eyes brimming with tears, Regina waved one hand in front of her face.

"Let me sit down."

They went to the far corner away from the others, and sat together.

"You remember that tumble-down old farmhouse Lou Ellen lived in?" began Regina.

"Yes," said Grace. "It was out in the country, with no neighbors nearby."

"Well, as Lou Ellen got older, she stopped using the back bedroom. She stored boxes of family papers there, but kept the door shut to save on the heating bill. About two months ago she went into that room for something and discovered bats had somehow gotten into the room and were roosting there and leaving droppings all over the boxes and furniture. She called the county extension agent to ask about how to safely get the bats out of her home. He called the state Wildlife Resources Commission, who sent one of their agents to visit Lou Ellen. He looked at the bat roost in the bedroom, and then informed her that this was a species of bat protected under the Endangered Species Act. Removal might result in the death of the young bats, he told her, and therefore it was illegal for her to remove the bats from her own home. He told her not to use the room, clean the room, or touch the bats in the room. That room now belonged to the bats, he told her, and had federal protection to be there. The bats had more right to her home than she did! Bats! Can you imagine?"

Regina stopped and dabbed at her eyes with a handkerchief. "Anyway, he taped a sign on her bedroom door saying that it was illegal to enter and remove or harm the bat population living there. It had a US government seal on it, and you know how Lou Ellen respected legal authority. She had nowhere else to go, so she just kept the door shut and kept living there on her little pension."

"I went to check on her and bring her some tomatoes from my garden about three weeks ago," said Bill. "She was listless and complained of a headache. I took her temperature and she was running a fever. I noticed she kept scratching at a place on her arm. When I looked closely, it looked like two small puncture wounds from a bat bite."

Bill sighed. "I asked her, 'Lou Ellen, did you go back into that room with the bats?' 'Just once, three weeks ago, to get Daddy's picture album,' she said. 'Only one bat got out, and I left the door cracked open for several days until he got back in,' she said. I took her straight to the county hospital emergency room. The doctor diagnosed rabies. Her throat had started to spasm, so the disease had progressed too far. There is no cure for rabies. She died within two weeks."

Regina leaned forward and looked into Grace's eyes. Grace saw a steely determination in Regina's eyes and heard a fierce urgency in her voice. "Grace, you know that I worked for the Federal Government as an FBI agent, and I respect the law. Thirty years ago I swore an oath to protect and defend the Constitution of the United States, so help me God. But so help me God, our government has gone beyond the Constitution and gotten out of control and beyond the consent of we the people. The Constitution says nothing about the inalienable rights of bats! This government has put the so-called 'rights' of diseased bats ahead of the property rights and right to life of my poor cousin Lou Ellen, who minded her own business and never hurt a soul in her life, including bats."

Regina leaned back, chin up, her torso ramrod straight in the chair. "This isn't the country I swore an oath to. I want my country back. I don't know this country we live in now, this country that would rather endanger the life of a harmless old soul like Lou Ellen Parker than allow her to remove rabies-carrying bats who invaded *her* house!"

Grace thought *she's not just grieving for Lou Ellen; she's grieving for her country, too.*

Several other friends and family members had drifted over to where Regina and Bill were talking and silently listened.

Regina looked up at them and tears glistened in her eyes again. "I want my country back! I want Lou Ellen back!"

The others murmured sympathetically, "Me too, Regina." "Amen." "That's right."

*   *   *   *   *   *

Isaiah began a weekly commute from his corporate offices in Silicon Valley. He arrived in Tuskegee each Thursday night and camped out in an extended stay hotel. He and Grace worked on the software design on Fridays. Saturdays he wrote software code and sent e-mails and code sequences to his team in California. He had asked Grace for a date that second Saturday night. She accepted his invitation, and then invited him to attend church with her Sunday morning. He agreed, delighted at the chance to hear her sing in the choir and spend more time with her. By the time he flew back Sunday night, he was hooked.

The third Friday, as they were eating a lunch of pizza delivered to Grace's office where they worked, she suddenly asked, "Why are you doing this?"

Taken by surprise, he looked at her across the work table and asked, "What do you mean?"

"You're spending a lot of money commuting here from the West Coast, not to mention your team of six software engineers dedicated to this project back at your office. This is costing you a lot of money."

"It's worth it, to see you and work with you."

"And I like seeing you too, but Isaiah, the airfares! My grandmother taught me never to waste anything."

Isaiah finished a bite of pizza and grinned. "Not a waste, an investment. I expect to make back the money and then some when I launch a commercial version of this software for medical research organizations, agri-business, and pharmaceutical companies. The basic principles and applications will apply to all of them. They will pay handsomely for software that will cut years off their development time for new products. Especially when I reveal that the software has been beta-tested by the Nobel Prize-winning botanist Dr. Grace Washington at the renowned Tuskegee University. And wait 'till I reveal that the beta test helped bring to market the new super-seeds that are going to feed a hungry world. The publicity will be huge!"

Her eyes suddenly got hard.

"Huge indeed! What makes you think you can use my name and the university's name in advertising your software? Is that why you've been romancing me? Hoping to trade off my reputation? Using me?"

She stood up, glaring at him.

"I should have suspected something when you put on a full court press with that charm Estelle Wright was raving about! And you even came to my church and charmed my friends. And it was all a con! It was all about marketing for your software!"

He looked at her, bewildered.

"Grace, *you* asked me out on our first date. You asked me to come to your church. I asked you for a second date because I'm attracted to you. It was not to entice you to partner with me on a software project."

Grace's face did not soften. "I think you had better leave now. Maybe it was a mistake to mix business with a personal relationship."

Isaiah closed his laptop and swept it and his papers into his briefcase. "I'd like a chance to explain myself."

"Not necessary. I've got the picture. Leave." She went back to her desk, shaking. As she sat down she looked at her computer screen and began twisting a lock of hair around her fingers.

He left.

*   *   *   *   *   *

When her office door clicked shut, Grace closed her eyes. A tear ran down one cheek. *Not again. I won't let it happen again.* She opened her eyes and reached up to wipe away the tear. She turned her head and looked out her office window, eyes on the horizon, unfocused, remembering.

It had begun three years ago. It had lasted five months. A handsome, smooth-talking con man had talked his way into her heart. She met Rashim at the home of friends in Birmingham. Rashim Alcazar was invited as a dinner companion for Grace. He was a financial advisor, a partner in a family-owned investment firm in New York. He was attentive to her and showed great interest in her work and her patents. Especially her patents.

He had charmed her into investing with him. Then he charmed Grace's university colleagues into investments handled by his firm. They knew Grace, so they trusted him. His big mistake came when he tried to fast-talk Carl, one of Grace's friends from church. Carl was no university egg head. Carl was an auto mechanic who dealt in tangible facts. He did some checking up on the Alcazar investment firm and found that it was a Ponzi scheme. He also discovered that Rashim had used Grace's name and Nobel Prize credentials as part of his advertisements without Grace's knowledge or permission.

Grace's friend Regina Bell was not only head of campus security, she was an ex-FBI agent. With Regina's help, the money was restored to Grace and her university colleagues. Rashim went to jail. Grace felt used and humiliated before her colleagues and friends.

Even after three years, the memory still stung. In her office, Grace's eyes refocused, and she turned back to her desk. She took a deep breath.

Not again. I won't let it happen again. She opened a file folder bulging with papers to grade.

 **Chapter Four**

The following Friday, George T'Chaka Wright was hanging up his suit coat after returning from lunch with several potential donors to the university trust fund. He sighed. With the stock market tanking, it was getting harder and harder to convince wealthy patrons to give to the college. The gifts were fewer and smaller these days. To top it off, the new administration in Washington had proposed phasing out the tax deduction for charitable giving. If that happened, the college would be totally dependent on federal and state funding. The strings attached to government funds were many and contradictory. *The academic freedom and research of the university is being strangled by those strings,* he thought grumpily.

There were three sharp knocks on his office door. His administrative assistant was taking a late lunch. "Come in!" he said loudly.

Isaiah Mercury entered, looking grim. "Isaiah! Come in. Oh! You've got troubles, I can tell by looking at your face. Sit down and tell me what's on your mind." Isaiah settled on the couch and put his face in his hands. George sat in a high-backed chair opposite the couch. "Is it that bad?"

Isaiah looked up. "George, we've known each other a long time. You were my faculty advisor when I was an undergraduate here, then my sensei when I first took up martial arts. You were a father figure to me, and then we became good friends. We've been friends for so long I can't remember when you first told me to call you by your first name instead of Dr. Wright. Yes, it's bad. I need advice from a friend." Isaiah sat up and then slumped back into the couch, looking defeated.

"Isaiah, you know I'll help you. I'll give you the best advice I've got, and pray that it's enough. First, tell me, is this business, or personal?" George looked concerned.

"Personal."

"Money, legal, or women?"

"Women. One woman." Isaiah's voice was dull and flat.

"Whoa! Then you're asking the wrong person. I gave up trying to understand women a long time ago. In the sixth grade, actually. I can't help you, but I know who can."

Isaiah looked up hopefully, "Who?"

"Estelle. She is wise in the ways of the world, and wise in the ways of women. But her renowned relationship advice will cost you big time. We're now talking about the best of the best for relationship advice. Oprah, Dr. Phil, and Dr. Laura come to Estelle for advice on their tough cases."

This got a smile from Isaiah. "Then I've come to the right place!"

"Here's the price tag: you need advice, and by coincidence I need advice too. I need advice from a hot-shot entrepreneur businessman."

Isaiah's eyebrows shot up. "You? Need advice from me? This will be a first. It's a deal!"

George stood up and hit a speed dial button on his cell phone. "Estelle? I'm bringing Isaiah Mercury home for some TLC and relationship counseling from you. Dinner's included. I'll cook. Thank you, sweetheart. We'll see you around six."

George opened his office door and spoke to his administrative assistant, who had just returned from lunch. "Christina, I'm taking a meeting with Mr. Isaiah Mercury of Promethean Software International off-site. I won't be back today. See you Monday."

*   *   *   *   *   *

The R&D team leader at the rival software firm made his report to the CEO. "We've studied the performance characteristics for this Adam Smith software project at Promethean Software International, and there is no way we can match it right now. The team estimates that it will take us six years of research and development to come up with an Alpha version of our own."

The CEO looked at him with narrowed eyes from under her ash blond bangs. "Why can't you steal a copy and reverse engineer it?"

"We've already tried that. Our operative was defeated by a firewall within a firewall. We hacked an early version three months ago before the firewall went up, but Mercury's encryption self-destructed the file when we tried to open it. It uses a ferocious virus that eats the file, and then starts wiping everything on the internal network. It's like Pac-Man on steroids. We damn near lost all of our own R&D files before we were able to pull the plug on the CPU running the stolen copy."

The CEO stared at her monitor and brooded over this bad news. *Six years to develop a comparable version. Play catch-up for six years?!*

This entire firm could disappear in the fiercely competitive software world within three years, let alone six. This is a major problem.

She looked up. "Thank you. That will be all." *Time for Plan B.*

After he left, she punched the speed dial for her CFO. "Peter? Start a crash acquisition study. The target is Promethean Software International. Actually, just their new selling software. I'll send you the intelligence we have on its performance characteristics and projected market penetration. Work up a scenario and proposal for a buy-out offer. Make it an offer they can't refuse. But, as back-up insurance, alert our friends in Washington that we may need some of their special powers of persuasion."

      *   *   *   *   *   *

Estelle stood in the doorway when George and Isaiah came up the walkway. "Isaiah, let's go sit in the garden. Would you like something to drink?"

"A beer would be wonderful."

"George, dear, would you bring a beer for Isaiah? And a glass of wine for me?"

Estelle led Isaiah to the garden out back. Wisteria vines grew up over an arbor. A few purple blooms had begun to spread their fragrance. They sat on a wrought iron bench under the arbor.

"Now then, young man, what seems to be the trouble?" Estelle called anyone under the age of fifty "young."

"Estelle, I've had two dates and two working meetings with Grace Washington and I'm crazy about her. I've done everything except carry her books to class."

"I've noticed. And so have others. Word gets around. You've been hovering around that girl like a big old black bumblebee humming around a yellow daisy." Estelle smiled her small serene smile.

"Today she asked me why I was spending the money to fly here and assign a team of my people on this software project. I gave her an honest answer. I told her I wanted to see her, and that I expected to make money selling this software when potential customers learned that it had been designed for, and with, the Nobel Prize-winning scientist Grace Washington at the famous Tuskegee University. Then she turned on me."

"Turned on you?" Estelle raised her eyebrows.

George appeared with a tray of drinks. He put it on the table before them, looked once at Estelle, and then walked back into the house without comment. Estelle turned back to Isaiah.

He bowed his head and said in a low voice, "She accused me of romancing her just so that I could use her name in advertising. She accused me of using her. She asked me to leave. I asked for a chance to explain myself, but she refused. Estelle, I'm miserable."

"I can see that." She sipped her white wine delicately. "Young man, is software design the only reason you have been flying here all the way from the West Coast?"

"Of course not. I could do telephone and video conferencing and get the same thing done. I fly here because I want to be near Grace. I come here so I can ask her out on dates. I fly here to look into her soft brown eyes. I travel here so I can hear her sweet voice sing in the church choir."

Estelle smiled her serene little smile and asked softly, "But you didn't tell her that?"

"No." The word came out with a sigh. He was still looking down.

"Did you ask her permission to use her name in your advertising?"

"No. . . . I had planned to, but then I just blurted it out." There was a long silence. Estelle took another sip of her wine. His glass of beer sat untouched.

Isaiah finally looked up at her with a mournful look on his face. "I guess I'm a big old *dumb* bumblebee. I thought the reason I was hovering and humming around was obvious to the pretty yellow daisy."

Estelle's kind eyes never left his face. "It probably was obvious, but she still needed to *hear it*. From you."

"But she thinks I'm a con man, just using her to sell something. If I tell her now, she'll just think it's part of the con." His shoulders slumped down even lower as he sank deeper in the chair.

"Tell her anyway. Tell her just the way you've told me."

"I'm afraid. What if she won't believe me?"

"Then you're no worse off than you are right now. Doing something is better than doing nothing. Tell that girl how you feel about her." Estelle patted his hand.

"OK, Estelle. I'll try. I don't know if she'll even talk to me, but I'll try."

"And one more thing."

"Yes?"

"Ask if you can carry her books to class."

This made Isaiah smile. "Will do."

"Good. Now go talk to George in his study. I believe he had something to ask you." She stood up.

Isaiah hugged her. "Thanks Estelle. I needed someone to talk to."

George was seated at his desk in his study, reading some financial reports from the university. He looked up when Isaiah tapped at the open door. "Come in, come in. I was just reviewing our university trust fund situation." He took off his reading glasses.

Isaiah sat in a chair before the desk. "That Estelle is one wonderful woman."

"Now you know why I married her. Looks, intelligence, and *wisdom*."

"Wisdom in the ways of women, which I definitely don't have. You were right. Estelle is better than Oprah." Isaiah sighed. "You said you needed my advice. What's up?"

George tapped the papers in front of him. "Donations to our trust fund are down. No surprise, since the markets tanked. You're a businessman who owns your own company. You've been a good donor. How can I generate more donations to support our university research programs and teaching?"

Isaiah leaned back and looked up at the ceiling for a long moment. Then he jumped out of the chair and said loudly, "Eureka!" He began to pace back and forth energetically.

"OK, Archimedes, what have you found?" said George, leaning back and crossing his arms.

"Ever hear of Gatorade?"

"Of course. Oh! You mean the royalties the University of Florida receives for licensing Gatorade to Stokely-Van Camp?" George now stood up himself and joined the pacing.

Isaiah clapped his hands and then rubbed them together. "Right! Quaker Oats owns it now, but the point is that some of the research discoveries here at Tuskegee University can be licensed out for their commercial applications, while you still retain the patent. In fact, much university research is financed by grants from corporations. When anybody here asks for a grant for research, you can also negotiate for a royalty percentage on the commercialization of the research patents. You might accept less grant money, but gain more revenue in the long run from the continuing royalties."

George laughed. "That's it! I knew there was a reason I wanted to be the faculty advisor to a certain bright young undergraduate! I've donated the royalties from my own patents to the university, but it somehow never occurred to me to do the same with other research. Harvesting royalties! Booker T. Washington would be proud. Woo-hoo! How do we get started?"

"Right here, right now, with my research software. You invest some of the time of your ace botanical scientist, and I invest my time and that of my project team. I hereby offer a royalty of five percent of sales of this biological research software to Tuskegee University."

"Deal! Thank you, Lord!" George danced a few steps excitedly.

"Just one problem."

"What's that?"

"Your ace botanical scientist Grace Washington is also my woman problem. She doesn't want to work with me anymore."

Just then Estelle stuck her head in the door. "George, you'd better get started on the supper. We have one more guest."

George looked a question at his wife in the doorway. She gave a slight nod, looking back at him.

"In that case, I'm going upstairs to change clothes and get started. That grill is calling for ribs!" He loosened his tie and picked up his suit jacket.

"Ribs? Did I hear someone say ribs?" asked Isaiah. "I just happen to be a great rib chef, and my secret recipe barbeque sauce won a blue ribbon at the Memphis Barbeque Festival last May. Got an extra apron?"

"I sure do. I'll make the potato salad while you grill the ribs." Estelle left, and George turned back to Isaiah. In a low voice, he said, "We'll talk about the woman scientist problem later. "

*   *   *   *   *   *

On her way home from work, Grace stopped at the grocery store to pick up a few things. She made a mental list: *Let me see, milk, eggs, butter . . . oh, and a bag of candy to share at choir practice.* She turned

47

down the candy aisle. She was shocked to find the shelves bare. The store manager, Mel, was sweeping the aisle.

"Mel! What's going on? What happened to all your candy?"

Mel looked up from his push broom and his face lit up. "Grace Washington! Good to see you. What's going on?" His face looked momentarily puzzled. "Oh, you mean this aisle? Well, the Food and Drug Administration has decided that since eating too many sugary foods is linked to diabetes, then candy should be a restricted dietary supplement, just like prescription drugs. The candy will be kept behind the pharmacy counter from now on. You'll need a prescription from your doctor to get any."

"Mel, you're joking!"

"Nope. Wish I was. Going to be a lot of work to add space for this stuff in pharmacy. Have to keep it locked up just like narcotics and other drugs."

"So, the food police have found a way to become the food Gestapo!"

"'Fraid so. Don't say that out loud, though. The same FDA regulation that now classifies candy as a drug also has penalties for any food retailer who makes critical comments about the new regulation. I can be fined $10,000 and sent to prison for six months. It's called making untruthful claims to the public about FDA health and safety regulations."

The busybodies who like to tell the rest of us how to live our lives have now acquired police power, thought Grace as she checked out at the cash register. *What is this country coming to? We are choking on a flood of regulations and control.*

Just then her cell phone rang. "Hello? Oh, hello Estelle. Sure, I have time to talk. Let me get these groceries paid for and I'll call you back from my car."

*   *   *   *   *   *

Isaiah was humming a hymn, "What shall I do?" while he combined the ingredients for his barbeque sauce in a mixing bowl in the kitchen. Then he took the bowl out to the patio. He set it down next to the grill and began putting ribs on the grill. He carefully basted each rib with his sauce, and whistled the hymn as he did so. *Lord, some things are looking up, but I still need help with Grace. I think she's the one, Lord. Help me do this right. I don't want to lose her.*

Estelle was setting the table on the patio. George came out of the kitchen with a bowl of potato salad. "Cole slaw coming up!" he said as he went back inside.

Isaiah heard the doorbell ring. "I'll get it," said Estelle, gliding into the house. He heard a babble of voices as George joined Estelle to greet their guest. Then his heart stopped. He heard Grace's voice. He turned from the grill slowly, still holding the basting brush with one hand.

"Don't you look good in that green apron," Estelle said brightly. Isaiah stood frozen, looking helplessly at Grace. Her face was a blank mask, revealing nothing.

George stepped up and took the basting brush from Isaiah's hand. "I'll take over the grill for a while. The wisteria is starting to bloom all over this neighborhood, if you two care to take a walk around the block. Estelle and I will finish here."

Estelle looked into Grace's eyes and touched her hand. "Honey, I think a walk will do you good."

Grace and Isaiah walked stiffly through the house and out the front door. At the street, Isaiah turned to Grace and said, "I'm sorry I hurt you with what I said today. Grace, I'm falling for you. Have been ever since I first saw you at the basketball game. You are the reason I fly out here from California. Nothing else matters to me but you. I'd a hundred times rather be with you than use the school's name to advertise my software. I don't want to lose you."

She looked into his eyes and then looked down. "I've been played before, and it sure sounded like you were playing me." She began to walk down the neighborhood street filled with stately brick homes. Isaiah walked beside her. They both inhaled the sweet wisteria. They both exhaled with a long sigh.

"Grace, I was so excited about how good this software is going to be that I got ahead of myself. I was going to formally ask your permission to use your name. But instead, I just blurted out my ideas when you asked. I'll drop the whole idea. I just want to be with you. I just want things to be right between us."

Grace slowed her pace. "When you said that, it took me on a flashback to a previous relationship where I got used. It was like you dug up the garbage from an old relationship, and it stank." She involuntarily wrinkled her nose.

"I'm sorry that you were hurt in that other relationship. I don't know what he did to you, but I'm not that other guy. I'm Isaiah Mercury, and I'm right here beside you, loving you."

She stopped, turned, and looked at him wonderingly. "I don't know, Isaiah. I don't know if I can trust you."

They heard a mockingbird call. "I had a long talk with Estelle today. She said that I should just tell you how I feel. So I'm telling you. Grace Washington, lady scientist with the soft brown eyes and the sweet soprano voice, I love you. I guess I'll have to let you and the Lord take care of the rest." He waited, looking into her eyes.

Her lips quivered a little, and her eyes moistened. "I talked with Estelle too."

Earlier, Estelle had said to her, "Honey, he's just like a little boy. An excited little boy who is in love with you and in love with his work. He just blurted out his idea and got ahead of himself. He's not devious like Rashim. Give him a chance to explain himself."

Grace took a deep breath. "I'm going to take a leap of faith and trust you, because I'm falling for you too." She began crying and lowered her head.

Gently, Isaiah cupped his hand under her chin and raised her face. He gently kissed her lips. They were warm. Slowly, she responded and kissed him back. She reached up and put both arms around his neck. Finally, she ended the kiss and pressed her face against his chest.

"Grace," he whispered, "I'll take care of you. When you hurt, I hurt too. I love you." He hugged her closer.

She giggled. "Your apron smells like barbeque sauce . . . with . . . with . . ." She sniffed again, "what is that smell?"

"That, my sweet Grace, is my secret award-winning ingredient. It's classified. You'll just have to taste it and decide for yourself. Are you hungry?"

"I am now. Falling in love makes me hungry." She sighed and looked into his eyes again. He kissed her again.

"Let's go eat some barbeque." He took her hand and turned back to the house. "I feel like I'm sixteen again. May I carry your books to class?"

"Yes. Will you go steady with me?" she teased him.

"Oh, yes! My steady date, Grace Washington. I'm so lucky! What more could a boy want?" He skipped down the sidewalk.

"Oh, I don't know . . . maybe some barbeque ribs and potato salad?" She laughed and ran up the steps to the front door of George and Estelle's home. He laughed and ran after her. The scent of wisteria drifted into the house after them.

*   *   *   *   *   *

The man with a broken nose placed a call to his contact at the Pristine Influence on Society Foundation in Chicago. "It's me. I've been able to do some hacking into the computers at Nutritional Abundance Industries. They're planning to commercialize Dr. Grace Washington's super-seeds and sell them around the world. When? In time for the next growing season in Africa, so you'll have to move fast."

He listened. "OK. That's doable. I know just the people for the job."

*   *   *   *   *   *

During the meal, Estelle exclaimed, "I love these ribs! Isaiah, you are almost as good a cook as George. What's in this sauce?" She took another bite from the rib she was holding.

"That's my secret. The judges at Memphis tried to get it out of me, but I've been trained by the Navy to keep secrets vital to national security." He smiled. "What if the formula for this barbeque sauce fell into the wrong hands? This sauce is like Garrison Keillor's Powdermilk Biscuits: it gives shy people the strength to get up and do what must be done! Navy beat Army last year after I fed them barbeque with this sauce. I'm going to patent it."

George snorted. "I normally don't have anything positive to say about squids, but in this case, as an ex-Marine, I have to side with Navy. Don't let Army ever get hold of this formula. It's more of a football advantage than Gatorade! Semper Fi!" He winked at Isaiah.

George sighed contentedly and licked the sauce from his fingers. "Speaking of Gatorade, I asked Isaiah to help me with ideas to improve funding for the university trust fund. As you know, donations have been down. Isaiah offered a five percent royalty from sales of this software

51

y'all have been working on. If it's as good as he says it is, that will give us buckets of money!"

Grace looked up from her plate at George and then Isaiah. A smile stole across her face. "In that case, I'll donate the use of my name in advertising the software. Just wait three months before you sell it to any other university with an agricultural research program, O.K.? I want to get my results published first."

Isaiah and George simultaneously shouted "Deal!" and slapped high fives with Grace and Estelle and each other. Everyone laughed.

Estelle said, "It's so good to hear you folks laugh. I'm going to bring out the old-fashioned ambrosia I made for dessert. It's my mother's recipe." She gracefully rose and left the table.

Grace looked thoughtful. "To really take advantage of this software, I'm going to need more graduate students on my team to help me. Minerva Stone, the CEO of Nutritional Abundance Industries, an agribusiness in the Midwest, has been funding my research. She will probably pay for the additional student researchers. She called me last week and asked for a meeting to discuss commercializing my research. She wants to produce the super-seeds in time for the next growing season in Africa. We could ask her for royalties for the university also."

"Now you're talking!" George was animated. "Minerva Stone is a good businesswoman. I've read profiles of her in business magazines. She supports research because it feeds her new product pipeline. She'll talk turkey!"

Estelle had returned and was passing around bowls of ambrosia. Miniature marshmallows glistening with sweetened mayonnaise nestled beside slices of apples, raisins, bananas, walnuts and oranges. She held up a spoonful. "Here's an ambrosia toast to royalties for Tuskegee University!" The others held out their own loaded spoons. "Hear hear!" "Yes, sister!" "Amen!"

Isaiah looked thoughtful. "We forgot to say grace over this meal. May I say it now?"

Estelle smiled her small Mona Lisa smile and said, "Please do." They all held hands and bowed their heads.

"Lord, we thank You for this wonderful meal. We thank You for opportunities to earn money for the university. I thank You for good friends who will counsel me and help me when I'm down. I thank you for sending a wonderful woman into my life. We thank You for the

52

fellowship and love around this table. Amen." "Amen," and "Yes, Lord," echoed around the table.

The stars came out in the warm Alabama evening and shone down on them.

 **Chapter Five**

After choir practice that week, Grace walked over to speak to her friend Eunice, who was the principal of the K-6 Christian School run by her church.

"Hello Eunice, how are you? I love that shade of purple in your dress."

"Grace Washington, bless your heart for noticing. Purple is my favorite color, as if you didn't know. But, I'm not doing so well."

Eunice's small smile fell into a frown, and worry lines radiated from her eyes.

"Eunice, whatever is the matter?"

"Oh Grace, pray for us. Jesus said, 'Render unto Caesar the things that are Caesar's, and to God the things that are God's.' But now Caesar wants the things that are God's too."

"Eunice, what do you mean?"

"We just got an official visit from a woman with the US Department of Education informing us that as an educational institution we're no longer allowed to talk about, teach about, or even mention God, Jesus, religion, morality, or the Bible."

"What? That can't be right. What did she say was the justification?"

"The letter she gave us says the United States was founded on the principle of strict separation of church and state. It says that since education is the exclusive responsibility of the state, the federal government can rule on what may or may not be taught in any school, public or private, religious or secular. She cited a new executive order by President Fletcher that says each instance of teaching religion in any school carries a criminal penalty of a personal fine of $10,000 and six months in jail."

"Eunice, we have to fight this! This is not right!"

"Grace, I had a long conversation with Reverend Longfellow and our lawyer about this. Our lawyer says there is nothing we can do. I have a family to support. I can't spend time in jail, and I sure can't pay a $10,000 fine. All religious instruction will have to go back to Sunday school. And we better not call it 'school' anymore either."

Just then Reverend Longfellow walked up. "Hello Eunice, Grace. How was choir practice?"

Grace skipped the pleasantries. "Reverend, how can we allow the government to tell us we can't teach our own religion in our own religious school? We don't take any federal money. This school is financed by tuition and donations."

Reverend Longfellow looked down. His voice was sad. "That is all true. But they threatened to take away our tax exempt status and slap a $10,000 fine on Eunice and me personally. We can't pay it, and we can't ask the congregation to pay it for us. That wouldn't be right. The deacons and I have already decided to rename Sunday school as 'The Children's Church Service.' That should keep us out of trouble with the feds. Eunice will remove anything religious from our school curriculum, and we'll go on."

Grace felt the blood rush to her face. She was fighting mad. She turned and left the church social hall. Walking to her car, she thought, *I can't believe this! What is happening to my country? First the food police, then the bat police and now the education police. Someone has hijacked the United States of America and I don't recognize it anymore. I want my country back.*

She remembered one of the complaints about King George III that Thomas Jefferson listed in the Declaration of Independence: ""He has erected a multitude of new offices, and sent hither swarms of officers to harass our people and eat out their substance [wealth]." *Our own government is sending swarms of officers to drown us in a flood of controls and regulations. Where will it all end?*

*   *   *   *   *   *

"Samuel! Well done!" The jubilant voice of the executive director of the Pristine Influence on Society Foundation barked in his ear. Samuel Solipsis winced and held his cell phone a few inches away from his ear.

"Thanks, Mr. Dunforth. Our supporter, judicial clerk Nancy Jones, deserves credit for making sure that we drew Judge Block for this case. With Judge Block, we couldn't lose."

The Pristine Influence on Society Foundation (PRIS) had been granted an injunction to block the activation of a wind farm in the California desert, even though PRIS supported "green" causes. Their objection was that the "pristine" desert would be disturbed, even though it was private land. PRIS waited until the wind farm had been

55

constructed before filing for an injunction. Thousands of investors had lost hundreds of millions of dollars, including a union pension fund.

"Nevertheless, my boy, knowing how to manipulate the system is as important as legal expertise. You made a major contribution. Yes, a major contribution. Our executive council will be so pleased. They are also the compensation council, you know!" Samuel shifted in his seat uncomfortably. He was sitting alone in a booth at a "gentlemen's" club. The next strip act would not start for twenty minutes. He looked down at his sloe gin fizz.

He spoke carefully and cautiously, fearful of offending his boss. "Now, Mr. Dunforth, you know the executive order from the president strictly limits how often and how much salaries can be increased. I've already had one increase this year and that's the limit."

"Nonsense, my boy, nonsense! I'm a close personal friend of the president, and if I want our compensation committee to give you a raise, you'll get it. Those rules don't apply to *us*," he continued jubilantly.

"Yes sir. If you say so sir." Samuel continued nervously. "I don't ask for any more salary, but I defer to your wishes," he said subserviently. Samuel sipped his drink again and thought that this statement sufficiently covered him in case of an official inquiry later. He was a lawyer, after all. His boss rang off, and Samuel checked his wallet to see how many twenty-dollar bills he had as the club performers began to strut onstage.

He smiled smugly as he watched the girls, and thought, *Beautiful women, and I have the power to control their actions. My power is right here.* His right hand moved to cover his stack of twenty-dollar bills. Then it moved to his left wrist, pulling back his cuff to reveal an expensive Rolex watch. He absently stroked the watch and glanced at it. *A Rolex. I've arrived. With my legal skills, I control what big corporations can do. With my money, I control what these beautiful bitches do.*

He thought back to high school, and how the jocks and popular kids had called him names and shoved him around in the hallways. The pretty girls never spoke to him. He knew that many of his classmates now worked for the companies he filed injunctions against. His injunctions often caused layoffs or bankruptcies. *Who's sorry now, you losers? Who has the power now?*

Spotting his stack of twenties, one of the strippers, a pretty girl, made eye contact and smiled at him. He smiled back. *Who has the power now?*

*   *   *   *   *   *

Grace parked at Ann's Dry Cleaning to pick up a suit she had left last week. She walked in the front door of the neatly kept shop. "Hello Ann, how are you? Hey Tina. I'm here to pick up my suit." Ann Mulcahy owned and ran the dry cleaning shop. Tina, working in the back, waved at Grace. Ann stepped up to the counter. Her face was deeply lined and her eyes were expressionless.

"Ann, you look worried. What's the matter?" Grace always enjoyed chatting with Ann and Tina whenever she came in.

"I got a letter notifying me of an EPA inspection," Ann said slowly.

Just then they both heard the deep rumble of a large vehicle engine outside. Grace turned and looked through the large plate glass windows in the front of the shop. A large black SUV had pulled up and double-parked beside Grace's car. Two men in dark suits got out and entered the shop, carrying clipboards.

"Ann Mulcahy?"

"Yes, I'm Ann Mulcahy," Ann replied.

"I'm Inspector Karvuth and this is Inspector Hamilton. We're here to conduct your EPA HVRCA."

"HVRCA? What's that?" asked Grace.

"Ma'am, are you one of the proprietors of this business establishment?" The EPA Inspector Karvuth had turned to her, his pen poised above his clipboard.

"No. I'm a customer."

Agent Karvuth tapped his pen against his clipboard. "Ma'am, interfering with an EPA Hazardous Vapors Release Compliance Audit is a misdemeanor offense under the Federal Code, punishable by six months in a Federal Prison."

"Asking a question is a misdemeanor offense?" Grace was incredulous.

"Ma'am, you have been warned. Any further talk from you will be considered interfering with an EPA Inspector."

Grace took a deep breath and stepped back.

Inspector Karvuth turned back to Ann. "Mrs. Mulcahy, you are to cease operations while this inspection takes place."

"How long will that take?"

"It will take two days, maybe longer."

Ann looked like a deer in the headlights.

"But, what about my customers? They'll need to pick up their dry cleaning."

"Ma'am, your customers will have to wait until after this HVRCA is complete."

Grace began to speak, "But my suit . . ."

Inspector Karvuth quickly turned to stare at her, his eyes hard. His right hand had pulled back his suit coat to reveal a set of handcuffs on his belt. *The dry-cleaning Gestapo!* thought Grace. Grace bit off her words and looked at Ann. Ann's eyes pled with her, *Don't make trouble.*

Grace turned and walked out of the shop. Inspector Karvuth turned back to Ann.

"As I was saying, you are to cease operations while this inspection takes place."

Ann turned toward the back of the shop and called out, "Tina, shut it down for today and go home. I won't be needing you anymore today or for the next two days. I'm sorry." Then Ann walked around the counter to her front door and turned over the sign so that it said 'closed' to the outside world.

Outside the shop, Grace found that the double-parked government SUV had blocked her car. Taking out her cell phone, she called 911. "I want to report a double-parked vehicle blocking my car on the corner of 13th Street and Main. Yes, it's a black SUV. No, I don't know who it belongs to. You'll send a tow truck? Thank you so much. I'll be here."

Half an hour later, a tow truck driver winched the black SUV onto his flat bed and left. Grace got into her car and drove away. The two EPA Inspectors were in the back of the shop lecturing Ann and didn't notice.

"Mrs. Mulcahy," announced Inspector Karvuth, "under the new executive order by the head of the EPA, these bi-annual inspections will be charged to you as a required user fee for services rendered. Each inspection will cost you $15,000. Failure to pay will result in fines of $100 per day. Here's your invoice for this week's inspection. Fines for any violations that we discover will be an additional charge to you."

Ann's face went white. "Inspector, I can't afford all of that on the little bit of money we take in from this small business."

"That is not our problem ma'am. We are the Environmental Protection Agency, and we protect the environment from people like you."

"People like me? What do you mean?"

"Mrs. Mulcahy, people like you pollute the environment while convincing the public they need unnecessary services like dry cleaning. People can wash their own clothes, but your industry brainwashes them into thinking they need dry cleaning. Europeans have a much more environmentally sound attitude about water-wasteful clothes washing and personal bathing. They don't do it as often as wasteful Americans do. We at the EPA applaud, emulate, and promote their example of sustainability."

Ann smelled their acrid sweat and noticed the ketchup stains on Inspector Karvuth's tie. *And you emulate their stink too*, thought Ann.

"Mrs. Mulcahy, it is now three o'clock, and our International Government Service Workers' Union contract protects our workers' rights to a reasonable work day. We'll be back tomorrow morning at nine a.m. Remember, no business is to be conducted until we complete our audit and release the property back to you."

They left and stood on the sidewalk, puzzled by the absence of their SUV. The junior inspector asked Karvuth, "What do we do now? Our motel is three blocks away."

"Call Washington for instructions, of course. Use your cell phone. Maybe they will send someone from the field office to pick us up. Then we'll fax in a missing vehicle report to the EPA motor pool accountability office. Use form EPA-3666."

What am I going to do, thought Ann as she locked the back door. *I don't know. Keep going until my money runs out, I suppose.*

When she got home, she pulled up her bank balance on her computer. The lines on her face grew deeper.

Lower than I thought. That EPA bill is due immediately. I'll have to lay Tina off next week and work fourteen-hour days by myself. Well, at least Tina's husband Bill has a good job at Carl's Auto Service. They'll get by.

*   *   *   *   *   *

Grace pulled into the parking lot of Carl's Auto Service in Tuskegee. A smiling black man in overalls came out, wiping his hands on a shop rag. "Carl," exclaimed Grace, "good to see you. How are Velma and the children?" Carl White was a good friend. After she had called to tell him about the arrest of Rashim (the crooked boyfriend) years ago, he never brought up the topic again.

"Hello Grace! They're fine. How about you?"

"Fine Carl, couldn't be better."

"I guess so, with that fine looking Isaiah Mercury hovering around you at church! Before too long, I'll get to ask you about *your* husband and children," he teased her.

"Oh Carl, too soon to think about that! But he is fine looking, isn't he?" Grace smiled a pleased little smile. Carl laughed.

"What can I do for you?" asked Carl.

"The air conditioning isn't cooling very well. Would you take a look at it?"

"I just had a cancellation, so this is your lucky day. Give me the keys, and I'll pull it in and check it out for you." He held out his hand and she gave him the keys.

She looked at the other three garage bays as she walked toward the waiting room. In all three, mechanics were working on cars, and the parking lot had seven more cars to be serviced. Carl had worked hard, developed a good reputation, and now had a steady stream of customers. She waved to Tony, a teenager, helping the mechanic in bay one. Tony was from Grace's church, and she knew his parents. He was working part-time after school and learning the business quickly, according to Carl. Carl himself had a fine brick home, drove a late model Mercedes, and was putting two of his children through college, one of them at Tuskegee University.

Pausing, she looked back at Carl, now bending over the engine of her car, hood open. He rose up, turned to a pegboard and selected the right tool. Then he bent back over the car. His movements were precise, with no wasted motion, the choreography of a skilled craftsman at work.

As she turned back, she suddenly stopped as a strobe light went off inside her head. *This is it! This is the secret, hidden in plain sight right here in front of me.*

Hard work builds prosperity.

60

The world was not divided into the 'haves' and the 'have-nots,' as some would have us believe. Carl did not 'have' because he took it away from someone else. Nor did he 'exploit' anyone. He started with $500, a box of tools, and a rented garage. He made his start working fifteen-hour days for his customers, and he now provides jobs for three other mechanics, plus a practical apprenticeship for the teenage Tony. They are all benefitting from Carl's hard work in building up a business.

Instead, the world was divided into the 'earns' and the 'earn-nots.' Carl earned, and four other people are the beneficiaries. They are earning and learning themselves, thanks to Carl.

Carl and tens of millions just like him are the economic engines of America, but few people know it. They, the little-known Americans, get up and go to work every day, and keep finding better ways to do the work. These hard working Americans are the secret of American prosperity.

The secret, hidden in plain sight, right here in front of me, marveled Grace. *The secret of everyday prosperity, as simple as a socket wrench, the will to work with it, and the willingness to learn how to troubleshoot and solve problems. Graduate-level economics, just taught to me by my neighbor Carl, the auto mechanic.*

*   *   *   *   *   *

When Carl returned her keys, she paid her bill to Tony at the cash register. Carl was sorting through his mail, and stopped and frowned at one envelope. Opening it, he scanned the contents, and then frowned again. Watching him, Grace asked, "Bad news, Carl?"

"Let me walk you to your car." Carl motioned with his head at the door. When they got to her car in the lot, Carl said, "I didn't want to talk in front of Tony. New federal regulations on professional certification requirements for auto mechanics have come down. To get the certification, we have to attend a training course that costs eight thousand dollars. It's stuff my guys and I already know, but the federal government is extending its tentacles into it. It's the equivalent of "no mechanic left behind." Without it, they aren't allowed to work. I'm assessed a twenty thousand dollar fine per uncertified mechanic."

"Carl, I'm so sorry. That's a ridiculous regulation. I didn't remember reading that Congress passed such a law."

61

"Congress didn't pass it. Some new bureaucrat with the EPA says unqualified mechanics put more emissions in the air every time they work on an automobile. No data, no proof, just his opinion. Because it's a supposedly 'Green' opinion, nobody will question it. Just like global warming, excuse me, climate change."

"Tell me about it. I'm a scientist, and when they intimidate the editors of scientific journals to suppress data contradictory to global warming, I know it's not science."

"Anyway, I can't ask my mechanics to pony up eight thousand dollars each for this. They have families to support. I'll have to cover it, but in this down economy, I'll have to lay off Tony and Bill. Tony's a good kid and a hard worker, but he doesn't have a family to support. Bill was the last one I hired, and he and his wife Tina have no children yet. Tina works at the dry cleaners, so they'll have one income to live on."

"Oh Carl, Tony is such a bright kid. I'll ask the maintenance chief at the university if he needs some part-time help."

Driving away, Grace meditated on her new insight and added a qualifier. *Hard work creates prosperity, IF you let it.* She had just witnessed the creeping control that exacted a price, a hidden tax that nobody voted for. Tony and Bill were paying the price. Carl is trying to build prosperity for himself and others, but the government won't let him.

She sighed. *The economy is bad, unemployment is high, and what do they do? Make it harder for small business owners like Carl to support the employees they do have.* She remembered reading a glowing bio on the EPA bureaucrat when he was first appointed by the president. His uncle owned the automotive training institute that was now the sole source provider for the required training for all mechanics in America.

This regulation of auto mechanics, thought Grace, *was just one of thousands of corrupt and costly rules, regulations, and arbitrary standards flooding over the land, forced on us without our consent by federal, state, and local politicians. Before, we were like people struggling to wade through knee-deep water. Now the flood of controls is waist high. People like Carl, the job creators, are struggling to move through the flood waters of corrupt rules and regulation. It's an economic tsunami washing over us in slow motion. What will we do when it reaches our noses? Where will it all end?*

Suddenly, she knew. She pulled the car over. She leaned her head on the steering wheel and gripped it so tightly her knuckles showed white for a moment. After a few minutes, she relaxed her grip and got out of the car. She stood, looking at the sky.

Where will it all end? I know. **I know where it will end.** *I've just been avoiding the obvious conclusion. I am a scientist, and I can connect the dots. I can project growth rates of disease and project trend lines into the future. It will end with America looking like North Korea, a fourteenth century subsistence economy with nuclear weapons. It will end with Americans living like refugees, with food shortages, repeating famines, neighbor informing on neighbor, and enforced political rallies to praise our 'dear leader.' The America I grew up in, land of the free and home of the brave, is dying, drowning in an economic tsunami of corrupt control and regulations. And ironically, the epicenter sending out this destructive tsunami is Washington, D.C.*

This pain, this numbness, this shock, was like . . . the pain of the impending death of a loved one. *I'm at the bedside, and my loved one, America, is moving less and less. Her breathing is more shallow and raspy.* Grace remembered the signs when her grandmother died. The pain in her heart now was like the pain she had felt then.

I had to let go of grandma, and I have to let go of the America I knew and loved. The America I knew is drowning in this polluted tide of smelly political floodwater. How can we survive a flood of corruption, controls, and coercion? Dry cleaning Gestapo intimidating middle-aged women like Ann and ordinary citizens like me in small towns all over America! Dear Lord, I don't know what to do. Help me figure out what to do. Help me, Lord, help me and help our nation. We are drowning and need your help, she prayed. She bowed her head, took a breath, and let go of control. She felt drained, weak, limp. *Help me to let go and let God,* she prayed.

A few minutes later, she raised her head. Tears were in her eyes, but also a look of determination. *The Lord our God is also the Lord of the floodwaters. He will provide and show us how to survive this man-made flood. Now I know what I have to do. I have to grieve for the nation I'm letting go of, as surely as I grieved for Grandma, but I know what I have to do. Thank you, Lord, for sending me inspiration. Now if I can just find some gopherwood . . .* She started the car and drove off.

 **Chapter Six**

Isaiah yawned as he flipped the egg in the frying pan. He and Grace now had a routine. He came early Saturday morning and cooked breakfast for the two of them. Then he went back to his hotel to write software code. He returned at six for their standing Saturday night date.

The dogwoods were still in bloom outside the kitchen window. He heard a "plop" on the driveway and turned his head to look out the other window toward the front yard. *Dang, he thought, they still deliver newspapers here.* He himself got all of his news from selected web sites downloaded to his iPad. Deftly sliding the egg onto a plate, he put bacon in the pan and then went to retrieve the paper.

Sitting down to his breakfast, he opened the paper. "Federal Government to Regulate Executive Pay," read the headline. In the fourth paragraph down, he read, "Treasury Secretary Gunther signed his name to the press release explaining that all pay of any employee, salaried, hourly, or contractor, is now subject to federal guidelines and controls, to be issued later this month. 'No one has the right to say how much he or she is worth,' said Secretary Gunther. 'Only the Treasury Department of the federal government can ensure that each person will be paid fairly. Federal employees above the level of G12 are exempt from this regulation, pursuant to Executive Order 616.'"

Oh brother, thought Isaiah. *I'll bet ninety-nine point nine percent of Americans don't even notice that the fourth paragraph says any employee. They think Gunther is going after the fat cats. Now we're all going to be skinny cats, after Gunther has grabbed yours, mine, and ours. Except the Feds of course.*

"Umm. Is that bacon I smell?" Grace slowly came down the stairs, tying the belt of her bathrobe. One slim brown leg was visible where the bathrobe opened in front.

"Umm-um. Is that my beautiful woman I see?" Isaiah stood up and looked her up and down appreciatively.

"A beautiful *hungry* woman." She smiled up at him and put her arms around him. They kissed.

"One egg, coming up for one beautiful, hungry woman. Bacon is on the platter. Coffee?" He was already breaking an egg into the frying pan.

"Yes, please." He brought the coffee pot over and poured a cup for her. Then he turned back to his cooking.

Grace pulled the newspaper over to her side of the table. "Gunther continues to be grabby for other people's money, I see." She sipped her coffee.

Turning to her with the frying pan, he served her egg. "What's on your agenda for this next week?"

She looked up at the ceiling, thinking. "Well, let me think. The work on the gene splices for the grains is done. The results are documented. I've almost finished my research article for *Science* summarizing the results and the applications in Africa and the rest of the world. Nutritional Abundance Industries is ready to begin sales and distribution of the grain seeds for the new strains into the African, Indian, and Asian markets. The university is on spring break, so no classes to teach. So, to answer your question, two things: finishing my article, and appearing at the press conference that Nutritional Abundance Industries is holding in Chicago."

"Grace, I've read your findings. You do know that your super-seeds have the potential to *end world hunger*? This is huge!"

"Yes, I know. It just hasn't sunk in yet."

"Why Chicago? Why not New York? More media there." He sipped his coffee.

"Well, Chicago is home to the agricultural commodities markets. Wheat futures, sow belly futures, that sort of thing. So it has the agriculture history, the Midwest "breadbasket of the world" symbolism. Also, Nutritional Abundance Industries is headquartered in Peoria, so Chicago is closer. Hey! These eggs are good!"

He smiled, "Don't sound so surprised."

"So? What's on your agenda?" She sipped her coffee.

He looked at her thoughtfully. "Well, I've been keeping this a secret, but I'm ready to announce the launch of my new marketplace software."

She dropped her fork. "So soon? I thought you had another six months of beta testing. Have you decided on a product name yet?"

"That's part of the surprise. I know more about your business than I let on. I know that Tuskegee President George T'Chaka Wright himself will be at your press conference to sign the royalty agreement between Nutritional Abundance Industries and Tuskegee University, based on your work. I also know that Nutritional Abundance will announce an endowment funding the Grace Washington Chair of Agricultural Science at Tuskegee University. Congratulations, sweetheart." He reached over the table and took her hand.

"Well! You certainly are well-informed! I don't know whether to be flattered that you're so nosy about me or offended that you're so nosy about me," she sniffed.

Isaiah smiled, "I'll answer that one. Flattered. I'm proud to be the royal consort of the queen of biotechnology. I make it my business to do research for your press clippings. It also helps to be the close personal friend of President George T'Chaka Wright."

"Ok, I'll choose to be flattered. Any more surprises?" She looked shrewdly at him.

Isaiah met her stare and chuckled. "You know me too well. Yes, there are two more surprises, but only if you agree to them."

"Oh?" She arched an eyebrow.

He took a deep breath. "OK, here they are. First, I am asking your permission to crash your party. I want to make it a joint press conference in Chicago to announce the release of my new marketplace software along with your new bio-engineered super-seeds." He held his breath, looking at her anxiously.

"A joint press conference? But why? What does your software have to do with my seeds?" She looked genuinely puzzled.

He took another deep breath. "Here goes. My new software is revolutionary. Not just because of what it does, but because of how easy it is to use. You know that I was trying to take the concept of E-Buyer type software for buying and selling to a new level. Here's the new level: My software works on ordinary cell phones with texting capabilities. No expensive iPhone or Blackberry required. I've concluded a deal with five of the biggest cell phone networks in Africa, India, and Asia to add my software service to their networks for the price of the text messages involved in accessing it. These network providers link to my software via satellite feeds. I have leased bandwidth on the HughesNet system of global communications satellites."

"So, you'll have global reach?" Her eyes shone.

"Yes. There's a simple graphical interface on the cell phone screen, so no computer is required. It's cloud computing, where the software is on my end, not in the cell phone. Small farmers in Africa and India will be able to market their crops for the price of a cell phone and a few dozen text messages. Buying and selling worldwide will be as simple as calling your cousin in the next town. The cost of doing business across great distances, even internationally, will come down to levels even the smallest subsistence farmer can afford. Trade will increase exponentially. Prosperity will rapidly grow for these folks at the bottom of the economic ladder."

He took another deep breath, looked down, and then refilled her coffee. "Now do you see the connection?"

She connected the dots at once. "Of course! When small farmers get my new seeds, they will have excess crops to sell, far above what they need for themselves. Your software connects them to the markets, so they can earn the money to improve the lives of their families. It's brilliant! And a true synergy with my product. If the crops don't get sold and moved from farm to market, *nobody* gets fed.

"Isaiah, when I was in Botswana last year, I remember one of the farmers, a Mr. Mantate Kubabupe, saying he didn't know how to contact the Kenyan markets that would offer the best price for his maize crop. If he can access your software with an inexpensive cell phone, he can make the sale. And his young and bright son can be sent to school with the money he will make.

"Yes! The answer is yes. I want you to share my press conference. Using these two products together enables the crops to flow to where the hunger is. But what will Nutritional Abundance Industries say?"

He grinned again. "They've already said it. I took the liberty of sounding out Minerva Stone on the idea. She said, and I quote, 'We're willing to do it, but only if Dr. Grace Washington agrees. This is her day, a celebration of her achievement.' Do you approve?"

"Yes, my darling, yes! What's the name of your new software application? You know that the brand name I chose jointly with the NAI marketing team is 'Carver's Legacy,' in honor of my hero and inspiration George Washington Carver."

This time his eyes shone. "I know, and it sends a thrill up my leg just to hear the brand name again. It reminds us of the achievements of a scientist who worked hard to create agricultural products that benefitted small farmers and enabled them to work their way up to prosperity. That ex-slave never whined that he was disadvantaged. He just up and invented better ways to farm and create wealth."

"You mean there is something besides me that sends a thrill up your leg? Should I be jealous? So what's the name of your new software?" She put her hand on his.

"Invisible Hand. The Marketplace Software that lends an invisible hand to your business, to your family, and to the prosperity of the people of our planet," he intoned in his best baritone radio voice. "I've signed up James Earl Jones to read those lines for us. ZNN, move over!"

"Even li'l ol me can connect those dots," Grace teased. "Economist Adam Smith's concept of the 'invisible hand' that guides the free marketplace for the benefit of all concerned, without anyone consciously planning it or trying to control it."

"Hey! You're good at connecting dots," he replied happily. "What, no thrill up your leg? I'm insulted."

"I think someone has just run a thrill up to my heart." She came around the table to sit on his lap.

"Umm. Me too."

"You haven't asked me what the second surprise is," he murmured after a kiss.

"OK, what?"

"Dr. Grace Washington, will you marry me?"

She looked into his eyes.

"Isaiah Mercury, you don't have to ask me twice. Yes. The answer is yes. Yes." She smiled her deep, dimpled smile and kissed him.

"Dr. Grace Washington, you have made me a very happy man."

"And you have made me a very happy woman."

He leaned his head on her chest and hugged her tighter. "I love you so much."

$$* \qquad * \qquad * \qquad * \qquad * \qquad *$$

That afternoon, giddy as a schoolgirl, Grace stopped into *Halo*, a beauty parlor she favored. She wanted to look extra nice for her date that night with Isaiah. "Hey girl! About time you came in here to get yourself more gorgeous!" called Tonya Soames. "Just set yourself down here in my chair, and we *will* make you a beauty fit to tame the beast. Not that that tall dark hunk of man you hang out with nowadays is a beast."

"What's new, girlfriend?" Grace asked.

"Nothing. That's the problem. Has that man of yours got a brother? What's his name? Isaiah?" She shook out the cape to cover Grace.

"Isaiah Mercury. And sorry, he's an only child, like me. And you know only children never learned to share, so don't even think about messin' with my man!" Grace dished out this trash talk in a lilt that was delightful to hear.

"Oohh! I hear that! You've got a good thing going girl, I hope you know." She winked at Grace. "Now, what can we do to beautify you to the max?"

"Well," said Grace, more slowly as she thought about it, "I have a hot date tonight, but I'm also traveling to Chicago for a press conference this week. So, I need hair that will last the week of traveling and meetings without major fussing. Any suggestions?"

"African braids. No doubt in my mind. Your hair is long enough so they'll hang down to your shoulders, making you look like an elegant African princess, and you don't need to do anything to them for a week. Do you have two hours?"

"Yes. That sounds perfect."

"Viola! Need help over here with braiding. Grace, you are one lucky girl. Viola can only do braiding under my supervision now. She was supposed to be off today, but she came in to get her check, and I need her help to get it done in two hours."

"Why can't she do braiding by herself anymore? Hi Viola." The two women began braiding Grace's hair, one on either side of her.

"The state cosmetology health and safety inspector came around and said that only licensed cosmetologists can do braiding, even though no color or heat or chemicals are involved. The license requires two thousand hours of training, plus tuition money for the school. So, she has to stop doing it by herself, or they will shut me down. Huh! Braiding has been done for three thousand years in Africa without any health problems and without any cosmetology board, thank you very much."

Grace relaxed and closed her eyes, enjoying the gentle stimulation of her scalp while they worked on her hair. "Tonya, I'm getting fed up with all this regulation and control from government. They treat us like little kids who have to be shushed and fed and put to bed, because the grown-ups in Washingon, D.C. or Montgomery think that only they know what's best for us. Like this thing with Viola. I can decide for myself

69

who's qualified to braid my hair. Nobody in Montgomery knows what's best for my hair."

"Amen, sister! I feel the same way. It's getting so complicated to run a simple business like a beauty shop. I'm good at hairdressing, not filling out long forms and interpreting complicated regulations. If I were trying to start up this business today, I don't know if I could."

"Oh Tonya, it scares me to think of that. You provide jobs. You're good for the community."

"I'm so glad you said that. I thought I was the only one who felt that way. It's not politically correct to say that business people are good for the community, but that's the way I see it."

Viola spoke up. "I agree. I was going to attend cosmetology school anyway, but I could have paid my own way if I could do hair braiding here at the shop without supervision. I've been doing it since I was seven years old, starting with my mother and sisters, so I've probably got three thousand hours of actual practice braiding hair. But the state cosmetology board wants to control it all."

Tonya snorted, "Them and a hundred other state and federal agencies who want to control us. It's the return of slavery."

Tonya did her best imitation of Butterfly McQueen's squeaky voice as the slave Prissy in the movie version of *Gone With The Wind*. "Massa, may I braid some hair? Yes massa, no massa, whatever you say, massa."

Grace, Viola, and the other customers and beauticians were laughing so hard tears were rolling down their cheeks. Viola was bent over laughing, and gasped, "Tonya! Stop! I'm laughing so hard my stomach hurts!"

After wiping the laughter tears from her eyes, Grace said, "So Viola, what will you do?"

"I'll keep working here as an assistant and start cosmetology school at night next semester. Tonya is going to loan me the tuition money. I'll pay her back each month after I graduate."

Grace opened her eyes. *The secret again. Hidden here in plain sight in a beauty parlor with two hard-working women. They are little-known outside of this community, but they have the secret.*

She looked around. Four other cosmetologists were working on hair, chattering away and laughing as they worked. *Four jobs. Four kitchen tables with groceries put on them, groceries earned by the work they did here. Four jobs made possible by Tonya.*

Ordinary Americans, hiding in plain sight with the secret unknown to most economists, politicians, and so-called activists. Hard work builds prosperity. Learn, work, and earn.

Tonya herself had worked part time while she attended cosmetology school. Like Carl White, Tonya had begun with little: one room in her mother-in-law's house. She worked on hair morning, noon, and night. She saved her money. Now she owned this building, an attractive shop built in the style of a cottage, with attractive touches like purple shutters on the windows and flowers in window boxes.

Why is this such a secret? thought Grace. *It's not that complicated unless other people make it complicated. Like the state cosmetology board, trillion dollar stimulus programs, and thousand-page laws that nobody reads until it's too late.*

Grace remembered a poem by Joseph Pintauro about Dr. Frankenstein wanting to create life the hard way, in a laboratory. He didn't realize that it was as easy as falling in love and having a baby.

It is as easy as falling in love with your work and doing it well, thought Grace. *If only these Frankenstein social engineers in Washington would quit experimenting on us.*

 **Chapter Seven**

The banner at the press conference read "Technology Conquers Hunger." It was scheduled for 8:30 a.m. at the Chicago Board of Trade, just before the starting bell for agricultural commodities trading. ZNN, Bloomberg, Reuters, ZSNBC, FBN, ZNBC, Yahoo Finance, FACTS Business News, Business Week, Investor's Business Daily, Forbes, Money, Financial Times, The Economist, Essence, Black Entrepreneur, and Fortune were invited to the press conference. Sausage biscuits and coffee were served on a buffet. Brief remarks were scheduled from the economist Sowell Thomas and the technology writer Geoffrey Guild. A videographer was covering it as a live feed and for later podcast on the internet. He was jointly hired by Nutritional Abundance Industries and Isaiah Mercury's firm, Promethean Software International.

"Ladies and Gentlemen, welcome to the most stunning technology breakthrough of our time: the end of world hunger. What you are about to see is the future of farming and the future of the worldwide marketplace," boomed Minerva Stone, CEO of Nutritional Abundance Industries. A self-made millionaire by age twenty-three, she now led the most research-intensive agricultural products company on the planet. She was of medium height but her steel-gray eyes flashed with authority and confidence.

"I'm Minerva Stone, CEO of Nutritional Abundance Industries. I would like to introduce a renowned thinker and author on innovation and creativity, Mr. Geoffrey Guild." Applause erupted from the appreciative crowd of business savvy investors and reporters.

"Thank you, Minerva," began Guild. "I can say without fear of contradiction that you live up to your namesake: Minerva, the Greek goddess of wisdom. You showed extraordinary wisdom in devoting research and development funds to radical new approaches to plant genetics and crop yields. I was delighted to accept your invitation to make remarks today about one of your chief researchers, Dr. Grace Washington. As you all will soon know from her scientific article to be published in *Science*, her genetically engineered crops will yield four times more food on just one-tenth of the land, with only one-tenth of the water and one-tenth the fertilizer. They are also insect and blight resistant, so that very little pesticides are needed.

"For their part, Nutritional Abundance Industries not only funded Dr. Washington's work, but they have discovered ways to produce the seeds more cheaply. The seeds will sell forty percent below the cost of conventional seeds, so that even the poorest of third-world farmers can afford them. In addition, NAI has dedicated the first year's production of these high-yield seeds exclusively for sale to subsistence farmers in Africa, India, and Asia. No seeds will be sold in the developed nations until next year."

"Ladies and Gentlemen, children around the world will be fed, and famines will end, as a result of this extraordinary invention." He paused.

"This is it, the beginning of the end of world hunger!" He reached over to an open sack of wheat, and pushed it over. The grain spilled out over the stage, an abundance of golden kernels.

"This unparalleled achievement is due to the analytical work, the genius, and the long hours of one woman and her dedicated team of research assistants. That woman is a visionary scientist and leader, willing to research where no one had researched before. I give you the once and future Nobel Prize winner, Dr. Grace Washington!"

Applause rippled as Grace stepped forward to the rostrum. She was elegantly dressed in a soft grey suit with perfect drape that said "business," yet revealed a few curves. She shook Guild's hand and pulled the microphone up to her height.

"Thank you, Mr. Guild, for your gracious remarks. I am proud. I am proud of my own hard work and my rigorous research that made this possible. I am proud of my team of researchers who worked so long and hard at my side. I am proud that our research was accelerated due to the special software created by Mr. Isaiah Mercury and his team at Promethean Software International. I am proud of the encouragement and support from Ms. Minerva Stone of NAI, and from my president, Tuskegee University President George T'Chaka Wright.

"NAI has given me the privilege of naming this new brand of seeds. Hard intellectual work, long hours, and the freedom to pursue radical new ideas are the ingredients that produced this new strain of seeds. In that tradition, I name it 'Carver's Legacy,' in honor of my childhood hero George Washington Carver, a fellow scientist who believed in the value of hard work. His work improved the lot of the small farmer and fed more people. So shall mine. Thank you."

Thunderous applause. Then a short photo session captured NAI CEO Stone presenting the royalty agreement to Tuskegee University President Wright. Grace looked on with a smile as Minerva then presented a check to endow the Grace Washington Chair of Agricultural Science at Tuskegee University.

Next, Sowell Thomas stepped up to be introduced by Dr. Wright. George took the podium. "I am the President of Tuskegee University. My name is Dr. George T'Chaka Wright. At Tuskegee University, we carry on the ideals of hard work, thrift, and entrepreneurship espoused by our founder, Booker T. Washington. We are proud of one of his descendants, our own Professor Grace Washington, for again showing how those ideals pay off in the real world. Now I am, we are, proud to introduce our next speaker, a world renowned economist and the author of forty-seven books: Dr. Sowell Thomas." More wild applause erupted from the traders and business reporters present.

"Thank you, President Wright. I'm proud to be on the same platform with you, Minerva Stone, and Dr. Grace Washington, achievers and producers who benefit families with their discoveries. It is indeed in the tradition of Booker T. Washington and George Washington Carver that we are here today honoring the new inventions of two extraordinary people of science, hard work, and entrepreneurship.

"I am an economist, a free market economist. I stand before you to honor the man who has brought us a tool to help us use the free market — a man who brought us a tool to make our lives better, as Prometheus brought the tool of fire to mankind in ancient Greek mythology. Fittingly, he has named his new software *Invisible Hand*, after the concept of the Invisible Hand, coined by the first free market economist Adam Smith. The invisible hand that brings mutual benefits to all who engage in free and honest exchange of goods and services by mutual consent."

Thomas paused. "You may ask, what has this got to do with ending world hunger? If we have the food, why do we need the software? Because the food has to move and flow from the farmers to the cities and countries where people will eat it. This means trade. This means buying and selling. The farmer has to sell the food crops he raised. I can give you examples of food rotting in the fields because it was not harvested, because nobody bought it, or a government didn't want it to flow to hungry people. No flow of food means no end to world hunger.

"*If you can't flow it, there's no sense to grow it.*" Appreciative laughter rose from the audience.

"Mr. Mercury's software enables the farmer to connect with world markets, so the food can flow. His new software is simple enough to be used by people unskilled with computers. It's cheap enough to be used for the price of several dozen text messages. You don't have to buy the software, you just use it. It leapfrogs over computers to offer itself on any cell phone with basic texting functions, much more available and affordable in developing countries than advanced G3 or G4 cell phones. It connects buyers and sellers all around the world. When the small farmers in Africa, India, and Asia raise a bumper crop, more than enough to feed their families, they will now be able to afford a simple but powerful tool that helps them to sell that crop at the best market price. If the local merchant doesn't offer a good price for his crop, that farmer can now sell to someone in the next province, or on the next continent. That better price will help the farmer and his family grow and prosper and continue to grow food for a hungry world.

"Thanks to Invisible Hand software, this bounty of food will flow around the globe.

"Ladies and Gentlemen, I give you Isaiah Mercury!" Dr. Thomas stepped forward to grip his hand, but Isaiah embraced him.

"You've always been one of my heroes," Isaiah said into his ear above the waves of applause.

"Thanks, Isaiah. That means a lot, coming from you."

Isaiah stepped up to the microphone. "Before I make my remarks, I want you all to be the first to hear some spoken words that will be part of the brand of my firm, Promethean Software International. I have a mystery guest who needs no introduction, Mr. James Earl Jones!" The audience exploded into applause.

James Earl Jones bounded up, and with his trademark impish smile, leaned close to the microphone and made the famous "whooo-cheee" aqualung breathing noise he had made famous as the voice-over for Darth Vader in the "Star Wars" movies. The crowd broke into laughter.

Then he drew himself up, leaned into the microphone once again, and with his majestic baritone, breathed, "*Invisible Hand. The marketplace software that lends an invisible hand to your business, to your family, and to the prosperity of the people of our planet.*" There were three seconds of dead silence. Then everyone broke into wild applause. With that, he turned, shook Isaiah's hand, and stepped away.

Isaiah came back to the microphone. "Now that, among other things, is what sends a thrill up my leg!" More laughter from the crowd ensued. "You'll hear that again and again.

"We're here today to announce two new products that will change the world and make it a better place. One will help grow the food to feed the world, and the other will help that food flow around the world freely and easily. I'm proud of my invention, and I'm proud of the invention of my colleague Dr. Grace Washington. But, ladies and gentlemen, there is something I am even prouder of.

"Today I stand before you a proud man and a lucky man. Dr. Grace Washington has agreed to be my wife!" More applause. He turned and motioned for Grace to come up. She did so, smiling and dipping her head coquettishly.

"Who do you think is prouder?" she asked the audience, pointing to herself and flashing a wide smile. She reached out and pulled Isaiah in for a big photo-op kiss at the podium. Dozens of camera flashes went off.

Minerva Stone announced, "Ladies and Gentlemen, this concludes our press conference. Help yourselves to Midwest sausage and biscuits, pick up our brochures, and enjoy the opening bell of this historic American marketplace."

Suddenly, from the back of the crowd, someone began shouting through a bullhorn. "Franken-foods deform babies! Franken-foods overpopulate the planet! Selling software enriches capitalists! Mercury exploits poor farmers!"

A dozen people removed their coats to reveal green T-shirts with the PRIS logo. They brought out concealed placards and began waving them above their heads. "Grace Washington mutilates embryos!" read one. Another proclaimed, "Promethean software steals from poor farmers!" "Put a wooden stake through Grace Washington's heart!" "Boycott Promethean Software!" "Franken-foods mutilate animals!"

One green-clad female protester ran forward and threw a container of pig's blood on Grace, covering her face and chest with it. Grace blinked and tried to use her hands to wipe it from her eyes.

"You fascist cow!" the protester screamed at Grace. "You kill babies! You mutilate animals! You have blood on your hands, and now you have the blood of your victims in your eyes. You deserve to die!" She reached down and pulled out a large knife from the waist of her pants.

Isaiah Mercury crouched like a tiger. You could almost see his rippling thigh muscles coiling for a spring. He slid forward and executed a Steven Segal-style takedown, left hand parrying the knife, right hand to the throat, while the right foot swept the attacker's foot backward. The chunky woman in green went down backwards. Her head hit the floor. Her knife-wielding hand cracked against a chair, but kept gripping the knife. Isaiah broke that forearm with one whip-crack kick. Then he kicked the knife away from the limp hand. The videographer he had hired for the occasion got it all on tape.

Police officers arrived and summoned an ambulance to take the woman away. As paramedics loaded her on a gurney, Isaiah saw the patches on their jackets. "Wait a minute! Where are you taking her?"

"Memorial Hospital," they replied.

"Take her to Cook County Jail. They have doctors to treat her there. She's a danger to the doctors, nurses, and other patients at the hospital."

"Mr. Mercury, she's unconscious. She's no danger to anyone." Isaiah stepped to the gurney. Quick as a flash, the woman's left arm whipped out another, smaller knife from her waistband. Isaiah, equally quick, caught the wrist in an iron grip and twisted her palm down and back. Another "crack" noise, and she dropped the knife.

"She's not a danger for the next thirty minutes until feeling comes back into her wrist. Officer, frisk her and escort these paramedics to take her to Cook County Jail." Isaiah turned back to where Grace was sitting, wiping off blood with a towel. The police officer handcuffed the woman to the gurney on both sides.

"You heard the man. I'm riding with you to Cook County Jail. I'm calling ahead for medical help to be standing by. No life-threatening injuries here." They began wheeling her off.

George Wright and Minerva Stone clustered around Grace in her chair. "I might have to give the name T'Chaka to you, Isaiah. You're quite a warrior," George said as he looked Isaiah over. "Are you all right?"

"Just shaky from the adrenaline," said Isaiah. He looked at Grace. "We should get you checked over and send that blood to a lab for analysis. There might be toxins or disease in it. There's an excellent private clinic only three blocks away. Let's go." He put his arm around Grace and helped her up.

"I'll drive," said George.

Minerva looked grim. "Drive my car, George. I'm coming too. I've got a carry permit and a Glock. I'll ride shotgun. Grace and Isaiah can ride in the back."

"You got it," said George.

 **Chapter Eight**

Executive Director Edgar Dunforth looked around the conference table at the monthly meeting of Board Members of the Pristine Influence on Society Foundation (PRIS). Samuel Solipsis, chief counsel and litigator, sat against the wall on his right, not at the table with board members. Dunforth unconsciously stroked the back of his left hand with his right.

The recording secretary, sitting against the wall on his left, read the roll call for the minutes of the meeting.

"Mr. Sonny Fremont." Fremont was executive director of ACANT, the Association of Community Activists Nonaligned for Truth. The "nonaligned" part of their name indicated that they were not formally aligned with any political party. Their most recent campaign involved protests and picketing at the homes of the county commissioners of Cook County. Their demand was that all unemployed persons be given two votes as a form of "political equity" and be made eligible for welfare payments in addition to their unemployment benefits. Picketers at the homes shouted threats at the children of the commissioners as they left for school each morning. One week later, the commissioners voted to give ACANT what they wanted. The picketers were withdrawn the next day.

"Ms. Diana Nomenski." Nomenski was executive director of the Feminist League of Professional Women (FLPW). Their current community outreach program was a public relations campaign to "Just Say No to Subservience." All working women were told to refuse all orders, directions, or communications of any kind from a male. All females were encouraged to shame, shun, and gossip about any other female worker who actually did her work in response to any request from a male, even if the male person was a customer.

Just last month, their members staged a sit-in at the local terminal of the Delivery Express Trucking Company. Whenever the female dispatchers gave a pick-up or delivery order to a male driver, it was OK. When male customers called in to schedule a pick-up or delivery, they were told to have a female employee call back with the order. They didn't bother. They called the competition instead. When the (male) terminal manager tried to reason with the women, they staged a sit-in and called the media. By month's end, all customers had switched to the competition. Two weeks after that, all employees were laid off and the terminal closed. Twenty two drivers, dispatchers, dock workers, and mechanics lost their jobs. Twelve of them were women. The FLPW issued a press release claiming a great victory for their cause.

"Maeve Franklin." Ms. Franklin was the chief executive officer of the Progressive Political Party national office. Their primary goal was the election of Progressive candidates for all political offices, national, state, and local. The mission statement of the Progressive Political Party read: "The most good is accomplished by the most government." A secondary goal was making all positions of power and public trust, especially those handling public money, into elected offices. The Progressive Party now held 70 percent of all elected offices in Illinois. A recent success was a law passed by the Illinois state legislature that made all garbage service manager jobs into elected posts. The legislation passed with help from a campaign by ACANT. The governor issued an executive order requiring all municipalities to hold a special election to fill the required post (even if there was no such job previously) and find the funds to pay the salary and the generous pension (courtesy of the taxpayers), even if the municipality did not operate a garbage service. In addition, the law required each municipality to hold a "collective bargaining" session with the garbage service managers every two years for increases to their salary and pensions. The bargaining was to be collective even if there was only one such position. Needless to say, Progressives "turned out the vote" for the special elections and elected pre-selected Progressive Party members into these positions.

"Gentlepersons, I hereby bring the meeting to order," intoned Mr. Dunforth. "First agenda item, a report on our injunction to halt wind farm construction in the California desert. Mr. Solipsis?"

Mr. Solipsis rose and addressed the table. "Mr. Chairman, our injunction was granted. The Solar and Wind Power Corporation was not only ordered to stop, but to pay for restoration of the site to its original desert state. This power source would only have encouraged continued human habitation on those parts of the state that should be restored to their original state before the arrival of humans. We can call this a success."

"Mr. Solipsis," Mr. Dunforth rumbled. "Well done on the litigation. Next agenda item?" He began stroking the back of his left hand again. He had planted the next suggestion, so he knew exactly what it would be.

Maeve Franklin shifted in her seat. "Mr. Chairman, for our next initiative, I propose a similar injunction against Nutritional Abundance Industries, to stop their release of the so-called 'Carver's Legacy' bio-engineered food crop seeds. These 'Franken-foods' would stabilize the current population base in Africa, India, and Asia. Infant mortality would drop. There is a real possibility that total population could increase and sustain itself with these new low-resource, high-yield crops."

Sonny Fremont spoke up. "Our protest intervention at their press conference backfired on us. Our PRIS-paid volunteers caused a scene, which is what we wanted. That scene was featured on all major newscasts that night, but there was a backlash of sympathy for Grace Washington, the inventor of these bio-engineered food crop seeds. Pictures of her splattered with pig's blood generated outrage and letters to the editor against PRIS. The film clips clearly showed our PRIS initials and logo on the green shirts of the protesters, and especially on the shirt of the woman who decided to attack Dr. Washington with a knife. Who was that woman, anyway?"

Diana Nomenski glared at him. "That was a long-time FLPW member who just happens to be my live-in at the moment. Watch your mouth, *male*."

Sonny persisted, "But why did she attack with a knife? I don't understand."

"A male can't be expected to understand post-modern feminist gender logic. Quintus felt the need to castrate this professional woman who took orders from a male."

Sonny missed the warning signs and kept talking, "But the CEO of Nutritional Abundance Industries is a woman. And who is Quintus?"

Nomenski snorted. "Typical male linear logic. Yes, the CEO of NAI is a woman, but the president of Tuskegee University is a *male*. Quintus uses her historically correct name, channeled to her by a past-life lover. In one of her own past lives, she was a Roman courtesan named Quintus Lucretia Aurelia."

Nomenski took a handgun out of her purse and placed it on the table. "Any more questions, *Mr. Male-at-this-moment*?" Sonny said nothing.

Maeve Franklin waited for a beat of three, and then proceeded. "Legal action does not have to be accompanied by a protest action. We can hold a press conference if we're successful, and control the kind of media coverage in that way. Our thirty-six web sites, blogs, and social networking organizations will spin the story our way after the fact. Live coverage of an event can always get out of our control. Mr. Solipsis could file for the injunction in the PRIS name. If it is not granted, we keep a low profile and don't mention it. News cameras are not allowed in court. If it is granted, we hold the press conference and crank up our spin machine." She looked around expectantly.

"I second the motion." This from Diana Nomenski.

The chairman acted quickly. "All in favor?"

"Aye."

"The ayes have it. So record it, Ms. Secretary," directed Mr. Dunforth.

"I declare this meeting adjourned." Dunforth banged his gavel.

In the hallway, Dunforth put his arm around Samuel's shoulder. "Looks like you've got your work cut out for you."

Samuel shrugged. "Another day, another dollar."

Dunforth winked, "You might start practicing saying, 'Another day, another yuan.' That political improvement is in the works, you know."

"Yes sir. Thank you sir." As he left the building, he tried to remember how many twenty-dollar bills he had in his wallet. The strip club was supposed to have a new girl tonight.

*   *   *   *   *   *

The next night in Chicago, over dinner, wine, and candlelight, Isaiah pulled out a little jewelry box and quietly placed it on the table. After the waiter finished refilling the wine glasses and left, Isaiah placed it on her side of the table. Grace smiled wide enough to trigger her dimple, the one Isaiah loved, the one visible only with her BIG smiles.

That dimple, thought Isaiah. *A man could get lost in that dimple. Do I love her, or just her dimple? I won't choose, and nobody can make me,* he thought. *I get it all. Dimples, hair, eyes, smile, everything.* "Open it," he urged her.

Shyly, Grace opened the lid of the plush velvet box. Immediately, gleams of reflected candlelight sparkled forth. "Isaiah, it's lovely." She held up the box.

"Try it on." She slipped on the ring that sparkled so brightly it nearly blinded her.

"Now that," she said, "is a sparkler." Reverently she held it close to the candle, turning her hand to see different angles. "Isaiah, I only love it."

Her dimple deepened with her smile.

"I have one more gift," Isaiah said softly, placing a larger jewelry case on the table before her. She opened the lid, and sparkles seemed to spill out of the box. She gasped. It was a diamond pendant necklace: three diamonds on either side of a centerpiece diamond that seemed to have depth as she looked into it. The design was elegant in its simplicity.

Isaiah stood. "May I?"

"Oh yes, please!" She demurely looked down as he stood behind her and clasped the pendant around her neck. He nodded at a waiter, who came up with a small mirror and held it up before her.

She looked at her reflection. A constellation of stars shone from her neck and left hand. "Isaiah, it's wonderful! I look like a fairy princess." The dimple returned.

"You are my fairy princess." Isaiah bent down and kissed the back of her neck.

"Would you take it off now?" she asked.

"Grace, please wear it. You make it look so beautiful."

She looked hesitant. "Growing up, mama would always say that stuff like this is too good to wear for everyday. Save it for a special dress up occasion."

"I'm looking at a woman seated at a five star restaurant, sipping a two hundred dollar bottle of wine, dressed fit to kill in a beautiful designer dress and Manolo Blahnik spike heels. If this isn't that special dress up occasion, what is?" He had taken her on a shopping spree that afternoon with his platinum credit card. He reached over to hold her hand. "I love you, Dr. Grace Washington."

"You make it special, not the clothes," she whispered. She took her hand away to look at the ring on her left hand. "I love you, my husband-to-be."

"Grace?"

"Yes?"

"Let's not set a date. Let's just do it."

"OK."

"Wow, that was easy. I thought you wanted a big wedding."

"I'm not a little girl anymore. I'm not in love with the big event; I'm in love with *you*. How about next Saturday at my house in Tuskegee?"

"Can I ask the warrior T'Chaka hisownself to be my best man?"

"Can I ask the warrior's wife Estelle herownself to be my matron of honor?"

"It's a date. I'll call the preacher."

"My preacher, Reverend Longfellow. You don't have a preacher."

"I do now."

*   *   *   *   *   *

The bride was brilliant in a sleeveless white satin wedding dress and a simple white veil. She wore a constellation of stars around her neck.

The groom was elegant in a black tuxedo and bow tie. The garden was filled with university staff and students. Five of Isaiah's friends and employees from Silicon Valley flew in for the occasion. Grace's friends from her church and neighborhood were there.

After the "I do's" were said, Reverend Longfellow concluded the ceremony in this way: "In the sight of God and man, you are now husband and wife. This is a sacred bond, which you are affirming by this public ceremony. We, as witnesses, now have a responsibility to help these two grow into an ever more loving and fruitful marriage relationship. We have a responsibility to help them stay married through hard times and good times. Do you all accept your responsibility?"

"We do!" the guests loudly affirmed.

"By the power invested in me by the bride and groom, I now pronounce it time to sample some of Mercury's Own Award Winning Barbecue Sauce. Let's eat!"

"Amen, brother!" shouted one of the guests.

Best Man George T'Chaka offered a toast after everyone had gone though the buffet line at the garden reception. "To the pairing of two geniuses, may their DNA be hybridized and replicated!" Loud laughs greeted this botanical reference to childbearing.

"Hear hear!" "Amen!" Isaiah grinned, and Grace bowed her head and blushed.

Estelle whispered to George when he sat down, "Married less than five months after they met. I'm collecting on our bet: twenty bucks. Pay up."

84

*   *   *   *   *   *

Grace had arranged for someone to cover her classes for her. On Sunday, they hopped a jet to Paris, took the high-speed LTV train to Strasbourg, and began a week of happy wandering through the villages, vineyards, and forests of Alsace-Lorraine.

Grace was fluent in French, and Isaiah had picked up a smattering of German while in the Navy. They hiked trails through woods and vineyards. In the fields, Grace chatted with local farmers about hybridizing, pest resistance and crop yields. They sampled the local wines and feasted on the famous quiche-Lorraine. At one inn, Isaiah talked his way into the kitchen and showed his barbeque secrets to his hostess. She taught him how to make quiche.

When he came out of the kitchen bearing a quiche on a platter, Grace smiled so big her dimple showed. He set it down and served a piece to her. She brought the plate up to her nose, closed her eyes, and inhaled the cheesy aroma.

"Mmmm. This smells wonderful." She opened her eyes and smiled again at Isaiah. "I must be the luckiest girl in the world. I married a successful genius who can design software for worldwide buying and selling, pilot a jet, speak a little German, and, most impressive of all, can cook!"

Nodding at the window, Isaiah said, "Look what else I brought you." He pointed at a vibrant rainbow above the valley.

He put his arm around her. "A regenbogen, just for you." She leaned against him with a sigh of contentment.

The honeymoon was short and glorious. For a week they drank each other in, as if each was water to the other after days without end in a desert. They sank into each other as if sinking into a dream sleep. It felt like they had always been together. It felt like they belonged together. It felt right.

*   *   *   *   *   *

The man with the broken nose was waiting for the Minister of Agriculture for Botswana in a café in Gaborone, the capital city. A man

85

in a suit and wearing eyeglasses entered, looked around the room, and approached his table.

"Minister? Please have a seat," said the man at the table.

"I don't know you," began the minister.

"You may call me Mr. Bruncali."

The minister sat and looked around nervously. No one was seated near them. "Coffee, minister?" The minister nodded, and the other man beckoned a waiter and gave the order.

After the waiter left, the man with the broken nose leaned forward. "Minister, your Ministry of Agriculture does good work for the people of your country. You protect the food supply and make sure nothing dangerous enters the ecosystem of agriculture in Botswana. The organization I represent wants to help you with that work. We believe that these so called "super-seeds" from Nutritional Abundance Industries are dangerous and could cause birth defects and paralysis."

The waiter served coffee and left. The minister took a sip. "I'm listening. What evidence do you have that this is so?"

"Minister, we have Ph.D.s who have constructed computer models based on data sets we have collected on the effects of eating crops grown with these seeds. The consensus of these Ph.D.s is that these crops are dangerous."

"Indeed? I would like to see these data sets, and study the algorithms used in these computer models."

Mr. Bruncali leaned back and sipped his own coffee. "Unfortunately, a careless computer technician accidentally erased the original data sets. The algorithms are complex, and our Ph.Ds do not want to reveal them until they have published their findings in a scientific journal. However, here is a pre-publication summary of their findings, which are also available on this web site." He slid a brochure with the PRIS logo across the table.

The minister studied the brochure. "I see. Conclusions with no data or methodology to back them up. This asks the reader to take it on faith. Not a very scientific approach."

"Trust us, minister, the science is there. We just can't release it at this time. Trust our expert Ph.Ds."

"I notice that the lead author for this article has his Ph.D in sociology, not medicine or epidemiology."

Ignoring this, Mr. Bruncali continued, "We also believe that there is no time to lose on this matter. We know that you began your career as a university researcher and that you respect scientific research findings. We're prepared to support your personal research with an endowed fund and a research station at this location."

He placed a document with the letterhead logo of a well known Swiss bank on the table. Then he produced a real estate brochure with a picture of a luxurious villa. The location was Switzerland. "Minister, you will notice that the fund is set up in your name alone, and the property title to the research station will be in your name alone. This will enable you to have the academic freedom to pursue your research interests as you personally see fit. You will not be required to make an accounting of the funds used."

"Research on tropical agriculture conducted in a Swiss villa? What a novel idea." The minister studied the real estate brochure and sipped his coffee.

"Minister, we will execute this personal research funding and finalize the purchase of this research facility as soon as your Ministry of Agriculture makes the importation and use of the super-seeds from Nutritional Abundance Industries illegal in Botswana."

The minister folded the documents and put them into his inside suit pocket. "Consider it done. Watch for a press conference and official proclamation from the Ministry of Agriculture two days from now."

The minister stood. "Thank you for the coffee, Mr. Bruncali." As the minister walked out, Bruncali took out his cell phone and pressed a speed dial number.

"Director Dunforth. Mission accomplished. Watch for a press conference in two days."

*   *   *   *   *   *

On a remote farm in Botswana, a farmer noticed black spots on his mealie corn. He frowned. *Blight.* He left his field and walked two miles to a neighbor's house.

"Setoki, there is a blight on my mealie corn. I must get help from the government agricultural agent, but he is far away. Will you take me to him on your motor scooter?"

When they arrived at the office of the agricultural agent, the farmer pulled a cob of mealie corn from his pocket and handed it to the agent.

After one look at the black spots, the agent said, "Blight. I must inform the Ministry of Agriculture immediately." He picked up the telephone.

*   *   *   *   *   *

The phone rang in Grace Washington's office at Tuskegee University. She picked it up. "Dr. Grace Washington."

"Grace? It's Minerva. The Ministry of Agriculture in Botswana held a press conference today to announce that the use or importation of your super-seeds is now illegal. The minister cited the so-called research findings posted on the PRIS web site that claim food grown from the super-seeds cause birth defects and paralysis. No data or research methodology, of course, just opinion and allegations. It's an op-ed piece masquerading as science, and we're supposed to take it on faith."

Grace slumped in her chair. The news hit her like a blow. "But we tested the crop harvests during my field trip to Botswana. Everything was safe. And after the lab testing, there were never any reports of health problems from the farmers we supervised eating food grown with the super-seeds. I ate it myself. I had no ill effects."

"Of course not. And this article does not cite concrete evidence either. The lead author is a Ph.D in sociology, not medicine or epidemiology. Here is his scientific observation, quote: *We have conducted telephone interviews with seven people in Kenya who have relatives who contracted a paralysis or delivered a baby with a birth defect. They are convinced it was something they ate. They are convinced it was food grown from the super-seeds being tested in Africa by Nutritional Abundance Industries. They have retained American lawyers to sue for damages.* Smell anything funny about that?"

"Yes. It stinks of opinion with no data. No actual patients are produced, just people who tell a story about an unnamed relative who is sick. Not to mention that we never tested the super-seeds in Kenya, so they could not have eaten food grown from them. All the test crops in African countries were bought from the farmers by Nutritional Abundance Industries in order to conduct further safety testing. None of it went into the food supply in those nations. These are all lies from the usual suspects. I'm so mad I could spit!" Grace gripped the phone so tightly her knuckles hurt.

"Amen, sister. Our lawyers tell us that the lawyers representing the alleged victims in Kenya are all on retainer from PRIS. This is another hatchet propaganda job set up by PRIS."

"Minerva, what are you going to do?"

"Fight it, of course. Our lawyers will ask their lawyers to produce these so-called victims. I'll be very surprised if any actual people are produced. I'll issue a press release with the facts about where our seeds were tested in Africa, and the fact that none of the test crops were sold to food distributors. Plus, our safety studies were conducted by researchers with degrees in medicine, not sociology. We'll post it on our web site as well."

"Sounds good. What do you need from me?"

"Nothing at the moment. Just wanted to keep you up to date. I'll call you if I need you. Hang in there, Grace."

"I will. I'll need help from my Higher Power, but I know I'll get it."

"Amen, sister, amen."

*   *   *   *   *   *

The blight spread rapidly through the farmlands of Botswana. The blighted crops were inedible, so the farmers didn't bother to harvest them. The fields were plowed under. Long lines formed at the food stores, and unruly crowds jostled each other at the village marketplaces. People tried to stock up on food from last year's harvest. Food prices went up with the shortage. Warehouses emptied as food supplies shipped out, but none came in.

In the second month of the food shortage, Mantate Kubabupe watched as his wife Lebo cooked a porridge made with the last of their mealie corn from the previous year. The baby girl, Tebogo, was born after Grace Washington's visit. She was healthy but thin. Mantate and his young son Moroka had begun to glean from the fields and search the forest for edible plants, but he knew that it would not be enough nutrition for Lebo to keep nursing the baby.

The test harvest from the super-seeds had all been sold at a good price to the seed company, Nutritional Abundance Industries, for safety testing. Mantate was now using the money to buy food at the village market like everyone else. But money could only buy what was for sale, and yesterday there had been little.

After the meager meal, Mantate motioned for Moroka to follow him outside.

"Moroka, go to our neighbor Tumelo Lukusa and ask him to telephone Mr. Phewai and ask him to visit us. We need his help."

"Yes, my father." Moroka began trotting in the direction of the Lukusa farm.

Mr. Phewai arrived the next day in his truck. Mantate greeted him. "Dumela, William, and welcome. Come into the house. Will you have tea with us?" Even in a time of food shortages, Mantate wanted to show hospitality.

"Thank you, no," said William. "I have a gift for you." He produced a bag and set it on the table. He took out a box of porridge mix and two cans of condensed milk. "For your newest child."

Mantate called out, "Lebo, come see the gift William Phewai has brought us." She came from the adjoining room with the baby on her hip.

Lebo broke into a big smile when she saw the cans of milk. "William! You are too good to us! Our cow gives less and less milk, and when I nurse this baby, I can no longer satisfy her. These cans of milk are a godsend. Thank you, my friend."

"You are welcome," said William. "May I hold her?"

"Of course!" She held out the baby to William. In his arms, the baby smiled at him, gurgled, and reached up and grabbed his nose.

He laughed delightedly. "What name have you chosen for this happy child?"

"Tebogo," said Mantate.

"How perfect," said William. "A name that means 'gratitude.'"

Lebo smiled and said, "We are indeed grateful for this child, a gift from God that brightens our lives and gives Moroka a new playmate. So, we named her Tebogo."

"I am grateful for her too," said William, smiling at the child.

"William," said Lebo, "would you be her godfather? We're taking her to be baptized next week."

"It would be an honor and a delight to be the godfather of such a beautiful child," said William. "Yes, I will be the godfather to Tebogo, who makes us all grateful to have her."

Returning the child to Lebo, William turned back to Mantate.

"Mantate, my friend, what can I do for you?"

"William, I sold all of my test crops to your company, and you paid me a good price, but now my money is useless when there is no food to buy in the village market. I fear my family may starve while this blight continues. Can you sell me some more super-seeds to plant? I must grow food quickly."

William frowned. "Mantate, I must tell you that the Ministry of Agriculture has forbidden the sale or use of those seeds. They say it causes paralysis and birth defects."

"But you had my crop harvest tested for safety. After your medical testing, we ate the samples you gave us for weeks. None of us was paralyzed. This baby was not deformed. Those seeds resisted blight. We could starve without those seeds."

William frowned again. "I will do what I can, but the Ministry of Agriculture is not friendly toward my company." The food he had brought was half of his own supply. He knew of five villages that had no market-day that week. There was no food to sell.

*   *   *   *   *   *

One week later there were food riots in the capital city of Gaborone. The Minister of Agriculture summoned William Phewai for a private meeting. They met in a small office in the Ministry of Works and Transport, so that no one in the Ministry of Agriculture would know that they had met. Through the office window they could see the square in the center of the government buildings at the top of the Main Mall.

"Mr. Phewai, thank you for coming so quickly. By some accounts the super-seeds your company tested here were blight resistant. Is this true?"

"Yes, minister."

"Mr. Phewai, this government will fall unless we can find a way to feed our people. The United Nations is sending humanitarian relief, but we can't rely on them forever. We must reestablish our own agriculture and our own food supplies. And we must do it quickly."

"Yes, minister."

"Can you persuade your company to send us an emergency supply of their super-seeds so that our farmers can begin re-planting immediately?"

"Minister, those seeds are illegal, by the proclamation you made."

The Minister looked down at his shoes. "Perhaps that proclamation was too hasty. Can you do this?"

"Yes, minister, I will try. I will talk to my employers. Are you going to publicly rescind your prohibition against these seeds? It will be difficult for me to get them across the border otherwise. Every customs official and every Ministry of Agriculture official will stop me and have me arrested."

"Here is a letter of authorization from me. Show it to any official who questions or tries to stop you. Here is my card with my private cell phone number. Use it if the letter does not work."

The Minister looked down briefly, then back up at William.

"Mr. Phewai, I do not wish to look like a fool. I will publicly rescind my prohibition against the super-seeds, but only after you assure me that Nutritional Abundance Industries will indeed ship us a new supply of blight resistant super-seeds. When I have a copy of the export authorization from the United States, I'll hold a televised press conference to publicly rescind the prohibition. Mr. Phewai . . ."

He paused and looked out the window at the statue of Sir Seretse Khama, Botswana's first President. "We have worked hard to become independent. Without our own food supplies we will not stay independent. What I am asking of you . . . it is a service to your country."

"Yes, Minister."

*　　*　　*　　*　　*　　*

The CBC Evening News, with Kathy Coeur-Saignant. "In breaking news today, the government of Botswana, in the face of food riots caused by a crop blight, has announced a desperate reversal of an earlier ruling to protect the safety of the nation's food. Here is the Minister of Agriculture at today's press conference." The picture shifted to a podium with the seal of Botswana on it. The blue, white, and black flag of Botswana hung in the background. The Minister of Agriculture read from a statement.

"Today we have rescinded the previous prohibition against the import, sale, and use of the food crop super-seeds developed by Nutritional Abundance Industries. We were too hasty in our previous prohibition. No hard evidence has emerged about safety issues, and the alleged victims in Kenya do not exist. These super-seeds are resistant to the blight which is currently destroying our crops, and they grow to maturity more quickly than traditional seeds, so they are exactly what we need.

"In our current agricultural crisis and food shortage, we have relayed a request to Nutritional Abundance Industries for an emergency shipment of these seeds for immediate re-planting. Their CEO, Ms. Minerva Stone, has personally assured me that shipments of super-seeds will be air-freighted to us within the week.

"While we will continue to rely on humanitarian aid for the months it will take to reestablish viable crops, we're confident that Botswana will eventually become self-sufficient in food again. Indeed, we expect to become a net exporter of food again within a few years. This is good news for Botswana and good news for the world. Thank you for helping us spread this good news."

Kathy Coeur-Saignant reappeared on the screen. "Many officials at the World Health Organization at the United Nations disagree with this breach of food safety protocols. One official commented that mass starvation was preferable to the risk of some people becoming paralyzed and babies being born with birth defects. This seems to be another case of a greedy corporation taking advantage of the desperation of starving people."

*   *   *   *   *   *

The intercom button on Samuel Solipsis' office phone began blinking. He pressed the button. "Yes?"

"Director Dunforth wants to see you immediately."

Dunforth scowled from behind his desk as Solipsis walked into his office. He raised a coffee cup from a silver tray laden with pastries. After a sip of coffee, he glanced down at some papers on his desk.

"It seems that the government ministers I buy don't stay bought. The Minister of Agriculture in Botswana has lifted the prohibition on the super-seeds from Nutritional Abundance Industries. He claims the seeds are needed to feed people starving from the corn blight. Like so many of the unenlightened, he just doesn't understand the greater good we're trying to achieve. What are a few million people dead of starvation compared to a planet in glorious green ecological balance?"

Dunforth placed one hand on his ample belly and reached for a scone with the other hand. Taking a bite, he talked with his mouth full.

"Starvation is simply one way of ridding the planet of excess people. That's part of our mission at PRIS. Samuel, I want you to move up the hearing date for our injunction. File for an immediate emergency injunction to stop the distribution of those seeds."

"Yes sir," said Solipsis. He backed out of the office to avoid turning his back on the imperial presence.

$$* \qquad * \qquad * \qquad * \qquad * \qquad *$$

Samuel Solipsis presented his argument in front of Judge Block. "Your Honor, these so called "Franken-food" crop seeds are known to deform children and mutilate animals who eat them. PRIS asks for immediate relief in the form of an injunction forbidding sale or release of these seeds in any form, and the destruction of all warehoused supplies of these seeds, to be witnessed and verified by an observer from PRIS."

Mr. Blunt was counsel for Nutritional Abundance Industries. "Your Honor, there is no evidence that the "Carver's Legacy" brand of bio-engineered seeds either deform children or mutilate animals. Furthermore, counsel for PRIS has not submitted any evidence supporting this notion. They merely assert it."

Judge Block peered over his half-frame reading glasses at Mr. Blunt. "Mr. Blunt, this court holds higher standards than the merely legal statutes passed by Congress, as you may recall from your last appearance in my courtroom. For our precedents and standards we adhere to international law and the moral law that the needs of the many outweigh the needs of the few. Can you offer definitive and authoritative proof that these foods won't mutilate animals? Or won't deform children?"

Mr. Blunt was about to ask about this standard, but remembered Judge Block's reputation for bias. "No, your Honor. You will see in our brief before you medical studies showing that grain grown from these seeds are safe for human consumption."

"What about the mutilation of animals?"

"Your Honor, we have no studies about animals, because these grains are not intended for animal consumption. However, veterinarians tell us that if a given food is safe for human consumption, it is safe for animal consumption."

"Not good enough, counselor. Then I hereby find for the plaintiff. Nutritional Abundance Industries will cease and desist from selling or distributing these seeds immediately, and they will destroy these seeds in the presence of a witness to be supplied by PRIS. Mr. Solipsis?"

"Thank you your Honor. We will file the name of our witness with the court in the morning. "

I'm going to the ATM for more twenties. I'm celebrating with lap dances tonight! He decided to go to his favorite San Francisco strip club, *Thigh High.*

*   *   *   *   *   *

The next afternoon a process server hired by PRIS served the injunction papers on Nutritional Abundance Industries at their headquarters in Peoria. The assistant to CEO Minerva Stone ushered the process server into Minerva's office. He handed the papers to Minerva. "You have been served." Without another word, he left.

Her assistant returned. "What was that all about?"

"Let's find out." Minerva began skimming through the densely worded legal injunction. "Cease and desist sales and distribution of 'Carver's Legacy' brand of grain, fruit, and vegetable seeds . . . destroy all seed stock . . . perform the destruction in the presence of a witness from PRIS . . . well, well, well."

The assistant stood openmouthed in shock. "Oh, Ms. Stone, whatever will we do?"

"We'll do exactly what we are told to do," said Ms. Stone calmly. "Get Dr. Washington on the phone for me, please." Her hands shaking, the assistant left Minerva's office.

"Grace? Minerva. Well, the other shoe dropped. We've been served. Just what we suspected. A cease and desist injunction filed by PRIS and granted by the lovely Judge Block. One nice additional touch though, probably added by our friend Samuel Solipsis. The destruction of seed stock is to be performed in the presence of a witness appointed by PRIS."

In her faculty office at Tuskegee University, Grace groped for the back of her chair and sat down. She suddenly felt a little faint. "Destroy all seed stock?" Her life's work, destroyed and taken by force by those who did not have the intellect or work ethic to create it for themselves. Her imagination leaped to an image of barbarians sacking the monasteries of Europe, burning books, burning knowledge, burning what they did not understand and therefore could not control. Then she remembered the starving babies she had seen in Africa. And the mass starvation in Botswana.

"Yes," said Minerva, "the lord our god Edgar Dunforth hath repented that he has allowed the sustenance of man upon the earth, and the end of sixty percent of all flesh is come before him. Behold, he will destroy them with starvation. But with PRIS shall he make his covenant, and forty percent after their kind."

"Copy that. What is this about sixty percent of all flesh destroyed?" Grace asked.

Minerva frowned into the phone, "Go to the PRIS web site. They make no secret of it. They have decreed that earth can only sustain forty percent of the current human population in order to achieve their version of ecological harmony and equality with all other animal and plant species on the earth. Their goal is to reduce the population of the planet by sixty percent."

"So what are we going to do?" asked Grace, still in shock.

"Exactly what we are told to do," Minerva again calmly replied. "It's time to activate the Noah Option."

Grace closed her eyes. *I hoped it would never come to this. The Noah Option.* She and Isaiah were the architects, and had laid the groundwork for it some time ago. *Am I ready for this? Life has just become more wonderful. My life now includes Isaiah Mercury as my permanent partner in life and work and play. Do I have to change it all now, after only two weeks of wedded bliss?*

"Are you sure, Minerva? What about the emergency request from Botswana?"

"Ideas have consequences," Minerva reminded her. "The Ark will provide for Botswana."

Yes, Grace thought, *Ideas have consequences. When one big government plus PRIS controls everything, the consequences will be scarcity, regimentation, and living like refugees, like the perennially hungry, wretched people of North Korea or Haiti. God, please help those starving people in Botswana.*

Grace knew that in biology, it is known as "monoculture," when every member of a given species population is the same. In a monoculture, the population is more susceptible to disease and other threats. Genetic diversity ensures adaptability to new threats and diseases. She thought, *For humans, who survive by their minds, diversity of thought and action ensures adaptability. But, diversity of thought and action requires freedom. "Monoculture" of thought and action is the opposite of freedom. It is the hive mind, the collective, and it makes mankind less adaptable to survival threats. The collectivist North Koreans can't even feed themselves.*

Grace shook herself. *Shake it off,* she told herself. *Just like when I was knocked down countless times in basketball. Shake it off and go on.*

She turned her attention back to the phone and Minerva. "OK, I'm in. What do we do?"

"We comply with the injunction. Can you be here in Peoria on Friday?"

She thought. Her classes didn't meet on Friday. She could take a series of red-eye flights on Thursday night and be there. "Yes."

"Then I'll schedule a press conference for Friday at six p.m., to coincide with the news cycle. The news networks will have to cover it live, or run tapes later and lose an opportunity for the live breaking news they all love. If they run it live, they won't have time to do one of their Orwellian edits of the footage. It will be a 'cover it live or not' decision."

"Does Isaiah know?"

"Just a minute." On her end, Grace heard a whistling noise.

"I just switched to encryption mode so we won't be monitored. Yes, Isaiah knows. I activated the Noah Option protocols from my cell phone, and he has acknowledged. He has started the countdown. We are officially at N minus 35."

"I'll see you on Friday. May I bring some guests?"

"Of course," said Minerva. "I'm planning to invite a special guest of my own: Edgar Dunforth."

"Excellent. My guests would love to meet him."

Grace hung up the phone and began her own preparations for the countdown to the Noah Option. Her eyes filled with tears. *All we want to do is help grow food for a hungry world. What's wrong with these*

97

people?   What has happened to our country?   Our country used to admire this kind of achievement that benefited so many people.

She wiped her eyes with a tissue. Her jawline tightened and her eyes took on the steely look of determination that they always got when she played basketball against a team that played dirty. Her fingers flew across the keyboard of her computer.

*   *   *   *   *   *

N minus 35. Edgar Dunforth's administrative assistant knocked discreetly at his office door, which remained closed at all times. She thought, *the wizard sees nobody, nohow.* "Come in." The assistant opened the door and stood subserviently next to it.

Samuel Solipsis walked around and stood in front of her. She left. "Our intelligence operatives monitored a phone call between Minerva Stone and Grace Washington. Apparently they intend to comply with our injunction. But I smell a rat. They're giving in too easily. They must be up to something, but I don't know what."

"What makes you think so?"

"They referred to scheduling a press conference late in the afternoon, in time to make the evening news, but leaving no time for our friends at the networks to edit the video to our purposes. I'm suspicious."

Dunforth's assistant knocked again and was admitted to the inner sanctum. "Sir, this FedEx letter just arrived for you from Nutritional Abundance Industries. It required your signature, but I signed for you."

Edgar opened the envelope and began reading. "Oho! An invitation to the press conference, for me personally. Samuel, amend our filing with the court. Appoint *me* to be the designated witness for the destruction of the seed stock. I want to savor our victory in person. Miss Cringe!" He began stroking the back of his left hand.

The assistant hesitantly stepped forward, eyes down. "Yes sir?"

"Make arrangements for my personal PRIS jet to take me to Peoria."

"Sir, from here in our Chicago headquarters it's only three hours by car. Shouldn't we be setting an example about fuel consumption and carbon emissions?"

"Miss Cringe, do I have to repeat myself?"

"No sir. Right away sir." She blushed and backed out of the imperial presence.

98

Dunforth gave Samuel an exasperated look, "As if those rules applied to me. Me!"

"Sir, I'm still concerned that they may have something up their sleeve. They referred to something called the Noah Option."

"What can that refer to?"

"I don't have a clue." Both men had been raised by mothers who militantly opposed all knowledge about religion on the grounds that the "Judeo-Christian-Islamic" Abrahamaic traditions were exclusively and aggressively paternalistic and male-centric.

"Sir, maybe you shouldn't go. There's a danger that this could backfire on us like the protest at their other press conference."

Dunforth stood up and looked at him dismissively. "A danger? You overestimate them. I want to savor this in person. I want to see the look of powerless defeat in Minerva Stone's eyes when she announces that she has to destroy her precious Franken-food seed inventories. I want to be present and in the camera's eye at our moment of triumph over these money-grubbing, planet-populating capitalists! I consider them rebels against the orderly control of a state that controls everyone for everyone's best interests. Who are they to think they can go feed humans all over the world, further upsetting the natural balance and equality of all species? We know what's best for the planet, and it's not more food for human beings."

"Yes sir," Samuel said in a properly subservient tone.

*   *   *   *   *   *

The Minister of Agriculture was at his desk when his secretary buzzed him. "Minister, Minerva Stone of Nutritional Abundance Industries is on line one for you."

He pushed the button. "Minister, this is Minerva Stone. I have bad news. We have been served with an injunction under the United States court system forbidding us to sell the super-seeds and actually requiring us to destroy all of our super-seed stocks. I promised you a shipment of the seeds, but I have been overruled by my government. I'm sorry, but there is nothing I can do."

"Ms. Stone, you know that this means starvation for many of my people."

99

"Minister, I am anguished for the suffering of your people. You know I would help if I could. I had a cargo jet chartered and ready to fly to Gaborone with a supply of seeds. I suggest that you ask your Minister of Foreign Affairs to make a humanitarian appeal to our State Department. Under our system of government, the executive branch cannot overrule the judicial branch, so I'm doubtful whether it will work, but it's the only thing I can think of."

"Ms. Stone, I will indeed ask that our government make an appeal to your government. What I fear is that they will give us food, which will make us dependent on them, but not the seeds, which would make us independent of them. Thank you for what you tried to do for my people."

As he hung up, he thought: *PRIS is probably draining my "research fund" and taking back the villa in Switzerland. But I must do the right thing for my people. If only I had not outlawed those super-seeds in the first place, we might have had a supply in this country. What am I going to say to the President? How can I look into the faces of my hungry children tonight?*

        *   *   *   *   *   *

Mantate Kubabupe slumped on a chair in the shade of his porch and listlessly fanned himself in the heat. With barely enough calorie intake to keep him alive, he had no energy for working in his fields. Inside, his wife Lebo attempted to nurse the baby, but she had little milk. The boy Moroka lay on his cot, moving but little. His ribs showed. Mantate moved his head to one side. Was that a vehicle he heard in the distance? Soon, a truck pulled up in the yard.

William Phewai got out of the truck and pulled a box from the seat. Mantate watched him without getting up. William opened the door and placed his box on the table. Lebo looked up at him with gaunt eyes. The baby's belly had begun to swell from malnutrition.

"Lebo," said William, "my neighbor's child died from malnutrition. They gave me this milk ration they had been allotted for him by the authorities. Drink a little. Here is a baby bottle we can use to feed some to Tebogo. I'll start a fire in the stove so we can sterilize the bottle and the milk." He began putting wood into the cooking stove.

When he had the fire started and a pan of water on to boil the bottle, he returned to the box. He took out two cans labeled "chlorine bleach." With a bottle opener, he punched openings into each. He took one over to Moroka and pulled him to a sitting position with one arm under Moroka's shoulders.

"Moroka, sip this. It is a liquid food called Ensure. Dr. Washington managed to air-freight a case labeled as laboratory chemicals directly to me." Moroka gulped it. "Take small sips, or your belly will reject it."

When he saw that Moroka sipped more slowly, he got up and took the other can to Mantate, still sitting outside. Returning, he boiled the bottle and the milk. Then he gave the bottle to Lebo to feed to the baby. Lastly, he poured a glass of boiled milk for Lebo to sip. Mantate shuffled in, walking like an old man.

"Mantate, I have a case of this liquid food called Ensure. I will leave it for you and Moroka. We have a chance to get American public opinion on our side and get the super-seeds released. Dr. Washington has sent plane tickets for me, Lebo, and Tebogo to come join her and the Botswanan Ambassador at a press conference in the United States. She says that when the American people see the suffering of a baby like Tebogo, their hearts will melt and they will say to the American Pharaoh: *Let the super-seeds go to feed these people.*"

Mantate nodded dumbly.

"Mantate," asked William, "will you let her and the child go to America with me? I will protect them and stay with them at all times. I will bring them back safely to you. You have my word."

"Yes," croaked Mantate. "*Tsamaya sentle* — Go well. Go with God."

*   *   *   *   *   *

N minus 32. That Friday afternoon in Peoria, the parking lot at Nutritional Abundance Industries was jammed with satellite feed trucks from the major news networks. ZNN, ZSNBC, FACTS News, CBC, NBC, and ABC were represented, plus internet sites like Drudge and the Daily Kos, and the few remaining print media: *Time, Fortune, Forbes, Wall Street Journal,* and *Investor's Business Daily.*

Oddly enough, there were reporters present from *Reason, The Weekly Standard, Politico.com*, and several other political publications.

"Why are you here?" asked the reporter from *Fortune*. "You don't cover business news. You cover politics."

The journalist from *The Weekly Standard* shrugged. "We were invited, and my editor sent me, so here I am." He shrugged again. "Who am 'I' to question authority?" He winked.

In the austerely furnished large room, commercial video cameras were set up to record the news conference. Cables snaked down the corridor to the satellite feed trucks outside. The room was designed for training large numbers of farmers about using new seed strains, so the floor sloped theatre style. Every reporter and every camera person had a good view of the stage in front.

The CBC reporter asked his producer, "So, are we going to feed this live? Or edit it first?"

"We're going live. When I told New York that FACTS and ZNN were airing it live, they didn't want to be scooped. Since it starts before the normal CBC Evening News, they're going to interrupt programming with a 'CBC Breaking News Alert' intro and put the press conference on live. You'll do your usual summary and critique at the end, not at the beginning."

"Got it. Who am 'I' to question authority?"

"Right," said the producer. He looked hard at the reporter, looking for signs of stubbornness or sarcasm.

"Remember," said the producer, "the 'i' in collective is in the last syllable, following; not in the first, leading."

This saying had been circulating in progressive circles for the past ten years, and every public school child had learned it by heart beginning in the first grade. Sports coaches were required to refer to 'collectives' instead of teams. The baseball collective, the soccer collective, and so on. Sports that required individual excellence, like track and gymnastics, had long been abolished in all K-12 public schools after President Fletcher had enacted Title XVI: *No sport shall be practiced that requires and records individual achievement rather than that of the group or collective.* All colleges received federal money, so they abolished those sports as well. The Olympics had deleted them five years ago. Only private schools like Sidwell Friends, in Washington, D.C. continued to field track and gymnastics teams. Wilma Rudolf, Jesse Owens, and Jim Thorpe were deleted from the American History textbooks used in public schools.

Minerva Stone stepped up to the podium. Edgar Dunforth sat in the first row, half turning so that his profile could be picked up by the television cameras. Television klieg lights went on, lighting up the stage and Minerva's lone slim figure at the microphone.

"Ladies and Gentlemen, thank you for coming to this press conference. As you know, Nutritional Abundance Industries was served with a cease and desist injunction last Tuesday. This injunction was initiated by the Pristine Influence on Society Foundation, PRIS, represented here today by their executive director, Mr. Edgar Dunforth." She gestured toward Edgar and the cameras swiveled for a close-up of his face. He rose and took a little bow, and then sat down.

Minerva continued, "This injunction requires us to stop selling and distributing the 'Carver's Legacy' brand of enhanced grain, fruit, and vegetable crop seeds, and to destroy all such seed stock in our possession. We shall comply, *to the letter of the law,* effective immediately. The scientist responsible for inventing these enhanced food crops, Dr. Grace Washington of the prestigious Tuskegee University, has requested to make a statement. Dr. Washington."

From a side door, Grace entered the room. She was again dressed in understated elegance, a simple, lavender suit that flattered her height and spare figure. She went to the microphone.

"Before I begin my remarks, I would like an assurance from PRIS Executive Director Dunforth that I won't be drenched in pig's blood and attacked with a knife by your agents this time?"

She held up a large green T-shirt, partially covered in pig's blood, with the PRIS logo plainly visible. An assistant propped up a four-foot by seven-foot poster next to Dr. Washington, showing the now famous news photo of the woman in the green PRIS T-shirt thrusting a knife toward Dr. Washington. The cameras zoomed in on the photo, then the bloody T-shirt, and then on Edgar Dunforth, who twisted uncomfortably in his seat, accidentally showing his unmistakable profile to the cameras again.

"I believe this belongs to you, Director Dunforth, literally and morally," Grace said as she tossed the bloody T-shirt to Edgar.

The cameras followed the arc of the bright green shirt through the air. Dunforth instinctively raised his hands and caught it. He felt something sticky and warm, and immediately dropped the T-shirt. He looked at his hands. They were covered in fresh pig's blood from the T-shirt. Involuntarily, he held them out to avoid getting the blood on his expensive designer suit. The cameras focused on his outstretched bloody hands.

"Now I believe the blood is on the correct hands," continued Dr. Washington. "The hands that are stopping the distribution of food crop seeds that would feed millions of malnourished children in India, Africa, and Asia. Children who may die without it."

Samuel Solipsis gave his handkerchief to Mr. Dunforth, who frantically tried to wipe the blood from his hands. The cameras swiveled to catch this. He glared into the cameras.

"One other requirement of Mr. Dunforth's injunction is that we are required to destroy the seed stock in the presence of a witness from PRIS. PRIS has filed papers with the court designating Mr. Dunforth himself to be that witness. We are prepared to fulfill our obligation to the requirements of this injunction right now, so that the world will know that we are in compliance."

She turned, and an assistant wheeled a large apparatus onstage, about the size of a refrigerator.

"This is an industrial microwave oven. Concentrated heat from this oven will destroy any plant seed." The assistant plugged it into a 220-volt outlet.

"Mr. Dunforth, you are now legally required to witness this destruction with your own eyes. Please step up here next to the oven."

Dunforth bent his head toward Solipsis. "Do I have to do this?" he whispered.

"I'm afraid so, sir. It was all specified in the injunction written by us and issued by Judge Block. If we don't comply, we could be held in contempt of court."

Dunforth stood up with a stony look on his face and stepped up on the stage to the left of the oven. The cameras followed him. Red smudges of blood were still visible on his hands.

"Here are the containers of seed stock," Dr. Washington announced as the assistant brought out a dozen paper-wrapped packages. Each one was about the size of a shoe box. She opened the door to the oven and placed the packages on racks, plainly visible to the cameras.

Dr. Washington continued, "We have some witnesses of our own for this legal relief demanded by Mr. Dunforth's injunction. I call upon the ambassadors from India, Botswana, and Thailand to join us, along with their chosen representatives."

The ambassadors, dressed in business attire, came up to the stage and stood in a line to the right of the oven, looking over at Mr. Dunforth. Dunforth fidgeted uncomfortably, stroking the back of his left hand. Next, three women in native costumes came in, bearing underweight babies in their arms. They lined up in front of the ambassadors. The cameras panned from baby to thin baby. Lebo Kubabupe's cheeks were still sunken. Her baby Tebogo still had a swollen belly.

Grace resumed, "The great economist Bastiat once explained that every time the government takes money or prohibits something for a project of its own, they can point to it and say, 'look at this project.' But there is also the *unseen*. The *unseen* are the good things that would have been accomplished if the money had been left in the hands of those who earned it, or the good results achieved if the government had not forbidden those actions.

"We at Nutritional Abundance Industries choose to show the public and Mr. Dunforth the *unseen*, three babies and mothers representing the millions who could have been nourished to grow up and achieve good things for themselves, their families, and their nations; babies who could grow up to be scientists, engineers, geneticists, and yes, even presidents. There are millions of *unseen* mothers and babies like these who could benefit from Carver's Legacy seeds.

"In particular, we have the Ambassador from Botswana, where crop blight has caused mass starvation. These super-seeds are resistant to that blight, and could help the farmers of Botswana feed their people and again become self-sufficient in food production. Since this injunction calls for the destruction of the seeds, they won't get the chance."

She paused, and then said in slower voice, in a chanting recitation, "And the idol PRIS-Moloch demanded a burnt holocaust as a sacrifice to appease and please him."

Grace nodded to the assistant. He closed the door on the packages of seeds and flipped the switch on the microwave. A hum was heard. After five seconds, he opened the door. Immediately the audience smelled the burnt, blackened packages. "There is your burnt holocaust, Mr. Edgar Moloch Dunforth."

"And now, on behalf of this entire group from foreign lands, one representative will speak. She is Lebo Kubabupe, the wife of a farmer in blight-ravaged Botswana." Grace nodded to Lebo. Holding her child in one arm, she stepped forward and pulled the blanket back to reveal the baby's swollen belly. Then she pointed a finger at Edgar Dunforth. The room grew silent. The cameras zoomed in on her, her gaunt baby, and her pointing finger.

She opened her mouth. *"J'Accuse!"* Then, trembling, she turned and left. The others also pointed their fingers while staring at Dunforth, then turned and followed her out. The cameras panned to a pale and perspiring Edgar Dunforth.

Minerva Stone reentered the room and went to the podium. "Ladies and Gentlemen, we have fulfilled our obligations as specified in the injunction filed by PRIS. This legal action has removed our biggest new product line and effectively removes seventy percent of our projected future revenue. Accordingly, we have this day declared bankruptcy and given severance pay to all employees of NAI here in Peoria and at seventeen other locations in the US. This injunction has put fifteen hundred people out of a job. Many of them will be lining the halls as you leave, ladies and gentlemen of the press, for a last photo op. Many of those laid off may want to thank Mr. Dunforth as he leaves the building as well. This concludes our press conference."

Edgar Dunforth started, as if suddenly shaken awake. "Wait," he shouted. "This can't be all of the crop seeds. You were planning to sell them all over Africa, India, and Asia. You must have a warehouse full of them. You are NOT in compliance!" he shouted toward the cameras.

"Oh, but we are," replied Minerva. You may inspect all of our warehouses, beginning with the one next door." She turned to the reporters, cameramen, and news producers. The cameras were still running. "I invite all of you to accompany me and Mr. Dunforth next door to our warehouse to document on film that we possess no further bio-engineered seeds. We offer samples of the destroyed seed that you may take for analysis to any independent lab to confirm that it was indeed the bio-engineered seeds. In fact, I insist on it."

She began handing out burned packages to the nearest reporters. "Here ladies and gentlemen of the press, get this picture," she said in a loud voice. The cameras zoomed in on her as she placed a charred package in the hands of Edgar Dunforth. She smiled at him, "You have been served." Then she walked briskly to the door. "Follow me for the first pictures ever taken inside our warehouses or research facility."

Cameramen jostled one another to get behind her as her high heels clicked down the corridor. Silent ex-employees lined the hall, staring at the reporters and cameramen.

Dunforth went to Samuel Solipsis. "Can they do this? How can they possibly be in compliance? There has to be more crop seed somewhere. Where can they be hiding it?"

Samuel put on his usual cautious legal voice. "We can demand to inspect every NAI warehouse in the nation. However, since she's going so public with this, I assume that we will find nothing. That makes them in compliance with the injunction as ordered."

"She can't do this," spluttered Dunforth. "This was supposed to be my, *our*" he caught himself, "moment of triumph. And that cheap theatre with the babies! Who cares about babies?! We represent the needs of the many, and that outweighs the needs of a few babies. Issue a press release! Say that PRIS is outraged by these cheap theatrics that distract from the larger issue of sustainability for the WHOLE PLANET! And who the hell is Moloch? Is there another way out of here? I don't want to walk down a hall full of laid-off employees."

"Yes sir. I don't know who Moloch is, sir. I think this is the only exit sir," said Solipsis subserviently.

*   *   *   *   *   *

The FACTS evening news broadcasted an interview with Lebo Kubabupe.

"This is Daily Report, with Bill Ursa. On our last segment, you saw clips from the remarkable press conference at Nutritional Abundance Industries. Now FACTS News legal expert Milly Karr brings us an exclusive follow-up interview with the woman from Botswana where crop blight is starving millions of people. Milly?"

"Bill, I am here with Lebo Kubabupe, her baby girl, and William Phewai, all from Botswana. Mrs. Kubabupe, what is your baby's name?"

Lebo held her baby in her lap. The camera zoomed in on the baby's pinched face. "My husband and I named her Tebogo, which means gratitude, because we were grateful to God for this precious gift. We are also grateful to our friend William Phewai who shared his scarce food with us to help feed our baby and our son Moroka."

Milly smiled at the child. "Mrs. Kubabupe, what is the situation in Botswana?"

"Most of our people are malnourished. Many in the countryside have died of starvation. Much of the food aid from the United Nations is siphoned off and sold by corrupt bureaucrats and does not reach the people. We need a reliable source of food we can grow for ourselves. My husband and I are farmers and we can do this. I cannot understand why America, a country known for its humanitarian aid, would forbid the distribution of these super-seeds that can feed my people. That man, Mr. Dunforth, who brought the legal injunction against the seeds, did you not see how heavy he is? A well-fed man who forbids others to feed themselves!"

The television picture shifted to a split screen showing the plump Dunforth on one side and the gaunt baby on the other.

Milly responded gently, "Mrs. Kubabupe, it is politically incorrect in this country to call someone 'heavy.' It could be considered a hate crime. Mr. Phewai, what is your role in this?"

William frowned as he looked at Milly. "I am the field agent for Nutritional Abundance Industries in Botswana. I supervised the first test crops using the super-seeds. I know that the crops are safe to eat. I saw the medical test results from the first harvest, and I ate the grain myself. I am healthy. I also know first-hand how the super-seeds resist the blight that is currently destroying crops in Botswana."

William looked directly into the camera. His face was stern. "In Botswana we have worked hard to achieve our independence. We are proud of this. Our farmers are industrious and work hard to feed our people. We want to be independent and self-reliant for our food. Botswanans are adults who have made our own evaluation of the safety and efficacy of these super-seeds. We simply want to perform "a capitalist act between consenting adults," as your philosopher Robert Nozick put it. Adults in Botswana want to buy super-seeds from the adults at Nutritional Abundance Industries. All we ask is that you leave us alone to do so. Then we can feed ourselves without becoming beggars at the door of the United Nations."

 **Chapter Nine**

N minus 31. The next day in Nairobi, Saturday, agricultural agents for Nutritional Abundance Industries, Ltd. (incorporated in New Zealand) loaded their trucks with sacks of Carver's Legacy seeds and drove out into the countryside to begin selling to local farmers. This scene was repeated in Botswana, South Africa, Liberia, India, Thailand, Vietnam, and other developing nations. Carver's Legacy was spreading into a dozen countries. Farmers gladly bought the enhanced seeds at a price forty percent lower than conventional seeds. Competitors complained to local government officials, who were angry that they weren't getting their usual bribes, and eventually word made it back to Chicago and the executive offices of PRIS.

"Oho!" exclaimed Edgar Dunforth after reading his e-mail. Hitting the button on his intercom, he barked, "Miss Cringe! Send in Mr. Solipsis." After Solipsis entered, Dunforth handed him a printout of an e-mail from Nairobi. "It seems our Ms. Minerva Stone lied to us. NAI did not destroy all of the seeds. They are busy selling them all over Africa, India, and parts of Southeast Asia. We can now have Ms. Stone and her executives found in contempt of court and jailed, can we not?"

Solipsis looked up from the printout with a smile. "Yes, we certainly can! I'll get right on it. I'll keep you informed."

After the chief counsel left his office, Dunforth looked up at the ceiling with a contented smile on his face. *I'll see that bitch in prison. That'll show her who's boss!*

Ninety minutes later, ten federal marshals showed up at the front door of the headquarters of Nutritional Abundance Industries in Peoria with a search warrant for bio-engineered seeds and an arrest warrant for Minerva Stone and six of her top executives. To their surprise, the doors were unlocked. When they entered, the offices were empty of employees. All the furniture was there, and even the computers, but all paper was gone. Not even a three-ring binder held any company documents or correspondence in it. The warehouses were empty as well. Not a grain of corn, not a grain of wheat, not one apple seed. The computer hard drives were wiped clean. Not even an operating system. With no personnel records to consult, the federal marshals, who were all from out of town, did not even know who had been an employee at the company.

After contacting the Peoria police chief, the marshals were able to question one woman who was the sister-in-law of one of the police officers. She had worked at NAI, according to the officer. "It was the strangest thing," the woman said. "Yesterday, just before the big press conference, all of the employees were told that the company was going bankrupt due to the injunction and destruction of the seeds. We were given our severance pay in cash, and told that we were free to stay for the press conference if we wished. We already knew that Mr. Dunforth of PRIS was going to be there. Some of us wanted to give him a piece of our minds for what he'd done. Some stayed; most left. Some people saw lights on in the building after midnight, and others saw trucks leaving the property at four in the morning. I guess they cleaned out what they wanted and left with it."

"Any idea where they were going?"

"No."

"Any idea where we can find the CEO and other executives?"

"No."

The marshals managed to find the home addresses of Ms. Stone and the other six executives. When they arrived, the scenes at the homes duplicated what they had found at the plant. Furniture, household goods, toys, and clothing were left behind. Computers were left behind, but the hard drives were wiped. Pictures were on the walls, but no personal or family photos were found anywhere. It was as if anonymous people disappeared into anonymity.

Word was relayed back to PRIS and Mr. Dunforth. His contented smile vanished. "Gone?!" he thundered. "How could they be gone that fast? They only announced the bankruptcy yesterday! Solipsis! Find them!"

"Yes sir," he said subserviently.

Through his contacts in the federal government, Solipsis managed to get the cooperation of the FBI for the warrants to arrest Minerva Stone and the other NAI executives and their families on material witness warrants. Now the Federal Marshall Service and the FBI, DEA, and ICE would be looking for these fugitives from the justice of PRIS. Solipsis even managed to get the arrest warrants put on a BOLO (Be On Look Out) on Interpol, the international police agency.

"There is no way they can escape us now," he confidently informed Mr. Dunforth. "It's just a matter of time before we have them."

*   *   *   *   *   *

N minus 30. Monday.   In Christchurch, New Zealand, Minerva
Stone decided to call another press conference. Sky News (which would
feed into FACTS News in the US), the BBC, and ZNN were the only
major news networks with local contractors in Christchurch, so she made
sure that the press conference would be uploaded to YouTube and a
dozen other social networking sites for maximum dissemination around
the world.

"Hello Ladies and Gentlemen of the press, my fellow citizens in the
United States, and interested people of the planet. My name is Minerva
Stone, and until last Friday I was CEO of Nutritional Abundance
Industries of Peoria, Illinois, in the United States of America. I have
learned that officials of the United States organization called Pristine
Influence on Society, or PRIS, have obtained US search warrants for our
bio-engineered seed that sells by the brand name 'Carver's Legacy.'
They have also obtained US federal arrest warrants for me and six of the
former executives of NAI, and have extended these warrants
internationally through Interpol.   They maintain that we're not in
compliance with the terms of the federal cease and desist order to stop
sales of the bio-engineered seeds, and to destroy said seeds. The arrest
warrants are for contempt of court charges based on the allegation that
we have not complied with the injunction. I wish to respond to these
charges."

Minerva paused. "Our retained counsel in the United States is this
day filing to have those charges and arrest warrants dropped. The legal
corporation Nutritional Abundance Industries was in fact in compliance
with the original injunction.   That injunction directed Nutritional
Abundance Industries to stop selling and distributing the bio-engineered
seeds. Nutritional Abundance Industries filed for bankruptcy last Friday
and ceased all operations in the US by close of business last Friday. The
injunction also directed NAI to destroy all bio-engineered crop seeds in
its legal possession on any of its properties. NAI did destroy all bio-
engineered crop seeds in its legal possession last Friday during a
televised press conference.   That conference is available on
YouTubeAsia, YouTubeAfrica, FreedomToobz.Ark, and the web sites of
the BBC, ZNN, and FACTS News, for those of you who missed it."

Steepling her fingers in front of her, Minerva continued, "What probably has confused our colleagues at PRIS is the fact that bio-engineered seeds are today being sold under the brand name Carver's Legacy in over twelve nations in Africa, India, and Southeast Asia. The entity selling those seeds is Nutritional Abundance Industries Ltd., chartered in New Zealand, and a totally different company from the one that went bankrupt in the USA. Two weeks ago, Nutritional Abundance Industries Ltd. of New Zealand purchased the intellectual property, 99.99 percent of the inventory of bio-engineered crop seeds, and the commercial rights to the brand name Carver's Legacy. The entity known as NAI in the United States complied with the injunction to the letter of the law - US law."

Pointing her index finger, as if pointing at an invisible Edgar Dunforth, she lowered her voice for emphasis, "The new entity known as NAI Ltd. of New Zealand was not the subject of that injunction, and is in any case beyond the jurisdiction of injunctions issued in the USA, since it is not a USA company, does not operate in the USA, and never intends to operate in the USA. I am now the CEO of NAI Ltd., and the other six executives named in the USA arrest warrants are now employees of NAI Ltd. here in New Zealand. We're immigrants and citizens of New Zealand now. Since we have now conclusively proven that we did in fact comply with the injunction issued in the USA, we're confident that the arrest warrants will be dropped.

"Some of you may recall that Nutritional Abundance Industries had chartered a cargo plane to airlift an emergency supply of the Carver's Legacy super-seeds to blight-ravaged Botswana. These seeds are resistant to the blight, and would help reestablish Botswana's agricultural base. The Minister of Agriculture had rescinded his previous prohibition of the super-seeds and asked us for this emergency shipment. The legal injunction filed by PRIS stopped that shipment from leaving the United States.

"Tonight I am happy to inform you that a shipment of Carver's Legacy seeds have been unloaded in the capital city of Gaborone, and are being trucked out to farmers even as we speak. Nutritional Abundance Industries Ltd. of New Zealand is not the subject of that legal injunction, and we are now free to do the right thing and help the farmers and the people of Botswana become independent and self-sufficient in feeding their own families."

"Ask yourselves, when and why did government decide that it could rule that helping to feed hungry people was illegal? Ask yourselves, since when does government decide whether or not I am *allowed* to feed hungry people? When did we start asking the government's permission for everything we do? I thought they worked for us. Is this out-of-control government a force for good? Or for evil? Judge for yourselves.

"Thank you for watching. Good day."

*   *   *   *   *   *

In Chicago, Edgar Dunforth went ballistic after he watched this latest performance by Minerva Stone on ZNN. "Send Samuel Solipsis in here! Now!" he shouted into his intercom. Outside his office, Miss Cringe cringed and summoned Solipsis.

"Where did you get your law degree, a correspondence school? You incompetent . . . how could you have let this happen?" Samuel Solipsis did a bit of cringing himself.

"Sir, I don't know. I crafted that injunction so tightly that not one grain of rice could escape being destroyed. How was I to know that they had formed an off-shore corporation that was beyond our control?"

"Because we pay you to know; that's why, you idiot. And to think that I was going to ask the compensation board to give you another pay raise! I'll give you forty-eight hours to come up with a counter-strategy. If you don't, you're fired! Now get out of my sight, you turd!"

"Yes sir," he said, keeping his eyes down subserviently.

*   *   *   *   *   *

Dust billowed up in the yard of Mantate Kubabupe as a truck came to a stop. William Phewai got out and walked around to the passenger side to help Lebo and the baby get down. Moroka came running.

"Mother! My mother, I am so happy to see you!" He hugged her and then looked at his baby sister. "Tebogo looks well." He extended his finger. The baby grasped it in her own tiny fist and gurgled and smiled at him.

"Yes. We had ample food during our travels." Lebo looked up to see Mantate walking toward her. "My husband! You look well."

Mantate hugged her with tears in his eyes. "I thank God you have returned safely. William, my friend, thank you for protecting them during this journey. Moroka and I have grown stronger from the food you left with us. Look! The baby smiles! She looks well." Mantate held the child in his arms and looked down at her with a look of wonder.

William went to the back of his truck and began unloading boxes.

"Mantate, I have more food supplies for you. And good news. I have a supply of the super-seeds! You can begin planting immediately. I will help. Oh, I almost forgot." He looked around for Moroka. "Moroka. I have a special gift for you, from Dr. Grace Washington in America. Do you remember her?"

Moroka ran to him, eyes shining. "Yes! I remember the tall lady from America."

William held a package out to him. Moroka slowly, almost reverently, slid his fingers under the tape to open the package. He would re-use the brown wrapping paper for his school work.

"A book! Two books!" exclaimed Moroka. His smile was so big, it could have been the crescent moon. "See, papa, Dr. Washington sent me two books."

He held out the books so that his father could see. *Up From Slavery*, by Booker T. Washington, and *The Story of George Washington Carver*, by Eva Moore. Moroka read aloud a note from Grace Washington.

Dear Moroka, I hope you enjoy reading about a man who loved plants and inspired me to become a botanist, George Washington Carver. The other man, Booker T. Washington, was my great-great-great uncle. He worked hard to educate himself, and went on to build the great Tuskegee University, where I work. I hope his story will inspire you to educate yourself, as it inspired me to educate myself. Your friend, Dr. Grace Washington.

Mantate took the book from his son and looked at the picture of Booker T. Washington on the cover. He looked up at William Phewai. "This man was once a slave, and built a great university? Truly, in America, anything is possible."

Chapter Ten

N minus 29.   On long, deserted sections of highways outside Chicago, San Francisco, Los Angeles, Pittsburgh, Atlanta, and Boston, roadblocks were set up.   At first glance, the people manning the barricades were in uniforms identical to that of the state highway patrol of each state.   Only a close inspection of the patches on their shoulders, and their badges, revealed that they were from another agency.   They were members of the underground Constitutional Resistance Movement.

As cars approached, they slowed down.   Uniformed officers directed them to drive on or pull over for inspection.   Officers positioned to see the rear of the cars as they slowed down gave signals indicating which cars to pull over.

Outside Chicago, Samuel Solipsis was on his way to Peoria to see if he could turn up any information about Nutritional Abundance Industries that would help him save his job.   He was directed to pull over for inspection at the roadblock.   An officer approached him along with a video cameraman.

"Sir, we noticed that your vehicle has bumper stickers that say, "No Blood for Oil, Go Green, Stop Driving" and Walk, don't Drive."

"So?"

"Sir, this is an SUV, is it not?"

"Yes, so what?"

"And it belongs to you?"

"Yes."

"And it does get less than 12 miles to the gallon?"

"I suppose so."

"Sir, I am issuing you a citation for contempt of integrity and second-degree hypocrisy."

"What!   Why? Because I drive an SUV?"

"No sir.   We have no objection to any type of vehicle being driven by anybody.   It is the combination of these types of bumper stickers on this type of vehicle that we object to.   If you do not understand the obvious flaw in logic and blatant hypocrisy, then I'm afraid I can't help you."

"I'll have you know that I have a law degree."

"Then I'm afraid you've been educated beyond your intelligence." The officer's Blackberry beeped.   "Just a moment."   He read the screen.

"My DMV augmented database is telling me that you are an employee of a government agency or a 503c public interest advocacy organization, is that correct?"

"Yes, that's correct. I work for the non-profit agency called PRIS."

"And their mission is?"

"Lower use of resources for a sustainable planet."

"Then I'm afraid that the second charge is elevated to first-degree hypocrisy."

"Is this a joke? Some kind of reality show? Is that what the camera is for?"

"This is not a joke. It is in fact a reality show, but not the kind you are accustomed to. Step out of the car, sir."

"What? Are you kidding?"

"No sir, I am not kidding. Step out of the car and move behind it." Solipsis stepped out of the car and walked to the back of his SUV. Another officer had placed a short camp stool in front of his rear bumper, in the middle.

"Sir, please sit here." The video camera framed him with his bumper stickers clearly readable on either side of him. The first officer read, "The charges are contempt of integrity and first-degree hypocrisy. How do you plead?"

"Not guilty."

"We, the court of reality find you guilty by virtue of the evidence visible on either side of you, slogans on your own automobile whose resource consumption clearly contradicts the slogans. The fact that you work for an organization that preaches these slogans raises the charge to first-degree hypocrisy."

Solipsis looked into the camera with his mouth hanging open, in shock. "You are sentenced to three punishments. The first punishment is social shaming. This video will be posted on the Green Hypocrites page of the Constitutional Resistance Movement web site on FreedomToobz.Ark. Hold this under your chin."

Samuel held up a bumper sticker with bright green letters, that read, "H: Enviro-Hypocrite."

The officer continued, "Links will be e-mailed to all of your friends listed on your social networking pages, plus major media outlets. The title will be 'The Green H is the new Scarlet Letter, the mark of Enviro-

Hypocrites who do not practice what they force on others.' This mug shot will be there."

He continued, "The second punishment is a fine for first-degree hypocrisy, defined as working for an organization that preaches and agitates for the very behavior that you choose not to do: walk instead of drive. Your fine is your automobile. It will be sold in South America, and the proceeds used to help retired people pay utility bills made too high by the cap and tax bill your organization helped to bribe through Congress without public hearings or public debate.

"The third punishment is that you live with the answer you attempt to force on others without practicing it yourself." Two husky officers forced him to his feet and removed his suit coat. They then applied the bumper sticker across his rear end. The adhesive was quick-drying super glue that would tear the pants fabric if he attempted to remove the big green H.

The first officer said, "You will now have to walk to the next exit, the very answer you try to force on others."

Solipsis raised his voice, "I want to talk to your commanding officer. I want an appeal of this verdict!"

"I am the commanding officer, as it happens. Every offender gets an appeal, an appeal to the judgment of his friends, neighbors, co-workers, and the general public. Ask them if they think you were treated unfairly."

The officer turned to the camera. "Friends, neighbors, co-workers, and fellow citizens of Mr. Samuel Solipsis, he appeals to your judgment. Have we been unfair to him? Tell him what you think the next time you see him. E-mail him. Call him. Text him. His address, phone number, Facebook page, and e-mail addresses will be listed on this video when it is posted to the internet today."

He turned back to Solipsis. "These web sites are hosted at an undisclosed location, so that your Orwellian friends in the government can't shut it down. Start walking."

The camera followed him as he walked away, zooming in once on the bumper sticker across the seat of his pants: *H: Enviro-Hypocrite*.

He walked seven miles to the next exit, and then another two miles into the small town. Along the way, many passing cars had honked at him. Several had slowed down to give him the finger and yell "Hypocrite!" The only store where he could buy a new pair of pants was one of the 'Dollar' type stores, which he hated, and which PRIS had tried to outlaw as "purveyors of cheap products unsustainable for the planet." He was glad one was here now, so he could get rid of the pants with the permanent green H sticker on the seat. He was able to rent a car, and then report the incident to the local police. He had several blisters on his feet, and he was exhausted.

"Mr. Solipsis," said the dispatcher for the local police, "we contacted the highway patrol and they have no such roadblocks out today. We will continue to investigate the theft of your car and get back in touch with you." He never heard any more about the incident from the police in that small town.

His so-called friends smirked when they told him they had seen the whole thing on FreedomToobz.Ark, and that he was a very funny-looking guy when he walked: bowlegged with a green H on his rear. His neighbors gave him dirty looks when they saw him. The Drudge Report posted the link under a headline that read "True Greens should PISS on PRIS: Enviro-Hypocrites!"

Reports of similar incidents poured in from all over the nation, but the mainstream media refused to run the stories. People talked about it where they worked after seeing dozens of these "get out and walk, just like you're trying to force other people to do" incidents on FreedomToobz.Ark. Other web sites picked up on this viral story. Some cable networks that specialized in reality shows began showing the videos in prime time. Sports bars, coffee shops, and restaurants that featured multiple television screens began tuning in. Patrons laughed derisively and cheered when the hypocrites got their "comeuppance." "Serves 'em right!" they said. "Boo! Hypocrites!" they shouted when another mug shot appeared: a well known woman bureaucrat standing in front of her big SUV, wearing a big green H on her derriere.

*   *   *   *   *   *

N minus 28. Samuel Solipsis had a headache. Twenty-four of his forty-eight hours were up. He had accomplished nothing in Peoria except creating an endless repeating virally spreading loop documentary of his humiliation at the hands of those vigilantes from the so-called "Constitutional Resistance Movement." *Just what we need, he thought. More crackpot vigilante groups pulling publicity stunts!*

People in the street looked at him, at first with recognition, then with disapproval. He got no sympathy from the staffers at PRIS, where he should have been able to count on their support. He had gone to his favorite strip club for a little distraction. Even two of the girls there glared at him and refused to give him lap dances. "Hypocrite!" spat one girl, "You want to make me bicycle nine miles to work in the rain, while you drive your SUV? Dance in your SUV's lap, you pig!"

Feeling sorry for himself, he had called in sick. He endlessly rehearsed reasons why it was not his fault. *Why me? It's not my fault. Why me? Someone else must be to blame.* Like a rabbit darting this way and that from a pursuing fox, he looked for ways to evade responsibility for his actions.

Finally he remembered an idea from law school. One of his professors, teaching the course titled "Legal Evasion Tactics for Criminal Defense Lawyers," had said, "When the finger points at you, push it aside to point at someone else." Elated, he got out his Blackberry and began calling some of his contacts.

*   *   *   *   *   *

N minus 27. Twenty-four hours later, Samuel Solipsis reported to work. At 9 a.m. precisely, he asked Miss Cringe if he could see Mr. Dunforth. "Well," growled Dunforth, "have you come up with anything we can use against Minerva Stone?"

"I've come up with something we can use. Not against Minerva Stone, but against someone close to her. Then we use this person as a hostage. We use her to blackmail Minerva into doing whatever we want. A show trial arranged by our friends at the Justice Department, for example."

"That sounds promising. Who is it and how can I use it against Minerva?" Dunforth's small beady eyes gleamed.

"Actually, sir, PRIS will be using this strategy, but you won't. You've used the word "I" too many times, and as you know, "i" is in the last syllable of the word collective, it follows; it doesn't *lead*. There is no room in the revolutionary consciousness of progressivism for egocentric leaders, only for leaders subservient to the consensus of the many."

He leaned over the desk and pushed the intercom button. "Miss Cringe?"

"Yes, Mr. Solipsis, the board members are here and have demanded that Mr. Dunforth come before them in the collective conference room."

Solipsis looked Dunforth straight in the eye for the first time ever. "I believe you have been summoned by your masters, our collective."

"We'll see about that!" Dunforth angrily stalked into the executive collective conference room that adjoined his office. The board members stared at him grimly. "What is all this?" he demanded. "I didn't call a board meeting. I didn't authorize . . ."

Ms. Diana Nomenski interrupted, "I, I, I. Too much I, Edgar. You've never learned that the first part of the word collective is *collect*. As in *collect* our opinions and *collect* our consensus before committing this organization to actions that have consequences, like that abortive press conference in Peoria. 'Who cares about a few babies, you said.' You fool! Millions of babies and millions of mothers comprise an international collective. Our friends in the mainstream media cut that comment out of their coverage, but someone got it on a cell phone video and posted it on the internet. PRIS and the associated sister organizations that make it up were made to look like insensitive uncaring villains. Once again, you think of yourself as an individual, and not as part of a collective to be consulted, soothed, and obeyed. Sit down."

Shocked at being interrupted, he sat, open mouthed. Diana Nomenski rose from her seat and assumed the role of prosecutor. "It has been brought to our attention, no, it has been subserviently and properly offered to our attention, that you have taken it upon yourself to make decisions all by yourself, decisions that have harmed PRIS and harmed our mission of taking control of society for its own good.

"In addition to this fiasco of allowing the executives of Nutritional Abundance Industries to escape our justice, the bio-enhanced seeds have been sold and planted all over Africa, India, and Southeast Asia and will begin feeding more people and more children within one short growing season. That means more people on the planet, not fewer, a direct violation of the mission statement of PRIS: *reduce the planetary population to a sustainable 40 percent of this year's population numbers.* You are not only an abject 'I,' you are incompetent to fulfill the mission of the collective you belong to."

"But that wasn't my fault!" he burst out. "I assigned Solipsis to design a legal injunction that would prevent that. He failed, not me!"

"Again with the 'I' Edgar. Not even a re-education camp will reform you, we're afraid. You should have made that a collective decision of this collective board, not an ego trip individualist decision by one *male!*"

Diana stepped closer, glaring at Edgar. "The last count in this series of indictments against you is the sin of bad publicity. Publicity that hurts the cause of PRIS. At nine o'clock last night, links to this YouTube video began to be virally circulated all across America. My Space, Facebook, ProgressiveHiveMind, The Daily Kos, and the *New York Times* all carried dozens of posts with the link to this video documentary titled "Planet Betrayed by PRIS Double Agent." The double agent named is YOU, Edgar. We of the board collective have already viewed it, and we have received thousands of e-mails demanding that you be removed and prosecuted for fraud. If you had bothered to check your own PRIS Collective web site, you would have found that tens of thousands of angry e-mails had shut down your servers."

Turning back to her fellow board members, Diana continued her lecture. "Suffice it to say it shows how you abused the planet by taking the PRIS corporate jet from Chicago to Peoria, when you could have bicycled the day before. Even your assistant Miss Cringe is caught on tape suggesting you at least take a car rather than the jet. You are on that same tape rejecting her sensible suggestion. If only you had learned to seek the opinions of as many people as you could before making these decisions!"

Samuel Solipsis, sitting against the wall out of sight behind one of the board members, looked down and placed his hand over his mouth to conceal a smile. He had spent the past twenty-four hours creating that video, posting it, and circulating the link to his networks of progressive, Green sustainability, gender issue, and depopulation issue groups. He had arranged for a manufactured grassroots campaign of outrage to be directed at Edgar Dunforth. He had made sure that the tens of thousands of e-mails would be sent to the PRIS board members, not Director Dunforth. Then he made discreet inquiries to PRIS board members.

"Ms. Nomenski? Samuel Solipsis here. Have you been receiving these e-mails from outraged PRIS members? Have you seen the video? You have? Has the board collectively thought about an emergency meeting without Director Dunforth present, in order to collectively

121

decide on damage control? Many people on the PRIS staff have collectively expressed solidarity with that idea (this was a lie, but Samuel knew that "collective" ideas from many people carried more weight). The board collective does want a meeting? May we of the PRIS staff offer any help in arranging this meeting? You want me to arrange it and attend it? I . . . , no, *we'd* be delighted to be of service to the collective," he had said in a deferential tone of voice.

He now looked up to follow the next act of this pre-determined drama.

"But, but," Dunforth spluttered, "then why did this board, excuse me, this collective board, vote to buy a corporate, excuse me again, a *collective* jet for PRIS? For what purpose were we to use it? It will always spew out more carbon than any other mode of transportation!"

"Edgar, you condemn yourself out of your own mouth. 'A foolish consistency is the hobgoblin of little minds,' a great committee once said. We will be inconsistent when it suits our collective purposes. Our collective ends justify our collective means. If we decide to burn up fossil fuel in our corporate jet, it is a politically correct decision, because *WE* have decided to do it. When an individual decides to burn fossil fuel, it is politically incorrect, because he made an 'I' decision. Your mistake was that *you alone* decided to do it."

"Then there were no guidelines for me to base a decision on?" Edgar meekly asked, finally sensing that he was in danger.

"There you go again, Edgar. *Guidelines for me, me, me.* It's WE, not me. WE decide the guidelines, and WE can change the guidelines whenever WE want. It's not guidelines or principles that matter, Edgar, it's whether the guidelines were approved by a collective, a We. It's WE, not me. You never understood that. WE *is* the guideline."

Edgar sat speechless, too stunned to speak, hoisted by his own petard.

Ms. Nomenski continued, "This board collective has already met to consider the matter and formulate a damage control plan. Speaking on behalf of the Board Collective who has voted on this already, we inform you, Executive Director Edgar Dunforth, that you are fired effective immediately. We can't place Minerva Stone on trial for our propaganda ministry to reshape the revolutionary consciousness of all American proletarians, so we're placing *you* in a show trial instead. This board has made formal charges against you for embezzlement of PRIS funds, based on your unauthorized use of the PRIS jet, costing the Foundation over $30,000 and spewing untold millions of cubic feet of carbon compounds into the atmosphere to poison us and further accelerate global warming, a clear violation of our prime directive. We have sworn out a warrant for your arrest. Miss Cringe?"

"Yes, Ms. Nomenski. The federal marshals are here to take ex-Director Dunforth into custody. Per your instructions, Judge Moody [a big contributor and supporter of PRIS] has waived the arraignment and denied bail. Mr. Dunforth will be taken directly to the Cook County Jail, where the US District Attorney, who is outraged at the crowded conditions at the federal prison, has instead subcontracted with Cook County for cell space to confine Mr. Dunforth in the jail wing reserved for violent sexual predators and deviants."

"Excellent." Ms. Nomenski cracked her knuckles as the marshals placed handcuffs on Dunforth. She looked at her watch. "Marshals, if you please, we're a little ahead of schedule. Please wait with him here for five minutes. The media hasn't shown up yet to film him doing the perp walk into the parking lot."

"This is outrageous!" Dunforth erupted. "I demand a lawyer. I demand my legal rights!"

"There you go again, Edgar my dear. '*I*' demand, and '*my*' legal rights. You still don't get it. It serves the greater good that the needs of the many, us, outweigh the needs and rights of the few, you. Those legal rights supposedly belonging to you are sacrificed by us so that your show trial will be staged more theatrically. Edgar, you are going to be famous! We plan to make sure the video of your show trial is available on the US Embassy web site in Moscow. My dear, we'll show those folks how to *really* run a show trial. By the way, you had better get used to people calling you 'dear' in prison, especially your cell mate.

"Next order of business. We of the Feminist League of Professional Women FLPW, being duly appointed board members of PRIS, hereby make a motion to hire Mr. Samuel Solipsis for the post of executive director of PRIS, with all the obligations of collective decision-making thereunto appertaining, effective immediately. Do we have a second?"

Maeve Franklin, of the Progressive Political Party, raised her hand. "We second the motion."

"All in favor?"

"Aye."

"All opposed?" Diana looked fiercely at Sonny Fremont as she said this. Silence. "The motion carries. Mr. Solipsis, you are now officially executive director of PRIS. What is your first suggestion for a collective board decision?"

Samuel Solipsis stood up. "Thank you, board member Nomenski, for your vote of confidence. For our first suggestion, we make a motion that we temporarily adjourn to the parking lot. We can witness the perp walk and be seen in the news footage wearing frowns of disapproval as the criminal Dunforth is perp-walked to the police cruiser. This will greatly repair the damage to our reputation caused by this enemy of the people and enemy of collective decision making."

He glanced around the table. Seeing approving nods, he said, "We hereby make a motion that we adjourn to the parking lot and give media interviews expressing our outrage about Dunforth. I further move that we demand that the US district attorney quickly stage a publicly broadcast trial. This will show the American people, and the citizens of the planet, that we move swiftly to punish the enemies of the people, and that we continue our dedication to making all decisions for them for their own good. Do we hear a second?"

Ms. Nomenski responded quickly and loudly, "Second!"

"All in favor?"

"Aye."

"All opposed?" Silence. "The motion is carried. We hereby adjourn this meeting for forty-five minutes." He banged the gavel and nodded to the marshals. They heaved Dunforth to his feet and marched him down the hall to the stairs. The board members followed, silent as they rehearsed their sound bites for their latest fifteen seconds of fame.

Chapter Eleven

N minus 26. The CEO of E-Buyer, Gina Manley, had asked for an appointment with Isaiah. Intrigued, Isaiah had taken the meeting. E-Buyer was the most popular buying and selling web site in the world right now. They were a thousand times the size of tiny Promethean Software International, with staff and resources he couldn't imagine. What could they possibly want with him?

At the appointed time, Manley and her CFO, Mr. Peter Largent, were shown into Isaiah's spartan office at his company headquarters in Silicon Valley.

"Ms. Manley! A pleasure. I've long admired your work. Mr. Largent, pleased to meet you." Isaiah gestured them into seats at the small conference table in his office.

"What can I do for the two top executives of the most successful online auction software service in the world?" Isaiah asked affably.

"Sell your newest software to us," Ms. Manley promptly responded, "so we can stop the worldwide small business community from discovering how much better it is than our product." Her stiff smile suggested an iron hand inside this velvet glove of politeness.

This immediate bluntness shocked the normally unflappable Isaiah. He involuntarily pushed himself back from the table.

"Whoa! Sell Invisible Hand? We aren't even offering it in the US, your biggest market. You are already well established in China, Europe, and South America. Why do you want my product?"

"Quite simply, Mr. Mercury, it's good, it's simple, and it's cheap to use. You will be a threat to us in our markets within eighteen months. Once people see how easy it is to use, and how much cheaper it is than E-Buyer, we will lose market share to you. We've invested a lot to bring our service to the world, and we want to enjoy the revenue stream from our near-monopoly a bit longer. Outside this room, I'll deny saying any of this."

Largent spoke up, "We are prepared to make you an offer you can't refuse. You and your top execs can retire on top of a mountain of cash and take it easy. We know that you stand to reap revenues of $134 million in your first two years. $34 million of that will go to pay debt on the infrastructure of server farms you established to handle the traffic.

This morning we're prepared to offer you $250 million for Invisible Hand proprietary software systems."

Isaiah was stunned. "What would you do with it?"

"Sit on it. Bury it for a few more years, and then offer it ourselves. Our web service is a cash cow, and we can milk its lucrative revenue stream for three or four more years, as long as we don't have a more nimble competitor offering a simpler and cheaper alternative." Manley sat back, poker faced. "We're not ready to cannibalize such a lucrative revenue stream with a new disruptive technology like yours if we don't have to. We have a lot invested in our existing infrastructure."

"What about the African farmers I'm planning to serve? They can't afford central electricity, let alone a computer and internet service to be able to use E-Buyer for selling their crops."

"They have gotten along for thousands of years. They can wait a few more years."

"And the farmers' children who could have been educated with the extra income from selling crops to a world market?"

"Not our problem," Manley evenly replied, "We offer a good service that helps people, at a low price. We can't solve everyone's problems."

Isaiah looked hard into their eyes, and then said, "Unless you have a better service that helps people, at an even lower price: Invisible Hand."

"Which we will eventually offer," said Largent.

Isaiah looked out his window at the horizon. "Two hundred fifty million is a big number to me," he said dreamily. He pictured the island home he had dreamed of buying in the Caribbean. White sand beach and a boat pier with a sailing schooner moored to it. *Jimmy Buffett, make room for me!*

"Of course," said Largent, "we would want you to sign a five year standard non-compete agreement as part of the sale."

Isaiah snapped out of his daydream. *Not doing what he did best, and loved, for five years? It was like a five-year jail sentence. Not offering those small farmers a tool to link them into the newly flattened world marketplace? Denying them their own shot at prosperity "for a few more years?" Or indefinitely?*

He sat up straighter. "Ms. Manley and Mr. Largent, my answer is no. I love my work, I love my product, and I love working on cutting-edge technologies. I love creating tools to make people more productive, and then putting them into the hands of people who work hard. Invisible

126

Hand is a dream I've worked to bring to life for five years. I have to be the one to bring it to life. My own product, my own self."

Largent and Manley looked at each other. Largent nodded slightly. Ms. Manley spoke. "Mr. Mercury, we will up the ante. In addition to the purchase price, we will make you Chief Technology Officer in charge of Research and Development at E-Buyer. You can bring your team with you. You can still work on cutting-edge products. Your salary will be $1.5 million per year, plus stock options." This was ten times what he was paying himself now.

"And Invisible Hand software?"

"We will sit on it for a few years." If they bought it, they controlled it, he realized, no matter what his new job title might be.

Isaiah shook his head. "The answer is still no."

"Take a few days to think it over. Here's my private cell number. Call me with any questions or additional details you'd like to work out. We are reasonable. We can make this work. Call me." Manley placed her card in his hand. Rising, she and Largent shook his hand and prepared to leave.

"We've made a generous offer for your software, far above your sales projections and what you've spent so far," Manley said. "I think you should take our offer. If not . . ."

Isaiah now detected renewed steel in her voice. "If not . . . what?" he asked evenly.

She smiled at him, "Let's just say that in this schoolyard squabble, we have a big brother we can bring to the fight. He lives in Washington, D.C." She turned to leave.

"I think you've just used my own government as a threat against me," he said quietly.

"But people from Washington are only here when they want to *help you*," she replied sweetly. "My offer stands for five days. Think about it." The door closed behind them.

Isaiah sat back in his chair, a scowl on his face. *So, Gina Manley and the giant corporation E-Buyer want to push me around. And they have the United States government to help them do it. Two of the biggest bullies on the block. Well, well. Time to find the right sling and the right stone to slay these Goliaths.* He stared into the distance, remembering his first encounter with a bully . . .

*   *   *   *   *   *

It was in the third grade. On his way to school, the bully pushed him down and took his lunch. Again. But this time, Isaiah said a quick prayer, *Lord help me, just like You helped David beat Goliath.* He came up swinging. *Boof!* A left into the bigger boy's stomach. *Crunch!* A right to his nose. Blood spurted from the nose and he began blubbering. As the bully left, Isaiah breathed *Thank You Lord.*

Isaiah was beaten many times by bullies after that, but he never backed down. And the same bully never came back for more. He learned, *stand up to a bully, and he will back off.*

*   *   *   *   *   *

Rocking a little in his office chair, Isaiah's scowl turned to a small smile. *The bigger they come, the harder they fall . . . what sling should I use . . . ?*

When a week passed without Isaiah calling Gina Manley, he received a congressional subpoena. He was being summoned to testify before a Senate sub-committee, under the penalty of contempt of congress, which carries jail time. The bully's big brother was now in the fight. He packed his bags for D.C.

*   *   *   *   *   *

N minus 18. Isaiah was in his hotel room the afternoon before he was to testify before Congress, reviewing facts and figures for his testimony the next day. There was a knock at the door. When Isaiah answered it, a smartly dressed young government staffer type introduced himself with a business card: J. Walter Obson, Under-Secretary for the Treasury in Charge of Bailout Exceptions. "Mr. Mercury, I have good news for you. Your firm qualifies for some of the bailout money from the most recent federal stimulus package: $300 million, direct from Uncle Sam. You don't have to do anything in return, except obey certain instructions from time to time from the Treasury Secretary, as relayed by me."

Isaiah offered him a seat. "I don't understand. My firm didn't ask for any bailout money. My firm is financially sound. We are not in debt.

128

We're privately owned, so there are no stockholders to report to publicly."

"Mr. Mercury, *actual need* is not the criteria for these bailout funds. There are exceptions to actual need. Perceived need in the national interest, as reported to us by our friends and colleagues in the industry, that is the real criterion. In our departmental mission, vision, and values, number one on the list of values, I quote the words of the great Secretary of Labor Robert Reich: *We hold to no higher truth than our own perceptions.* In this case, we hold no higher truth than our own perceptions of need and the national interest, and we often accept the perceptions of others, if they come recommended to us."

Gina Manley and E-Buyer came recommended to you, thought Isaiah. *Came recommended and came offering perceptions of Isaiah Mercury and Promethean Software International. Perceptions like bail him out, and then you control him, and then you can block the introduction of Invisible Hand marketplace selling services that threatens our near monopoly.*

"Mr. Obson, what is your higher truth perception about how Invisible Hand software fits into the perception of need and the national interest?" asked Isaiah.

"Oh, the Treasury Secretary was very specific about that. Our position is that we need more cooperation in the marketplace, not more competition. We don't need one more software product competing with *our* big established companies with hundreds of thousands of jobs, and hundreds of thousands of people in those jobs who *vote*. We want you to delay the introduction of Invisible Hand Software Services," J. Walter said earnestly.

"*Our* big established companies?" Isaiah raised one eyebrow.

"We at Treasury like to think of big companies with hundreds of thousands of employees as ours, because we have their best interests at heart," replied Mr. Obson.

"And what about the millions of smaller companies like mine?" asked Isaiah.

"Oh, we have their best interests at heart too, but it's more difficult to analyze and understand the role and impact of millions of small companies, so we start with the big ones first, the ones we understand."

The ones you have an understanding with, thought Isaiah.

129

"Mr. J. Walter Obson, I don't want your bailout. I think your bailout will sink me. I think your bailout will make me dishonest," Isaiah said while looking steadily at him.

"Oh now, Mr. Mercury, don't go making unsubstantiated charges. There is nothing dishonest here. There are laws about making false charges, you know." Mr. Obson rose and reached for his briefcase.

"Those laws only apply to *false* charges," Isaiah said carefully, holding up a small tape recorder he had kept running in his jacket pocket. He did not mention the hidden surveillance video camera he had set up for just such an eventuality.

"Mr. Mercury, that was quite unnecessary, and quite useless. I'll be watching your testimony before Congress tomorrow. Good day." The small man let himself out. Isaiah smiled and began whistling softly as he went back to review his notes again.

*   *   *   *   *   *

N minus 17. The next day, Isaiah Mercury was testifying before Congress. The Senate sub-committee on Inter-State, Intra-State, and Extra-Territorial Business Control, Regulation and Taxation had subpoenaed him to offer testimony on a Senate bill that proposed additional taxes and regulations on transaction fees and the ways in which software was used. Sub-committee Chair Senator Hiden had the floor. One of his aides passed him a note. Looking up at the network cameras, he nodded. This was his pre-arranged signal for the network director to switch the feed to the camera that captured his "best" side, the right, with his leonine mane of white hair. He cleared his throat.

"Mr. Mercury, am I to understand that your firm, Promethean Software International, now sells software internationally?"

"No, Senator, we do not sell the software, but we charge a fee for transactions made over our software site."

"I don't understand."

"Well, compare it to the telephone companies. They now have software that switches your calls automatically when you make a phone call, connecting you to your party. When you make a call, they charge you for the call, not the software."

"It sounds like your firm should be regulated by the Federal Communications Commission, just like the phone companies."

"No sir, that would not be correct. Phone companies are required by law to offer universal service for basic voice communications. My software operates over a cell phone, but only when someone chooses to use it, and the users are only charged for the transactions they make. My users do not have to pay a monthly subscription or access fee. Every use of *Invisible Hand* marketplace software is a voluntary act between consenting adults. Nobody is forced to use it; nobody is told how much to use it. It's there if they want it. If they don't want it, they aren't paying any fees to subsidize its availability. I bear the cost of making it available in the marketplace of the internet."

"Mr. Mercury, how many countries now have access to your software?"

"I'm concentrating first on the developing countries where it can leverage the efforts of small farmers and small entrepreneurs. Twenty countries so far. We're three weeks into the launch of this new service, and we have already had fourteen million transactions from six million individuals and small businesses and small farmers."

"And what is the average transaction fee collected for those fourteen million transactions?"

"Senator, we're averaging sixty cents per call." The senator's aide made a rapid calculation on his laptop and passed a note to the senator.

He whistled. "Young man, you have revenues of eight million four hundred thousand dollars after only three weeks in business! I'd call that windfall profits."

"Senator, that figure is gross revenue before expenses, not profit. We pay fees to the cell phone providers. We pay corporate taxes here in the US. We have invested thirty-three million in R&D and start-up costs without collecting one cent in revenue. We have high payroll costs for trained software and network engineers. We have had to build server farms to carry the high-volume traffic and back up the data. We pay fees to the market exchanges that we access, like the Chicago Board of Trade, for agricultural commodities sold by these small farmers in Africa. It will be a while before we break even on this venture. But I'm confident that we will, eventually."

"Son, I don't know a thing about all of those costs you mentioned, but I know a cash cow when I see one. You are making a killing on all these transaction fees in foreign countries, and not paying one dime in taxes on them here in the US. Do you think that's fair?"

"Senator, we pay substantial taxes here in the US, based on our profit after expenses."

"Young man, what I'm talking about is a direct tax on the consumer, like the federal taxes that appear on everyone's phone bill."

"Senator, are you asserting the right to tax small subsistence farmers in Botswana for a service they purchase in Botswana, simply because the man who invented it, and the company providing it, is American?"

"That makes perfect sense to me," replied the senator serenely.

"Then you had better inform the government of India that you expect to collect taxes every time an Indian citizen purchases electronics from another Indian citizen, because the man who invented the transistor was an American, William Shockley."

"Oh? I didn't know that." He turned to his aide. "George, look into that will you? We can schedule testimony from the Indian ambassador next week on that matter."

Isaiah spoke, "Senator, may I request a brief recess? Say one hour?"

"Certainly. This session will reconvene at 4 p.m." He banged the gavel and people began filing out. The Senator's aide gestured him over to look at some figures on his laptop.

Isaiah took out his cell and punched in a coded sequence: *Noah is loading, 2x2.* Then he made a call. "Grace? Noah 2x2. Yes, sweetheart, like you, I'm shocked that it began happening this quickly. I'll see you on Saturday sweetheart."

Isaiah began texting his key people with coded instructions. His last two calls were to the Indian Embassy and the Embassy of Botswana. In fifteen minutes he was done. *Now we wait, he thought.*

When the sub-committee was gaveled to order at 4 p.m., additional media were on hand with live feeds. FACTS News, ZNN, ABC, the Indian National News agency, the BBC and the People's News Network of Botswana were on hand and filming with live feeds. Even tiny Reason TV had sent a crew. The senator noticed the additional cameras and preened, pleased that he would have additional coverage. *My aides must really be on the ball, he thought. I must compliment them.* Actually, Isaiah's public relations people had done it.

"Mr. Mercury, during the recess the sub-committee staff and I have made an assessment of the situation, and we do not wish to be unreasonable. We propose, and I shall offer as a bill in the Senate, a flat consumer surtax on every one of your software transactions from

Invisible Hand marketplace software. In this way, we do not take directly from your firm, and you can continue to pay down your debts from R & D, etcetera. The consumer would pay a flat rate surtax of twenty-five cents on each transaction he makes on Invisible Hand marketplace software. Your firm will be required to collect this tax and remit it to the US Treasury. At your current rate of business transactions, we conservatively estimate that this will generate forty-two million of badly needed dollars for the US Government in the first year alone. Promethean Software International would not pay a dime extra. A win/win for both parties. Surely you have no objection to this?"

"Senator, I now exercise my prerogative for witnesses to testify on my behalf." Isaiah turned and looked to the back of the room. A stately gentleman in colorful African robes came forward. The cameras zoomed in for this unexpected drama.

"Senator and members of the committee, I bring forward Ambassador Zingale of Botswana to answer your question about objections to a tax on users. Ambassador?" The dignified man sat down.

"Thank you, Mr. Mercury. Thank you for your indulgence, Senator and esteemed committee members," the Ambassador began in a rhythmic cadence that was a delight to listen to. "A surtax of twenty-five cents may seem like a small thing to you, Senator. With all due respect, you are a well-fed man and a well-paid man in a prosperous country. Did you know Senator, that 25 cents in my country will buy a one week supply of mealie corn to feed a family of three? Did you know, Senator, that a twenty-five cent surcharge might be the difference between making just enough to finance next year's crop, and no more, and making a little extra to pay for schooling for his child, or medicine for his pregnant wife?"

The ambassador slowly moved his gaze to make eye contact with every senator sitting at the raised platform above him. "A small thing can make a big difference. Senator, have you ever read the short story called *A Piece of Steak* by your great writer Jack London?" The senator shook his head.

"A pity," said the ambassador with a sad shake of his head. "An aging prize-fighter is training for one last prize fight to win a purse to feed his family. He knows that a little extra nutrition the day of the fight, a piece of steak, might give him the extra endurance to win against the younger competitor. He cannot come up with the price of the steak and he loses. A tragedy for his family." The ambassador paused. "We are a nation of struggling prize-fighters, Senator. An extra 25 cents might be the small difference that makes a big difference in their lives."

The Ambassador stood. He stood tall, and his colors seemed to magnify his dignity.

"Now then, Senator, there is also the question of national sovereignty. You may think that a strong military power like the United States of America, who cannot mind the till of their own shop and their own economy, can simply reach out across the sea and seize money from the small, poor farmers of a small and poor nation. I tell you, you cannot. We will resist you. We will not pay. If we have to forgo the use of this marvelous software that has already made life better and business cheaper for tens of thousands of our farmers and shopkeepers, so be it. We will have to struggle harder, but we know how to struggle, and we will continue our struggle with dignity.

"If the bully Uncle Sam suddenly shows up in the village marketplace where Mr. Isaiah Mercury and one of our farmers have shaken hands on a deal, and steps between them to suddenly demand more money for himself, simply because he is like a small child who cannot resist spending all the money in his hand that day, I tell you we will not pay the bully!

"Our smallest and humblest shopkeeper keeps his books balanced and his shop and family out of debt. He saves. If he wants something he cannot pay for, he saves and waits until he can afford it. He puts this mighty assemblage of spoiled children with the political power to take money from others to shame, to shame I say! He does not ask his national government to reach out and take from others in another land. He has too much pride and self-respect to shamelessly steal from others because he has no self-discipline. He saves and serves his customers. I am proud to say that I come from a family of such honest and thrifty shopkeepers."

He paused and drew himself up tall once more. "I know that I am a guest in this house rich with history and past greatness. Like any guest, I hesitate to speak so bluntly. Like any guest, I *will* speak out when unruly children are grabbing the possessions of the guests and doing violence to them. In my land, if the parents will not control and discipline the children, then the guest will do so. I must speak truth to power and tell

134

you congressmen and senators, you are acting like greedy spoiled children. I call upon your parents, the citizens and taxpayers of this great land, to discipline the children and not allow them to destroy the house of their fathers and grandfathers, this great land that once stood for freedom and prosperity. I thank you again for your indulgence in allowing me to speak."

The ambassador turned to go with a sweep of his colorful robes. As he did so, he faced the galleries and the cameras. Applause began in the galleries, and continued in wave after wave, each one building to a louder crescendo. The ambassador stood, eyes lifted, taking it all in. The cameras continued to roll with the live feed. Some panned the crowd.

One camera zoomed in for a close-up of a woman standing, applauding, with tears streaming down her face. Then it moved to a man, a working man dressed in work clothes. His face was deeply lined and tanned by the sun. He too was standing and applauding, with tears glistening in his eyes. Next, an African-American Army sergeant in uniform, standing and applauding with tears running down his face.

The cameras returned to the face of the Ambassador as he looked wonderingly up at the galleries of citizens who were not his own, but who were his spiritual blood brothers. Tears began to well up in his own eyes as well. He silently mouthed, *thank you,* and strode out of the senate chamber.

When the applause had stopped, Isaiah Mercury moved back to the microphone. "Senator, I now call on the Indian ambassador to speak in my place."

The senator banged down his gavel and interrupted, "Mr. Mercury, there will be no further testimony today. I pay my respects to the Indian ambassador and say that we will hear him another day. This session is adjourned." He banged the gavel once more and then rose and quickly left the room, skipping his usual photo-op preening and glad-handing for any media in attendance.

Isaiah's cell phone rang. "Wow, Isaiah, you know how to put on a show! I want to shake Ambassador Zingale's hand! He was impressive in Peoria, but this was magnificent! Will we see him anytime soon?" Grace was breathless.

Isaiah smiled into the phone, "Next time we're in Washington. Or in Botswana, as the case may be. I gotta go now. Lots to do. Love you.

Bye." Isaiah strode out like a man on a mission. Which, of course, he was.

*   *   *   *   *   *

N minus 17. Evening. That night on the FACTS cable channel, the news program *Daily Report with Bill Ursa* led off with the story of Ambassador Zingale's dramatic testimony. Doing his trademark stand-up intro, Bill announced, "Tonight's top story. Ambassador Zingale of Botswana lectures a Senate sub-committee on fiscal responsibility. He said they are like spoiled children in need of discipline, and that the citizen voters are the parents who need to administer a spanking. American citizens in the galleries gave the Ambassador a standing ovation."

The picture changed to footage panning over the applauding galleries.

"Then we will meet the man who started the fireworks. Will Goughnager gets his own exclusive interview with software genius and entrepreneur Isaiah Mercury. We'll get reactions from the FACTS Panel. All this, here now." The theme music played.

After the red, white, and blue logo sequence for the show, Bill reappeared. "Our top story tonight is surprise testimony in front of the Senate Sub-committee on Inter-State, Intra-State, and Extra-Territorial Business Control, Regulation and Taxation. Sub-committee Chair Senator Hiden had subpoenaed software CEO Isaiah Mercury to testify before the committee concerning proposed new taxes and regulations. After an adjournment, Senator Hiden asked Mr. Mercury for comment about a proposed new tax on software usage by citizens of *other countries*. Carlton Cantwell has the story. Carlton?"

"Bill, witness Isaiah Mercury, seen here testifying before the adjournment, exercised his right to call a witness in his place. And what a witness! He called Ambassador Zwingale of Botswana, where the new software is beginning to be used heavily, to comment on Senator Hiden's proposed twenty-five cent tax per transaction on users of Mercury's Invisible Hand marketplace software. Let's listen."

There followed video footage from Ambassador Zwingale's testimony, culminating in the "spoiled children" comparison and shots of the applauding citizens with tears rolling down their faces.

136

"Bill, this unscheduled and unexpected testimony prompted a three-minute standing ovation from visiting American citizens in the galleries. Let's listen to this woman's reaction."

The camera now focused on the tear-streaked face of the first woman shown when the cameras originally panned the applauding galleries.

"It was just so moving," she said, still wiping her eyes with her hands. "There stood this majestic African man, who spoke so plainly and simply about financial discipline and getting your own house in order. *And he told the children to behave!* And he told the American citizens, the taxpayers, to suck it up and act like parents and control these spoiled children, our own congressmen and senators. I was ashamed of my government, but proud to be in the same room with a man with the integrity, the moral courage and the intellectual honesty to say what needed to be said to these spoiled brat congressmen who treat *us* like children. They go and spend all of our money, and then our children's money, and then have the nerve to try to take money from poor farmers in Africa. I just wish this man could run for president of the United States! I want my country back." Tears began to roll down her face again.

The camera cut back to Carlton in his stand-up pose. "That sums up the reactions of many, both here in the Senate galleries, and across the nation watching this dramatic testimony. Bill, it's as if a neighbor came to us to complain about our children running wild and playing with financial matches. Except that we *elected* these children. Back to you, Bill."

"Thanks, Carlton. Next up, Will Goughnager interviews the man who put the match to the fireworks, software entrepreneur Isaiah Mercury."

After the break, Bill appeared on camera again. "Where did all these fireworks start? Will Goughnager interviews the man originally subpoenaed to speak to this sub-committee, Isaiah Mercury, CEO and owner of software company Promethean Software International. Will?"

"Thanks Bill. We caught Mr. Mercury as he was leaving Capital Hill today." The camera showed a close-up of Isaiah, standing on the steps of the capitol. "Mr. Mercury, how did this all come about?"

"Will, I was subpoenaed by this sub-committee to comment on additional regulations and taxes that they were considering on software in general. I knew they really wanted to leech off the revenue stream from the successful launch of my new marketplace software for the developing countries, *Invisible Hand*. Since they were caught attempting an unconstitutional bill of attainder a few years ago during the AIG bonus scandal, they had to disguise it as a tax on all marketplace software from an American company, but used overseas. Sweet for them, since they would tax poor farmers in Botswana to raise money for their earmarks and boondoggles. No American taxpayer would scream, since the tax wasn't on them.

"Will, it isn't right. It's unconstitutional. No taxation without representation. The small farmers of Botswana, Asia, and India are not represented in the US Congress. We have no right to tax them. So I decided to take a page from the book of my friend Minerva Stone and make Bastiat's unseen *seen*. These senators would hold press conferences and show pictures of bridges to nowhere and talk about all the jobs they would temporarily create with this tax money. That is the seen. What is unseen are the families of these small farmers struggling to make ends meet and get the best prices for their crops. The money taken from them, however small, could deprive them of the small margins in their business that they could use for medicine or education for their children. We have no right to take that away, however small an amount. It's theft.

Isaiah sighed. "So, I invited Ambassador Zwingale and the Ambassador from India to come to the party to put a human face on this proposal, to make the unseen effects of this tax *seen*. I have never heard so moving and eloquent a case as that made by Ambassador Zwingale. He's right. Our congressmen and senators are spoiled children. We do have to step up to the plate and discipline the children. They have torn up our back yard. Unemployment is high, retirement funds are gone, sorry companies who mismanaged their shareholders' money get bailed out by our spoiled children using *our* money, the taxpayers' money."

"Now these spoiled children want to go over to the back yards of the neighbors and vandalize them too. Today we heard from one of those neighbors, Botswana, saying *discipline your own children or we'll do it for you*. And they can do it too. Botswana with international shunning, and India and China by unloading their US treasuries; cutting up our national credit card financed by them. Like that lady from the gallery said, 'Suck it up! Control the kids! Put them in time out! They are supposed to work for *us*!'"

"Bill, this business leader sounds mad as hell. Will he take it anymore? Back to you."

* * * * * *

N minus 16. The next day, three dozen more "Hypocrisy Exposed" videos were posted on FreedomToobz.Ark. Several were of congressional staffers offering bailouts to companies in return for jobs for their wives and relatives. One was of Treasury Under-Secretary of Bailout Exceptions J. Walter Obson offering unneeded bailout money to Isaiah Mercury. By that afternoon, several cable networks were rebroadcasting them under the banner "Bailing Buckets of Money to Friends and Family."

The next morning, when those same staffers came down to the street from their tony Georgetown apartments, they found their cars egged and an upturned bucket of rotten eggs sitting on one of the hoods with the graffiti, "Bail this out!" J. Walter Obson wondered if he could make a case to his boss for Secret Service protection. After all, his job contributed to national economic security. He wrinkled his nose as he inhaled more rotten egg smell from his SUV.

In several prosperous Maryland suburbs, hundreds of congressmen and staffers started their SUVs and drove to work. They didn't notice a bumper sticker that had been added to the back of their cars. It was a large green "H," followed by the words "Enviro-Hypocrite." On several street corners in downtown Washington, D.C., protesters marched with signs reading "You want Green? You go first: Walk!" and "Ride a bicycle, hypocrites!" Whenever one of the SUVs with the large green H on the back bumper passed, they threw rotten eggs at it and shook their signs. The action was captured by FACTS News, ZNN, and, of course, several grassroots citizen videographers planning to post the action on FreedomToobz.Ark.

"What is the matter with these people?" said one young woman staffer to another in a senator's office. "They egg my car. They act like they don't realize that driving a big car is on a perceived need basis. I need to drive an SUV for safety reasons. They don't."

She sipped from her bottle of designer water. "Somebody needs to educate them that we do these things for their own good. That gives me an idea . . ." She sat down and began scribbling notes for her morning briefing meeting with the Senator. Another earmark was in the offing.

Chapter Twelve

N minus 15. Grace Washington sat in her office reading research papers submitted by her graduate students at Tuskegee University. She had her red pen ready. *Good research design,* she wrote on one. *Where is your evidence for this?* she wrote on another.

There was a knock on the door. "Come in," she said without looking up.

"Dr. Washington?"

She looked up. "Yes?" A man dressed in a dark suit stepped into her office. A second man at the door opened his jacket to reveal a gun.

"Dr. Washington, I have a warrant for your arrest, and a message for you." He flashed an FBI badge in one hand, and handed a cell phone to her with the other.

Speechless, she put the phone to her ear. "Dr. Washington, you will now regret that you released your so-called super-seeds to feed the people of the third world. You will be punished for your crime against the sustainability of the planet and the equality of all species."

She heard the click ending the call. She did not recognize the silky voice of Samuel Solipsis. The man took the phone back and pocketed it. She noticed that he was wearing latex crime scene gloves.

"What is this?" she exclaimed, her eyes wide. "Who was that on the phone?"

"I was only instructed to do two things: deliver a message and arrest you."

Her eyes now flashed angrily. "Let me see that badge, an ID, and the warrant."

She examined the badge and the ID card. Special Agent Franklin Connor. The warrant alleged that she defrauded the government of $70,000 by paying her graduate students for their work on the research for the bio-engineered crop seeds, a private project, with government funds.

"This is bogus!" she exclaimed. "These funds were provided under a contract with Nutritional Abundance Industries. They were not government funds."

"You'll have to take that up with the federal district attorney. Please stand and place your wrists behind you."

"Is this necessary? I'll come voluntarily."

The agent shook his head. "This is standard procedure."

Grace put her wrists behind her back and he snapped on the cuffs. As she passed through the outer office, she asked the department secretary to call her husband and President Wright. When they got to the parking lot, four news media trucks were set up with cameras rolling.

Is this standard procedure? Who leaked this to the media? she thought. *Somebody is orchestrating a big PR campaign to make a political point.*

At a gesture from Agent Connor, another agent placed his hand on Grace's shoulder to walk her past the cameras. Agent Connor unobtrusively stepped over to a trash dumpster next to the building, turned his back to the cameras, and slipped the cell phone and latex gloves into it.

The ZNN reporter was narrating as the cameras followed Dr. Washington doing the "perp walk" through the parking lot to the FBI vehicle. It was strategically parked at the far end of the lot, so that she and the FBI Agent had to walk a gauntlet of network cameras and news reporters commenting for their audiences.

"Lew, ZNN investigative specialists have learned that Dr. Washington misused government funds. She used taxpayer funds to pay high salaries to her graduate students for private research benefitting a for-profit company, and then collected kickbacks from the struggling graduate students. The Attorney General has said that such abuses of the struggling taxpayers' money will not be tolerated. We can expect that he will make an example of Dr. Washington. He has already filed a brief with the Federal District Court in Birmingham to move the trial to Washington, D.C. He has filed a brief with the Federal District Court in Washington to allow live network broadcasts of the trial. We will be seeing the cross-examination of Dr. Washington on live TV. Lew?"

The various camera crews began putting their equipment away. Charging through the parking lot, Tuskegee University President George T'Chaka Wright looked like a fullback slicing through a weak defensive line. The FBI vehicle pulled away just as he arrived.

"This whole charge is a fake and a frame-up!" he shouted. "I'm the president of Tuskegee University, and I'm here to give interviews, sound bites, or whatever the hell you people want. This is wrong!"

The crews continued securing their equipment, and the news reporters turned away. The fix was in. "I'll give an exclusive to the first person who puts a microphone in my face!" President Wright shouted. The ZNN truck began backing out.

"Damn cowardly suck-ups! Not one of you wants to show the other side of the story!" President Wright stood watching them go, fuming. Suddenly he dug his phone out of his pocket and hit one of the speed dial buttons.

"Christina?" he barked at his administrative assistant, "Send our attorney to represent Dr. Washington. Birmingham. Tell him to bring cashier's checks to post bond."

The nearest federal court was in Birmingham. Next he called his wife.

"Estelle, those eco-loons have trumped up some kind of bogus federal charge against Grace. They just arrested her. They want something, but I don't know what it is. I'm driving to Birmingham to meet our attorney at her arraignment. You want to come too? Good. I'll pick you up in ten minutes."

Now, he thought, *Federal Justice Department, beware! T'Chaka and Estelle are on the case.*

When they arrived at the federal courthouse in Birmingham, Grace was not there. Nobody in the federal court system in Birmingham knew anything. The FBI office in Birmingham knew nothing. One of the federal judges was a friend of George. He agreed to make some calls to find out what was going on. Thirty minutes later George's phone vibrated.

"George, they played dirty. The Attorney General filed a brief to have the trial moved to Washington, D.C., and they granted it on the spot. He also filed to move the arraignment to Washington so that your lawyer wouldn't be there to post bail. She's en route to D.C. in a Justice Department Gulfstream jet."

Cursing, President Wright called another number. "Carl? Can you represent a Tuskegee University professor on short notice? You will? Thanks, Carl, I owe you one. Dr. Grace Washington. Yes, the genius botanist. Some bogus trumped-up charge about fraud with government funds. She's en route in one of the AG's jets. The arraignment should be late this afternoon in federal district court there in D.C. You'll use your firm's accounts to post bail? I owe you two. After you spring her, would you put Dr. Washington up at your house? She'll be safer there than at a hotel. I'll be there by morning. See you then."

*　　*　　*　　*　　*　　*

Attorney Carl Wainwright arrived at federal district court in downtown D.C. within five minutes of Dr. Washington's arrival in FBI custody. The assistant federal district attorney addressed the judge, "Your Honor, the defendant is charged with five counts of fraud against the United States Government."

The judge looked over at Grace. "Do you have counsel?"

Before she could answer, Carl Wainright walked forward and said, "She does now, your Honor." The assistant federal D.A. started and looked around, surprised.

"How does your client plead?"

"Not guilty, your Honor."

"The people on bail?"

The assistant United States attorney studied his Blackberry for three seconds, and then said, "The people request remand, your Honor."

"This professor is no flight risk, your Honor," Carl quickly replied. "Dr. Grace Washington is a Nobel Peace prize winning botanist who works at Tuskegee University and has numerous ties to her community."

"Your Honor, the people may be adding a charge to the indictment that involves national security and possible bio-terrorism. She is a Ph.D. botanist with access to a state of the art botanical laboratory, your honor. For this reason, the people ask for remand."

"National security? Bio-terrorism?" the judge raised his eyebrows. This trumped any other argument in a post 9/11 world. "Granted. The defendant will be held in custody pending trial."

The guards would not let Carl Wainwright confer with his client until after she had been processed, forced to change into prison overalls, and deprived of her reading glasses.

"Mr. Wainwright, I don't know you, but I'm glad you're on my side. What's going on? Nobody will tell me anything," Grace said. Carl smiled at her and polished his horn-rim glasses.

"Your boss George T'Chaka Wright was my sergeant in Operation Desert Storm. Saved my life, twice. He called me after he had done enough detective work to find out where the Attorney General was whisking you off to. As for what's going on, here are the charges." He passed the legal document to her.

144

She shook her head sadly. "I'm sorry; they've taken my reading glasses. Metal frames could have been used to stab a fellow inmate, you know." She began twisting a strand of her hair. She squinted at the document, trying to bring it into focus.

"I'll summarize it for you. You are charged with using US Government funds to pay five of your research assistants (that's where the five counts come from) to do their research work on the bio-engineered crop seed contract you and they performed for the for-profit firm of Nutritional Abundance Industries."

"But I never did that! All funds for the bio-engineering research contract were handled by the university administration. NAI made progress payments, which went directly to the university. The university in turn paid the assistants after I signed their time sheets."

Carl sighed. "I'm sure that everything was above board and accounted for in any organization run by President George T'Chaka Wright. And God help the accountant who misplaced one decimal point! However, in a remarkable stretch of logic and linguistics worthy of George Orwell's *Doublespeak*, the Justice Department maintains that since the Department of Defense rents the Tuskegee University Auditorium twice a year to hold a recruiting event for the armed forces, and that since the rental money is deposited by the university into a general administrative account at the university's bank, and that since the NAI contract money was also deposited into the selfsame administrative account at the same bank, and that since money is fungible, some government money ended up in the paychecks of your five research assistants. Whew! Longest sentence I've spoken in years! And the most nonsensical."

Carl wiped his forehead with his handkerchief.

"What utter nonsense!" spat Grace. "What kind of logic do they teach in law school these days?"

"Jefferson weeps," the attorney sighed sadly. "Logic, the law, and the Constitution don't matter much these days. When somebody gives the order, they do it, law or no law. How do you suppose you ended up here in Washington, D.C. instead of Birmingham, which had jurisdiction?"

Grace rolled her eyes. She somehow managed to look attractive even wearing an ugly pair of orange prison overalls.

Carl resumed, "Dr. Washington, this is political revenge, not a criminal prosecution. I can smell it. The question is, who in this all-powerful administration have you offended? Or, who in your circle of friends has offended this administration or one of their non-profit liberal-issue advocacy group toadies?"

Grace was silent for a moment. "When they arrested me, the FBI agent said he had a message for me. He handed me a cell phone. A voice told me that I would regret releasing my super-seeds to feed third-world people. I didn't recognize the voice, and I was too shocked and surprised to make any sense of it."

Then it hit her. "Nutritional Abundance Industries! That envirofascist group PRIS got a federal court injunction against them to stop the distribution of my invention, the Carver's Legacy crop seeds. NAI reincorporated offshore and bought the seeds and the intellectual property rights from NAI North America. NAI Ltd. was not named in the injunction, and is beyond the reach of the US Court injunction anyway. They have been selling the seeds as originally planned in Africa, India, and Southeast Asia. Since PRIS can't punish NAI, they are punishing me instead."

"Say!" another thought struck her. "Maybe they're using me as a hostage to get at Minerva Stone, the CEO of Nutritional Abundance Industries Ltd." Her eyes glowed with the intensity they always got when she made a scientific breakthrough or solved a puzzling problem.

Carl nodded. "I remember the case. And Minerva's televised press conference. Say!" he exclaimed, as another memory hit him. "You were there too! You and Minerva really outfoxed and embarrassed old Edgar Dunforth, the Executive director of PRIS. On national TV, too. Dr. Washington, you have made some powerful enemies."

"But I read that Dunforth is no longer with PRIS. He was even put on trial for embezzlement."

"Yes," said Carl, "but the new Executive director is even more dangerous. Samuel Solipsis, formerly chief counsel to PRIS. That man has more venom than a king cobra. Don't make the mistake of underestimating him. Some rumors say that he sabotaged and framed Dunforth to avoid the blame about the useless injunction that he wrote and filed."

Grace stood up, agitated. "So what is our legal defense?"

Carl remained seated, staring straight ahead. "The AG went to law school with Samuel Solipsis," he said stonily. "They were fraternity brothers. I don't think there is a legal defense. They'll twist the law to suit them no matter what evidence we submit. This will have to be a political deal, or else you'll be creating hybrid bees in the agriculture wing of the federal penitentiary."

A guard rapped on the small window in the door of the room. He held up three fingers.

"Three minutes." Carl thought quickly. "I'll see you again in the morning, and hopefully we will know more then." He looked her over. "You have a cell mate?"

"Yes. They told me she's a drug dealer named Twisty Turner."

"Twisty is an old client of mine. The bunks attach to the walls. Sleep facing out. You can wake up seeing and using your arms to defend yourself that way. They may try roughing you up."

"Thanks."

"I'm a criminal lawyer. I have a few ex-clients on the inside besides Twisty who owe me some favors. I'll put the word out: hands off Grace Washington."

"I owe you one."

"Be careful what you say. I might collect one day." As she was led out, she briefly flashed a smile at Carl Wainwright.

*   *   *   *   *   *

The assistant federal district attorney from the arraignment called Samuel Solipsis. "We got her."

"Any problems?"

"Not yet. Bail denied, as planned. One surprise though. An attorney showed up to represent her. We couldn't slip in our handpicked public defender, so we got no insider information about her. Not just any attorney, but Carl Wainwright, no less. Best federal criminal defense lawyer in D.C. The judge and the AG see eye to eye on this one, so I don't think he can do much against us."

Samuel spoke carefully into his phone in his office in Chicago. "Gianni, well done. When can we schedule a televised trial? The sooner the better."

Gianni Fusco had come into the world of federal prosecution from a long-time Mafia family. The family had "friends" in the Justice Department, who had "friends" on the law school admissions board.

"Today is Monday. We can begin the trial on Thursday. That gives us time to line up the media coverage. It's a slow news week. They'll jump at the chance."

"Sounds good." Samuel punched *end call* on his encrypted cell phone.

*   *   *   *   *   *

That night in her cell, Grace told her cellmate that Carl Wainwright was her attorney.

"Mr. Wainwright is a stand-up guy. He did his best for me. Me and the others in this cell block got the memo from him: *Hands off Dr. Washington.* You'll be safe in here." Twisty smiled briefly.

"Thanks, Twisty. I'm going to sleep."

"Good night, Doc."

"Twisty?"

"Yeah?"

"Why do they call you Twisty?"

"I've got a nervous habit of twisting a strand of my hair all the time." Grace smiled in the dark. "Me too. Ever since I was a little girl."

Twisty chuckled. "So Doc, you and me got at least one thing in common."

"Yes, we sure do."

"Good night, Doc."

"Good night, Twisty."

*   *   *   *   *   *

N minus 14. The eastern sky in front of him began to lighten, with a few hints of pink predicting the sunrise to come. Isaiah Mercury piloted his corporate Gulfstream jet eastward over the Mississippi River. As soon as he had gotten the call from Grace's department secretary at the university, he had dropped everything he was doing at his headquarters in Silicon Valley and called his fixed base operator to prep the jet for immediate takeoff. He and his staff had been working through the checklist for executing the Noah Option. They were now at N minus 1 for the operation of his company. He told them to keep on the countdown schedule.

He managed to get a call through to George Wright's cell phone. "George? Isaiah. I've just passed over the Mississippi. I should land in D.C. in about two hours or so. Can you pick me up at the airport?"

"Will do," growled George. "Estelle and I are taking turns driving all night. We should get there about the same time you touch down. I'm going to be one cranky son of a bitch when I pick you up."

"And how will I be able to tell the difference from your normal cranky gunnery sergeant son of a bitch self?"

"Just tell your beautiful cabin attendant to make fresh coffee before you land and prepare an IV for me. Be sure it's good coffee, not that nasty stuff you used to make in the Navy."

"The beautiful cabin attendant is my co-pilot and ex-Navy Seal Douglas Soto. He can be pretty cranky himself, but he writes some mean software code. He also makes a mean cup of coffee. I'll relay that request."

"It's not a request, dammit!"

"I won't tell him that, and I don't advise you to either, unless you're toting your assagai."

When the Gulfstream braked to a stop at the corporate FBO hanger at Reagan National, George and Estelle Wright rolled up in their Lincoln Town Car. When the jet door folded down into stairs, a short, wiry man with oriental features and jet black hair stepped out with a thermos of coffee held in front of him.

"I was told that if I handed this over quietly, no one would get hurt. I'm Douglas Soto, Isaiah's head of software development and chief factotum."

T'Chaka chuckled and held out his hand. "George Wright, and this is my wife Estelle."

"I'm sorry we have to meet under these circumstances. I better get the bags."

Isaiah came down the stairs quickly. "Estelle! Where did you pick up this scruffy hitchhiker? He looks dangerous."

She smiled shyly. "Only when I unleash him. And I may, if we don't get your lovely wife back."

Isaiah embraced George, then Estelle. "We can talk in the car. Let's roll." Douglas Soto put bags in the trunk and closed it. He climbed into the front passenger seat. Estelle drove. George and Isaiah began talking in the back.

*   *   *   *   *   *

After checking in and cleaning up at a hotel, the four grabbed bagels and more coffee and headed for the federal lock-up. Carl Wainwright met them there.

Isaiah whistled. "Carl Wainwright! The most famous federal criminal defense lawyer in D.C. What did we do to deserve you?"

Carl nodded his head at George. "Best RPG man in my platoon during Desert Storm," beamed George.

Isaiah whistled again, "My man George T'Chaka is *connected.* A good man to know, and I'm glad I know you."

Carl briefed them on what he and Grace had deduced the day before. Then they talked strategy.

As family, Isaiah was allowed ten minutes to see Grace alone first. They hugged. "Oh Grace, baby, are you OK?" Grace pressed her face into his chest.

"Yes. But this is an awful place." He put his hand under her chin and raised her face up for a kiss.

"Baby, I don't know how, but we'll get you out of here. And as for those sons of bitches who put you here on those trumped-up charges . . ." He trembled in his whole body and fell silent.

When Estelle, George, and Carl Wainwright came into the room, Estelle rushed forward to hug Grace. "We've been praying for you," she whispered into Grace's ear.

After George hugged her, he stepped back and said, "Damn, girl! How do you manage to look good in prison overalls?" Grace bobbed her head and gave a little smile.

Carl took charge. "OK, we now know this is political payback, not a real criminal case. The Justice Department intends to manufacture any evidence they want, and reinterpret any laws they want, aided and abetted by activist progressive judges, in order to get a conviction. My office has already learned that they have alerted the media to broadcast directly from the courtroom, and their sources say it starts Thursday. So, no time for us to prepare our case."

"This is to be a Soviet-style show trial to make an example of Grace. This trial is a message, a warning to anybody who might think of opposing the policies of this administration or their quasi-government stooge organizations like PRIS: *don't cross us*. We know they grabbed Grace because they couldn't get Minerva Stone for contempt of court with their injunction to destroy the enhanced crop seeds."

Isaiah looked worried. "So what can we do?"

Carl smiled, "Piss in their pool party. I have some ideas, but I want to wait until we hear from Assistant Federal District Attorney Gianni Fusco. I'm playing along with their charade, and have filed a discovery motion to get what evidence they have. They'll fake it, but at least they'll have to fake it faster in order to give it to us. I have a meeting with him scheduled here in forty-five minutes. George, I'm afraid you and Estelle can't be present for that meeting, only Grace and Isaiah."

Forty-five minutes later, AFDA Fusco came into the room with his assistant. He nodded to Grace and Carl, "Ms. Washington, Mr. Wainwright."

"That's Doctor Washington," Grace said icily. He shrugged. He ignored Isaiah, who said nothing.

Carl began, "Mr. Fusco, we know . . ."

"That's Assistant Federal District Attorney Fusco to you."

"Of course. We know that the charge is bogus, and that you have manufactured evidence, witnesses willing to perjure themselves, and a judge willing to accept a new theory of the fungibility of money. It says that if drug money is laundered at my bank, and I withdraw from my ATM one of the bills used to buy drugs last week, then I am guilty of conspiracy to sell illegal drugs."

Fusco was doodling on his legal pad. Carl continued, "As a matter of fact, the paper in your legal pad was manufactured with wood from old-growth forests, and that makes you part of a RICO conspiracy to violate statutes forbidding the logging of old-growth forests. That carries a fifteen-year sentence, Mr. Fusco." Fusco stopped doodling and looked up sharply, fear on his face.

"Of course I'm not going to file a complaint," continued Carl, "but you never know who's going to take a dislike to you and find some law they can bend to make you guilty of something or another you never knew you were guilty of, do you?" Carl leaned across the table, "Today Dr. Washington is on the menu to be sacrificed. Next week it may be you." Satisfied with his fun, and gratified to see that flash of fear in the other man's eyes, he sat back. "So, AFDA Fusco, what deal have you got to offer us?"

Gianni took a deep breath to regain his composure. Then he said evenly, looking into Grace Washington's eyes, "Conviction on five counts of fraud against the federal government carries a sentence of five years on each count. Twenty-five years total. How old will you be when you get out, doctor?"

She looked evenly back at him. "I should be out on bail now. Why was it denied?"

"Why doctor, you're a well-known geneticist. You could be concocting biological weapons of mass destruction to set loose on America. We couldn't take that chance." Grace was silent. Isaiah's eyes hardened.

Carl said, "What do you want?"

"Two things. Destroy all Carver's Legacy seeds in any country where they are located, and give us Minerva Stone."

Grace flinched. Her face looked ashen. "Destroy all seeds . . ." she whispered. Images flashed through her mind. *Millions of malnourished babies in Africa, India, and Asia, crying from hunger. Swollen little bellies . . . the chance for life for an entire generation of children, crushed . . . my life's work. Destroyed.*

Carl leaned forward and said, "Minerva is not guilty of anything either. She complied with that injunction. What can you possibly want with her?"

"Let's just say that certain parties are eager to find new grounds to hold her in contempt of court."

"The new company is chartered in New Zealand. Everything she has done, has been done legally. The original company named in the injunction complied to the letter. You have no case against her."

Fusco leaned over the table. "Oh, you of all people should not be surprised when I say, *we will have a case against her*. We can make up a case against anybody we want. We just need Stone back in the country again. Dr. Washington can arrange that."

Grace looked up, "How?"

"Just tell her that when she reenters the country, and submits evidence that all the Carver's Legacy seeds have been destroyed, the charges against you will be dropped. Otherwise, say so long to Dr. Grace Washington for twenty-five long years."

Grace looked at Fusco with her varsity game face. "So I'm a hostage, to be traded for destruction of the seeds and Minerva Stone. You should go into business with the Somali pirates, Mr. Fusco."

She paused. "There are millions of third-world babies who may die of malnutrition, Mr. Fusco. Babies my seeds could save. You are giving me a choice: go to prison, or be complicit in the starvation of millions of babies around the world. I thought this administration was devoted to compassion and helping the weak and hungry."

"Oh, we're compassionate, in our own way. We are compassionate when and where and how we choose. We choose, not you. Compassion is our business, Dr. Washington, not yours, and not Minerva Stone's. You pretend to care about babies, but the way you distribute your seeds is through a for-profit company. All you really care about is making money."

Grace kept looking into his eyes. "As of this moment, Minerva Stone and I have fed more babies, and made more farmers' families prosperous, than your entire administration. And we made money doing it, without forcing anybody to buy our seeds. We're proud of that. We do care about those babies, and we're good at what we do: growing food for them. Which is why we make money doing it: because we're good at it. Have you grown any food for babies in Africa, Mr. Fusco?"

"I'm not here to debate policy on world population survival and crop production, Dr. Washington. That's for our policy partners at PRIS. Either you destroy the seeds and give us Minerva Stone, or you go to jail. Then you can analyze the nutrition in the prison cafeteria for the next twenty-five years."

"Even if I were cowardly enough to betray her, I don't know how to reach her. She's been moving from country to country setting up her new distributors."

"Well then, we have a trial scheduled to start the day after tomorrow. All the major media, including international media, will be there to broadcast live. Maybe Ms. Stone will catch the trial on Skynews or some such. We'll put you on camera to ask her to return."

153

Carl interjected, "We'll need some time to consider your offer. And if we do accept, we'll need time to track down Ms. Stone and reason with her. We can't have a two-way conversation with her on television."

"Work fast. The trial starts Thursday. The charges can be dropped at any time during the trial, but once sentence is pronounced, it's out of my hands. And Judge Nance likes to wrap up his trials in five days or less. Good day counselor. Dr. Washington." Again he ignored Isaiah and walked out, assistant in tow.

Then he stuck his head back into the room. "By the way, Dr. Washington, you might counsel your husband that he should reconsider the bailout offer he was given. Someone might use his software to buy a gun and use it in the commission of a felony. Then we would prosecute him under the RICO racketeering law for enabling a criminal conspiracy. He would face hard prison time and forfeiture of all his assets, including his company and the patents for all the software he created."

Isaiah rose and took a step toward Fusco. "You make blackmail threats like a Chicago thug."

"And I suppose you as a martial arts black belt are going to show me how to threaten?"

"You, Mr. Fusco, are a prosecutor for the United States Department of Justice. The only threat you should make against me or anyone else is justice."

"I do threaten you with justice."

"Then, to quote Sir Thomas More, I'm not threatened."

"I threaten you with *our* justice, the social justice of social equity enforced by a progressive administration."

"Then I stand by my first statement. You make blackmail threats like a Chicago thug."

Fusco closed the door. Isaiah turned around and let out a long breath.

Then he came around the table, bent down, and hugged Grace in her chair. In her ear, he whispered, "And God remembered Noah. Look for a rainbow as a token of a covenant between me and thee."

Then he turned to Carl. "Counselor, how do we pee in their pool party?"

Carl grinned, "We use the secret Promethean weapon, the weapon of Odysseus, the Scarlet Pimpernel, and Br'er Rabbit: the mind, our mother

154

wit. I believe you, Dr. Washington, were a proponent of the mental game? I recall that you had an awesome head fake."

Grace looked up, "How . . . ?"

Carl smiled again. "I saw you play an exhibition game against my alma mater, Georgetown."

He paused, and his face grew serious. "As your counsel, I must ask what your wishes are. Do you want to accept this deal with the prosecutor? I can't guarantee acquittal in a trial like this. It's not about the facts, it's political. You're facing twenty-five years, and they're likely to make it hard time as an example to their political enemies. We don't know that Minerva Stone would agree to destroy the seeds and give herself up, but we could at least ask."

"Mr. Wainwright, if I did that I couldn't live with myself. I can survive twenty-five years of prison, but I could not survive a lifetime of self-hatred for what I had done. I would be creating my own hell on earth. No. Let's fight them." She looked at Isaiah and managed a small smile. "It's the right thing to do."

Carl Wainright clapped his hands and rubbed them together. "Let's cook up a head fake for the courtroom." They put their heads together.

 **Chapter Thirteen**

N minus 11. Thursday morning. Network voiceover: "Today, a special daytime edition of *Court Record with Gabrielle Vandervoss*." Gabrielle was standing in front of the Federal Courthouse.

"Gabrielle Vandervoss here with the show trial of the month: Dr. Grace Washington, famous scientist and botanist, inventor of Carver's Legacy, the super crop seeds. Now being cultivated by small farmers in Africa, India, and parts of Southeast Asia, these crops are said to yield four times the amount of food on one-tenth the acreage, with one-tenth the irrigation water. Her crime? Accounting irregularities that the Justice Department alleges are fraud and embezzlement of taxpayer funds. The evidence? The funds she used to pay her graduate student researchers were drawn from the same university general administrative bank account that was used to deposit rent checks from the Department of Defense for renting a university auditorium. I know, I know, it's a stretch, but we report, you make up your own mind.

"We will be broadcasting live from inside the courtroom. Live broadcasting is usually not permitted during court proceedings, but in an odd twist of events, the Attorney General himself filed a brief requesting the broadcasts. Seven major networks, including the BBC and PBS, are here to broadcast live. Someone in this administration wants major publicity for this trial, reminiscent of the 1930s-era show trials in the totalitarian Soviet Union under dictator Papa Joe Stalin. When we return, we will be in the courtroom."

*   *   *   *   *   *

Carl Wainwright watched as Grace was led into the courtroom by the bailiffs. She was dressed in the stylish suit she had worn when she was arrested. They didn't take the handcuffs off until she was seated.

"Were you OK last night in the cell?" Carl asked.

"Yes, thank you. Twisty says to tell you everyone got the memo. Memo?" Grace arched her eyebrows inquisitively.

Carl allowed himself a small, wry grin. "They're good with passing along messages on the inside. They call them memos."

156

Carl leaned closer and said in a low voice, "Look over your right shoulder and you'll see the king cobra himself, Samuel Solipsis, the new executive director of PRIS."

Grace found herself looking into vacant but venomous eyes. Solipsis gave her a tight smile and a nod.

"Now I remember him," said Grace. "He sat beside Dunforth when we destroyed the seeds in Peoria."

They rose as the judge came in. "All rise," intoned the bailiff. "This court is now in session. The honorable Judge Cyrus Nance presiding." The judge sat down. "Be seated," barked the bailiff.

AFDA Gianni Fusco rose to make his opening statement to his handpicked jury. Citing national security concerns, counsel for the defense had been excluded from jury selection proceedings. The allegation had been that terrorist cells could threaten the jury in order to influence their deliberations. The logic was that since Dr. Washington's work was in the field of bio-engineering, and since bio-engineering *could* be used for a biological weapon, then she *might* be working with terrorists.

Carl thought, *Yeah, and since the prosecutor's surname was Italian, and since the discoverer of America was Italian, and since Italians then carried contagious European diseases like measles that killed hundreds of thousands of native American tribespeople, then AFDA Fusco was guilty of genocide. So much for actual evidence and direct links to the crime.*

"Ladies and Gentlepersons of the jury," began AFDA Fusco. Especially for his television debut, he had bought a tailored designer Italian suit that made him look slimmer.

"The prosecution will show beyond any reasonable doubt that Dr. Washington signed pay vouchers for her five graduate student researchers. We will prove that the checks cut, based on these pay vouchers, were drawn from the First National Bank of Tuskegee. We will prove that the specific account these checks were written on was called the General Administrative Fund Account of Tuskegee University. We will prove that on two separate occasions checks from the Department of Defense were deposited into this account, thereby co-mingling government funds with funds from other sources. And finally, we will prove that the work these graduate students did was for the exclusive benefit of a privately owned, for-profit company, Nutritional Abundance Industries.

"We will connect the dots for you, Ladies and Gentlepersons, showing that funds derived from hardworking and struggling taxpayers such as yourselves were used for the benefit of a corporation which only existed to squeeze profits out of unfortunate customers. Using government funds for private benefit, unless specifically authorized by one of the sixteen stimulus bills passed by Congress in the last twelve months, is fraud and embezzlement."

Half of the jury were welfare recipients who had never paid taxes in their lives. They had been promised a bonus above the normal jury pay to sit on this particular jury.

"And how will we prove all of this? Ladies and Gentlepersons, we will bring witnesses who will offer dramatic testimony about who signed the pay vouchers and who cashed the checks drawn on those pay vouchers. We will show you the actual checks cashed and a graphic display showing how checks are cleared by the Federal Reserve Bank. We will show you clips from documentaries aired on the BBC about the near-starvation levels of sub-Saharan subsistence farmers, farmers who are preyed upon by the predatory Nutritional Abundance Industries extorting high prices for their inferior crop seeds. Your taxpayer dollars, Ladies and Gentlepersons, spent for the benefit of a private company making private profits, a company dangling the false promises of better crop yields to poor, illiterate farmers, just so *they* can make a profit. *Fraud*, Ladies and Gentlepersons, is a legal term for that kind of theft. Look at the defendant, Ladies and Gentlepersons."

Here he nodded to his assistant, who turned and gave a cue to the camera operators, who had been briefed when to zoom in for close-ups to amplify the drama of the AFDA's words. The prosecution had hired a producer of television reality shows to advise them on how to block camera angles, how to pose themselves in the courtroom, and how to coach and sequence their witnesses to make good television. He didn't need to worry about how to make a good legal case, since that was guaranteed by an understanding between the Attorney General and the judge. They dutifully zoomed in for a close-up of Grace. Her suit had been returned for her to wear, so she would look richer than the jury members.

"Take a good look, Ladies and Gentlepersons. Notice the rich cut of the expensive silk suit. Notice the expensive pearls she is wearing. This rich person stole from you, the struggling taxpayer. Stole for what? Stole for the benefit of her rich friends at Nutritional Abundance Industries, so that they can practically steal from poor African farmers. Ladies and Gentlepersons of the jury," here AFDA Fusco made a dramatic quarter turn to the cameras at the back of the courtroom, as the television producer had coached him to do, "taxpayers of America, and my fellow citizens of the planet, after seeing and hearing the dramatic testimony, seeing the graphics, and viewing searing documentary videos, we know there will be no doubt in your minds that this person, this rich person who thinks she is smarter than you, is guilty. I thank you."

One of the television producers at the back of the room raised her hand in a pre-arranged signal to the prosecution table. It was time for a break for commercials. The Assistant Counsel to the AFDA rose and said, "Your Honor, the prosecution requests a brief adjournment to marshal our many witnesses." His Honor had been apprised of this arrangement. The prosecution had provided a make-up artist in his chambers to make him look good for the viewing citizens of the planet.

Carl Wainwright rose, "If I may, your Honor, I have a brief but dramatic announcement of my own to make before we adjourn." The judge looked at the back of the courtroom, where the producer for ABC news, elected to give the signals for all of the news producers, gave a nod.

"Proceed, Mr. Wainwright."

"Your Honor, the defense, now and for the record," here he copied the prosecutor's turn to face the cameras at the back of the courtroom, "stipulates to the allegations of fact the prosecution has made as to the pay vouchers, the cashing of checks, and the near-starvation level of certain African farmers filmed by the BBC. What we do not stipulate is that any of this constitutes fraud. So, your Honor, under the rules of evidence, we can dispense with the eight witnesses testifying about who signed the pay vouchers and who cut the checks. We can also skip the graphics and the BBC documentary about Africa."

Eight make-up artists watching the trial on a monitor in a hastily arranged green room down the hall cursed and threw down their brushes. The eight witnesses, disappointed about losing their few seconds of planetary fame, joined in the curses. One of them thought, *I wonder if I get to keep the wardrobe they gave me?*

Carl watched the disappointment on the faces of the news producers with satisfaction. "One piece of evidence the defense *will* offer in dramatic and graphic form," he paused to raise the hopes of the producers, "is a receipt from Target for $69.33, which includes $39.99 for one microfiber silk-look suit on clearance sale, plus one string of genuine imitation pearls, also on clearance for $9.99, plus state sales tax, the US carbon use tax, and the UN surcharge on consumers of non-developing nations, of course. While my client may be guilty of signing a pay voucher, of all the evils in the world that she might be guilty of, never let it be said that she is rich. Now, your Honor, we may go to commercial break."

He sat down. The judge glared at him and started to say something, but noticed that the little red lights on the cameras were off, so he banged his gavel and barked, "Adjourned for a fifteen-minute recess."

The networks had been promised lots of time to sell commercials for this highly watched event. Even as the gavel banged down, advertising managers were pushing their speed-dials to the networks to demand a reduction in the rates they were paying for their ads. Counsel for the Defense had just lost them 20 million viewers in North America alone. No drama, fewer viewers. Fewer viewers, lower ad rates.

On ABC, a commercial began to run a split second after Carl sat down. "Are you sitting at home surfing channels? Have your parents begun nagging you to get a job and move out? Now you can! In all probability you may be a victim of Video Gamers and Channel Surfers Syndrome, or VGCSS. This highly addictive condition has been shown in clinical studies to render its victims incapable of performing the daily repetitive activities of most jobs, such as getting up at a certain time in the morning to go to work. The national law firm of Rostand and Kollend is enrolling victims nationwide for our class action law suit against Japanese and Korean manufacturers of televisions and game station equipment. You could collect big, move into your own apartment and get your own cable TV with adult channels! Call the number at the bottom of your screen to enroll. The number is 1-800-GET-YURS. Call today and get yours."

Prosecutor Fusco met with Judge Nance and the lead TV producer in chambers, a meeting normally unethical by legal standards without the presence of counsel for the defense.

"What can we do now?" wailed Fusco. "We can't waste my best dramatic moments. I've rehearsed with my witnesses too long for this moment. I even have blocking for my movements marked on the courtroom floor where the cameras can't see it, just like a professional production."

"Judge," said the producer, "every network will lose millions in revenue for ads with fewer viewers, now that the drama has been cut. Can he do this?"

The judge looked unhappy. "I'm afraid he can. If we try to admit testimony and evidence for facts he has already stipulated, then he can comment after each and every one, 'Your Honor, these facts have already been stipulated, why are we wasting the court's time?' And when he does, all the drama is gone anyway, so we're back to the same thing." He brooded. "No time for planning now. Meet here in chambers at the lunch adjournment and we'll think of something."

Gabrielle Vandervoss was providing her trademark legal commentary during part of the adjournment.

"In a stunning development, defense counsel Carl Wainwright has stipulated to all of the prosecution's allegations of fact. Deprived of his most dramatic scenes of testimony, can the Prosecutor get the ratings that the Attorney General wants? More importantly, can he get the worldwide ratings that PRIS wants?"

Her investigative staff had turned up the link from the Attorney General's office to PRIS. She didn't have to prove a direct link to back up what she had just said, as the web site for PRIS had posted a link to the PBS internet live broadcast of the trial. The headline over the link read, "Click here to see the latest criminal betrayer of the planet - on trial at last for her enviro-crimes."

At the defense table, Grace looked around at the gallery. "Where is Isaiah? And George and Estelle?"

"You'll see them at lunch," Carl said reassuringly. The judge reentered the courtroom.

"All rise," intoned the bailiff. Carl and Grace stood up. The judge sat down.

"Mr. Wainwright, your opening statement?"

161

Grace sat, and Carl began, "Your Honor, if it so please the court, I'll keep my opening statement brief. And since we have stipulated to the allegations of fact, I would like to keep the trial moving by proceeding to some witnesses of my own."

The judge looked at the prosecutor. "We have no objection, your Honor." Since his carefully planned stagecraft for the cameras was now not to be staged, AFDA Fusco had no witnesses to call anyway. Indeed, since the facts had been so obligingly stipulated by the defense, he had nothing left to do but rest his case and make his summation.

"Ladies and Gentlemen of the jury," Carl began, and then turned to the cameras, "and impartial and fair-minded citizens of the planet, as my learned colleague has appelled you," he turned back to the jury, "we have stipulated to the allegations of fact. Yes, Dr. Washington signed pay vouchers. Yes, the checks came from an account that also had government money deposited into it. We stipulate to that.

"We will offer testimony to clarify this new legal theory introduced by the prosecution, which he refers to as the Legal Theory of the Culpability of the Fungibility of Money."

Fusco jumped up. "Objection, your Honor! Relevance?"

Carl looked at the prosecutor calmly and then at the judge. "Your Honor, this is a new legal theory which does not exist in the federal statutes, or in any codes of law in any of the fifty states. If my client is to be tried on the basis of such a theory, and we cannot find it in the federal code books on the shelves behind your Honor, then we must admit into testimony, and for the record, the basis and meaning of this theory. Otherwise we risk the finding of this court being overturned on appeal."

Judge Nance hated to have his verdicts overturned on appeal. "Objection overruled."

"Your Honor, for my first witness, I call an expert, Professor Stanford of the Georgetown School of Law, who published the first article advancing this theory in the *International Journal of Relativistic Law Interpretation* just last month." A thin man with a wispy goatee in a denim jacket and carpenter jeans took the stand and was sworn in.

"For the record," began Carl, "you are Professor Stanford, author of the article on the Legal Theory of the Culpability of the Fungibility of Money?"

"And why would you doubt that, young man?"

"For the sake of the jury, who expect a professor testifying in court to dress in a suit and tie; they may doubt your identity and your credibility."

Stung by the last comment, he replied irascibly, "I affirm that I am indeed Professor Stanford. I wear working denim as a political statement to show my solidarity with the workers of the world. Anyone who confuses the clothes someone wears with their expertise, or their possible guilt or innocence, for that matter, is a fool!"

"Is that your expert legal opinion, professor, speaking as a professor of law and the author of the widely used textbook *Legal Theories to Suit the Times*?"

"It is."

"Let the record show that the author of the legal theory we're using to prosecute this defendant says that the clothes someone wears is no indicator of their guilt or innocence."

"Your Honor," interrupted the AFDA, "are we here to try a case or conduct a class in first-year law?"

"It's too late for the first year law class, Mr. Fusco," Carl replied, "and in this the seventh year of our lord President Fletcher, probably irrelevant. However, it does pertain to this trial, Judge, if you'll allow me to proceed?"

Glancing nervously at the cameras, the judge said in a clipped tone, "Mr. Wainwright, be careful that you do not find yourself in contempt of the Presidency, as defined in presidential executive order of this year number 714: *no person shall make any remark derogatory to the current President of the United States. Doing so constitutes hate speech punishable by imprisonment.* Be warned. Proceed."

"Now then, Professor Stanford, please explain for the jury this legal theory as it applies to this case."

"Gladly, young man, uh, young person, that is," he glanced apologetically at the cameras. "This legal theory, which I published last month, is now adopted by twelve nations around the world, including Cuba, Venezuela, and North Korea, I'm proud to say. It holds that any money drawn from 'the poisoned well' is part of a criminal act, and the mere act of drawing out that money, let alone using it, is a criminal act that should be punished."

He looked at the jury and leaned forward. "This is very simple. If everyone in a village got their water from the same well, and one person came along and poured a bucket of poisoned water into the well, the poison spreads to all of the water. Then any water from that well would poison anyone drinking from it." His eyes twinkled triumphantly. "If you came along and drew water from that well, you are drawing out poisoned water that could kill someone. You are guilty of actual or attempted murder, and ignorance of the fact that the well was poisoned is no excuse!" He smiled for the cameras.

"And please explain about the fungibility, Professor Stanford."

"Certainly. We say that money is fungible; meaning that money that enters a common fund can be used for anything the owner of that fund chooses. I may give my nephew money to buy textbooks, for example. He may use that money to pay off a gambling debt instead. It doesn't matter that I intended the money for textbooks. Once he has it, it can be used for anything. I may say that I didn't give him the money to pay gambling debts. It doesn't matter. Money will purchase anything.

"So, like our poisoned well, once the government money was put into the bank with the other money from Tuskegee University, all the money mixed together, like the poisoned water mixed with the well water. It is fungible. There is no way to know if any dollar bill I get from that bank was originally government money or not, so legally we have to treat all of it as government money. Anyone drawing on that money without the express permission of the federal government is therefore guilty of fraud, which is a form of theft, and there is the thief!" He rose from his seat in the witness box and pointed at Dr. Washington.

The cameras panned from his outstretched index finger to Dr. Washington. She looked steadily at the witness. *We're not in Kansas anymore Toto*, she thought. *We've left the world of objective fact, physical laws, and reality.*

"Thank you, Dr. Stanford." Carl sat down.

"Any questions for this witness?" The judge looked at the prosecutor. "No questions, your Honor." Fusco thought, *Counsel for the defense is making my case for me. Is he another one of the AG's many friends?*

"Professor, you may step down." The professor strutted for the cameras as he marched down the center aisle and out of the courtroom.

"Your Honor, for the sake of clarity, would you stipulate for the record that the professor's legal theory of the Culpability of the

Fungibility of Funds is indeed the legal basis for the charges against Dr. Washington?"

The judge looked at the prosecutor, forgetting that the cameras caught this interchange between them. The prosecutor nodded. "Mr. Wainwright, this court so stipulates."

"Thank you, your Honor."

Carl looked at a list. "Your Honor, for my next witness, I call upon Ms. Frederica Zimmer, assistant prosecutor for the great state of Maryland."

Gianni stood. "Relevance, your Honor?"

"Professor Stanford has explained the theory of The Culpability of the Fungibility of Money. I want to be sure the jury fully understands it by offering an example from a recent case."

Gianni's jaw dropped. *Wow, he must be a sleeper cell guy for the AG. This will be easier than I thought.* "Your Honor, I withdraw my objection."

"Proceed, Mr. Wainwright."

Ms. Zimmer was sworn in and seated. She was an attractive redhead with a serious demeanor. "Ms. Zimmer, please give us your real-life example of the legal culpability of someone due to the fungibility of money."

She looked at the jury earnestly. "We're investigating a case right now involving this theory. A twice-convicted drug dealer is out on parole. After evidence surfaced that he was back into drug dealing, we kept him under surveillance. He was caught on tape collecting money from his street distributors. As part of the process of building a case against him, we marked some money with ultraviolet ink, invisible to the naked eye. One of our undercover agents used it for a buy. Our suspect had that money in his possession and personally deposited it in a bank. He has a bogus business account there, so he can launder the money. The bank surveillance cameras show him doing this."

"And may we see this surveillance video?"

"Yes. May I use the large screen display that AFDA Fusco provided for his videos?" The judge nodded. The network cameras were already calibrated to rebroadcast these screen videos clearly. They focused on the screen.

Ms. Zimmer narrated, "Here you see the suspect in a metal-studded jacket depositing cash at the teller window. Now we cut to video from the back room of the bank, showing employees sorting money and taking some of the cash deposited by our drug dealer and placing it into the cassette device that dispenses money at the ATM machine that's mounted on the outside of the bank building. Now you see them loading it into the ATM dispenser on the inside." She paused and looked at the back of the courtroom. Six Maryland state troopers in uniform were seated there.

"This next video is from the outside bank security camera covering the ATM outside. We will next witness a high-ranking federal official taking possession of this fungible drug money. Possession of this drug money under the RICO statutes makes him part of a criminal enterprise, and criminally culpable under the professor's legal theory."

The video showed Judge Nance at the ATM withdrawing money. "Notice the time stamp on the videotape," Ms. Zimmer said. The date and time was the previous evening.

She stood up and withdrew a warrant from her jacket. "Judge Nance, you are served with this arrest warrant charging you under the RICO criminal racketeering statutes with acting in a criminal conspiracy by taking possession of money used in a drug buy."

She nodded toward the back of the courtroom. Six tall troopers put on their hats and walked forward. Judge Nance sat open-mouthed, too surprised to speak.

AFDA Fusco jumped up. "You can't do this! Court is in session! Bailiff! Stop those men! Let me see that warrant!"

He rushed up and grabbed it from the judge's hands. Scanning rapidly, he shouted, "This is a John Doe warrant! The judge isn't named here!"

"Yes," Ms. Zimmer replied evenly. "We didn't know who the co-conspirator was who would take possession of the money when we got the warrant yesterday afternoon. We were tapped into an internet feed directly from the ATM camera, waiting for big fish to show up. We just didn't know how big the fish would be. I had this warrant cross authorized and signed by the chief of police of the District of Columbia. The bank with the laundered money is in Maryland, my jurisdiction. The transfer of drug money, the crime, took place in Maryland. The judge resides in Maryland. Officers?"

The burliest state trooper gently raised the judge to a standing position and handcuffed him. The cameras zoomed in. He removed the judge's wallet and handed it to Ms. Zimmer. She reached into her handbag and brought out an ultraviolet light.

"Since we're very much on the record here with cameras from seven networks feeding live and to the internet, I want to be fair and test the money in the judge's wallet for all to see if we're mistaken. Cameramen, will the glow of ultraviolet light be visible on your video feeds?"

"You bet!" one of them shouted from the back. "Show it!"

Shifting so that members of the jury and the cameras both had a clear view, she spread out the cash from the judge's wallet on the judge's desktop. Then she turned on her ultraviolet light. The glow was unmistakable.

"Members of the jury, do you see this ultraviolet glow?" They all nodded. She nodded in satisfaction. "Good, I may subpoena you all to testify in the judge's trial. How about the cameras?"

"We got it clear as a bell," shouted a cameraman, forgetting that he was on the air live.

"Good, I may subpoena your videotape too."

AFDA Fusco pounded the table, but stayed away from the tall troopers now escorting the judge in an impromptu perp walk down the aisle of his own courtroom while the cameras rolled.

"He's a federal judge! This should be an FBI matter! He's wearing judicial robes! You can't take him into Maryland's custody!"

Ms. Zimmer stepped up to the prosecutor's table. "Maryland crime, Maryland custody, Maryland jail time. AFDA, did you sleep through first-year law on jurisdiction? And as for the judicial robes, check the trial transcripts for Professor Stanford's testimony. *'Anyone who confuses the clothes someone wears with their expertise, or their possible guilt or innocence, for that matter, is a fool!'* " She walked down the aisle, doing a bit of strutting of her own for the cameras.

Carl looked Gianni in the eye. "Enough drama for you?" Gianni pushed his way out of the courtroom with a panicked look in his eyes.

The courtroom was in chaos, with everyone suddenly talking at once, including the network reporters. They all scrambled to get in front of their own cameras.

Gabrielle made it first. "Breaking news and sensational news. You witnessed all of it live. Federal Judge Nance was just arrested in his own courtroom, in front of the jury and seven network live feeds, charged with a crime based on the same legal theory the prosecutor was using against Dr. Washington: culpability for fungibility of funds. To add salt to this wound, Judge Nance stipulated to the use of this theory in open court, for the record, and on the videotapes of seven news networks. Maryland state assistant district attorney Zimmer dramatically shined her ultraviolet light on cash from the judge's own wallet. The blue glow of guilt proved it was drug money from an investigation she was conducting. In a stunning reversal of fortune, Judge Nance is now charged with a criminal conspiracy under the RICO laws. More on this breaking news in a minute."

Grace was looking down at notes she had made on a pad when a rainbow of light glowed on the white paper. A hand placed a small prism on the table in front of her. Grace looked up to see Isaiah next to her. "Pursuant to my covenant with you, may I take you to lunch?"

"Oh Isaiah, don't joke at a time like this. Did you see what just happened?"

Carl spoke up. "On that note, I can't see what *will* happen next. The bailiffs have all chased down the hall after the judge. We're adjourned and I'm going to lunch. Good day." He abruptly turned and walked out with his briefcase.

Suddenly Samuel Solipsis was at the defense table with them. He reached out and gripped Grace's arm. "Don't think for a second that this is over!" he snarled. Isaiah grasped his hand, peeled it off Grace's arm, pirouetted with the arm to lock it at the elbow, and pulled it down abruptly over his shoulder. There was a sharp crack from the elbow, and Samuel cried out and sank to the floor, sobbing, "It's broken! You broke my arm!"

Isaiah leaned over him and said in a low tone, "If you ever touch my wife again, I'll break your neck!"

Isaiah pulled Grace up. "Don't talk. Just come with me. I have a lovely lunch waiting for you." He took her by the arm and walked her briskly through the back door into the judge's chambers, out into the crowded corridor, down the back stairs and into the street. A Lincoln Towncar was at the curb. The back door popped open and Isaiah handed her in.

As he closed the door, Douglas Soto gunned the car away from the curb and headed for the beltway. Grace was in a state of shock. "Where are George and Estelle?"

"At a D.C. police precinct, filing a report on their stolen car. Don't worry. This is my friend and colleague Douglas Soto. He has already switched plates with an identical Towncar from a D.C. limo service."

Douglas glanced back from the driver's seat. "Pleased to meet you, ma'am. I've heard a lot about you from the boss."

She looked out the window. "Where are we going?"

"To an undisclosed location, from where you will be led, like one of the seven clean animals, directly into Noah's Ark."

"But we'll be fugitives."

"Yes, fugitives. Fugitives from a system taken over from within and a nation, not of laws, but of corrupt men. Excuse me, *persons*. No, not even men. Spoiled children who smash and destroy in a tantrum when they can't have what they want. You can't win in that court, Grace, because it no longer has objective rules of law and evidence. The law is whatever they say it is. And 'they' are your enemies. As Gabrielle was saying to her viewers, this is a stunning reversal of fortune, a reversal in which the lawful are hunted as fugitives by the lawless."

He looked grim, but suddenly his face softened into a smile. He reached into the front seat and brought back a wicker picnic basket. "Reuben sandwiches, grilled in butter, just the way you like them. And would you care for . . ." he rummaged in the basket and came up with a wine glass and a bottle, "a Pinot Grigio with your luncheon?"

*   *   *   *   *   *

After leaving the police station, George and Estelle went to a nearby deli for lunch.

As their food was served, the ABC noon news began on the television. "ABC News has learned from our on-the-scene reporter at the federal courthouse, that in an incredible theatre of the absurd, the judge presiding over the trial of Dr. Grace Washington for fraud against the United States government has himself been arrested for a similar crime under the selfsame legal theory used to prosecute Dr. Washington. Maryland Assistant District Attorney Frederica Zimmer, appearing as a witness for the defense, served an arrest warrant on Judge Nance and had him escorted off by Maryland state troopers. ABC correspondent Nancy Flanders reports from the courtroom."

"Charley, the scene in the courtroom was chaos after Judge Nance was led away in handcuffs by the Maryland state police. Unfortunately, we had technical difficulties which destroyed our tape of the scene, so we can't show it to you, but some of you may have seen it on the live feed." A producer stepped into the picture and handed her a piece of paper. "Charley, in yet another stunning development, when bailiffs returned to the courtroom after attempting to retrieve Judge Nance, they couldn't find the defendant! Dr. Grace Washington, the most famous scientist and botanist in America, is now officially a fugitive from justice. Charley, back to you."

George was speechless for once. Estelle was amused. "So this is what it takes to get you to be quiet for five minutes? The disappearance of a dear friend of ours? Well, I guess there's no point in taking a taxi to the courthouse. I'm calling Isaiah." She stared intently at her cell phone for a minute. "No answer. It goes to voice mail."

George spoke. "Let's get a taxi to the hotel. We can get an afternoon flight to Atlanta and then pick up a rental car to drive home to Tuskegee."

"Hadn't we better file a missing person report on Isaiah and Mr. Soto?"

George looked thoughtful. "No. They're grown men who know how to take care of themselves. Give them another forty-eight hours. If we don't hear from them by then, we'll file the report."

*   *   *   *   *   *

N minus 10. The next day was Friday. Attorney General Handford was meeting with AFDA Gianni Fusco.

"What have you got to say for yourself?"

Gianni was studying his fingernails. He looked up. "I didn't see it coming. Everything was set. I could see that the judge was on board with me and you by the cues he gave."

The Attorney General frowned more deeply. "Mr. Fusco, for the record, (and for his own record the AG was secretly recording the conversation) the judge was not on board with anybody, and certainly not with me. Are you saying that you improperly colluded with the judge to fix the trial? The Bar Association would certainly have to be informed about that."

170

Gianni hastily backpedaled. "No, no! I only meant that the judge had agreed to the brief you filed, which allowed broadcasting from the courtroom. What I didn't see coming was this grandstand play by the defense counsel, with the courtroom arrest and all."

"For the record, Mr. Fusco, Counselor Wainwright has already voluntarily filed an affidavit with the justice department, complete with lie detector test taken and verified by the same outfit employed by us and the FBI. It backs up his story that he knew nothing about the drug investigation by the Maryland State Assistant DA. He claims that she called him and said that someone told her he was looking for active cases where The Culpability of Fungibility of Money Legal Theory was being used. She said she had such a case and offered to testify. He accepted. He didn't know that the object of her investigation was Judge Nance himself."

Gianni looked down again. "When I called her boss, the Maryland State Attorney General, he said Zimmer didn't know that the object of the investigation was Judge Nance either. Zimmer only found out when she was called and told by her surveillance officer the night before the trial began, he says. He did say that she was ambitious and never missed a chance to score some publicity with a big collar in front of the cameras. We already had the cameras arranged for her, so it made it hard for her to resist. He said she had not informed him either, and that he only knew it when we did, from the broadcasts. She's probably bucking to run for Maryland Attorney General herself some day."

The AG had patiently let him finish. "So, you took it upon yourself to call the Attorney General of the State of Maryland without my say-so?"

Gianni was already looking down, but he seemed to shrink into himself. "Sorry. I panicked. I had no facts, and I knew that you would be asking for some."

"When I need facts, Gianni, I can find them. Any facts that I need, for any purpose that I need them for. Do we understand one another?"

"Yes, sir."

"That affidavit, and the fact that it was broadcast live, means that we can't touch Mr. Wainwright on this." He paused. "I want," he paused again, "*We* want, you to investigate Ms. Fredrica Zimmer. Find something against her: jaywalking, anything. We'll find a way to use it against her. Even if it is a gray area, we have appointed enough judges that we can find one to see it our way. Get on it."

"Yes sir. . . . sir?"

"Yes?"

"What about the disappearance of Dr. Washington?"

"I have the FBI working on that. I'll let you know when she's found." Gianni turned to go.

"And Gianni?"

"Yes?"

"This isn't personal; this is business, *federal government business*. So don't go crying to your old man and the *famiglia* over this. I have people watching him too. Dismissed." Gianni slunk out of the room.

The AG buzzed his administrative assistant. "Miss Conyers?"

"Yes sir?"

"Send in my next appointment."

"Yes, sir."

The CEOs of Microware, E-Buyer, and PurchaseAll came into his private conference room. "Lady and Gentlepersons, welcome. Coffee? Something with more kick?" They all shook their heads. "Thank you, Miss Conyers. That will be all for now."

"Lady and Gentlepersons, what can I do for you?"

William Portal, the CEO of Microware, spoke first. "Frankly, Mr. Handford, we need your help. We want to cooperate with the administration. We want to cooperate fully. We only want cooperation in return."

The Attorney General smiled benignly. "Call me Earnest. What kind of cooperation are we talking about?"

Gina Manley of E-Buyer spoke next. "We know that you and the President want to impose wage and price controls on the software industry above and beyond the wage regulations recently enacted by Treasury Secretary Gunther. We're willing to cooperate. We won't oppose it through our public relations departments and lobbying firms. We're all willing to take a hit on our public executive compensation. We will even issue public statements of support for the President's plan." She stopped.

"And in return?" prompted the AG.

Gina said carefully, "In return, we want three things, for starters. One, we want the next stimulus bill to include special legislation that requires all software companies to submit to an independent audit to certify that they are doing their share for the planet, and that they are financially transparent and ethically responsible in the way they use and distribute their software. They will pay for this at the rate of two percent of their yearly revenues as the audit fee." This Administration and Congress were averaging about one stimulus bill every six weeks.

"Two, we want an earmark in that stimulus bill for creating a non-profit agency to be called *Software Ethical Transparency Agency*, or SETA. This will be the agency that performs the audits. We want the President to appoint the three of us to serve as board members, and designate the internal finances of the agency to be confidential under presidential executive privilege. We want to be compensated for our services on contract at twenty million dollars each, plus one-third of one percent of the revenues of the software companies that we audit, to each of us, for our services in achieving and enforcing software transparency and ethical responsibility to the planet. The public is not to know what we are paid. The other one percent goes to the US Treasury."

The AG nodded. "That's doable. And number three?"

Now the third CEO spoke, Geoffrey Bricknell of PurchaseAll. "Number three, we want legislation passed that limits the market share of any one software company to what it is today. In the field of buying and selling software, commonly called marketplace software, PurchaseAll has fifty percent market share. E-Buyer has thirty percent and William's Microware has nineteen point nine percent. William, of course has other software products besides marketplace software."

The AG looked puzzled. "The three of you already dominate your industry. Why do you need this help?"

The three CEOs looked at one another, a little shamefaced. William spoke again. "Uh, Earnest? Earnest, we have not made a major innovation or technology breakthrough since we achieved dominance in our respective markets about ten years ago. Times have been good for us. Like the hare in Aesop's fable The Tortoise and the Hare, we sprinted ahead in the early days, and then we rested. We've made cosmetic improvements to our software, but nothing that was a game changer.

"Right now we're still the largest in each of our markets. As long as we can sit on the board of the new non-profit, semi-governmental agency we outlined, we don't even mind having our salaries cut. We each own enough of our own stock to do well with dividends and occasional stock splits and sell-offs."

"But?" prompted Earnest.

"But," continued William, "remember that I have nineteen point nine percent market share in the US for marketplace software? Guess who has the majority of the one tenth of one percent that is left? *Isaiah Mercury of Promethean Software International.* And he's gaining on us exponentially. Thank God, or thank someone, that he chose to launch his new Invisible Hand software in the developing markets first and not the domestic market. His software operates through cell phones. Cheap, simple, "non-smart" cell phones! This makes access much cheaper. And he doesn't even sell the software like I do. He offers it as a free interface like Gina and Geoffrey do over the internet. You don't even have to have internet access to use his system, just a cell phone, always cheaper than a computer. Not even a G3 or G4 cell phone. And his price! You can use his software for the price of a few text messages, for God's sake!

"Earnest, when he enters the US market, and he will eventually, he will blow the three of us out of the water. We need protection. We need time to catch up, like you gave the car companies, only we don't want direct bailout dollars and federal control of our companies. We want to keep control of our companies. We know that if we don't work out a menu with you, we *are on* the menu."

The AG shrugged and spread his hands. "What else do you want then?"

William leaned forward, "That's all for now, just three things. Number one: enact the transparency audit requirement into law, which generates revenues for you and for us. Besides that, it gives you (and us) a sneak peek into proprietary research and development work done by these upstart, excuse me, *start-up* companies, all in the name of transparency, ethical responsibility and the public welfare. It's a win/win. Both parties get additional money. Both parties get to inspect technology developments that we can copy, but which someone else paid for. Since this is a semi-governmental agency like Freddie Mac, that means the government can reach in and help themselves too. We can always add the justification of national security."

Gina added, "And the other two items. Number two, put us on the board of this new agency. Limit the board to the three of us so that we don't have to share our audit fees. Number three, limit market share of

174

marketplace software to today's split of percentages. Increasing beyond that could be punishable by fines and jail time, like insider trading. Make the fines as big as you want; we don't care. You control the enforcement."

The AG looked thoughtful. "I think all of this is doable. There may be some minor changes here or there as it works its way through this Congress and all the congressional staffers. How many jobs will this create?"

The three of them looked blank. "You know, jobs? A wink used to be as good as a nod. And you call yourselves captains of industry! Jobs? Hello-o? This will be done through a stimulus bill that is supposed to create jobs? Earth to software titans? Come on, how many cushy jobs in PR, sales, marketing, and governmental relations can you create for friends and relatives of congressmen and congressional staffers?"

The three CEOs came to with a start. Now they understood. "Yes," said William. "At Microware, we can probably create . . . two hundred jobs."

"Gentlepersons and lady, need I remind you that there are nearly six hundred congress people and senators? Let me also remind you that according to one textbook on marketing, a marketing influence factor of three to one is needed for effective salespersonship." This time they recognized the wink, and rapidly re-calculated what their nod would be.

"Now that I've had more time to think, I think this stimulus package will create . . . nine hundred jobs at Microware worldwide," William said. He looked a little worried. "Uh, Earnest, with the Presidents' wage and price controls, I may have to ask for a little price increase to cover this expense."

"No problem, William. Ask, and those who cooperate shall receive."

Gina spoke up, "And at E-Buyer, I believe that a stimulus package of this magnitude could create . . . four hundred jobs world-wide."

All eyes turned to Geoffey. "At PurchaseAll, we could stimulate employment growth of . . . five hundred jobs."

The AG smiled, "Lady and Gentlepersons, I believe we have just stimulated enough jobs to convince Congress of the great prosperity this will bring to their friends and family. Congratulations. You have just stimulated yourselves. Shall we drink to it?"

William said, "I believe I could use a good stiff drink right about now. Does the 'Buy American' provision of the seventeen stimulus bills preclude me from asking for Scotch?"

The AG leaned over to him confidentially, and said in a low tone, "Those rules are for 'we the people.' We are the government. We make the rules for others, not ourselves." He pushed the intercom button on the conference phone on the table.

"Miss Conyers? Please bring in my stimulus acquiescence celebration Scotch and four glasses." He turned back to the others. "You see, this type of government-business cooperation is not as rare as you might have thought. You're among friends here. Come, a toast." He poured the drinks and raised his glass. "To cooperation over competition."

They each raised and clinked their glasses. "To cooperation over competition!"

Chapter Fourteen

N minus 10. The corporate jet for Promethean Software International touched down at the airport. The "undisclosed location" was Christchurch, New Zealand. After nearly eighty years of a Euro-socialist economic model of heavy regulation and control of the economic actions of individuals, New Zealand had grown tired of economic stagnation. They began to roll back government to its proper trio of roles: national defense, police protection of citizens from violence and fraud, and adjudication of disputes via a court system. The rollback was just beginning, but was vigorous enough to raise their standard of living noticeably. Unshackled, the citizens had begun creating new businesses and hiring one another. There was even a cluster of technology innovation at Christchurch.

"Welcome to Ark Pacific," Isaiah said to Grace as they walked from the aircraft.

"Where are we?" Grace asked, blinking in the sunshine.

"Christchurch, New Zealand. This way." They went through Customs and Immigration. After their passports had been stamped and their bags cleared, Isaiah steered her to another small office.

"Mr. Mercury?" asked the official at the desk.

"Yes."

"We've been expecting you." He turned to Grace, "Dr. Washington, I presume?"

"Yes."

"A pleasure to meet you. My name is John Canaan, minister of immigration and talent recruitment. Please sit here while my assistant snaps a photo for our archives."

Bewildered, Grace sat on a chair before a digital camera connected to a computer and monitor. A young woman said "Smile!" and a light flashed in her eyes.

Isaiah then gave her some papers to sign. "What is this, Isaiah?"

"I know you want to know what you're signing line by line. You can take the time to read it, or you can trust me. I did read it line by line three months ago and signed it myself. It's OK."

She looked into his eyes. His gaze was strong and steady and full of love for her. She smiled at him and then signed. The Minister's assistant took the papers and left. After ten minutes, she returned with a dark, slim, bound document the size of a small notepad.

"What's this?" Grace asked as she studied the cover. It was embossed in gold with the sovereign seal of New Zealand.

The minister stepped forward and shook her hand. "I formally welcome our latest and greatest citizen, with the possible exception of her husband. You are now a Kiwi." Grace looked down at the document and opened it. It was a New Zealand passport.

Isaiah raised her hand to his lips. "To my lady of the dual citizenship."

She gave the minister a dazzling smile. "Thank you. I'm proud to be here."

A car was waiting for them at the curb, with the redoubtable Douglas Soto at the wheel.

They drove through city streets luxuriant with blooming trees. Flowers spilled out of window boxes on nearly every building.

"This reminds me of Alsace, in France," remarked Grace. She put her hand on Isaiah's arm and smiled at him. She leaned against him and sighed with contentment. She was safe. She was with Isaiah. That was all she could think about for now.

*　　*　　*　　*　　*　　*

N minus 9. The next morning, Isaiah woke early when his cell vibrated under his pillow. It was Douglas Soto.

"What's up?" asked Isaiah in a low voice, rubbing sleep from his eyes.

"Our servers in Mexico. Someone executed a hack attack at 2 a.m. Mexico time. Isaiah, the method of attack shows that they were trying to hijack a copy of *Invisible Hand*."

"As we suspected. Status?"

"The attack was unsuccessful, but we didn't set off any alarms. They think they were undetected, so they may try again tonight."

"Can you trace the origin of the attack?"

"Working on it now. Should know in about an hour."

"Good. Keep me posted."

He looked over at the still-sleeping form next to him in the bed. *Sleeping Beauty*, he thought. He leaned over and kissed her. She stirred and whispered, "Good morning."

"Good morning, sweetheart. I have to go to work. Two big things on my agenda today. This morning, I have to defend against hacker attacks from the US government. This afternoon, I have a date to take my wife to her new lab."

Her eyes widened, "A new lab? Today? But I don't have my list of protocols, and my data, and, and . . ." She sat up, suddenly overwhelmed.

"My dear, I took the liberty of backing up all of your research files from the University several weeks ago. They're here, in a hard drive back up. I also took the liberty of giving George Wright a beta copy of my next generation encryption software, to guard against cyber hacking attacks against his copy of your research at Tuskegee University."

"Well . . . it sounds like you've thought of everything."

"Probably not. Here's the number for a cab service and a map of Christchurch. There's also a list of lab equipment suppliers. Here is the blanket purchase order Minerva has set up for your use with industrial suppliers. Here's a new credit card in your name established though a local bank for any personal purchases. Have fun. I'll see you at noon for lunch at this restaurant." He handed her a card.

She read aloud, "Tuskegee Barbecue Down Under! What on earth?"

"Friend of mine. Maori exchange student at TU developed a passion for southern-style barbecue. Can't imagine who influenced him. Set up this restaurant when he returned to Christchurch. Tuskegee sounds like a Maori word, kind of. Been doing a great business ever since. Kiwis love barbecue!"

*   *   *   *   *   *

At his new office for Promethean Software International, Ltd., Isaiah conferred with Douglas Soto and his team of cyber-security specialists. "So, what have we got?"

"Isaiah, we traced the cyber-attack to the US Treasury Department, Department of Bailout Exceptions."

"Oh, so Mr. J. Walter Obson and his master want revenge, do they?"

"Seems that way."

"Tonight, when they attack again, let's give them what they came for."

"Sir?" the team looked puzzled.

"They want something of ours; let's give it to them, code name Odysseus."

Comprehension dawned on their faces. Douglas whistled. "The old Trojan Horse gift. Well this time, if they're smart, they'll look this gift horse in the mouth. As the sorority girls used to say about the fraternity boys at my alma mater, 'Beware of Greeks bearing Trojans!'" Laughing, they went to work.

*   *   *   *   *   *

Tipuna Akuhata greeted Isaiah at the entrance to Tuskegee Barbecue Down Under. "My brother! You look well! And who is this lovely woman? Is she not shamed to be seen with such an undesirable as you?"

"This, Tipuna, is my bride, Dr. Grace Washington. Grace, you can see that Tipuna acquired the fine art of trash talking during his four years at Tuskegee University. Tipuna, you must give her respect. She's a botanist who is not only smart, but she has a mean turn-around jump shot!"

Tipuna tipped his head back and laughed heartily. "You married wisely then. When you go walk-about, she will find edible plants to keep you alive. When you come to the city, you can win bar bets on her ability to sink free throws. There was a time when she would have been worth many kune-kune pigs to my people." This time Isaiah tipped his head back and laughed heartily.

"When you two have finished bartering me for pigs, would you introduce me to this gentleman?" Grace said lightly.

"My dear, this is Tipuna Akuhata, a good friend from university days at Tuskegee."

She shook his hand and smiled, showing dazzling white teeth. "I am pleased to meet you, Mr. Akuhata."

"Tipuna, I bring you a gift from Tuskegee," Isaiah held out a box.

"A Golden Tigers jersey!" he said delightedly. "But please, Dr.Washington, you must call me Tipuna."

"Please call me Grace."

180

He donned the jersey. "I must enjoy this immediately." He escorted them into the restaurant, which was decorated with Tuskegee University sports posters and memorabilia.   He called out to one of the servers, "Arapera! A menu for my esteemed friends."

When the server arrived with menus, Tipuna said, "Arapera, look! A new Golden Tigers jersey! Is it not beautiful?"

Arapera looked at it and remarked drily, "Beautiful and just in time. His other jersey is so ragged and faded the tiger's teeth are falling out." Everyone laughed.

*　　*　　*　　*　　*　　*

After lunch, Isaiah drove Grace to the newly rented corporate offices of Nutritional Abundance Industries, Ltd. Minerva Stone greeted them at the door. "Welcome!" She hugged Grace tightly. "We were so worried when we heard about your arrest."

"I'm OK, thanks to Isaiah."

Minerva turned and gave Isaiah a hug. "Thank you for keeping her safe. I owe you a debt, and hungry people around the world owe you a debt, though they don't yet realize it."

She walked them through the administrative offices and into the back, where a gleaming laboratory stood. Some equipment was still in crates waiting to be installed. "Grace, this is yours, if you'll accept it."

"Oh Minerva, it's beautiful. Is this crate an electron microscope?"

"The finest." Grace walked through the lab like a child on Christmas morning, wonderingly touching the stainless steel equipment, digital read-outs, and glass beakers. She turned back to face them from across the lab.

"Oh Minerva, I can't accept this. This represents millions of dollars in equipment, and I could never pay for it."

Minerva smiled. "You don't have to. Just accept the post of Vice President of Research and Development for Nutritional Abundance Industries.   Then you are entitled to use it whenever you want.   A generous salary, plus royalties from all inventions you create."

Grace looked dazed. "I don't know what to say."

"Say yes!"

"Yes!"

"Come meet your staff." Minerva led the way.

181

While Grace was chatting with her new staff, Minerva took Isaiah by the elbow and led him back to the adjoining lab. "Isaiah, I want to pay my debt to you."

Isaiah looked puzzled. "Minerva, you don't owe me anything. I was saving my own wife from those vultures who were using her to get at you. You read my e-mail on that deal they offered, didn't you?"

Minerva looked out the window. Her face grew as stern as the famous bust of Pallas Athene, Greek goddess of wisdom and war, her namesake. "Yes, and I can't tell you how despicable I think those people are, to threaten an innocent person with false charges in order to get at me. Isaiah, I owe you a double debt. If you had not rescued Grace, I would have returned. She's that important to me, and to the world, whether they know it or not. You saved me as well as Grace." She turned back to Isaiah with a smile. "I think you're going to like my proposal to repay you. It benefits my business and yours, a win for both of us, and it discharges my debt of honor."

*   *   *   *   *   *

Grace closed the door of her new office, overwhelmed by all these new developments and wanting some quiet time for herself.

Arrested, put on trial, rescued, flown into exile, made a citizen of New Zealand, offered a new job and new lab, all within one week. At least your life isn't boring, girl!

Suddenly shaky, she sat down in the desk chair, hyperventilating. After her breathing returned to normal, she stood and went to the window of her new office and looked at the harbor. The lush foliage made for a beautifully framed picture. The window was open and a fresh-smelling sea breeze gently blew in. She took a deep breath. A small frown was on her face. *How did we ever end up here? What has our world come to?*

She remembered when she and Isaiah first fully committed to this desperate idea, and her doubts about it. Those doubts came back to her now. *Is this the right thing to do?*

*   *   *   *   *   *

It had been in the clinic in Chicago, after the knife attack by the PRIS protester. She had been checked out by the doctor. She took a long, hot shower to wash off the pig's blood that had been thrown on her. She felt so dirty. She leaned against the shower wall and let the hot water course over her back. *Oh, it feels so good to be clean again. Why did that woman want to kill me?* She shivered despite the hot water.

Afterward she put on a hospital gown and slipped between the clean sheets of the hospital bed. She pulled the cotton blanket up to her chest. She wiggled to snug herself into the bed. Minerva was on her way back to Grace's hotel room to bring back fresh clothes for her. At Grace's request, the nurse took away her blood-soaked suit and shoes, to be incinerated.

There was a knock at the door. "Come in."

Isaiah entered and sat beside her. He reached over and took her hand. "Are you OK?"

"I'm still shaky, but I'm much better now that I've had a hot shower." She gave him a weak smile.

"We got the lab results about possible toxins or contagious diseases from the pig's blood. It was negative. No toxins. I promised a large expedite fee to the clinic administrator for a rush job."

"Thanks, baby, for taking such good care of me." Her smile deepened into her dimple.

Then she sighed and said, "Let's see what the rest of the world thinks about this attack."

She picked up the TV remote and snapped on the TV. It was tuned to ZSNBC. Keiffer Umlaut was reporting on the attack at the news conference. "Well America, it turns out that the 'new' 'improved' (here he made 'air quote' gestures with his hands) food crops trumpeted by the greedy Nutritional Abundance Industries were rotten. At their news conference this morning an alliance of green organizations sponsored by PRIS exposed the fact that the rotten Franken-fruit products of this company cause birth defects, horrible mutations, and an unsustainable population level in the third world. In addition, PRIS revealed that NAI mutilated animals in the testing of these mutated harmful food crops. When I think about those unscrupulous, greedy business people, it triggers my gag reflex."

Grace started to get out of the bed, but then sank back. "I'm so mad, I want to pace the floor, but I can't do it in this dang hospital gown with my tee-ota-laytee showing in the back!"

Isaiah chuckled. "Tee-ota-laytee. That's what my grandma called it too."

The angry energy abruptly left her face. She pressed the off button and looked wanly at Isaiah. "All lies. No attribution, no data, no witnesses. Just lies made up by PRIS and reported with no fact-checking. And no mention of the knife attack and the pig's blood thrown on me."

Grace stared at the ceiling with a blank look on her face. "Isaiah, the situation in the country just keeps getting worse. I try to keep faith, but I'm losing hope. What kind of country is it where those who want to feed hungry men, women, and children are attacked, vilified, and despised, and those who want to deny food to starving children are the acclaimed 'saviors' of the planet?"

Isaiah squeezed her hand. "Remember what we talked about? Our plan?"

Grace closed her eyes. "The Noah Option? Yes. When I first told you about my idea I was so relieved to find out that you and your friends had already reached the same conclusion and had already begun preparing places. But . . . Isaiah, I know that I gave it the name and began preparing for it myself and that it's probably the right thing to do, but it's so hard!" Her eyes filled with tears. "Let go of everything? I keep hoping that things will turn around."

He leaned closer. "What does your heart tell you after this morning's events?"

Grace opened her eyes and calmly looked into his. "Isaiah, this morning I looked into the face of evil and saw its knife thrust toward my heart. I know that pretending it doesn't exist won't make it go away."

She looked up at the ceiling again. "But to be the first ones to activate The Noah Option? I'm like Moses before the burning bush. I don't *want* this assignment. What if we lead, but nobody follows?"

Isaiah took a deep breath. "It would still be the right thing to do. Remember what you told me about the secret hidden in plain sight?"

She sighed, "Yes. My neighbor Carl the mechanic and his hard work and creating a good life for his family and jobs for his employees."

"Grace, we've seen enough by now to connect the dots to the larger picture, to the menace threatening Carl and you and me and every other hardworking American. The dots led us to the one thing all these groups have in common, from PRIS and other progressive do-gooder organizations, to the companies seeking bailouts, to the companies convincing the government to force us to buy their products, to the government agencies trying to control every little thing we do. The one thing they all have in common is the desire for power and control: an oligarchic dictatorship."

"Isaiah, I know that all their propaganda about 'the public welfare' and 'do it for the children' and 'the good of the planet' is a smokescreen for what they really want, which is the power to tell the rest of us what to do. When the East German communist government controlled all aspects of their citizens' lives, the people lived as slaves and tried to escape every chance they got. When the Berlin wall came down, we discovered that the all-controlling East German government had created terrible pollution in the air, the rivers, and the cities. So much for 'give us all the power so we can save the planet.'"

Grace looked Isaiah in the eye. "I'm a scientist. It was a perfect control group design for a scientific experiment. The same German people, the same German culture, and the same resources. The western half under a Western style democracy with economic freedoms, the eastern half under a fascist socialist dictatorship that controlled everything. Well, the results of that experiment are in. The half with economic freedom prospered and lived well. The half with socialist fascism lived like refugees and polluted everything. No honest scientist can mistake the data."

Isaiah took her hand again. "The people in these politically correct groups never did the hard work to create a technology like you did, or create a business with jobs like your neighbor Carl did, but they claim the right to control those who did do the work.

"Grace, I'm scared too. But, remember Who was in that burning bush. A Power so Absolute He couldn't even have a name. When Moses asked His name, He said I AM WHO AM. Let's pray for faith, courage, and the strength to do what we know needs be done."

He knelt down beside her bed. He kept her hand in his. "Would you pray for us, Grace?"

She closed her eyes. "Dear Lord, we know that all things are in Your hands. Please give us the faith and the courage to do the right thing. We worry about what we're giving up, but we know that You will bless us many-fold. Amen."

Grace sat up, her eyes shining. "Isaiah, would you hand me the Gideon's Bible from the bedside table?" She thumbed through it until she found the verse she was looking for.

She read aloud, "Try me now, and I will open the windows of heaven and pour you out such a blessing that you can scarce hold it all. Malachi 3:10."

Isaiah took both her hands and looked into her eyes. "I can scarce hold it all."

He hugged her. When he sat back, she asked, "How will it start?"

"As the Lord said unto Noah, two by two, sister woman, two by two. We be two, you and I."

"Amen, brother man, amen." Her smile was radiant. Isaiah felt warm and happy, basking in the glow of that smile.

"Now then, how about some barbeque take-out for lunch? I know of a great little barbeque place not far from here, and I can be back in forty-five minutes. You want fries with that?"

"Oh you! Everything must be back to normal, because Isaiah Mercury is thinking about barbeque again!" She threw a pillow at him. Then, in her little girl voice, "Would you bring me extra sauce?"

*   *   *   *   *   *

Remembering that bedside scene, a small smile crept back to her face. She whispered a prayer into the soft Pacific breeze coming through her office window. *Lord, it's me again, Grace. I have doubts again. I am trying You and relying on You again, because I can't do it by myself. But You can. Amen."*

She inhaled and smelled bougainvillea. *I have Isaiah, and I have a brand new lab. I can scarce hold it all.*

Chapter Fifteen

N minus 7. It came at 4 p.m. New Zealand time, which was 2 a.m. Mexico time. The Treasury Department pirate hackers tried to gain access to the Mexican server for Invisible Hand Software. This time they succeeded. As soon as they had downloaded the software successfully, Isaiah and his team knew it. Isaiah's team then remotely wiped the server in Mexico clean of all data, and put it up for sale on Invisible Hand. All other PSI servers physically located in the United States had been similarly disposed of. Now, no trace of PSI was left in the United States, other than a few ads in old issues of business magazines in the lobbies of businesses across America.

The team at Promethean Software International activated hidden control and surveillance subroutines buried in the guts of the Trojan Horse version of the Invisible Hand software they had allowed the pirates to download. They were able to access surveillance video and audio from the hackers' secret den in the basement of the Treasury Department building in Washington, D.C. The PSI team had hacked the hackers. They began recording the proceedings for later use on FreedomToobz.Ark. The security camera showed two hackers side by side at their computer monitors. Their faces were clearly visible.

"We got it!" exclaimed Hacker One as he exchanged high fives with Hacker Two.

"Treasury Secretary Gunther will be pleased. He can pass the word to Attorney General Handford that we can now auction off our copy of Invisible Hand to the highest bidder for reverse engineering. Whoever has it can make knockoff copies to compete against Mercury, without putting in five years of work and investment in research and development. The AG told him that Gina Manley of E-Buyer was especially interested in obtaining a copy. She will now owe this administration big time. She can maintain her competitive advantage for the next ten years with this stolen software. And Secretary Gunther and Attorney General Handford can call in favors from Manley and E-Buyer any time they want. We own them! Hackers rule!" (More high fives.)

"I can see it now," said Hacker Two. "We get to make the first and only low bids for whatever we want on E-Buyer! Waiting for the end of the auction is for the little people. We, the elite hack force of the Treasury Department, can claim even better administrative privileges than the rest of these government drones. What's next? Kim Jong Il, give us your slave girls! Wooo Hooo!"

Treasury Secretary Gunther entered the room and was clearly identifiable in the video feed. "Alright, geeks, report!"

"We've done it, sir!" said Hacker One. "We stole a copy of Invisible Hand software, just as you ordered!"

"Good work, Harrison. You too, Garland. I knew I picked the right men for the job."

Douglas Soto looked at Isaiah. "Boss, I think we have our smoking gun."

"Do we ever!" Isaiah looked thoughtful. "I don't want them to know we have this capability yet. Set this video feed to record. The Justice Department has a reputation for snooping around a lot. We can leak it to someone in Justice from an "unnamed source" in Treasury. He or she won't be able to resist scoring his fifteen minutes of fame with the media. They will never know that it really came from us. Then Treasury will think this leak to the media came from Justice."

*   *   *   *   *   *

N minus 6. Minerva and Isaiah videotaped a joint press conference and posted it on FreedomToobz.Ark. It was for Nutritional Abundance Industries and Promethean Software International together. Then they e-mailed a joint press release (with a link to the videotaped press conference) to all major media, including media in their target markets of Africa, India, and Southeast Asia. They also bought text-ads and podcasts for distribution to the chosen cell phone network providers in the target markets. It acquired the "viral spread" so coveted by modern marketers, as friend after friend e-mailed links and/or posted the link on their Facebook pages, or LinkedIn pages.

Soon, it had enough buzz that ZNN, Sky News, FACTS News and several other cable news networks picked it up and played portions in prime time news. Some excerpts:

"Hello, members of the worldwide community of small farmers, shopkeepers, and entrepreneurs. I'm Isaiah Mercury, owner and CEO of Promethean Software International, and chief designer of the new Invisible Hand selling and buying software service for all cell phone users. As many of you may know, the US government has proposed a tax on all users of my buying and selling service, anywhere in the world, simply because it is an American company operating in the United States. This is an unconscionable penalty on my customers, and an arrogant act of usurping the sovereignty of other nations, *all because our politicians can't keep their hands out of other people's pockets.* I have removed that rationale, and that threat.

"How? Following the example of my colleague Minerva Stone, I have liquidated my company in the US, and reincorporated in New Zealand as Promethean Software International, Ltd. Our web site address will remain the same, but I have made arrangements to host it overseas. Our customers will continue to be served seamlessly. All buying and selling with US suppliers will be done through unidentified third party middlemen. The addition of the middlemen will add cost to all transactions with US suppliers, placing them at a competitive disadvantage, but that is the price of electing politicians who can't run a simple passenger train service like Amtrak, but think they can run all the businesses in the country, or the world, for that matter.

"And now, an exciting announcement for farmers large and small, from Minerva Stone, CEO of Nutritional Abundance Industries. Minerva?"

"Thank you, Isaiah. We're pleased and excited to announce an additional benefit to our customers, as a result of our marketing partnership with Promethean Software International. Starting today, and retroactive to last month, any customer who buys a supply of our Carver's Legacy crop seeds, in a quantity big enough to seed at least five acres, will receive a free cell phone preloaded with Invisible Hand access numbers on speed-dial. It will also be prepaid for service for one month with the local cell phone service providers affiliated with PSI. At the end of the month you may continue prepaying for service, or convert over to a longer-term agreement with the affiliated cell service provider. You pay for the Invisible Hand service only if you use it, in the form of charges for text messages to Invisible Hand. If you don't use it, you still get to keep the phone.

"Each of our representatives have over a hundred phones to begin this program, so if you haven't already, order your supply of Carver's Legacy seeds. We know you'll harvest enough to sell some, and then you can sell to a worldwide market with Invisible Hand. When Carver's

Legacy shakes the Invisible Hand, you just got more prosperous! Isaiah?"

"Thanks, Minerva. Our new slogan is *'Tell it and Sell it to the Hand!'* The Invisible Hand, that is. Tell it and Sell it to the invisible helping hand on your cell phone, because that other BIG SELLING SITE *can't hear you* on your cell phone."

Isaiah and Minerva, both clearly enjoying themselves and "hamming it up," stood shoulder to shoulder on the video screen. They both held up the backs of their cell phones to the camera. Both phones bore a graphic of a hand outlined on the back. They both put their cell phones to their ears and said to the camera, "This Hand is listening, so tell it to the Hand. If this service is not offered where you live, call this new international access number for a direct link: CARVERSHAND."

*   *   *   *   *   *

The "Carver shakes the Invisible Hand" video on FreedomToobz.Ark got five million hits the first day it was posted. By the end of the week, the stats showed twenty-five million hits.

At week's end, over ten thousand cell phones had been given away with purchases of Carver's Legacy seeds. Invisible Hand transactions hit seven million that week.

*   *   *   *   *   *

N minus 5. A low level Deputy Assistant Counsel for the Assistant Attorney General for Corporate Enforcement received an intriguing e-mail that morning with the subject line, *Interesting Video from Treasury*. There was a video attachment, and an origin e-mail suffix showing that it had come from within Treasury, but no name traceable to any specific person or specific computer within Treasury. The body of the e-mail said only, *"This ought to be made public, as a service to the planet."*

One hour after receiving it, the Assistant Counsel's personal cell phone rang. "This is Amanda Bernata, of the Washington DirtDig news blog. I understand you have some interesting video from Treasury?" A leak was in progress.

By ten a.m. the video was posted on Washington DirtDig.com, with a breathless introduction from Amanda Bernata: "Breaking news. A

190

source within the Justice Department leaked this video of a secret cyber hacker unit in the Treasury Department, operating under the explicit orders of Treasury Secretary Gunther. The video also reveals a link to Attorney General Handford, and implicates both cabinet officers in a conspiracy to steal the intellectual property of private American business firms. A major American software firm is also implicated in this government corruption. No firm can have secrets from these hackers, and no firm can keep proprietary data safe from these government pirates. The hackers can be clearly heard on the videotape, scheming to auction off software stolen from African-American entrepreneur Isaiah Mercury to the highest bidder. Entrepreneurs of America, disconnect from the internet, because no one's intellectual property is safe while these pirates cruise the new Spanish Main, the internet, looking for victims to pillage and loot. And now the video."

This report enjoyed a viral spread to the usual suspects: Politico.com, the Drudge Report, and others. At noon ZNN and FACTS News, each seeking to scoop the other, mentioned it and directed viewers to the website. Before two o'clock, talk radio hosts across the country were playing excerpts and taking phone calls about it. Feeling the viral pressure, even CBC and ABC mentioned it briefly on their evening news reports. NBC held out and ignored it.

Around the country, CEO after CEO and entrepreneur after entrepreneur pulled the plug on internet connections to their servers containing sensitive information. The flow of business transactions and business communications in the US slowed to a crawl. Hotmail and G-mail added millions of new accounts in a matter of hours, finally shutting down their servers. Business people everywhere shifted to anonymous e-mail accounts to communicate. Congress, Justice, and Treasury were flooded with angry e-mails. Their servers overloaded and shut down by eight o'clock that evening.

Someone had managed to get the private home numbers and e-mail addresses of congressmen and posted them on the internet. Their home phones rang continuously long after midnight. One congressman found four thousand e-mails waiting to download into his home computer.

*   *   *   *   *   *

N minus 4. At ten o'clock the next morning, under intense pressure from congress and other cabinet level departments, the President directed Treasury to hold a press conference and release this statement: "The recent publicity scare about the so-called cyber-hacking pirates at the Treasury Department was due to internal security footage that was leaked and taken out of context, and some juvenile comments by IT personnel who have now been fired. The comments on the video were in fact code language used for security purposes, and referred to routine, ongoing cyber-surveillance of criminal conspiracies that are under a joint investigation by the Justice Department and the Treasury Department. There is no cause for concern.

"Both the Justice Department and the Treasury Department reassure all American businesspeople that their private proprietary data is treated as confidential. Their data is merely under regular government agency review for the appropriate transparency and conformity to the latest policy pronouncements of this administration. This is routine and normal and no cause for alarm."

This did nothing whatsoever to reassure business people, who watched with incredulity while the Treasury Department spokesperson spoke of "regular review" of their data for "appropriate transparency."

On one of the big three television network news shows, Charles Gibbon observed, "Maybe I don't understand the meaning of words anymore. The Treasury spokesperson said that 'private proprietary data' is merely under regular government agency review for appropriate transparency? In my dictionary, *transparency* implies that the proprietary data is not private. This is a contradiction of what they were trying to reassure us about, or at least what I think they were trying to reassure us about, that no one is snooping into our private data. But if there is 'regular government agency review,' then they are saying that they ARE snooping into our private data. Without warrants. I hope the President will clarify this during his long-awaited speech scheduled four days from now."

By midnight, millions of databases had been shifted to offshore servers, and thousands of US small business and corporate servers had been wiped clean. Secretaries of State and Commerce in other countries received over ten million e-applications to create foreign corporations by 2 a.m. Trillions in small business capital was shifted to millions of overseas bank accounts by 3 a.m.

192

*   *   *   *   *   *

N minus 3. When the morning television news began, everything was normal. By 9 a.m., the bankers had seen what had happened with their millions of small business customers. They informed the appropriate agencies, who informed the FDIC that the cash reserves of thousands of banks across the country were now technically in default by FDIC standards. The transferred assets were far too much for the FDIC to cover with its established reserves.

The chairperson of the FDIC called Treasury. "Earnest, you're going to have to tell the Federal Reserve to speed up the printing presses. Small businesses have shifted massive amounts of money overseas, overnight. We need more money to cover the losses we're projecting for the banks. This fleeing capital has created the perfect storm of bank defaults, and we can't cover them all."

"Oh s__t. What will we tell the President?"

"Tell him what you told him the last six times: that this is a complex financial crisis, that Treasury needs to inject more capital to avoid a worldwide financial melt-down, and that if he reassures the American people, we will come through this all right."

*   *   *   *   *   *

N minus 2. Minerva, Isaiah, Grace, and Douglas Soto conferred.

"Do we stick to the countdown? Is it still the right time to tell them?" asked Grace.

"I think so," said Isaiah.

He looked at Douglas. "I concur."

Minerva nodded her head emphatically. "Let's do it."

Their video team prepared for another video press release. The four of them got to work.

*   *   *   *   *   *

N minus 1. The President's press secretary asked the major networks for more airtime for the President's speech scheduled for the next day, so that he could include a special announcement to reassure the

American people. Sensing something major, they alerted their sales departments, who hastily called advertisers to tell them that the new rates would be higher for ads immediately preceding and after the presidential address. They double-checked their satellite feeds from the White House press room.

*   *   *   *   *   *

Noah minus 0. At 8 p.m. President Fletcher walked to his podium adorned with a special logo reading "Press Conference of the President of the United States." The networks had been running teaser ads alerting people to tune in for a special reassurance announcement from the President. They used the "branding tag line" for the press conference given to them by the White House Press Secretary. The crawler at the bottom of the screen read "Tune in at 8 p.m. for the *Concerns & Reassurance Address by the President.*" Sometimes it was the acronym.

"Ladies and Gentlepersons, my fellow Americans, and my fellow citizens of the planet, I come before you today in a time of grave economic crisis. I speak particularly to our small business entrepreneurs, to offer them reassurance about their privacy and confidentiality under this administration.

"Recent events have led some businesspeople to take certain actions, in what they thought was a reasonable and prudent move to protect themselves. Let me both reassure them and warn them. I reassure them that under my administration your private and proprietary business data will be kept confidential. We only review and monitor the business transactions of American businesses, small and large, because, as I've always said, we have your best interests at heart, and we know what is best for you.

"I warn all Americans that moving capital without authorization from the Treasury Department is a violation of my new executive order 3678, issued this morning, and made retroactive to last week. I've always said that your capital is held in trust for future generations. Let me be clear: I am now that future generation and I am the one who holds your capital in trust . . ."

The screen flickered for a minute, and the face of Isaiah Mercury came on the air, replacing that of the President. "My fellow Americans, this is not a presidential teleprompter malfunction. I make no apology for this interruption. This President's men hijacked one of my data streams, and now I am hijacking one of his.

"In the New Testament, John 8:32, Jesus said: *'And ye shall know the truth, the truth shall make you free.'* A wise man from my youth, a Mister Charles Greige, added this pearl of wisdom attributed to President James A. Garfield: *'The truth shall make you free, but first it will make you miserable.'* Unfortunately, you are beginning to learn the truths about current events and corruption within your own government, and these truths will make you miserable. But they can make you free, if you act on these truths. If you are prepared to work through your misery, like General George Washington worked through his misery and despair at Valley Forge, then go to this web site to start your journey to truth and freedom: www.thetruthwillmakeyoufree.Ark. You can also go to channel 1776 on your television. A special TV broadcast will be there, overriding the normal channel.

"I am now showing you a painting of General Washington kneeling in the snow at Valley Forge to pray for divine help and guidance. These are dark times for America, but if you can kneel down and pray like the father of our country, we may get some help like he did."

Here Isaiah kneeled, and the camera drew back to show him on one knee, bowing his head, and closing his eyes. "Heavenly Father, help our nation in this hour of need." He opened his eyes and looked into the camera. "Thank you, and may God bless America."

The President reappeared on the screen. ". . . when you make the sacrifices I ask of you, you will be sacrificing for your country. As I've always said, these are the sacrifices we've been waiting for, and when you sacrifice, you will realize that by making these sacrifices, I know what is in your best interests, and I will tell you what your best interests are. Trust in me, for I am the trust you have been waiting for.

"Moving on to other matters, We have today signed seventeen new executive orders, and this means that We will no longer allow Americans to do the following seventeen things . . ."

Very few people heard the last sentences uttered by the President, as they were scrambling to find the television channel 1776 or the .Ark internet domain suggested by Isaiah. Once there, they saw Isaiah and heard this video message:

"My fellow Americans, my name is Isaiah Mercury. If you haven't seen the surveillance video smuggled out of the Treasury Department, go to the link shown on this page. It is firsthand proof that, in the words of American humorist Mark Twain, 'No man's life, liberty, and property are safe while the legislature is in session.' His statement is also true for the executive branch. The government's explanations are self-contradictory lies, as you have seen. They admit that they are snooping on your private business data, *'for your own good'* as if we are children and they're our parents.

"I speak now to all Americans: working men and women, tinkerers, inventors, entrepreneurs, and plain old independent contrarian cusses who like to run their own lives their own way. Running your own life your own way *is the American way.* If you are ready to fight back, then fight like Mohammed Ali: *float like a butterfly, sting like a bee.* Float like a butterfly and duck the punches of your opponent. When he swings, don't be there. He just took a big swing at me, and I wasn't there. I moved my business to New Zealand!

"Several years ago, some friends and I could see that there was a rising flood of government corruption and coercion starting to drown the hardworking families of America. Increasing taxes and regulations have made it hard to earn a living and raise a family without government busybodies telling you how to do every little thing. Talk about oppressed groups! Soon we will all live like refugees. It will be like the aftermath of hurricane Katrina for everyone in America.

"We began to realize that the constant barrage of new taxes, new regulations and government takeovers of industry after industry are part of a plan to eliminate personal freedoms in America. We started to connect the dots, and the dots revealed that the various 'activist' groups, environmental groups, social justice groups, businesses wanting bailouts and favors from the government, the major political parties, the government agencies themselves, and the so-called special interest groups, all have one 'special interest' in common . . . *they want power and control over you and how you live your life.* They all think they know better than you and have the right to tell you what to do.

"So, my friends and I planned a way to protect ourselves when it got to the point that power-hungry politicians forced too much control over our lives. My wife, the Nobel Prize-winning botanist Dr. Grace Washington, came to the same conclusion and the same idea independently. She invented the perfect name for it: The Noah Option."

Grace joined Isaiah on the screen. Then the camera focused on her alone.

"My fellow Americans, you recently saw me in a televised show trial in Washington, D.C., on phony trumped-up charges. Do you know what they really wanted? They were blackmailing me. The Justice Department of the United States of America was in collusion with the Pristine Influence on Society Foundation. They wanted me to lure Minerva Stone into the country so they could imprison her. Her crime? Feeding the hungry people of Africa, India, and Asia with the seeds I invented. They also wanted to destroy the supplies of those seeds around the world. Why? Because they in their god-like wisdom have decided that the population of the world is 'unsustainable' and has to be cut back by sixty percent. Go to the PRIS web site if you don't believe me. If they change it today, you can see what they originally said on an archived copy of their web site on .Ark. You can also click on the link on this web page marked 'blackmail' to see the video my husband secretly made of the Assistant Federal Prosecutor blackmailing me in the pretrial conference.

"Eliminate sixty percent of the population of the earth! That means the starvation of living human beings, individuals like you and me with families, children, and grandparents. This goes beyond genocide. This is humanicide. Hitler killed six million Jews. They want to kill hundreds of millions of all ethnic groups. PRIS and all of their sympathizers are mass murderers. They are happy to starve you and your family if it suits their purposes."

Grace paused and held up a picture of Noah's Ark to the camera.

"Those of you who went to Sunday School will remember the story of Noah. God had decided to destroy all of wicked mankind in a flood. But God decided that Noah and his sons and daughters-in-law were worth saving. So He instructed them on how to construct an ark and bring two of every animal in it, male and female, so that they could survive the flood and then repopulate the earth and start fresh. So the animals went into the ark, two by two. After the flood, mankind started over. God sent the rainbow in the clouds as a sign of his promise that He would never do it again.

"We decided that we would find or create little "Arks," places where honest people, whether businesspeople or craftsmen or just people who didn't mind doing an honest day's work, could live and be safe from this flood of corruption, coercion and control. Safe from the corrupt politicians in America or anywhere else; politicians who want to take your money and run every little detail of your lives. If the flood of corruption ever subsides in America, maybe we'll come back, two by two, and start over, like Noah and his family. We'll look for a rainbow of economic and personal freedom to know when it is safe to come back. Maybe then we can re-found America on the principles that once made her great.

"I'm not going to tell you where these places are, but if you really want to come to one of Noah's Arks, keep coming to these web pages or occasional messages on television channel 1776, and look for clues. Talk to people you trust; talk to people in your church. If you are sincere, 'seek, and ye shall find. Knock, and it shall be opened to you.' When you've figured it out, just get out. Don't tell everyone. Close up shop and come. Disappear. You probably won't be able to bring many of your possessions with you, but you will be bringing the most valuable possession you own: your mind. All the works of civilization, all of healthcare and agriculture and art and technology came from the mind of man. You can rebuild anything with that one tool: your mind.

"Once you figure it out, if you need help getting your family out, contact us through this web site. We'll help. But be sure everybody in your family *wants* to leave. Remember Lot's wife. If they hesitate and look back, they'll be lost. I'll say no more about this part, because the powerful bureaucrats would love to find us and stop us.

"One requirement, though. Don't come to an Ark if you like to control other people, tell them how to live their lives, and dream up and enforce a bunch of rules on other people. In the Arks, one of our principles is *Mind Your Own Business*."

The camera switched back to Isaiah.

"I will tell you about one Ark place, because I'm here and I've been assured by people I trust in this government that we are safe here. Safe from extradition on trumped-up charges, and safe to pursue our livelihoods, raise families, and grow our businesses. I've moved to New Zealand and set up my business here. Like Minerva Stone, I will make this my home and headquarters and do business with the rest of the world from here. Americans can do business with me through my access numbers that connect them through other countries, if they want to.

"When you decide you've had enough of busybodies trying to run your life, enough of government tax-thieves taking your money and your ideas, enough of special interest group Pharisee hypocrites preaching to you how to live but not ever doing it themselves, then get out. Find an Ark and come into it. You are welcome to come alone, or with your mate, or with your family. Together, we will wait for the waters of corruption and power-hunger to subside. And while we wait, we will build a new world for ourselves, as Noah and his family did. Maybe we'll never come back. Their loss.

"I speak again to all American tinkerers, inventers, entrepreneurs, hard workers, and plain old independent contrarian cusses who like to do things your own way. I am one of you. The special interest groups, the media elite, and the government all try to make you feel ashamed of what you do. They call you selfish, greedy, money grubbing, all because you want to be paid for what you produce. I say to you that people who are not paid for what they produce are *slaves*. We are a free people.

"I say, be proud of what you do. Be proud that your hard work, your inventions and the services of your businesses, large and small, make life better for everyone. Be proud that you make a payroll and create jobs for other people to support their families. God bless the man who invented the electric drill! I hope he got rich off his invention. He makes my life better every time I have to drill a hole. He didn't exploit me. He helped me. He didn't make me buy his drill; I *wanted* to buy his invention.

"Making money is a by-product of serving others with goods and services that they like well enough to voluntarily pay for. Greed is taking money from others against their will. The only way to do that is through theft, government taxation or regulations. So, for example, one company 'persuaded' enough congressmen to make their type of light bulbs required by law, instead of inventing a light bulb that saved enough on electric bills and was easy to use, so that customers would *want* to buy it. Now you don't have a choice about buying the best light bulb for yourself; they have the government enforced monopoly, and they rake in unearned profits.

"Grace and I have retreated into an Ark, floating and safe from a flood of corruption, control, jealousy, and persecution against those who work for a living and prosper in their work. Someday this flood will subside.

"When that dove flies onto the windowsill of my Ark with an advertising flyer for green olives in her beak, then I'll know it's safe again for people to engage in buying and selling and entrepreneurship in America. Buying and selling the best we have created to offer each other, without being treated like criminals or children or slaves. Then, as Dr. Martin Luther King told us we would, we will all shout together, black and white, male and female, Christian and Muslim and Jew and Buddhist, in the words of the old spiritual, 'Free at last, free at last, thank God Almighty, we are free at last.'"

Chapter Sixteen

N plus 1. Stephanie Jones of Jones Systems pulled into the parking lot of her small engineering company the next morning and got out with her "to go" cup of coffee from home. Russell Myers, her quality control engineer, was closing his car door next to hers. "Good Morning, Russell."

"Morning. Say, Stephanie? Got a minute?"

"Sure, Russell."

"I mean here, before we get inside with the others."

"OK." She took a sip of her coffee and turned to face Russell.

He moved close to her, closer than he normally did. He lowered his voice, "Stephanie, when you go, Marge and I want to go too."

She instantly knew what he was talking about. "OK. I don't know which Ark yet."

"Whither thou goest . . ." She nodded. He nodded. They both walked into the shop.

*   *   *   *   *   *

N plus 2. Felix Trayler usually opened up the office at the ten-person CPA firm where he worked, Alexander & Sons, LLC. Felix had been with the owner, John Alexander, for over twenty years. He was an early bird who liked to start early and make the coffee. John Alexander and his son Jack had long ago given him a key. He brought out his key chain as he walked to the front door, and then stopped short. On the door was stenciled in day-glow orange paint a symbol:

Felix stared at it a moment, and then whispered, "Godspeed, old friend." On the receptionist's desk inside he found eight envelopes. He opened the one addressed to him. It was a generous severance check.

*   *   *   *   *   *

N plus 3. Sue Hart pulled her panel truck up to the loading dock. The sign read "Courier Express. Local express delivery service." She had been delivering late airline luggage and picking up packages all day. When she went up the stairs to begin unloading, she saw an envelope with her name on it. "Dear Sue," she read, "Here is your severance check. Federalized Express has already agreed to come over tonight and transfer all packages to their facility. I've enclosed a letter of reference that should help you get another job. You are a reliable and hard worker. I'll miss you. Mary and I have gone 'two by two." Take care of yourself. ~ Joe." On the other table she saw envelopes with the names of the other six drivers. She sat down and began to cry.

*   *   *   *   *   *

N plus 4. Caldwell Cameron watched as the last equipment operator parked his backhoe and walked to his pickup truck. "Good night, Bart."

" 'Night." He drove out the gate.

Caldwell had been in the grading business for thirty-three years and had built up the business from himself and one bobcat to fifteen pieces of equipment and eleven employees. He called his auctioneer on his cell. "Barry, I'm mailing the key for the front gate to you. You'll put them in your Saturday auction? Good. You have the bank routing to send me the proceeds. Thanks." He drove out of his gate and stopped. He swung the chain link gate shut and clicked the padlock. He put severance envelopes in the rural mailbox and raised the red flag for outgoing mail. Then he hung a hand-made cardboard sign on the gate that read: 2 X 2.

He smiled, remembering Genesis *"They went in two by two unto Noah into the ark . . ."* Then he sighed, thinking, *Noah only had to wait a hundred and fifty days. We might have to wait several generations.*

*   *   *   *   *   *

N plus 7. By week's end, thirty thousand small businesses across the nation had shut down and the owners disappeared. The unemployment rate across the nation ticked up from 14 percent to 18 percent. Thousands of photos and videos of the Ark logos and "2 x 2" signs stenciled and hand-painted on doors and gates of closed businesses were posted to FreedomToobz.Ark and other sites. Local television news began showing the signs and reporting on the closings and the disappearances. Network news ignored it. The grapevine spread the news.

*   *   *   *   *   *

N plus 30. By the end of the month, one hundred and fifty thousand small businesses had closed. Three trillion dollars of capital had slipped out to overseas accounts. The Treasury Department took notice and began looking for more ways to shut off the dollar drain.

Word along the Mexican border was that the coyotes could now pick up some extra money going the other way: smuggling Americans into Mexico. The influx of illegals into the US had slowed with the worsening economy. Some of the old Underground Railroad routes into Canada were reactivated by the Constitutional Resistance Movement. The CRM let it be known that they would help people who wanted to get to an Ark safe zone. In Montana, North Dakota, western Washington state, and Idaho, hunting and fishing guides put up hand-painted "2x2" signs. This signaled that, for a cash fee, they would smuggle you across the border into Canada. Family vacations to the border states became popular. Motels in even the smaller towns along the northern border were booked full for months in advance.

There were rumored to be several Ark locations within the United States, but no one could confirm this. This was officially listed as an urban myth on one of the web sites devoted to debunking popular rumors.

Bumper stickers began appearing that said "Pray for the Arks," "Lord, send the dove of Capitalism." "My son/daughter is an Ark-Angel" "2x2 — Who's next?" and "Pray for a Rainbow." Others popped up: "Constitutionalists unite! Strike off your chains!" "Fascists Fear Our Constitution."

*   *   *   *   *   *

N plus 60. By the end of the second month, every town in America had lost a dozen or more businesses. Unemployment nationwide had ticked up to 20 percent. Whenever businesses shut down to "go Ark" there was a ripple effect of tipping other businesses into shutdown or bankruptcy. There were critical shortages of harvesting contractors and crews and equipment in the Midwest. Many quarterly tax payments to the IRS/Treasury were late due to the disappearance of many CPAs who had handled this for local businesses. At least fifty percent of infrastructure road projects were behind schedule (even more than usual) due to contractors closing down, and thirty-five percent of scheduled airline flights were cancelled due to the shutdown of a number of aircraft maintenance companies and the disappearance of key engineers from the remaining aircraft maintenance companies.

*   *   *   *   *   *

N plus 90. By the end of the third month, sixty percent of American towns were experiencing periodic brownouts and outages due to interruptions in coal deliveries to power plants. Railroad engineers and dispatchers were "going Ark." Technicians and engineers in the power plants themselves were "going Ark." Food processing and canning plants were at 70 percent of capacity due to key manager and technician shortages.

*   *   *   *   *   *

N plus 92. At the start of the fourth month, the President began to sip his morning coffee as he looked over his briefing papers. He suddenly made a face. "What the hell?" He looked into his coffee cup. It was black. "Frederick!" he called to his steward.

"Yes sir?"

"Where is the cream for my coffee?"

"Sorry sir, we did not get our delivery of milk and cream this week, and we're fresh out."

"What!"

"Sorry sir, that's all I know."

The President picked up his phone. "Send in the chief of staff, *now*."

"Yes Sir."

The chief of staff hurried in. "Sir?"

"Sim, there is no cream for my coffee! What the hell is going on?"

"Sir?"

"The chef for the President of the United States of America can't get cream for the President's coffee. I want to you to find out why and report back to me."

"Yes sir."

He returned in thirty minutes. "Sir, the restaurant supply company lost their dairy source. The dairy farmer shut down and "went Ark" as they're saying nowadays. It will take them several days to find another supplier."

"Tell the chef to get another restaurant supply company."

"Yes sir."

At lunch, the White House chef asked to speak to the President. "Good afternoon, Mr. President. How do you like this lunch?"

"Very well, thank you, Ramon."

"Sir, I wanted to tell you in person that no other restaurant supply company can guarantee a supply of milk every day. They're all having supply problems from the dairies."

"What's the problem?"

"It seems that many of the maintenance contractors for the automatic milking machines have "gone Ark," and the machines are breaking down. It seems there's a big dairy industry in New Zealand and Australia, sir, if you take my meaning."

"I understand. Thank you. Oh! Does this mean a shortage of my ice cream too?"

"Sir, we're down to our last half gallon."

*   *   *   *   *   *

N plus 93. At a special emergency cabinet meeting the next day, the President addressed his cabinet officers. "Ladies and Gentlepersons, we're now seeing economic dislocations and shortages reaching all the way into the White House. I can't get cream for my coffee because many of the independent maintenance contractors for the milking machines have 'gone Ark,' and we all know what that means."

The assembled secretaries of various departments looked at one another uneasily. They did not like to admit that this "Ark" thing was real.

"CIA Director Smythe, have you found out any locations of these so-called Arks?"

"No, Mr. President, other than New Zealand, we don't know. We suspect some in Australia, but that's not confirmed yet."

"Well, find them! We want to put pressure on those countries to repatriate our citizens."

"Yes sir."

"Secretary of State Carlyle, what luck are you having pressuring New Zealand to stop harboring these fugitives?"

"None, Mr. President. The prime minister said that unless we had evidence that they had committed crimes against persons or property, they would not be extradited. He claims that they are legal immigrants."

The President spoke again. "Madame Director of Homeland Security, I, we, want increased patrols on the Mexican and Canadian borders to stop these skilled personnel from escaping to these "Ark" places. Air travel is down, so shift some TSA people from the airports to the borders. General Friedman, help her on the Mexican border with some army units. We know it's not legal to deploy our military within our own borders, but put out a cover story that these are training missions for desert warfare. General, we also want you to prepare labor camps in the West, Midwest, and Atlantic states, — enough to accommodate fifteen million people, with appropriate guards and trucks and buses for transporting these people to work on a daily basis. See to it."

Next he turned to the Secretary of Labor. "Secretary Tianin, we want you to create work crews in these labor camps organized by skill shortage and where the skills are needed. For example, we can put unskilled people on crews to do the milking at these dairies where the milking machines are breaking down. We can put people on crews to man these food processing plants and canning plants. We can put people on these construction crews building roads. Create other crews to meet other needs, particularly where technology and organization is involved. This is a national emergency."

To the Secretary of Homeland Security and the Chairman of the Joint Chiefs of Staff of the Armed Forces, he said, "We want you to plan to put any persons that you pick up at the borders into these camps. We need the labor. We need precisely the kind of skilled labor, brains, and initiative that these 'Ark' people have."

Turning back to the Secretary of Labor, "Secretary Tianin, plan on taking people collecting unemployment compensation into these camps too. Make these Ark people the supervisors of your work crews for any unskilled unemployed people that you sweep up. Make the usual exceptions for our friends, but get us people."

To the Attorney General, Director of the Census, Secretary of Commerce and Secretary of the Treasury, he directed, "We want you four to make up a list of people who have skills that would fill our national skills shortage." He paused, "Especially people with the skills to repair these milking machines. I want cream for my coffee."

To his Chief of Staff, "Mr. Smythe, we want you to prepare legislation that will empower me, us, We, to intern as many of our citizens as we deem either a security risk, a flight risk, or vital to the national interest. Call it the American Skills Preservation Act."

To his press secretary, "Mr. Damon, prepare a speech for us that will justify interning citizens to these labor camps in the name of the greater good and the national interest. Don't call them labor camps; call them American Prosperity Camps, where our motto is 'Work together for national prosperity. Be happy in your work, for you are the workers we have been waiting for."

*   *   *   *   *   *

N plus 107. A group of Wisconsin dairy farmers and their families were camping outside Ely, Minnesota, near the Canadian border, waiting for the fishing guide to show up and guide them to their 'fishing spot' in Canada. It was early dawn, and several dads had put coffee pots on their camping stoves. They were preparing to cook breakfast for their families. The smell of hot coffee drifted across the misty campground.

Near one picnic table, a soldier in full combat gear emerged from the mist, holding an M-16A2 combat rifle across his body.

Startled, the father stepped back and said, "Who are you?"

The soldier smiled and replied, "Going somewhere?"

"We're camping."

The farmer's wife and eight-year-old daughter came out of the tent. The soldier raised his rifle and pointed it at them. "Sir, what authorization do you have to be camping here?"

The farmer stepped in front of the gun.

"Please! Don't point that gun at my family!" The soldier was joined by two others.

He kept the M-16 trained on the family. "Sir, I'll ask you again, what authorization do you have to be camping here?"

"None! We've camped here dozens of times in the past. We've never needed authorization. This is America. We don't live by permission in a free country. What is this?"

The soldier motioned to his teammates to fan out. "Sir, what is your profession?"

"Dairy farmer."

The soldier smiled again. "Oh, we've got work that will make you happy. You and your family will be interned in an American Prosperity Camp on a dairy farm near Washington, D.C. The President needs cream for his coffee." He lowered his weapon; the wife and daughter hugged the father and looked at the soldier fearfully.

The other families (about thirty people including children) walked toward them, herded by soldiers with rifles. A black government SUV drove up. A man in a suit and tie got out and walked toward the group guarded by the soldiers.

He held up a piece of paper and announced, "We are the Superintendent of American Prosperity Camps for the Mid-Atlantic States. You are hereby interned under the American Skills Preservation Act. You were attempting to leave the country with skills you acquired in this country. The United States gave you the opportunity to learn those skills, and those skills rightfully belong to the people. You will now be taken to camps where you will use those skills on behalf of their rightful owners, the citizens of the United States."

The farmer spoke up again, "We *are* the citizens of the United States. Interned? But we don't want to go. You can't own our skills without owning us. Owning another human being is prohibited by the 13th Amendment to the United States Constitution." He pulled a small copy of the US Constitution from his overalls pocket, flipped a few pages, and read, "Neither slavery nor involuntary servitude, except as a punishment for crime whereof the party shall have been duly convicted, shall exist within the United States, or any place subject to their jurisdiction." He looked at the superintendent. "Unless we're being punished for a crime, you can't force us to work. This so called 'internment' of yours is slavery."

"Oh, a campground lawyer, eh?" The superintendent looked him over. "You'll do well for a working crew leader, interpreting and enforcing rules for the others. Well, as it so happens, you are being punished for a crime — the crime of fleeing the country with valuable skills that belong to the people."

The farmer met his gaze calmly. "We're camping in the United States of America, so we haven't fled. Each person's skills belong to each individual person who worked to learn them, not to some vague group you call 'the people.' 'The people' have never exercised skills. Only individuals demonstrate skills. 'The people' never milked my cows. I did."

"That's an old-fashioned way of thinking. After all, 'It takes a village . . .' Skills aren't learned in isolation, they're learned in a group, and so that group owns the skills, and that group owns those who learned the skills. You belong to the group."

"Belonging to someone, even a group, sounds like slavery to me, Massa."

The superintendent's face grew red. "I am not your master; the people of the United States are your masters. We are only their duly appointed agent. As to the technicality of you still being on US soil, we're going to convict you and every member of your party of criminal conspiracy of *intention* to flee the country with skills that don't belong to you. So, it does not matter that you are still on US soil. We have a witness who will testify about your plans to escape to one of those 'Arks' after you got into Canada."

He turned and nodded toward the black SUV. A soldier got out of the back and pulled out a man in handcuffs. It was the fishing guide. He looked sorrowfully at the farmer.

"They threatened my family! I had to tell them what they wanted to know. I'm sorry." He looked at the children in the group. "I'm sorry," he said again, looking down.

"Jefferson weeps," said the farmer.

A prison bus pulled up. The soldiers began putting ankle shackles on everyone, including the children. As one soldier knelt to put shackles on a child's ankles, a nearby mother looked sharply at him.

"Barney?"

He looked up, "Aunt Rose?"

"Barney, how can you do this to children? And your fellow Americans?"

He looked back down. "I'm sorry, Aunt Rose. I'm under orders. The National Guard reports directly to the Commander in Chief now." He clicked the shackles closed around the child's ankles. The prisoners were shuffled into the bus.

As the bus pulled off, the superintendent looked at a clip board given to him by a soldier. "Five families of dairy farmers. Excellent. The President will be pleased. Now he'll get cream for his coffee. More American skills preserved for the nation." He looked at his watch. "It's still early. We can round up more at the next campground. Let's go." He got back into the passenger side of the SUV. It pulled out of the campground.

*   *   *   *   *   *

N plus 108. George T'Chaka Wright and his wife Estelle were just sitting down to their morning coffee. There was a sharp knocking at the door.

"Can't they see the doorbell? No need to knock the door down!" said George as he got up from the table. Three men in dark suits stood on the porch. A black SUV was parked in the driveway.

"Citizen George Wright?" the closest man asked.

"President George T'Chaka Wright, of Tuskegee University," George answered. "And who might you be?"

"Citizen Wright, we are FBI agents, here to serve you and your wife Estelle with an internment order under the American Preservation of Skills Act. You and Mrs. Wright are to come with us, sir."

"And you, sir, are out of order," replied George, struggling to hold his temper. "Mrs. Wright and I do not have any of the skills listed on the government's shortage of skills list, and we are not in the act of fleeing the country. We're sitting down to our morning coffee, which, under more civilized circumstances, we might have invited you to enjoy with us. You may call my lawyer, Mr. Carl Wainwright of Washington, with any further inquiries. He's in the book. Good day to you." He started to close the door.

The lead agent put his foot in the door, forced it open, and stepped into the house. George reacted instinctively with a kempo karate take-down. The agent's head cracked against the floor and he lost

210

consciousness. The other two agents drew guns and shouted, "Step back! Hands on your head and kneel!"

As George complied, Estelle rushed into the room. "What in the world?"

One agent pointed his gun at her and barked, "Hands on your head and kneel!"

She looked at him in shock. "By what authority do you invade our home with guns?"

"Ma'am, put your hands on your head and kneel, NOW!"

"Estelle!" said George. "Do what he says, please."

She carefully knelt down, using her hands to steady herself, and then placed her hands on her head. One agent then holstered his gun, walked behind George and Estelle, and handcuffed them both.

The agent on the floor stirred, groaned, and moved his head carefully, as he slowly rose to a sitting position. "What happened?" he asked groggily.

"Young man, you forced your way into my home without a warrant or proper identification, so I defended myself and my family," George replied from his kneeling position.

The agent gingerly rose to a standing position, holding his head with one hand. He reached into his jacket pocket and produced a piece of paper, then a badge.

"Citizen Wright, this badge identifies me as an agent of the people's Federal Bureaus of Investigation. This warrant for the internment of you and your wife specifies your skills as a geneticist and DNA bio-engineer. It's signed by Secretary Tianin of the Department of Labor."

Sizing up the situation, George saw that there was no way out. Thinking quickly, he said, "I'm the one with the skills, not Estelle. Let her go."

"Sorry, Citizen Wright, the warrant for internment specifies both you and Mrs. Wright are to be interned."

George pleaded, "But why? She doesn't have the skills you want. Let her go."

The agent looked back at the warrant, reading quickly. He flipped a page over. "Here it is: 'Mrs. Wright is to be interned for her skill in retaining the skills of Citizen Wright within the country.'"

George's mouth set into a stern line. "So, she is a hostage to ensure that I don't attempt to escape?"

The agent looked at him, and then at the warrant. "She is to be detained in a women's facility in Maryland not far from where you will work in an American Prosperity Camp, doing your patriotic duty to use your skills for we the people."

He nodded at the other agents. "Let's go." They pulled Estelle and George to their feet and force-marched them out the front door. The two cups of coffee sat on the empty kitchen table, steam rising.

*   *   *   *   *   *

N plus 110. Two days later, George was taken from the camp dormitory room (housing eight people in bunks), and loaded into a prison van, wearing orange overalls and shackles on his ankles and wrists. The van drove out of the camp gates manned by guards in Army fatigues and carrying automatic weapons. The camp was surrounded by high, chain-link fences topped by barbed wire. Forty-five minutes later the van stopped in front of a large complex of buildings. During the drive, George had noticed that they passed through the small town of Denton, Maryland. *I'm on the Eastern Shore of Maryland,* he thought.

George was taken from the van and shuffled into the front doors, which the guards unlocked with a security card. "Citizen Wright, this is where you'll work from now on," said the guard on his right.

"So, the return of slavery," said George sarcastically. They entered a laboratory room where stainless steel equipment and instruments gleamed.

"High-tech slavery, but still slavery," he repeated.

A short man in a lab coat walked up. "Dr. Wright?"

George looked down at him. "That's *Citizen* Wright to you," he said.

Ignoring this, the man extended his hand and said, "I'm Dr. McClellan, director of the ethical trans-genetic harvesting operations substation, known as ETHOS. You'll be working for me here at ETHOS. You have well-known and valuable skills, Dr. Wright. I especially requested you when the Department of Labor asked me for my requisition of needed citizen skills."

George did not extend a shackled hand. Instead, he shuffled in a manner to make the chains clink. "Yes, Massa." The director dropped his outstretched hand.

"Dr. Wright, I know that you must resent being brought here against your will, but this is a matter of national priorities and national skill shortages. I requisitioned your skills because your country needs them. And, I was pretty sure that you wouldn't come voluntarily."

"Why didn't you simply ask me politely first, and find out?" George looked angry.

Abruptly, the director turned. "Let me show you your new work. Guards, escort the skills internee, if you please." He pushed open the swinging door into an adjacent lab. It was a large warehouse-sized room, and long row after long row of cylindrical incubators stretched off to the far side of the room. George recognized the type of incubators used for intensive care of premature babies. One of his nephews had been born prematurely and placed in such an incubator at the hospital. George looked into the glass window on one of the incubators and saw a tiny child attached to feeding tubes.

The Director swept one arm over the incubator farm in a gesture of inclusion. "Here we have taken stem cell research to the next level. We do not yet have the knowledge to stimulate stem cells to grow specific organs for use in organ transplants. So we take embryos and grow them to maturity in this embryo farm. Then we harvest the human organs from them."

He turned to the wall where glass containers had nutrients pumped in. George turned and looked. He turned pale and felt nauseous. He was looking at small hearts and livers.

"Did you say embryo farm? For harvesting human organs?" asked George in a faint voice.

"That's correct," said the director briskly.

George fell to his knees, bent over and vomited on the floor.

"A common first-time reaction. Take him to the washroom and clean him up," said the director briskly. "Call for the janitor to clean this up." The guards pulled George up and shuffled him back through the swinging doors. After cleaning him up, they brought him to a smaller lab with windows looking out over the embryo farm. They placed him on a lab stool in front of a work table.

The director entered.

"You are slaughtering babies like farm animals and using their organs for human transplants?" asked George, still in a weakened voice.

"Your words are judgmental, but the facts are correct," said the director tonelessly.

"How much a pound for human hearts?" whispered George.

"I beg your pardon?" asked the director.

"How much a pound for human hearts? You're farming them as a commodity. I'm sure commodity prices have been set. How much? A pound of human flesh. We have come to it at last, dear God. Some of the Nazis made lampshades of human skin from the extermination camps during WWII. You raise human babies and butcher them for their organs. Like any other commodity . . . Jesus wept."

He looked up at the Director, then added, "And Moloch rejoiced."

"Moloch?" asked the director quizzically. "I don't believe I know that name. Is he a researcher at one of the other Ethical Harvesting Substations?"

George grimaced. "He was a researcher at the Substation for the ethical treatment of children as commodities and consumption for idolatry at the city of Carthage over two thousand years ago."

The director continued his puzzled look. "I'm afraid my field is genetics and ethical tissue harvesting, not ancient history."

"And so you doom us all to repeat it," George replied, his voice a little stronger. "The ancient Carthaginians sacrificed their small children to the pagan god Moloch. They threw living children into a furnace and burned them alive."

"That's barbaric," the director said calmly.

"Unlike your more pretentious scientific barbarism. Yes, they were so unscientific and environmentally unfriendly" said George. "They didn't even eat the infants, as the thrifty Dr. Swift modestly proposed."* His voice grew strong and cold, "I'm sure you, on the other hand, as worthy modern acolytes to Moloch, waste nothing. You sacrifice babies to the scalpel, not the fire. What do you do with the bodies?"

"Yes, we're environmentally-conscious and committed recyclers here. We grind up unused embryo tissue to mix with animal protein, recycled for the lab cafeteria. Waste not, want not."

George's face went ashen. "Mad human disease! Cannibalism! As a dog returneth to his own vomit, so a fool returneth to his folly," he managed to say, before he fell to his knees and bent over again, with dry heaves this time.

214

"Take him back to the dormitory," said the director without emotion. "We'll finish the new worker orientation tomorrow."

As the prison van pulled away from the building, George looked at it closely. "What was this facility before it became an embryo farm?" he asked the driver.

The driver shrugged. "There's a lot of chicken farming around here. This used to be a meat packing plant." *And it still is,* thought George.

Jonathan Swift, in a famous satiric essay called "A Modest Proposal," tried to prick the consciences of the English into helping the starving people of Ireland during the potato famine. He "modestly proposed" that the poorest people of Ireland be allowed to sell their own babies to the prosperous English as a food commodity, a delicacy.

*   *   *   *   *   *

That night, back at the dormitory, George was lying down, feeling weak. Two of George's fellow internees came to his cot. "Are you OK?"

"No, I'm not OK. They showed me the embryo farm. These people treat human beings as commodities, to harvest like crops. It's inhuman. It made me sick to my stomach."

One man said, "The first time I saw it, it reminded me of that scene in the movie *The Matrix,* where thousands of big pods containing inert human bodies have nutrients pumped in so that the machines can harvest their energy. Spooky. Demonic."

George sat up. "Demonic is right. I thought of the archaeologist Otto Eissfeldt. In his 1921 excavations in Carthage, in an altar to Moloch, he found the remains of thousands of animals and human children, many newborns. This new generation of Moloch worshippers redefine Moloch as 'me.' Me, me, me. Anything is acceptable if it serves me/Moloch. Other human beings are commodities to be 'harvested' for the benefit of me/Moloch. They never stop to think that this way of thinking leaves no distinction between themselves and the others they treat as commodities. Sooner or later, they too become commodities, to be used by others in their turn. From dog eat dog, it's come to parents eat children.

"I come from Tuskegee University in Alabama," concluded George. "Some black people there were treated as commodities, as lab rats, as a

215

means to someone else's end. The federal government let many black people suffer and die of syphilis as part of the infamous Tuskegee experiments. That's why the Director here guessed that I would never come voluntarily to his little shop of horrors."

Just then, another internee dressed in the regulation orange overalls, indistinguishable from prison garb, approached the small group at George's cot. "Anybody here know of a good barbeque place nearby? Of course, to get there, we have to plan a jailbreak first."

"Isaiah! How did you get in here? Did they catch you too?" George jumped up and embraced him.

"Shhh. Keep your voice down. I had to break into this place, and I'd like to break out without attracting too much attention."

Isaiah looked at the other two internees. "Gentlemen, are you in?"

They looked at each other once, and then nodded. "We're in."

"Follow me," Isaiah said.

The four of them walked down the hall to the toilets. The wall had fresh cuts in the shape of a rectangle around the middle urinal. Isaiah carefully pulled on the middle urinal, and it slid back from the wall surface.

"Crouch down, go through, and turn right. Then wait for me." They did so.

"OK," said Isaiah, "the laundry truck is here picking up bed linens and towels from the guard's dormitory. I'm afraid we're all going to come out of this smelling like sweaty guards, but it beats the alternative. The side door of the truck has been left open. We're going down this hole into the crawl space, and then crawl to the north side of the building to an opening near where the truck is parked. When I say go, crawl outside, sprint to the door of the truck and burrow behind the bags of laundry. Got it?" The other three nodded.

They went down the hole and crawled on hands and knees to the opening, but stayed back in order to remain unseen. When the driver left the truck to go back for another load, Isaiah said "Go!" The four of them sprinted, and then burrowed into the bags of laundry.

"Phew!" said the first man. "I think I smell our night-shift dorm guard already!"

"Shhh!" said Isaiah. The door closed and the truck started up. After five minutes, Isaiah turned on a flashlight. "OK, the driver is one of us.

In about ten minutes, he'll stop and open the doors. Get into the van that's waiting and immediately change your clothes."

"Gladly," said George.

Fifteen minutes later, the van was speeding away with five men. The driver turned his head briefly. "Why Mr. Soto, it's good to see you again!" said George.

Douglas Soto smiled and said, "There's a thermos of coffee back there. It's gonna be a long night."

George laughed, "Trust Douglas Soto to remember everything."

"Except the barbeque!" teased Isaiah.

Isaiah turned to the other two internees. "Gentlemen, would you like to go to one of the Arks?"

"Yes!" they both shouted at once.

"Done!" smiled Isaiah.

He turned to George. "It may interest you to know that a certain young lady named Estelle will be waiting for us."

"Estelle! Isaiah, God bless you!" George's eyes shone with tears.

"Well, I read somewhere that you can do two jailbreaks cheaper than one. You know how I like efficiency," Isaiah's eyes twinkled.

Just then, blue lights started flashing about a half mile behind them.

"Boss!" said Douglas Soto.

"I see them. Slow down just after the next curve. I'm jumping out. I can slow them down. Get George and Estelle and these two gentlemen out on the Gulfstream and all the way to Ark Pacific. Don't stop until you get them there. Got it?"

"But boss, we can fly to the alternate airfield and wait for you."

"No. Too risky. I'll be OK. Fly all the way to the Ark. Clear?"

"Crystal." Isaiah then pulled the orange overalls back on.

Grabbing one of the internees by the shoulder, he said, "Quick, what is your name, ID number, and job at the lab?"

"Don French. ID 2782008. I refill the nutrient I.V.s for the embryo incubators."

When Douglas turned the corner and slowed, Isaiah jumped out, rolled, and went behind some bushes. Then he rubbed dirt on the overalls and his face. He stepped onto the berm next to the road.

When the prison van with the blue lights came around the corner, he waved his hands frantically. The van screeched to a stop and guards

217

jumped out and grabbed him. "Hey, this isn't my fault! They grabbed me for a hostage! I jumped out when they slowed for the corner."

The guards looked him over. "Name, number and job?"

"Don French. ID number 2782008. I do nutrient I.V. refills at the embryo farm." He cowered and hunched over to disguise his height.

The guards checked against a clipboard. "That's him. Let's go for the others." One guard shoved a nightstick into his throat. "Where were they headed?"

Isaiah coughed and gagged. "I heard them say they had a fishing boat waiting for them on the Chesapeake somewhere."

"Where?"

"They didn't say. One of them was driving."

The guard punched him in the ribs with the nightstick. "Where?"

Isaiah bent over in pain. "Cambridge! I think they said Cambridge."

The prison van picked up speed. The radio crackled. "BOLO on escapees from the Prosperity Work Camp at Denton. Believed to be heading for the Cambridge area to rendezvous with a fishing boat. Alert the Coast Guard."

The PSI Gulfstream jet took off from the Easton Airport as the prison van from Denton pulled up at the Cambridge waterfront.

*   *   *   *   *   *

Back at the American Prosperity Camp outside Denton, the camp superintendent was attempting to verify who was missing from the prison break. He verified George Wright and one other internee. He decided to interrogate Don French, the recaptured internee. It was his only link to those who escaped. It was the only clue that might save his job. The problem was that beyond name, ID number, and job, they didn't much care about any personal details of their internees. They just wanted them to do their jobs and not make trouble. The guards didn't fraternize much with the internees, and nobody knew much about this Don French.

The camp superintendent took a photo of French and e-mailed it over to the ETHOS Labs. Director Mitosean took one look and phoned the superintendent.

"That's not French. That's that Isaiah guy who interrupted the President's television speech months ago. He can tell the FBI where these Ark places are."

Within two hours, a black FBI SUV had picked up Isaiah and taken him to Andrews Air Force Base.

"Where are you taking me?" Isaiah asked one of the agents.

"You are a high escape-risk person of interest. We aren't taking any chances with you. Off you go to Gitmo."

"I thought nobody was detained there anymore."

"Nobody is, as far as the world knows." Shackled at wrists and ankles, still wearing the orange detainee overalls, he was loaded into a military jet inside a hangar. Three hours later, he was at the Guantanamo Bay detention center.

Chapter Seventeen

N plus 111. The next day, photos of Isaiah in his orange prison garb and shackles were in every newspaper (those still in operation with stimulus money) and on every news network show. The headline in the *New York Times* read, *"Architect of Noah's Ark Scam in Custody. Associated Press. Isaiah Mercury, the sometime software robber baron guilty of bilking millions from unsuspecting customers of his fraudulent Invisible Hand software, is today in custody at an undisclosed location. Mercury is best known for his hacker prank of intruding on the President's address to the nation months ago. He used this prank to lure millions of unsuspecting victims into his Ponzi scheme of 'Noah's Ark' locations where he claimed everyone could be prosperous. Victims of his scheme were bilked out of tens of thousands of their life savings trying to buy a spot on these so-called 'Arks.'"*

With the same picture of Isaiah in shackles and prison orange, Kathy Coeur-Saignant on the CBC Evening News intoned, "Isaiah Mercury, the infamous hacker who intruded on the President's speech and then defrauded millions out of their life savings with his 'Ark' scheme, is now in government custody. Acting on an informer's tip, federal agents apprehended Mercury late last night. Sources at the Department of Justice say that we can expect a trial with full transparency and full media coverage before the end of the month. CBC News will bring you full coverage when this trial begins. Remember, Corporate Broadcasting Collective reports what's good for you to know, when it's good for you to know it."

*   *   *   *   *   *

The President was on the phone with the Attorney General. "Earnest, I want you to cut this guy's nuts off. We want to make an example of him, so that people will stop these ridiculous unpatriotic attempts to leave the nation and go to these mythical 'Arks.' You got that?"

"Yes sir, Mr. President. We're planning a televised show trial that will demonstrate how silly his ideas are, and show how people leaving for these 'Arks' will be punished."

"Good plan, Earnest. Keep me informed."

*   *   *   *   *   *

On FreedomToobz.Ark, these photos were posted with a different headline: "The New Slavery." The byline, instead of "Associated Press" or "Reuters," read "The Constitutional Resistance Movement." The copy read, *"Entrepreneurs and those with needed skills are forced into a new slavery. Look at the shackles on this man. Now look at these photos of people interned into the President's "American Prosperity Camps." Notice what they are wearing: shackles and chains.*

"Who wears chains? Slaves. If this is a voluntary program, why the chains? What happened to the 13th Amendment to the Constitution? The one that outlaws slavery? Our Congress and our President seem to have forgotten about it, or they have decided that they are above the law. The principle was that we are a nation of laws, and not of men. Our congress-people and our President seem to think that we are a nation of men, not laws, and that they are the men who are entitled to control us."

*   *   *   *   *   *

N plus 112. During the night, Attorney General Handford experienced great abdominal pain and was taken to Walter Reed Hospital. His lab tests were put at the head of the queue and rushed back to a team of top medical specialists reserved for top government officials. In the morning, a hepatologist entered his hospital room. Mrs. Handford sat by the AG's bedside. She was his latest trophy wife, a young blonde.

"Mr. Attorney General, I'm afraid this is bad news. You have advanced liver disease, cirrhosis. I see from your medical records that your personal physician has counseled you over the years about your drinking."

The AG looked disgusted and snorted, "That old fool wanted to take all the fun out of my life. A little drink now and then never hurt anybody. So, I've got cirrhosis. So what? Fix it."

The hepatologist shook his head, "I'm afraid it's not that simple. You require a total liver transplant. Not just a piece from a living donor, but the entire liver from a recently deceased person. The numbers of organs available for transplant are always fewer than the number of people needing them. Normally, that would not be a problem for you,

221

since members of government always take precedence over the average citizen. However, you have a rare blood type and a rare genetic make-up. There are no livers in the organ bank that are a match for you. I'm sorry."

The AG's wife gasped. *What about my position in D.C. society,* she thought. Wives of cabinet members were on the "A" list for social invitations. *Widows* of cabinet members were off the radar screen entirely.

"Doctor," she asked, her voice trembling, "how long does he have?"

"About three months, I'm sorry to tell you both." *Three months. That under-secretary of commerce was giving me the eye at last night's dinner party. I can hook him and reel him in within three months.* Under-secretaries' wives were on the "B" list, but at least she'd still be on a list.

The AG did not look concerned. "Doc, call the head of the CDC and ask her to get you my top match on her database called Backup American Anatomical Listings. See, Doc, the CDC prepared an emergency medical preparedness plan for all cabinet level officials. They compiled a list of compatible organ donor matches for all cabinet members from a medical database they created on all living American citizens. The follow-up report I received showed two young and healthy matches for me, perfectly matching my rare genetics and blood type."

The doctor looked puzzled. "I don't understand. A medical database on living Americans? How does that help us? We can't take the entire liver from a living person. That person would die without it."

The AG smiled. "All citizens are created equal, but some are more equal than others. CDC medical directive number 6.24.33 rules that all bodily organs were nurtured by the state with our federal medical programs for citizens, and therefore the state has a proprietary and overriding interest in all bodily organs of all citizens. Rule number 6.24.33 gives government the right to requisition any citizen's bodily organs, at any time, for any reason the government decides is in the national interest. I'm the Attorney General, and I've decided that it is in the national interest that I get a new liver."

The doctor's mouth hung open. "Don't worry, Doc. The CDC will take care of the requisition. It's all legal. I drafted the rule for the CDC."

*   *   *   *   *   *

That afternoon at 3 p.m., Samuel Solipsis' secretary, Miss Cringe, buzzed him. "Mr. Solipsis, there are some gentlemen from the Center for Disease Control here to see you. They said it's urgent."

"Send them in." Samuel eased to his feet to greet his visitors. His arm was out of the cast, but it was still painful to move it, despite the medications. Three fit young men in dark suits and ties entered his office. *They don't look like medical researchers,* thought Samuel.

"Mr. Solipsis, we're with a department of the CDC called RCA, the Requisitions Collections Agency." He flashed a badge. "I am RCA Agent Fourens, and this is a CDC requisition for your liver, all of your liver, duly authorized under CDC rule number 6.24.33." He handed over a legal document to Solipsis. "We're here to escort you to the ETHOS harvesting facility in Maryland."

Samuel sat down, stunned and confused. "What? I don't understand. You can't just take my entire liver! It will kill me! I, that is we, have rights!"

Agent Fourens looked impassive. "Sir, CDC rule number 6.24.33 explicitly established the property rights of the government over all bodily organs of all citizens. A high-ranking government official needs a liver transplant. Your rare genetic make-up and rare blood type are the optimum match for him, given that you are younger and healthier. The CDC is simply exercising the proprietary rights of the government."

Solipsis looked stricken as he heard this recitation of legalese that he had often used against others. "But, I've never even heard of this CDC rule!"

Agent Fourens remained impassive. "Sir, as a lawyer yourself, you know that under current legal interpretations of international law superseding US law, ignorance of the law is no excuse and allows no exceptions."

Agent Fourens nodded to his two colleagues. They stepped forward and handcuffed Solipsis. He gasped, "Is this necessary?"

Fourens replied, "Standard procedure. We often have people who try to escape a duly authorized requisition." Samuel's face was ashen.

"But, but, you are treating me like property to be disposed of, like a mere commodity!"

Fourens allowed himself one small smile. "Sir, in preparing to execute this requisition I researched you and your organization, PRIS." Here he pulled out a document from his suit pocket. "I saw this on the PRIS web site and printed it, so I quote verbatim, '*All species are commodities to be kept in balance, including humans. To restore that balance with species as diverse as algae and insects, our mission is to reduce the planetary population of the commodity species Homo Sapiens by sixty percent.*'"

Agent Fourens folded the paper and replaced it in his suit pocket. "Mr. Solipsis, just think of it as doing your part, of setting a leadership example. The commodity — your liver — will reduce the planetary population of Homo Sapiens by one life: yours. A noble sacrifice for the PRIS cause. You could be a paragraph in the government history books as a martyr, if you play this right.

"You could be an inspiration for millions of young Americans to kill themselves for the planet. Isn't that a legacy you can be proud of? Don't you want to use your one phone call to call the PRIS publicity department?"

"But, that was never intended to apply to me! I'm one of the progressive elite. Just ask the Attorney General!"

Fourens again smiled briefly. "We have."

As he was escorted out, a FreedomToobz.Ark citizen videographer was on the street filming, tipped off by a source. He mentally composed the narration as he filmed: *One who treated other humans as commodities is now commoditized himself, a mere transport system for a liver.*

One of the agents put his hand on top of Samuel's head to load him into the back of the black government SUV. Before his head went down, Samuel glimpsed one of the resistance movement bumper stickers on a nearby telephone pole. It read, "Live With Your Answers."

*　　*　　*　　*　　*　　*

N plus 113. Meanwhile, at the new headquarters of Promethean Software International, in Christchurch, New Zealand, Douglas Soto briefed Grace, George, and Estelle.

"They've moved Isaiah to the Guantanamo Bay detention center, because they believe that he's an escape artist. We have a back door into the computer systems of the Treasury Department, and from them, into the Justice Department. He is detained with dozens of other 'high flight risk, high interest' detainees of this administration. Of course, this administration supposedly closed Guantanamo. These are secret political detainees. They do have television privileges, so they saw Isaiah interrupt the President on national TV months ago. He's quite a celebrity with the other detainees, who are all political enemies of the Administration, not true criminals. He's healthy and doing well. Would you like to see him?"

Grace gasped, "Can we do that?"

"Yes, and hear him too, if he's talkative," said Douglas. He tapped out some commands on the computer keyboard. A video feed from Isaiah's cell came on the screen. Isaiah sat reading a Gideon's bible. He had a small smile on his face. After a few seconds, he closed the bible, closed his eyes, and folded his hands in prayer.

Grace said, "Let's pray with him." She reached out and held Douglas's hand, and Estelle and George completed the circle. "Dear Lord," prayed Grace, "please watch over and protect my husband Isaiah. Please deliver him from this captivity and bring him home safely to us. Amen."

"Amen," said Estelle, George, and Douglas. They looked at the screen again. A guard had come to escort Isaiah for mealtime.

As the guard opened the cell door, they could hear Isaiah say, "Hey man, how can you call that cafeteria swill food? I mean, it's bad even for a *prison*. When are you guys going to get some barbeque in this place? Is barbeque deprivation part of your enhanced interrogation techniques?" Then the prison cell was empty. Douglas turned off the video feed on his computer screen.

"Well," said George, "we know they haven't broken him yet! He's still trash talking and asking for barbeque!" Everyone laughed.

Douglas cleared his throat. "I'm leading a PSI team to rescue Isaiah. Dr. Washington, I believe that some of your graduate work was with infectious childhood diseases?"

"Yes."

"That could help us with our plan. Would you work on that with my team tonight?"

"Of course."

George spoke up. "Anything I can do to help?"

Grace looked up at him. "George, you could help me in the lab."

"You got it."

Estelle smiled. "I'll keep the coffee coming." She and Grace exchanged a high five.

Douglas said, "Dr. Wright, the lab is down the hall on the left."

As George and Estelle left the room, Douglas motioned for Grace to stay behind. "Grace, at 8:00 tomorrow morning it will be midnight Guantanamo time. At that time, we can chance a conversation with Isaiah for about fifteen minutes. I thought you'd like a few minutes of private conversation with him."

Grace was again dumfounded. "We can do that?"

"Yes. All cells are equipped with microphones for eavesdropping on prisoners, and speakers for announcements. We can hack into that system, isolate the circuits to Isaiah's cell and safely have a conversation with him, if we keep it short. We won't be able to see him, because it will be after lights out at the prison, and we can't risk the guards seeing a light and coming to investigate."

"Douglas, you are a gift from God. God bless you."

"Thank you. Be here at 8 a.m. for your private chat."

*   *   *   *   *   *

Promptly at 8 o'clock, Grace was in Douglas's office. The video feed screen was on, but showed a black screen. "Lights out," said Douglas. He tapped his keyboard for a few minutes, and then whispered into a microphone set up in front of the keyboard, "Boss? Boss, if you can hear this, stand on your bed to get near the ceiling microphone and whisper." He paused.

They heard scraping noises, then a hoarse whisper, "Doug, is that you? I had to drag the bed to the middle of the cell first."

"Boss, it's Doug. We only have fifteen minutes, and we have to review some procedures with you. But first, someone wants some private conversation with you. Five minutes." Douglas stood and motioned for Grace to take his chair. Then he left and closed the door.

"Isaiah? Baby, it's Grace," she whispered.

"Grace? Grace?" Isaiah's voice cracked. "Oh, there is a God in Heaven. Thank you, Jesus. Thank you God. Grace, baby I love you so much. I'm sorry this happened. It wasn't supposed to go down this way."

"Hush," she whispered. "Are you all right?"

"Yeah, so far."

"You must be. We heard you trash-talking the cafeteria food and whining for barbeque yesterday!"

They whispered secrets for each other's hearts. They shared loneliness, heartache, and fear. They whispered and immersed themselves in each other's whispers. Grace felt like Isaiah was holding her hand across thousands of miles.

There was a tapping at the door, and then Douglas Soto stuck his head in. "Grace? Grace, we have to brief Isaiah now."

Grace nodded, and then whispered, "Goodbye my sweetheart. I'll see you soon." She rose and left.

Douglas leaned over the microphone. "Boss, here's what we've worked out . . ." Douglas whispered.

When he had finished, Isaiah whispered back. "Roger that."

$$*\quad*\quad*\quad*\quad*\quad*$$

N plus 117. Three days later, it was time for a new duty rotation of guards to take over at the detention facility at Guantanamo. They had flown in the day before, and the off-going rotation would fly back to the states for three weeks to be with their families.

This was a new rotation of guards who had never been to Guantanamo before. The normal rotation of guards had mysteriously caught a mild new form of the measles that was highly contagious and had spread to all the guards and their families. The entire unit of guards was under quarantine. They were over it within a week. Later investigation by the CDC would determine that this strain of the measles had been artificially produced in a lab. The researchers at CDC concluded that only a person with a Nobel laureate level of biological expertise could have created a measles strain that was simultaneously mild and highly contagious.

As an extra security precaution, the Guantanamo guards used a database with the prisoners' photos to take roll call. The photos were scrolled up on the guards' cell phone screens, so they could visually confirm that the correct prisoner was indeed in the cell. Four military guards with cell phones walked four cell blocks daily, visually verifying the presence and identities of forty-eight political detainees.

These new guards had never seen the prisoners before, but were confident in their new prisoner facial recognition system. If they were not sure that the prisoner matched the photo, the two accompanying back-up guards would bring the prisoner out to good light. Then the PPC (Prison Population Checker) would scan the prisoner's face with his cell phone camera into the Prisoner Facial Recognition System (PFRS). It would tell the PPC the prisoner's name, number, and cell number. It was foolproof. Prisoners were forcibly shaven once a week so their facial hair could not disguise facial features and trick the PFRS.

Before the first official roll call, the commandant of the Guantanamo Detention Facility received a priority-one prisoner transport requisition for one Pierre La Fontesquieu, a gentleman of Cajun descent arrested on suspicion of smuggling citizens out of New Orleans to Mexico. They were ready to begin his show trial in New Orleans. It was hoped that this local trial would send a message to other Cajuns (known for their fiercely independent streak and their ability to find hiding places in Louisiana swamps) and deter them from any further Ark smuggling activities.

The prisoner transfer went smoothly. The computer system for prisoner and cell location showed Pierre La Fontesquieu housed in the cell formerly occupied by Isaiah Mercury. The system showed that Isaiah had been transferred to another cell. The guards sent to remove him matched the picture on their Prisoner Facial Recognition System. It was Isaiah's face. Citizen La Fontesquieu was delivered to New Orleans via military transport plane, and then transported via prison van with two US Marshals.

En route to the county prison, the van was stopped at a traffic checkpoint manned by the Constitutional Resistance Movement. The dozen police officers at the checkpoint wore the uniform of the Louisiana state patrol.

The van driver and guard flashed their badges. "Federal Marshals transporting a prisoner to the county prison in New Orleans pending trial in the federal courthouse."

The 'state trooper' looked at their badges and then looked at their prisoner. Pierre La Fontesquieu was Isaiah Mercury. The trooper turned back to the driver, "Fellas, we're searching for an escaped prisoner from the next county. It will take fifteen minutes to search and clear the cars ahead of you. We have some coffee and doughnuts. I know you have to stay with your prisoner, but Cecil over there could bring you a cup."

The driver said, "Sure," and the guard nodded and said, "OK by me." The trooper nodded at Cecil, who brought over a cardboard take-out tray with two coffees and two doughnuts. Four minutes after their first sips, the driver and guard were fast asleep.

Douglas Soto, in a perfectly fitting Louisiana state trooper uniform, opened the passenger door and liberated the guard's keys. "Isaiah, you OK?" he asked as he quickly unlocked the shackles.

"Yeah, buddy. I owe you one."

George T'Chaka Wright, also in state trooper uniform, came up with a take-out food container. "This barbecue came straight from New Orleans, so it's primo: Cajun-spiced to perfection."

Isaiah smelled the container, then grinned, "Well, maybe I owe you two. Hey, you two look good in those uniforms."

Soto was all business. "Later with the wisecracks. We're on a tight schedule. Get in the patrol car over there. Here are some clothes. We need your prison overalls." Shucking out of the overalls, Isaiah quickly changed clothes.

Turning back to the prison van, he told Douglas, "Just a second. I want a souvenir." Reaching into the back, he retrieved a set of shackles. Climbing into the highway patrol car, he sampled the barbeque while Douglas returned to the prison van.

A private service ambulance had been staged at the traffic stop by the local CRM, following the plan developed by Douglas Soto and his team from Christchurch. The driver and guard were loaded into the ambulance and sent to the hospital. Probable diagnosis: food poisoning. A wino who had been sleeping it off behind a tavern was quickly put into Isaiah's orange prison overalls and shackles and loaded, still sleeping, into the prison van. Two CRM 'troopers' took over as driver and guard. Douglas Soto downloaded a photo of the wino into the prisoner identification system of the guard's cell phone and gave it to the 'trooper' acting as guard.

When the prison van arrived at the prison, the two troopers explained that the Marshals had been taken sick by food poisoning and sent to the hospital.

"We had extra officers at the traffic stop, so we volunteered to bring the prisoner in. Here is the Prisoner Identification System. One of the marshals showed us how to use it before going to the hospital. Here's this prisoner's photo ID."

The trooper showed the cell phone prisoner photo to the intake clerk. The face was that of the wino they had between them.

"The prisoner has been acting drunk. He may have eaten some of the same food that gave the marshals food poisoning. Better get him checked out by a medic."

After getting an official receipt for prisoner delivery and the cell phone, the two 'troopers' left.

*   *   *   *   *   *

N plus 118. The next day at Guantanamo, the daily roll call check began. The four prison population checkers and their back-up guards fanned out across the complex to begin their electronic roll call. As each of the four stopped in front of the first cell on their rounds, they punched in the cell locator number. Each of the four got an identical picture, though they didn't know it at the time. It was a head shot of the actor Kirk Douglas, in his starring role as the Roman slave, Spartacus. The guards were too young to have seen the movie or the actor.

"This is wrong!" said the first PPC aloud.

"What is it?" asked one of his back-up guards.

"This prisoner's face does not match the photo from the PFRS photo database."

"Let me see," said the back-up guard. "You're right."

"Let's check the next one. Could be a computer glitch."

"Right." At the next detention cell, the face shown was the same: Kirk Douglas.

"Dang." He got on his two-way radio. "Lieutenant, Sergeant Andrews, cell block A. We have a problem. We get the same face photo for the first two prisoners, and neither matches the prisoners in the cells."

"Lieutenant, ditto cell block B."

"Ditto cell block C."

"Ditto cell block D."

The lieutenant frowned. *Oh God, trouble on my first day on my new duty assignment.* "All PPCs, you have twelve prisoners in each cell block, except A, where we transferred a prisoner yesterday. Verify twelve prisoners, whether the photos match or not. Call in your numbers

230

as soon as you're done." He turned to his top sergeant. "Get the captain on the horn."

After urgent communications with the Justice Department in Washington, D.C., the prison commandant was told that his first priority was to locate and isolate prisoner Isaiah Mercury, who had the know-how to pull off such software tricks. The captain ordered all prisoners brought to the exercise yard and lined up by cell block designation.

When all forty-seven prisoners were in the exercise yard, the captain stood on an observation platform and addressed them.

"We're looking for prisoner Isaiah Mercury. Prisoner Isaiah Mercury, please identify yourself." Silence. "If the prisoner will not identify himself, and no other prisoners will identify him, then the entire unit will go on bread and water rations until he is so identified." Silence.

Suddenly a voice was heard from the back, speaking up loudly, "I am Isaiah Mercury." He held up his shackled wrists.

Then another voice was heard. "I am Isaiah Mercury." Shackled hands went up.

Then another, "I am Isaiah Mercury."

The refrain was taken up in each row, until the entire group held up their shackled hands and shouted in unison, "I am Isaiah Mercury!"

The captain raised a bullhorn and shouted "Silence! The prisoners will be silent!" Silence descended on the yard.

Then one lone voice rang out from somewhere in the formation, "I am Spartacus." He held up his shackles and shook the chains defiantly. The entire group laughed, cheered, whistled, hooted and clapped.

The captain turned to the lieutenant. "Start fingerprinting every prisoner. Take DNA samples too." *It's going to be a long day,* he thought wearily.

Unknown to the Captain, the entire scene had been hacked from the base security cameras, and broadcast live on FreedomToobz.Ark. It was then picked up and re-broadcast by the new FreedomToobz.Ark communications satellites on the new underground CRM television channel 1776. Anyone with a satellite dish could pick it up for free. It somehow came through the filtering software of every satellite dish network and every cable TV network. Millions of Americans and Canadians watched at restaurants and sports bars, in their homes, and on the internet.

Cheering and clapping broke out in the bars and restaurants; high-fives and fist bumps were exchanged all over America.

The FreedomToobz.Ark announcer crowed, "Woo hoo! Isaiah Mercury busted out of Guantanamo, the highest-security prison there is. And did you see the faces of the other prisoners? Americans who dared to speak out, every one. I saw Larry Elder and Glenn Beck on the back row. They can intern us, they can imprison us, and they can continue to enslave us with rules and regulations, but they can't break our spirit! Their tool is the chain. Our tool is the mind. Retake America! This breaking news video feed brought to you by the Constitutional Resistance Movement. God bless America."

Chapter Eighteen

N plus 119. Isaiah stepped off the PSI corporate jet at Christchurch, New Zealand. Grace met him halfway down the steps and engulfed him in a big hug and a passionate kiss.

"Isaiah! You're safe! You're safe! Thank you God, for bringing him home safely to me." She hugged him tighter.

"Baby! Grace. My own sweetheart. Thank you Lord, for bringing me home safely to Grace." He did not want to let her go.

Grace caught sight of Douglas Soto over Isaiah's shoulder. "And God bless you, Douglas Soto, for bringing Isaiah home safely to me. I will be forever in your debt." Douglas winked at her. Then catching sight of Estelle Wright down on the tarmac, he gave a thumbs up sign to her.

"Grace!" called George from further up the steps, "Let him step to the ground! He's not on the sovereign soil of his new country until he steps down." Grace wiped her eyes, then turned around and came down, followed by Isaiah.

Isaiah turned back and called, "Doug! Get out your video camera, please. I want to capture this moment for FreedomToobz.Ark." When Doug was on the ground with the camera at the ready, Isaiah knelt down and kissed the ground.

"Got it!" said Doug, "Any words for the fans, patriots, freedom lovers, underground Constitutional Resistance Movement folks, and sojourners in Arks around the world?"

Isaiah put his arm around Grace and looked at the camera.

"Yes. I am Isaiah Mercury," he paused and took a deep breath.

"My fellow Americans in exile, my fellow constitutionalists and capitalists in exile or in the underground, and freedom lovers everywhere, be of good cheer. As you can see, I am no longer in a government prison for political prisoners, thanks be to a good God. You and I are fighting the good fight. We are lighting candles of freedom in the darkness. We may not win the fight in this generation, but we will win. We will win because the lust for power, the anti-life equation of total control of others, and the charade of total government control of economies always fails, fails under its own contradictions.

"Socialism and fascism don't work. These systems exist only as parasites, as blood sucking leeches on the bodies of free economies and free peoples. When they kill the host bodies, when the economies are no longer free and the people are enslaved under the control of their keepers in government, then they run out of blood to suck, and they die. North Koreans would starve if it weren't for the food they extort from the rest of the world. Their rulers are evil, because they take tens of millions of people down with them, down into lives of poverty, lives of ill health and disease, and lives that are short, brutish, and miserable. Read your history. Read *Modern Times* by Paul Johnson. Mao, Pol Pot, Kim Jong-Il, and Stalin starved and murdered millions of their own people.

"Dr. Adrian Rogers once said, 'What one person receives without working for, another person must work for without receiving.' When someone has to work without receiving the fruits of his labors, he is by definition a slave. He also said, 'You cannot multiply wealth by dividing it.' This is what socialist governments do: forcibly seize the fruits of your labor, and then divide it among those who did not labor to earn it."

Grace released her hold on Isaiah's waist and stretched her hands in front of her in a gesture of supplication. "My name is Dr. Grace Washington. The Carver's Legacy super-seeds I developed can literally end world hunger. The special interest group PRIS and their corrupt allies in the US government conspired to try to destroy my seeds. Why? They want to control and reduce the world population, as they brag about on their web site. Who elected them God, to control who lives and who dies around the whole world?

"I want to tell you about a secret I discovered, *a secret hiding in plain sight* in every town in America, *a secret acted out by millions of little-known Americans every day.* There is the story that the scientist Isaac Newton 'discovered' the secret of the law of gravity when an apple fell and hit him on the head. Gravity had been hiding in plain sight since the first day of creation. It just took the apple to get him to realize it."

Grace dropped her hands to her side. "The apple hit me when I took my car for a repair to one of my neighbors, Carl. Carl has a prosperous business with three full-time mechanics on his payroll. Carl works hard and lives well and is paying college tuition for two of his children — an American success story. Thirteen years ago Carl started with $500, a box of tools, and a rented garage. Today he owns a modern garage on a busy street and a fine family home. Who spread this wealth and shared it with Carl? No one. The wealth didn't exist thirteen years ago. Where did all this wealth come from? From Carl's hard work. He created the wealth from a box of tools, a rented garage, $500, and *hard work.*

"That's the secret hidden in plain sight: *hard work creates prosperity, if you let it.*

"Carl and tens of millions of little-known Americans just like him act out this secret every day, hidden in plain sight, as ordinary as apples. They, the ordinary Americans, get up and go to work every day, and keep finding better ways to do the work. When they do it better, they make more money. It's as simple as that, if you leave them alone to do it.

"Graduate-level physicists study principles discovered by Isaac Newton, but basically it's as simple as a falling apple. My neighbor, Carl the auto mechanic, hiding in plain sight, showed me how simple it is: hard work creates prosperity. Carl, you are as good and as sweet as an apple. I hope you see this.

"The secret hidden in plain sight is that hard work creates prosperity if you let it. What stops hard work from creating prosperity? What holds it back?

"I am a scientist, a botanist. I study how to make crops prosper. One thing that won't let crops prosper is a parasite. Parasites suck out nutrients provided by the host and harm it. If parasites are allowed to become too big and too numerous, they eventually kill the host. Those of you with pet dogs know that parasitic heart worms can kill your dog if untreated.

"I am a botanist, and I know a parasite when I see one. From a scientific point of view, our government has mutated from the original constitution into a swarm of parasites, sucking out the money from hard-working Americans and giving nothing in return. Eventually they will kill the hosts, the hard workers like Carl, and the great economy of the once-free United States of America will die. You can already see for yourselves that our country is sick, like an anemic person with a parasitic tapeworm, not getting enough nourishment.

"If you ask any county agent, any veterinarian how to cure this, they will tell you: *control the bloodsucking parasites!*" She said this last phrase with emphasis and a frown.

Then she smiled her dimpled smile and then looked over at Isaiah.

Isaiah flashed his toothy grin, "Amen, sister. You folks at home in America, keep exposing the hypocrisies, corruption, and evil on the internet and television and through word of mouth. Telling and showing what they do shines a light on their actions. Evil things hate the light. They scatter like cockroaches when a light is turned on in a basement.

"We discovered that so-called special interest groups have one special interest in common: power and greed. The only way they can enforce their will on the rest of us is by allying themselves with the one institution in our society that has a monopoly on the use of force: the government. Unfortunately, government also attracts those personalities who like to enforce their will on others through power and control. Once these special interest groups corrupt the government (and they don't have to work too hard to corrupt the government), the government helps them force us to do what they want. They are both parasites, as Grace explained.

"These groups and government officials tell us that capitalism is evil, because it is built on profit. Profit is when you keep the fruits of your labors.

Only slaves cannot keep the fruits of their labors. When I work hard and create software and sell it, I make a profit. Profit is my pay for my hard work. Socialism and fascism are all about *taking* the fruits of your labor. Socialism and fascism are built on slavery. Socialism and fascism are evil because they make you into slaves."

He paused and pulled out the prison shackles from his backpack. "Here is their tool." He held the shackles aloft and rattled the chains.

"Here is our tool." He pointed to his forehead. "The free mind. Our God-given ability to reason and think things out for ourselves.

"When the barbarian hordes overran Europe in the fourth century and destroyed Roman civilization, smashing artworks, burning cities, schools, books, and churches, they wiped out knowledge and plunged Europe into the Dark Ages. The Christian monks saved books and manuscripts that they gathered into their own 'Arks,' the walled and fortified monasteries. They defended their monasteries against barbarian attacks and preserved the learning of antiquity in mathematics, medicine, astronomy, agriculture, and countless other subjects. They kept learning alive in their monastic arks, like small points of light in a sea of darkness. They waited for centuries for civilization to return, so they could share the knowledge again.

"We may have to wait for centuries in our Arks, until the world is ready for our knowledge and skills again, until the world will respect us and leave us in peace to use our minds to create goods to offer in voluntary trade with our fellow man. Until then, we will not cast our pearls before swine, lest they turn and rend us, as they have rent and torn so many of our fellow patriots and entrepreneurs.

"One day the flood waters of this socialist fascism will subside, and freedom and capitalism and constitutionally restricted government will once more bring prosperity, health, and the laughter of a free people to the United States and other places around the world. It is already growing here in my new country of New Zealand. We of this generation, waiting and raising our families in the Arks, may not live to see it, nor the next generation, but it will come, as surely as there are rainbows.

"So, be of good cheer, my brothers and sisters in freedom and capitalism. With faith in God, and courage to do the right thing, as God gives us to see the right, we can build a new life for ourselves and our children in our Arks. Our Arks can be a beacon of hope for the rest of the world. We want to be able to tell our grandchildren, and our God, in the words of the Apostle Paul, 'I have fought the good fight, I have finished the race, I have kept the faith.'"

*　　*　　*　　*　　*　　*

Doug Soto had dropped Grace and Isaiah at their cottage and returned to his office. Within the hour, he had the video with Isaiah and Grace's speech posted on FreedomToobz.Ark. He next sent links to all of his contacts in the various resistance movements in America, plus selected media outlets. Isaiah had stepped off the plane at 8 a.m. New Zealand time. By 5:30 a.m. Eastern Standard Time in the US, it was linked on the Drudge Report and dozens of other internet news aggregators. By 5:45 a.m. thirty-five million people had the link waiting for them in e-mails or on their social networking pages. At 7 a.m., it was the lead story on ZNN and FACTS morning news. ABC mentioned it briefly near the end of their morning news show. CBC and NBC ignored it. At 7:15, the speech was the subject of seventy-five million text messages and fifty million tweets.

At 7:15 a.m. the President snapped off the television set in the Oval Office and turned to Sim Smythe, his chief of staff. "I thought we had ZNN on board with us to ignore all stories relating to this Ark nonsense?"

237

"Mr. President, we did, but my source tells me that they are so far behind FACTS News in the ratings that their advertising revenue is down by forty percent. They are desperate not to allow FACTS to scoop them on any stories."

"Can't we offer them stimulus money like we did for NBC and the *New York Times*?"

"Mr. President, Edward Revolver is still their major shareholder, and he vetoed accepting any stimulus money after you fired the CEO of NBC and nationalized General Electricity. He wants to stay in possession of his extensive western properties."

The President wrinkled his nose as if he had smelled something bad. "Possessions! That's all these CEOs and shareholders care about. Nobody wants to sacrifice for their own good until We force them to do it. No one person 'possesses' anything. Everything belongs to everybody, in trust, and we in the government are the duly authorized representatives of everybody's trust. We decide who gets what, not the owners of shares of companies."

"Yes sir."

"Why wasn't I informed that this Isaiah person had broken out of jail? How could he do that? I thought Guantanamo was the most secure prison we have."

Smythe squirmed in his seat. "Mr. President, we thought it best to allow you deniability in case this incident revealed anything more, like the fact that we're still using Guantanamo, but as a prison for political prisoners, not prisoners of war."

The President looked thoughtful, "Oh. Good thinking." Another thought occurred to him and his brow wrinkled. "Who is 'we'?"

"Sir?"

"You said 'we' thought it best to preserve deniability. Who is 'we'?"

"Sir, myself, the chairman of the joint chiefs, the director of the CIA, Attorney General Handford, and Secretary of the Treasury Gunther."

"I see." He turned away from Smythe. *Those bastards are making decisions behind my back! I'd better schedule some more Town Hall meetings across the country to consolidate my power base.*

Turning back, he asked Smythe, "Anything else for today?"

"Yes sir. Secretary of Agriculture Zubrinski asked to see you. She said it's urgent."

"Very well, send her in."

Sharon Zubrinski, a heavyset woman in tweeds and sensible shoes walked in with short, nervous steps. "Mr. President, thank you for seeing me on such short notice."

"No problem. As I've always said, my ear is the people's ear. What's up?"

"The harvests in the Midwest, Mr. President. They're not going well."

"What seems to be the problem?"

"Machinery maintenance, sir. When so many of the harvesting contractors and their families 'went Ark' we had a shortage of skilled harvesting machine operators and maintenance technicians."

"Didn't Secretary of Labor Tianin send you enough skilled people? She's rounded up millions into the Prosperity Camps."

"Mr. President, the people she sent either don't know how, or won't operate and repair the thousands of harvesting combines needed for this year's harvest. Nobody in my department knows how to teach them. In addition, the equipment for tilling and planting is also short of maintenance for the early spring planting. Sir, we're facing a major food shortage for this fall and winter. The harvests may be down by forty percent."

The President looked shocked. "But, I ordered the cabinet to get the skilled people to take care of problems like this. I gave the order! Why isn't it happening?" He pounded the desk with his fist.

She struggled for the properly subservient tone of voice, "Sir, with all due respect, skills can't be seized the same way you confiscated those shipments of arugula for the White House kitchen. Skills aren't a tangible item. You can intern the people, but not the skills. There is no way to tell if these interned people ever had the skills in the first place, or if they do have the skills and are just playing dumb."

"Then threaten them! Force them to repair the machines. This is a matter of national security!" A sudden thought occurred to him. *Golly! I wonder if I'm going to run out of coffee cream again?*

"Sir, I will relay your wishes to Labor Secretary Tianin, who runs the labor, I mean, Prosperity Camps. In the meantime, I strongly recommend that we plan for rationing food beginning next October. Remember, harvests may be down by forty percent. We already have an organization for distributing ration tickets to the American public, the

Asset Substitution Regulatory Board over at the EPA, in charge of toilet paper rationing. Since there is a direct relationship between food consumption and toilet paper consumption, we can simply task this agency with distribution of food ration tickets as well. Since food comes under the jurisdiction of the Agriculture Department, I ask in fairness that you issue an executive order that directs this board to have dual reporting responsibilities: that it report both to me at Agriculture and to Director Mason Underwood at the EPA, and that either one of us will have veto power over decisions made by the other. That's only fair."

The President looked left in an unconscious move to see what the teleprompter would tell him to say. He jerked his head a little when he realized there was no teleprompter. "I've always said that the fair thing to do is what we should do to be fair. Consider it done. Anything else?"

"Sir, rationing the American people to sixty percent of their current caloric intake will in all probability lower people's immune systems, and the usual wintertime flu season may affect people more severely. We should alert the CDC to be prepared to execute the Stressed Population Triage Protocols that we worked out with the Pristine Influence on Society Foundation (PRIS) last year. When the oldest fifteen percent of the population and the youngest fifteen percent of the population is severely ill with influenza, or any other disease, the CDC will direct all doctors and hospitals to implement the Euthanasia Protocols with humanely administered toxins.

"This would reduce the number of people we have to feed by thirty percent, putting us closer to the forty percent reduction in available food. The PRIS people will protest that it is nowhere near their target of sixty percent population reduction for a sustainable planet, but it's a major step forward."

The President nodded, then lifted his chin in his trademark upward gaze. "Yes, regrettable, but We warned the American people that I would ask them to make sacrifices. Tell the CDC they have Our authorization to activate the protocols. Say! I just had an idea. What about those enhanced crop seeds that company was selling to Africa? Let's use those for the early summer planting, and we should get a better crop yield. That would alleviate the food shortage, wouldn't it?"

Secretary Zubrinski looked unhappy. "Sir, that company, Nutritional Abundance Industries, 'went Ark' to New Zealand and it has refused to sell its seeds in the US market."

The President, undeterred, replied, "They left their labs and equipment behind. Send our top USDA scientists to their labs in Peoria and replicate their work. With the same equipment, it can't be that hard, can it?"

The Secretary looked doubtful, but said, "Yes sir. We'll get right on it sir."

     *   *   *   *   *   *

N plus 120. The USDA top 'scientists' had been in the business of telling other scientists what research they could and could not do for the past twenty years. Few of them had ever done research on their own, and that was back in their graduate school days. They grumbled about being sent from Washington, D.C. to Peoria for a six-month assignment.

"This is a matter of national security and you will do as ordered," said their Director of the Department of Research on Research. "Or would you prefer that I intern you?" he asked darkly. "There is a Prosperity Camp near enough to Peoria that we could have you commute to work via camp buses." No one spoke up.

On their first day on the job in Peoria, the USDA scientists wandered through the labs, looking helplessly at the equipment. "What is this thing?" asked one, looking at the electron microscope last used by one of the research teams of Nutritional Abundance Industries.

"I don't know," said his colleague.

"Has anyone found any research notes about the work on the Carver's Legacy seeds?" Ten people shook their heads.

The team leader said, "Sift through every file cabinet you can find and every desk drawer. Don't waste your time on the computers. The hard drives have been wiped. We have to find their research notes. I know all paper documents are missing, but there must be some scraps of paper left behind somewhere!"

One woman raised her hand. "What if we can't find them? How will we know how to do our own research?" she whined.

The team leader furrowed his brow. "I don't know. Does anyone remember your design of experiments class?" All heads shook no. "How about gene splicing for DNA sequences?" All heads shook 'no.' "Well, we'll think of something. You, Shultz. Find a phone book and

241

look up the number for the Illinois State Agricultural Extension Service. Ask for the closest county agent and get him out here. Go!"

The agricultural county agent for Peoria was in the hospital for appendicitis. His doctor ordered a CT scan. The nurse came back to him, "Sorry, Doctor Robins, the CT has been down for the past week waiting for repair. The medical technology maintenance company we contract with 'went Ark' three weeks ago and we haven't found another one yet."

The doctor sighed. This was the third technology delay in the past three weeks. "Then I'll have to operate without it. We can't wait. It will take longer without the scan, but it has to be done. Book an OR for me." Repeated calls to the county agent from the USDA team went to voice mail on his deactivated cell phone in his hospital room. He was unconscious for two days and nights.

The USDA team did an internet search for crop seed enhancement and found several of Dr. Grace Washington's research articles. At a staff meeting, the team leader scratched his head. "I understand her general approach, and even the specific DNA sequences that have to be manipulated, but I don't see how she did the actual manipulations. Twenty-five years ago when I was in graduate school, we got some statistically insignificant improvements by exposing seeds to radiation. I know how to do that. So, call the local feed-and-seed supply store and order a truckload of each major crop seed cultivated in the Midwest. Call the chief and tell her we need to requisition the radiation chamber from the state university. Make it a priority federal confiscation for national security and get it trucked over here. Shultz, set up an assembly line for irradiating bags of seeds. We'll ship those out to the farms as USDA certified enhanced crop seeds. That should satisfy Secretary Zubrinski."

Later that summer, a few of those seeds yielded crops two percent above previous yields. Most did not. The shortage of working machinery and skilled crews led to reduced planting and reduced harvesting. The harvest was forty-five percent below projected yields. It would be a winter of discontent and food rationing. The elite at PRIS were pleased.

*　　*　　*　　*　　*　　*

N plus 121. The next day, in his comfortable, security guarded and gated community, Treasury Secretary Gunther walked to the end of his driveway to pick up his morning paper. He had his morning cup of coffee in his hand, enjoying the early morning coolness. Abruptly, he dropped his coffee cup. It smashed on the concrete drive. He was staring at his mailbox at the end of the driveway. It was wrapped in a chain and padlocked. He tugged at it, but the chain was wrapped too tightly. *I'll need bolt cutters*, he thought.

He looked up and down the street. Some other mailboxes had chains and padlocks on them. Many other government bureaucrats lived in the upscale neighborhood and commuted to D.C. *What the hell is going on?*

His driver picked him up in the black government-issue Towncar for his drive to work.

"Mr. Secretary? What's with all the chains on mailboxes?" his driver asked.

"Tom, I have no clue." When they got on the D.C. Beltway, Gunther's eyes were caught by a large electronic billboard they passed every morning on the commute. This morning it showed a picture of himself holding chains in his hands. The text read, "He's a Chainer, enslaving us with regulations. Every new regulation is a link in our slave chains. Resist the Chainers! Resist the New Slavery!"

"What the hell?" he blurted out.

The driver said, "Look! Here's another one." The next large electronic billboard had a picture of a mailbox wrapped in chains. The text said, "They enslave us with chains of rules and regulations. Chains mark the slave masters!"

Gunther hit the speed dial on his cell phone. "Get me Attorney General Handford. Earnest? Tom Gunther here. Have you seen this chaining thing? They got your mailbox too? We have to get the FBI on this chaining thing. They somehow hacked into these electronic billboards on the beltway, too. Get your forensic IT guys on that. They have my picture hanging out there, for God's sake! What's that? Oh, right, I know it's illegal for any government official to say the word 'God,' but it just slipped out. By the way, how is your new young liver?"

The Attorney General tagged this portion of his automatic phone recording "Treasury Secretary" and filed it for evidence against Gunther at a future show trial, if needed.

Two hours later, an investigative assistant to the Attorney General called Treasury Secretary Gunther with an update. "Mr. Secretary, here's what we have so far. A new covert action was begun by the Constitutional Resistance Movement. Links were spread across covert social networks known as freedom networks. The "followers" and other linked people are kept confidential through encryption. The latest links shared over this underground network revealed home addresses of government officials involved in actively enforcing rules and regulations by a multitude of government agencies. Police and law enforcement agents enforcing laws against violence and fraud were excluded. A new slang word is now in use: 'chainers.' They are calling those who enforce regulations 'chainers.' The campaign is to publicize the names of regulatory enforcement personnel and ridicule them."

Secretary Gunther frowned, "I assume you've cracked the encryption and are rounding up these petty vandals?"

The investigative assistant hesitated, then said, "Sir, we're working on it. Their encryption is military grade, and extremely difficult to crack. Vandalism is not a federal crime unless it's done against federal property. Private mailboxes are technically considered property of the federal government, but there are too many for the FBI to investigate. Local police are investigating the vandalism to mailboxes."

"But surely the fact that these people acted in concert on the same night proves it's a criminal conspiracy?" argued Gunther.

"Sir, the only possible link is a web site that we assume they all looked at. However, we cannot prove that they all looked at it, so we have no conspiracy case. We did find a printout of one web page instigating this vandalism, dropped by one of the vandals in a Georgetown neighborhood. I'm faxing it to your office."

Gunther's assistant came in with the fax. The page said "They put the chains of slavery on us when they enforce these thousands of rules and regulations over our daily lives. Read the Declaration of Independence. Like King George III, our own government *has erected a multitude of New Offices, and sent hither swarms of Officers to harass our people and eat out their substance.* Patriots! Use a new and random covert action to shine some publicity on them and expose them for what they really are: 'Out the Chainers.' ~your friendly neighborhood Constitutional Resistance Movement (CRM)."

Gunther crumpled the sheet and threw it into his trash can. "Patriots my foot! Petty vandals!"

Hardware stores and home improvement stores around the D.C. suburbs sold out of bolt cutters and hacksaws that day. That afternoon, many houses with chains on the mailbox were egged. Gunther's house was egged. On the way home his driver stopped for him to buy bolt cutters, but they were sold out.

As he entered his home, his wife was in full nagging mode, "Tom, this is unacceptable! I can't hold my head up at the country club. Members of the Junior League have been calling me all day long asking 'What do those chains mean on your mailbox?' When I walked into the country club dining room, I heard whispers saying 'slavery' and 'chainers' and 'slave masters.' Tom, I tell you I will not tolerate this! You and I are contributors to the United Negro College Fund. We're not racists! How dare they call us slave masters!

"And Tom, what about the eggs all over the house and windows? You know our maid doesn't do windows! Those eggs will stink in the morning! My tennis partners will see it when they drive up!"

Tom Gunther wearily called a janitorial company and scheduled them to clean the rotten eggs from the windows and brick exterior of his home.

"Lovey, it has nothing to do with racism. They're using slavery as a metaphor for what we do when we expect them to conform to regulations designed to force them to share their wealth with the planet and live a sustainable lifestyle."

Just then, his two children ran into the room. "Daddy," sobbed the oldest, "Someone called me 'Princess Slavemaster' on my Facebook page!"

The youngest added, "I'm getting tweets about my slavemaster daddy. We saw your picture on a billboard when we went to school. Do you really put chains on people? Our friends are making fun of us! It's not fair!"

This little domestic crisis was repeated in thousands of homes in the D.C. suburbs that night. Hundreds of pictures of the outed officials using bolt cutters and hack saws to cut chains from their mailboxes circulated on the internet. Not even FACTS News dared to cover the story. By the next day, everyone except the humiliated "chainers" were talking about it at work and in coffee shops. The outed ones got stares whenever they appeared in restaurants and other public venues. Often, someone in the crowd would play "clinking chains" sounds from their cell phones. At federal office buildings, employees kept their eyes downcast subserviently to avoid angering their bosses.

Chapter Nineteen

N plus 130. After ten days had passed, chains started reappearing at random intervals on mailboxes, dragging from automobile axles, on office doorknobs and on anonymous e-mails adorned with pictures of chained mailboxes. Many of the regulatory compliance personnel got a little jumpy, looking over their shoulders often when on the streets, and began driving home by varying routes. Some had packages delivered to them with chains inside. Some found their cars chained to lampposts, and graffiti spray painted on their vehicles:

"Let my people go! – CRM" "Laissez nous faire! – CRM" or "Don't Tread on Me! – CRM" were some of the graffiti slogans spray painted on windshields. Others found their cell phone ring tones had been replaced with the "clinking chains" sounds. The rate of early retirements among the regulators began to rise. So did the divorce rate.

The President summoned Attorney General Earnest Handford to the Oval Office. "Earnest! You look good. The new liver must be agreeing with you."

The AG flashed a wide grin and said, "Yes sir! It even comes with a warranty: good for ten more years of hard drinking before another replacement. Ha! Not to worry. The CDC says they've located a six-year-old girl in their database who is a match for me. In ten years I'll have another young Government Motors certified replacement liver waiting for me."

What the President didn't know was that the six-year-old girl was his daughter.

"Well, good, Earnest. Now, down to business."

"Earnest, I want you to confer with these internet search engine people and find out what they did for the Chinese Communist government to restrict access to the internet. Then do it here. We've got to shut down access to these Constitutional Resistance Movement web sites, but we've got to do it surreptitiously, so no one realizes they're being shut out. They should get messages like 'server temporarily down' and so on. At the same time, I want you to compile a database of who is attempting to access these subversive web pages. We need to round them up into high-security intern camps where we can quarantine them to prevent spreading the contamination of their thinking to the general population. We can certainly use the manpower, uh, the *personpower*, to pick corn and beans and to milk cows. Fewer and fewer people seem willing or able to keep agricultural machinery running."

"Yes sir. I'll get right on it."

"Dismissed."

*   *   *   *   *   *

N plus 132. At the Saul Alinsky American Prosperity Camp south of Chicago, the interned skilled workers and unemployed were being checked in after a day of picking corn and green beans in farm fields. The harvesting machines for corn and wheat were still broken, and nobody seemed to know how to repair them. The straw bosses of the work crews (usually those with no technical skills) set everyone to work harvesting corn by hand. They used buckets. There was a shortage of buckets, so everyone harvesting green beans were told to use their shirttails as makeshift baskets to hold what they picked. Every few feet they had to stop and walk back to the end of the cultivated row to empty their shirttails into a farm trailer. This fourteenth-century feudal-system technology was the best the straw bosses could come up with. The harvest proceeded slowly.

The interned field hands turned in early, exhausted from a twelve-hour day in the fields.

At ten p.m., commandos from the Constitutional Resistance Movement cut the barbed wire on the south end of the labor camp and crawled inside. One by one, they took out the guards with dart guns filled with a powerful narcotic. They would sleep until morning. The internees were awakened by the sound of diesel engines outside their dozens of tents and trailers requisitioned from FEMA. A few sleepy souls stumbled outside to see what was happening. A dozen big tour buses were idling in the assembly yard where the guards lined everyone up for roll call each morning. Two dozen armed commandoes with an American flag patch and a triangular "CRM" logo patch on their sleeves stood guard over the buses.

CRM, thought one woman, tucking in her shirttail. *That's the Constitutional Resistance Movement!* She turned back to the tent where her husband was emerging, "Dave! It's the Constitutional Resistance Movement! Get the kids! We're getting out of here!"

The refrain was repeated throughout the camp, "It's the Constitutional Resistance Movement! They're here to free us!"

The leader of the CRM commandoes brought out a bullhorn and called, "Attention, my fellow American citizens! We're commandoes of the Constitutional Resistance Movement, and we're here to liberate you. Grab what you can and proceed to the nearest bus. Hurry! We have less than forty minutes to get out of here. When the guards don't send in their hourly report, government troops will be sent to investigate. Hurry! Families, stay together and get on the same bus together. GO!"

Nearly a hundred internees stood back. The CRM leader approached them. "What is it? Don't you want to escape?"

One man gave a sullen reply, "We get fed and clothed here. We get free medical care here. If we go with you, can you guarantee we'll be fed and clothed?"

The CRM leader looked sad. "No, we don't guarantee any of that. Nobody will force you to work, like they do here in the camp. But if you don't work for a living on the outside, you'll starve."

The man crossed his arms defiantly. "Then we aren't going. They feed us here."

"How long were you on unemployment benefits before they brought you here?"

"Four years."

"Just remember this: cattle are fed, but they are property, commodities to be consumed. You can act like cattle, or act like free men and women. Your choice."

The commando turned and walked away. Five of the group followed him. The rest shuffled back to their tents.

The chartered buses pulled out with three hundred or so people from the camp. They drove the rest of the night and stopped at a farm field before dawn. CRM commandoes in each bus spoke up. "Everybody out! Take your things. We have to go on foot from here." When they were assembled in the field, the buses pulled away.

The leader spoke again. "We're guiding you into Canada from here. We'll be following one of the old Underground Railroad routes used to smuggle slaves to freedom before the Civil War. Tonight we're using it to smuggle slaves to freedom again. If you get separated from our group, conceal yourselves in the woods by day and travel by night. Look to the

Big Dipper to find the North Star and keep heading north. Your CRM commandoes will show you how to do this if you don't know how.

"The guides for the Underground Railroad called the Big Dipper the Drinking Gourd. They had a song to help the escaped slaves remember how to find the direction to go: 'Follow the Drinking Gourd.'" He stopped and looked around, then sang, "A*nd the old man is awaiting for to carry you to freedom, if you follow the Drinking Gourd.* We have an old man at the Canadian border who will carry you to freedom in one of the Ark locations, if you want to go there. If not, you're free to go where you will. You are all free men and women and can make up your own minds. Good luck, and may God bless us and protect us all in our journey to freedom."

A long ragtag line snaked northward in the starlight, following in the footsteps of other slaves before them; the path to freedom, made by individuals choosing to walk it, under the guiding stars of the Drinking Gourd.

*   *   *   *   *   *

N plus 133. In Judge Nathaniel Green's chambers at the federal courthouse in San Francisco, a federal prosecutor stood in front of the judge's desk. He had applied for an arrest warrant for a "coyote" who was now actively smuggling American citizens into Mexico. The northbound human smuggling of illegals was sharply down in volume, due to the crumbling American economy.

"Young man," said Judge Green, peering at him over the top of his reading glasses, "I see no citation here of a federal statute allegedly being broken."

The young prosecutor had been daydreaming, and suddenly jerked himself upright. "Your Honor, I thought, I thought . . ."

"You thought what?" *I know exactly what you thought, you punk apprentice Gestapo officer. You thought that I was safely liberal and progressive and would give you anything you wanted because you are from this liberal and progressive administration.* "I'm waiting, Mr. Federal Prosecutor."

"Your Honor, this man has been observed by our informant smuggling American Citizens into Mexico. The President has ordered that we stop this talent drain. If we arrest him, we will prevent the estimated loss of over three hundred valuable American skill sets in the next month alone."

"Skill sets? You mean three hundred American citizens?"

"Yes, your Honor."

"Were any of these American citizens taken against their will?"

"Well, no your honor, but . . ."

"Have any Mexican authorities complained that these people are illegally entering Mexico?"

"No, your Honor.

"Again, I ask you, what US federal statute has been allegedly broken by this man?"

The prosecutor shifted his feet nervously. "Well, actually, none, your Honor, but the President has directed that we stop this outflow of valuable American skills."

The judge dropped the warrant application papers into his trash can. "Then I suggest the President ask Congress to pass an actual law making it illegal to leave the country. Warrant denied."

The young man's face fell. Then he looked up. "Your Honor?"

"Yes?"

"May I speak off the record?"

"If you wish."

"I agree that this would work better if we had an actual law. I'm doing some research on this, looking for international laws that we could use as a model for drafting similar legislation here. I've requested a study assignment to the eastern part of Germany. In their legal archives there, I believe I will find old laws making it illegal for people called East Germans to escape to a place called West Germany. Also, blueprints and plans for the guard towers and machine guns they used to make East Germany one big, highly secure internee camp that kept people and their skills and talents in. I'll draft legislation based on this for use here in the United States. I think this will help my career. Until I began researching, I never knew there was ever an East Germany. Did you?"

Judge Green kept a poker face and nodded. "I've heard of it."

"Your Honor, you've been in the legal profession a long time. Any advice for a young lawyer about this?"

"No."

The young lawyer turned to leave.

Judge Green sighed. *Of course you never heard of it, you sheep. Because they don't teach history anymore. So they can do it to us all over again. But we can fight the good fight.* "Wait." The young man turned back. "Yes, here's a suggestion for you. You know how higher-up politicians and Congresspeople like impressive sounding titles?"

"Why yes, I've noticed that."

"My suggestion? Call your proposed legislation 'The Final Solution.' They'll like that."

"Yes sir. It does sound impressive. I'll do that. Thank you sir." The judge sighed and thought, *those who refuse to learn from history . . .*

After the door closed, Judge Green punched a code number on his phone that activated the encryption mode. Then he punched another set of numbers. The judge spoke rapidly, "Code name Scarlet Pimpernel. Alert your CRM and FreedomToobz.Ark agents for another surveillance video special. A young federal prosecutor is traveling to Germany to find the old East German laws that made it illegal for citizens to leave the country. And the blueprints for the guard towers, barbed wire fences, and probably the Berlin Wall itself. He proposes legislation to replicate all of it here in America. I'll send his photo and contact information over an encrypted line later tonight. Authentication code: Madison wept."

As do I, as do I, meditated the judge as he turned off the phone.

*   *   *   *   *   *

N plus 134. In the federal prison near Washington, D.C. it was time for mail call. The trustee pushing the mail cart came to Twisty Turner's cell. "Twisty? Package for you."

Twisty looked up from her bunk. "Me? Who'd want to send me anything?" She got up slowly and reached her hand through the bars for the package. It was a thick envelope, resealed with scotch tape after the prison officials had inspected it for contraband. *Return address New Zealand. I don't know nobody in New Zealand.* Popping open the flap, she found a baby blue scrunchy for holding back her ponytail, and a note.

For your hair, from the other Twisty. Enjoy. You are in my prayers. Staring at it, she whispered, "Doc!"

From the top bunk, her cell mate said, "What was that?"

"Nothing." Twisty lay back down on her bunk. She cradled the scrunchy to her chest with both hands, and smiled a small, secret smile.

*　　*　　*　　*　　*　　*

In the soft twilight of the Botswana countryside, the Kubabupe family sat together after the evening meal. In the glow of the lamp, young Moroka sat at the kitchen table reading aloud from his book. His father Mantate sat contentedly across the table, holding the baby, Tebogo, and feeding her tiny spoonfuls of porridge from a bowl. Moroka's mother, Lebo, sat at the table too. She was knitting a blanket for the baby. The lamp cast a warm yellow circle of light around the family.

Lebo's cheeks were no longer sunken. They had a healthy shine. The pantry was well stocked with mealie corn they had harvested, and other foodstuffs bought with the money earned from selling the ample harvest from the Carver's Legacy seeds. On a shelf lay the cell phone with the "hand" logo of Invisible Hand marketplace software. Beside it lay a pad of paper and pencils for Moroka's schoolwork. He had started attending the school in the nearby town, thanks to the harvest money.

The baby smiled up at her father and gurgled a small happy noise. Moroka looked up from his reading and reached over to touch the baby's small waving fist.

"Tebogo is such a happy baby," he said.

"Moroka, will you not continue reading to us?" asked his father with a smile.

Flashing a big smile, Moroka answered proudly "Yes, my father."

Looking back down at the book sent to him by Grace Washington, *Up From Slavery* by Booker T. Washington, he began to read, ". . . and I had the feeling that to get into a schoolhouse and study in this way would be about the same as getting into paradise."

*　　*　　*　　*　　*　　*

N plus 135. In New Zealand, at her lab at Nutritional Abundance Industries, Grace Washington worked on developing the next generation of enhanced crop super-seeds. She saw several promising possibilities. By the end of the day, she had outlined a research plan and schedule for her staff. The lab hummed with activity.

In his software lab at PSI, Isaiah Mercury worked on improvements for the next release of Invisible Hand software. He had already thought of ways to accomplish certain tasks with fewer lines of code, thereby speeding up the selling transactions. Each transaction would be cheaper. "Doug," he called out, "take a look at this and tell me what you think."

*　　*　　*　　*　　*　　*

N plus 135. Earlier that same day, President Fletcher toured a nationalized dairy farm in the Maryland countryside. The farm overseer led the presidential retinue through the milking barn. Over fifty internees in orange overalls were milking the cows by hand. The President paused at one stall where a young woman sat on her milking stool.

"How's it going?" asked the President. She looked up at him with a dull blank stare. Then she turned back to her work.

"They don't talk much," commented the farm overseer. "Mr. President, step over here and try this freshly skimmed cream." He offered a glass.

"Mmm. That's good." Someone handed him a towel to wipe off his milk moustache. The President looked directly at the farm overseer. "I want one hundred gallons of that cream requisitioned for the White House kitchen every day."

"Yes sir."

Hearing this, the young woman bent over her milk pail and spat into it, unobserved. Then she straightened up and resumed working.

*　　*　　*　　*　　*　　*

N plus 136. The next day, over breakfast in the kitchen of their newly rented home, Grace told Isaiah about her work. "Isaiah, the next generation of Carver's Legacy seeds will be even better. I believe that I can tweak their DNA to produce more surface compounds that repel insects. Another DNA sequence promises to be the key to absorbing and utilizing nutrients from fertilizers more efficiently, so less fertilizer is needed. We can feed more people than ever."

Isaiah held up his fork covered in gravy. "Can you find the DNA sequence for spontaneous gravy production?" She threw a biscuit at him.

She riposted, "Have you found grits at a local supermarket yet?"

254

"Nope. We'll have to grow our own corn and make our own hominy grits. How about some fast-growing corn seeds from that lab of yours?"

She grinned, "Coming right up."

"Guess who I saw yesterday?" said Isaiah. "Joanne Hancock of Solar Power and Wind Corporation. She wants to build wind farms in Australia and New Zealand. She never took federal subsidies, and her designs are actually efficient. Another refugee in Ark New Zealand."

Grace nodded, "Good for her! I'm glad we have another valuable talent free to create. Guess who I got in? My friend Regina Bell from the university. She got out with her daughter, son-in-law, and the grandchildren. I sound just like a basketball recruiter, don't I?"

Isaiah looked into her eyes, "I'm glad you recruited *me.*"

Grace smiled, "Who recruited whom?"

"I'm not saying, and you can't make me!" Isaiah ducked another flying biscuit.

He brought the coffee pot over and poured a cup for Grace. "Mmm. I love our new life together," she sighed.

"Don't get too comfy yet," said Isaiah, "What are we going to do with George T'Chaka Wright? He'll go crazy without something to do. How about a job in your lab? He's a bio-engineer like you, with a long string of patents to his name."

Grace snorted, "That lab is not big enough for the two of us! It will end up with a battle of the beakers. Uh-uh. I am very firm about the way I run my lab, and he's just too stubborn to work with me."

Isaiah laughed, "What George Bernard Shaw called the declension of an irregular English verb: I am firm, you are stubborn, he is pig-headed." Grace laughed with him.

After another sip of coffee, she said, "Not to worry. George has already been in talks with the people at FreedomToobz.Ark. The next time you see him, he will be the new Editor of the FreedomToobz.Ark news and analysis pages. A bully pulpit for someone with a lot to say."

Isaiah helped himself to another biscuit. "Perfect. That's perfect for George. A job where he can make a difference, and a job he will be good at."

Just then there was a knock at the kitchen door. "Come in!" Isaiah shouted. George and Estelle came in smiling.

"Good morning! Just in time for coffee. Sit down." Isaiah stood up and went to the stove.

"What, no barbeque for breakfast?" said George.

"I invite the man for breakfast, and he's ragging on me already. The hell I go through, just trying to be decent! Cream for your coffee?"

"Thanks," said George. "Guess who you are now speaking to?"

Isaiah returned with the coffee pot. "Let me guess . . . The new editor of news and analysis for FreedomToobz.Ark?"

George glared at him, "How did you know? Ruined my surprise."

Isaiah sat down next to Estelle and gestured at Grace with his coffee cup. "My secret source. She was so happy you weren't going to work at the NAI lab that she blurted the news."

George looked at Grace, but his glance softened. "Just for that, I ought to go give Minerva my resume."

Estelle intervened. "Oh no you don't! I've wanted more time with George for years, and this is a job he can do at home: writing." She put her hand over his. "I'll have my man in the house during the day! Imagine that." She smiled sweetly as she looked into George's eyes.

"Now *that's* an offer I can't refuse," George said slowly and contentedly, looking back at her. "Well, anyway, it is a perfect job for an educator. I'll have a chance to educate some of those nincompoops back in the States and around the world."

George looked at Isaiah. "So, Isaiah, O awesome prophet of freedom and capitalism! What's next for you?"

Isaiah smiled. "We hit twenty million transactions last week with Invisible Hand software. We're approaching the viral marketing stage where it will spread like wildfire. We have sixteen employees here in New Zealand and we need to hire eight more."

"And some of the first crops from Carver's Legacy seeds are starting to be harvested in Africa," Grace put in. "The yield is slightly better than the fourfold increase my research predicted. Excess crops will be waiting to be sold, and the cheapest way to sell it is with Invisible Hand. So, you can do well for yourself by doing good for others. That's the real moral principle of capitalism that none of those socialist busybodies ever understood. Or wanted to understand."

George looked thoughtfully into his coffee cup, then said slowly, "Grace . . . you, Isaiah, Minerva, me, and countless other scientists, engineers, entrepreneurs, and ordinary people, we are the creators. We bring to our fellow man the fruits of our minds and our hands: technology, medical advances, better nutrition, inventions, businesses small and large that serve their needs. And what do we get for it? Punished and shamed. Like the original Prometheus that you named your company after, Isaiah. What if all workers and inventors finally had enough and stopped using their brains? Acted like the dumb slaves the government wants them to be. What then?"

Grace replied, "Then we would no longer be human. To be human is to use your brain. Our tool of adaptation is our brain, not our bodies. When we no longer use our brains, we won't be able to adapt to new threats. The laws of evolutionary biology say those who do not adapt become extinct."

"Good!" said Isaiah. "We who do use the brains God gave us will survive, and those who wait for big brother government to come up with an idea to save them will starve. They'll just keep doing the same thing harder, like the pea-brained dinosaurs they are."

Estelle said, "Look at that cruise ship entering the harbor. I didn't know they called at this port."

Grace stood up and handed her a pair of binoculars that were hanging near the window. "Tell us what you see."

Estelle trained the powerful binoculars on the bow of the liner. "There's a banner draped over the bow of the ship." Her voice rose in excitement. "It reads *S.S. Noah's Ark*! I see hundreds of people lining the rails!"

Grace smiled, "The Constitutional Resistance Movement bought it six months ago through a holding company. That banner is covering up the real name of the ship. Officially, it's still a cruise ship, picking up people in Canada and America. Those are people who escaped into Canada. They used the old Underground Railroad routes; the routes used to guide escaped slaves to freedom before the American Civil War. And now those routes are helping slaves to escape once more. Thank the Lord."

The four of them looked at each other and said, "Amen."

George turned his head and gazed out the window. There was a magnificent view of the ocean. He loved panoramic views. Almost dreamily, he quoted, "And God saw everything that he had made, and, behold, it was very good. . . . and He rested on the seventh day from all his work which he had made."

George looked around the table. "My friends and fellow laborers in the vineyard, we have done much work, and there is much work still to do. I declare this an extra day of rest and gratitude to our good Lord. 'This is the day the Lord has made, let us rejoice and be glad in it.' Psalms 118:24. Look at that sunshine!" He rose and took Estelle's hand. "Anybody care to join Estelle and me for a walk on the beach? I plan to rejoice in this day and be glad in it. It is a freely given gift from our Creator, and I plan to accept the gift and enjoy it as He intended us to."

Grace rose and took Isaiah's hand. He looked at her. "You don't have to ask me twice." Together, the four of them walked into the sunshine. On the horizon, a departing raincloud sent down a rainbow.

Epilogue: Carver's Legacy

In the porte-cochere entrance to the Promethean Software International building sat a brass bas-relief sculpture of Noah's Ark, commissioned by Isaiah. It depicted Noah, his family, and the animals leaving the Ark, all looking up at a great rainbow in the clouds above them. Grace placed a brass plaque on the door with this inscription:

Dr. George Washington Carver's favorite poem,
from his memorial site at Tuskegee University, Tuskegee Alabama

EQUIPMENT

Figure it out for yourself, my lad,
You've all that the greatest of men have had,
Two arms, two hands, two legs, two eyes
And a brain to use if you would be wise.
With this equipment they all began,
So start for the top and say, "I can."

Look them over, the wise and great
They take their food from a common plate,
And similar knives and forks they use,
With similar laces they tie their shoes.
The world considers them brave and smart,
But you've all they had when they made their start.

You can triumph and come to skill,
You can be great if you only will.
You're well-equipped for what fight you choose,
You have legs and arms and a brain to use,
And the man who has risen great deeds to do
Began his life with no more than you.

You are the handicap you must face,
You are the one who must choose your place,
You must say where you want to go,
How much you will study the truth to know.

259

God has equipped you for life, but He
Lets you decide what you want to be.

Courage must come from the soul within,
The man must furnish the will to win.
So figure it out for yourself, my lad.
You were born with all that the great have had,
With your equipment they all began,
Get hold of yourself and say: "I can."
--Edgar A. Guest

Go ye and do likewise. ~ Grace Washington and Isaiah Mercury

*(Author's note: this poem is posted on the web site
of Tuskegee University)*

The Noah Option is Michael McCarthy's first novel.
He is now at work on the sequel, **The Rainbow Option.**

To visit ".ARK" go to www.TheNoahOption.com and click on .ARK

A sneak peek at the upcoming sequel:

The Rainbow Option.

(Note: some scenes in *The Rainbow Option* overlap the time frame of *The Noah Option.)*

That same night, Judge Barry Block pulled his Mercedes Roadster into his garage and triggered the garage door closer. Walking up the stairs he loosened his tie.

"Arjana! I'm home. What's for supper?" No answer. Walking into the kitchen, he opened the refrigerator and grabbed a bottle of beer. It was warm. *What the hell, he thought.* Feeling the milk cartons, they were warm also. Everything had spoiled. *Odd, the power was on to open the garage door.* He went to the light switch and flipped it. Nothing. *Not again!*

"Arjana! What the hell is going on?" No answer. He walked upstairs to their bedroom. Taped to a poster of the four-poster bed was a note.

Barry, the power is off again. I called the power company. Gone to the deli for take out. Back by 6:30. ~ Arjana.

He looked at his watch. 6 p.m. He would have to wait for supper.

Cursing, he went back downstairs. Picking up the phone in his study, he intended to call the power company. It was dead. He took out his cell. It was dead too. *And I just recharged it in the car on the way home. This is the same as the last time. What's going on?*

Apprehensively, he opened the front door. No poster taped to his door this time. Sighing with relief, he started to walk to the neighbor's house to use the phone. Then he saw the power company truck pull up, a crew cab with four doors. Grunting with relief, he changed direction and walked over to it. As before, three men in power company uniforms got out of the truck. They were the same men who had responded to his previous power outage.

"Why does it take three of you to do a simple repair job?" began the judge angrily.

"Union rules, Judge. Two for safety and one more just in case."

"Just in case of what?" asked the judge.

"Just in case we encounter a ruthless narcissist armed with arbitrary government power like you," said the tall man. One man slipped behind the judge and clamped a chloroformed cloth over his nose. The other one hoisted the judge in a fireman's carry as the judge lost consciousness.

"Time for the next lesson, Judge," said the tall man. They placed Federal Judge Barry Block in the back seat of the truck. They drove away, unnoticed by the neighbors watching the CBC Nightly News in their living rooms.

*   *   *   *   *   *

Judge Block woke up feeling cold. He didn't know it, but he was deep in the Sierra Nevada Mountains. Before him was a small stream. Behind him was an old log cabin, nearly invisible under the trees in the darkness. Three men wearing goose down parkas sat on logs around a fire. Their hands were extended toward the fire. Shaking, Judge Block got to his feet. He was wearing only the dress shirt and pants he had worn to the office. He went to the fire and extended his hands to warm himself.

"Good evening Judge," said the tall man. "Blanket?" He held out a woolen blanket. Block took it without a word and wrapped it around himself.

"Where am I?"

"That's for us to know and you to find out," one of the men said.

"Ever been a boy scout, Judge?" the third man asked. Block shook his head. "Too bad. Have a seat." Block sat down on a log across from the three and looked at them across the fire.

The tall man spoke. "Here's the deal, Judge. This is a *Course In Reality*. It's not optional, because reality is not optional. This part is called *Living With Your Answers – Part II*. You issued an injunction last Tuesday blocking the sale of high-yield crop seeds, a legal transaction between consenting adults. That was your "answer," your legal answer, even though there is not one law, not one precedent, not one article in the US Constitution that supports that position. You cited a higher standard, although jurisprudence does not admit any standards not in the US Constitution or US legal code. You unilaterally made up your own standard instead of waiting for our elected representatives in Congress to

262

pass a law. Your standard, your answer, was that 'the needs of the many outweigh the needs of the few.' You never considered the rights of the few, or of the many, because you decided that you alone had the right to decide who has rights.

"Very well. Now you will learn to live with that answer, *your answer*. The rights of millions of third-world farmers to freely decide to buy enhanced seeds, or not, outweigh your need to abuse your power and exceed your legal authority. You will now have to live as they do, as a refugee, and *eat like they do*, on their meager subsistence diet. For the first time, the answers you impose on others, others who are guilty of no crime, you will have to live with yourself.

"This section of *A Course in Reality* lasts ten weeks. You will live here through your own efforts. Then we will bring you out of the woods. Guards are posted at a one-day's march in every direction, so if you try to escape, you will be captured and returned. We have given out a story that you are visiting your in-laws in Albania for ten weeks. Your wife Arjana is in fact on her way to visit relatives in Albania. She was told that you're in de-tox. She was delighted to hear it. So, there will be no search for you.

"There is your cabin for shelter. You have your blanket. Here's a down parka. We're leaving you with enough food for ten weeks, if you confine yourself to one can of food per day. If you want more, we've left you some seeds, *conventional seeds*, which you can plant. It's April, so if you plant immediately, you will have some edible vegetables to eat by late May. Of course, these seeds will require you to give them a lot of water, pick insects off the sprouts before the vegetable is ruined, and manually mulch them with leaves for fertilizer. Then you will eat a bit better, with a fresh food supplement to your canned goods. If your gums begin to bleed, it means you need fresh vegetables for vitamin C.

"You have a shovel to garden with, and an axe to cut firewood. There is a grill, a spit, and a fry pan for your cooking in the cabin fireplace. You have only one day's worth of firewood, so you will have to begin cutting firewood first thing in the morning. Burns calories. Good exercise for you. Except that it burns more calories than you will get from your one can of food a day. If you eat more than one can a day, you will run out of food before the end of the two months and starve. Your choice. You also have a bow and three arrows, if you

263

would like to hunt for a food supplement. There is also a knife for gutting and skinning any game you shoot.

"There are also some books that you can read by firelight, if you wish. The Wilderness Survival Guide, the Bible, Milton Friedman, Thomas Sowell, Walter Williams, Ayn Rand, the Federalist Papers, the US Constitution.

"Subsistence living, for a man who forced subsistence living on others. Live with your own answers. Any questions?"

The judge looked terrified. "This isn't safe! What if I'm injured and need medical help?"

"There's a first-aid kit in the cabin with the same supplies that any family in rural Botswana has. Not much. Good luck, Judge. You'll need it. One other thing helps."

"What?"

"Prayer. If you're humble enough to ask for God's help, you may get it. But often, His help comes in a way you didn't expect."

With that, the three men stood up and walked away. The judge stared numbly into the flames of the campfire.

*   *   *   *   *   *

Three days later, Judge Barry Block was still in the denial stage of his predicament. He kept thinking, *A Course in Reality? What are they talking about? Living with Your Answers? Don't they know I give the answers? I'm a federal judge!* He couldn't believe he was really abandoned to live on his own in the woods, and kept hoping that someone would show up to rescue him.

He did nothing for the first three days. He had burned up his one-day supply of firewood the first night in the cabin fireplace with a big roaring fire. Since then, he had chopped no firewood. He lay curled in a fetal position at night under his blanket in the cabin, shivering and listening to owl hoots and coyote calls. Once he thought he heard a panther scream. During the day, he had sat staring at the ashes of the campfire, feeling sorry for himself. *Why me? Who are these people? If I get out of here alive, I'll see that they rot in jail!*

On day four, he had had enough of being cold all night. He tramped around in the woods with the axe, looking for fallen wood. He found plenty, but he had to chop it into lengths he could carry. He gathered wood all day long. That night, he built a tiny fire in the fireplace and moved his blanket to sleep as close to the fire as he could. Several times in the night he woke up cold and put more wood on the fire, but only a little.

On the morning of day five he had plenty of wood left to build up the fire and heat his can of food. He ate half and set the remainder of the can on the rough wooden mantelpiece. He began digging and planting the garden that morning. In the afternoon, he went in search of more firewood. In the evening, he picked up the half-full can, intending to heat it on the fire. It was covered with ants. He shrugged and put it on the grate over the fire anyway. *Extra protein.*

On the afternoon of day seven, he decided he was ready to practice with the bow and arrow. Only three arrows! He spent an hour firing arrows at a stump. Finally he managed to hit the stump on three out of five tries. Now he decided to try for a rabbit. He had seen a lot of them in the woods. When startled, they zigged and zagged in spurts of speed that he could never hope to follow and lead with his aim. He would have to sneak up on a rabbit that was standing still. Suddenly, he saw one. Carefully, he stepped closer. A twig snapped under his foot. The rabbit ran off. *Damn!*

He threw down the bow in a temper tantrum. "I'm a federal judge!" he screamed. He kicked at a downed tree trunk. "Ow!" he yelled, hopping on one foot. Finally he sat down on it. After three minutes of deep breathing, he started thinking about his situation. *I can't overrule a rabbit as if I'm the judge of the forest. This is reality, not my courtroom. An injunction won't make this tree into firewood. Only me and an axe. A brief won't put a rabbit to roast on the spit. Only me and the bow and arrow. Get to work, Barry.*

He carefully began to look for another rabbit.

By day eight, Judge Barry Block was a mass of blisters: blisters on his feet, blisters on his hands. And sore! Sore legs from walking. Sore arms and back from chopping wood and spading the garden. Sore legs from walking back and forth from the stream with small cans of water to water his planted seeds. He had so far opened and eaten thirteen cans of food. He couldn't help himself. He was so hungry! Taking stock, he realized he would be fasting for the last five days of his exile. Unless . . . he could get these seeds to grow, or catch fish and game. Or find edible wild plants. Or all of the above.

By day ten, the relative quiet and loneliness of the woods began to bring him some small measure of quiet in his mind. Instead of the constant *why me, why me, why me,* his thoughts began to follow the sequence of the task at hand. *There's a downed limb. Chop it into two-foot sections that I can carry easily. There's another. Chop.* At night, he used the sharpening stone left for him to sharpen the axe blade.

The repetition of the manual work of digging and chopping and honing began to take on a rhythm as his muscles grew stronger and less sore. Without realizing it, he was acquiring the spiritual discipline known to monks as working meditation. He took satisfaction in the solid *chunk* sound of the axe biting into the wood, and the solid resistance he felt in his arms as it hit.

*   *   *   *   *   *

Judge Block settled into a routine in his *Course in Reality* in the woods. In the morning, weed, spade, and water the garden. After lunch, search out firewood and split it for the evening fire. At twilight, when the rabbits were more active, practice stalking them. On day twelve, he got one. He gutted it as best he could and roasted it on a spit over the fire. After eating a small portion that night, he raised the spit and left it to smoke the rest of the night. According to his Wilderness Survival Guide, smoked meat would last longer. He disciplined himself to eat sparingly, and made the rabbit his only food for two days. On the third day after that, he got another rabbit. He grunted in satisfaction when the arrow struck its target. He became aware of his own feeling of satisfaction and then lowered the bow, thinking, *am I taking satisfaction in killing things?*

He sat down on a log and thought about it. *No, I don't pull the wings off flies or look for things to kill for the fun of it. I am taking satisfaction in my own increasing competence at surviving in the woods.* He got up and retrieved the rabbit and headed back to the cabin, whistling. Another two days of food without opening cans. He had made up for four of the five cans that he had consumed above the one can per day supplied to him for the ten weeks.

Suddenly, he stopped. He had an epiphany. *When I ate those five cans, I was borrowing against my own future. Except that out here, there is no "next generation" to pay back what I borrowed. I borrowed from myself, and it was up to me to pay myself back, or starve the last five days. This is what the government does with deficit spending, except that they evade the issue by assuming that the next generation will pay the debt. Now, I understand why that's wrong. Out here, I have to work to earn the extra food to pay myself back. I've had to painfully learn to use a bow and arrow, and then learn to stalk rabbits, and then figure out the best time of day to hunt, and then spend that time each day hunting. This rabbit is the fruit of my labor.*

He started walking back to the cabin. He gutted the rabbit and hung it up in the cabin. *I'll cook it tomorrow morning*, he thought. Amazingly, he wasn't hungry. He stoked the fire and went to bed.

The next morning he built up the fire and found the spit. Then he looked where he had hung the rabbit. It was gone! He nearly panicked. *What could have happened to it?* Then he saw the note on the mantelpiece. "Hi Judge. We needed food and didn't want to hunt today, so we took your rabbit. There are four of us, and only one of you, so our needs outweighed yours. Your friendly guards." *Damn! It wasn't fair! They have access to food from the outside world and I don't. I worked hard to get that rabbit and they just took it!*

He slumped, realizing that now he was still three cans down on his food budget. He sighed and opened a can for breakfast. After breakfast, he sat on a log at the campfire pit and tried to come to terms with his loss. *I tried, I learned, I worked, and now this. All my effort and it still wasn't enough. No matter how good I get at this, I can't do everything that is needed. I give up.* His shoulders slumped and he hung his head.

Suddenly, his head popped up. He had another epiphany. *That's right. I can't do everything. The tall guy said to pray and to ask for help. Ask God for help. I've never believed in God, but I need help from someone or something bigger than myself. I'm going to try.*

Judge Barry Block knelt down in the dirt in his filthy clothes and folded his hands together. Lord God, I've never believed in you before, so I'm not sure what to say. I can't do everything I need to do to survive. I can't do it by myself. I'm stuck and I need help. I need your help, and I ask you to give me help to survive out here. I hope there is something in this universe bigger and wiser and more powerful than me, who cares enough to take an interest in me. I'm calling that something God and I'm asking you, God, for help. Thanks for listening.

He rose up. Oddly, he felt better. He began to tend the garden. That evening, he got another rabbit. This time, he cooked it that night and let the remainder smoke. He blocked the door with the heavy wooden table before he went to bed.

*   *   *   *   *   *

On day eighteen of his coursework in the woods, Judge Barry Block woke up with a start early in the morning. It was still dark. He felt rain on his face. He threw back his blanket and stood up. Lightning flashed, revealing a hole in the roof where a large tree branch had fallen during the storm. For protection from the rain, he moved his blanket under the large table and tried to get back to sleep. When it was daylight, he surveyed the damage. A pine branch had punctured the roof. There were no materials to repair the cedar shake roof. He looked around at his surroundings. *Aha! I think I see a way to improvise.*

When he made his foraging trek for firewood, he looked for low-hanging pine boughs with lots of pine needles. He brought some back with each load of firewood. When he judged he had enough, he dragged out the table and bench from inside the cabin. He placed the table next to the cabin wall, and then the bench on top of the table. Next he piled all the pine boughs on top of the bench. He climbed up and stood on the bench and threw the boughs onto the roof. This brought him high enough to pull himself up and shimmy his way onto the roof. He then pulled out the branch that had caused the damage, and made a kind of thatch of pine boughs over the hole. He used pieces of firewood to weight it down.

Back on the ground, he surveyed his work. *Funny,* he thought. *I take as much satisfaction with this work as I do with legal work. Maybe more, because it's tangible. I can see the results, and they're pretty good, for a repair without proper materials or tools.* Whistling, he took his bow and arrows and went hunting. He got his rabbit.

When he returned to the cabin, he found three filleted trout, a package of butter, and a filet knife on his table with a note. "Judge, The Lord helps those who help themselves, and so do we. After we saw how you went to work and repaired your own roof, we thought we'd lend a hand. These filets can be broiled on your grill, or fried with the butter. There's a fishing rod in the corner with three hooked flies. Best spot is a

268

pool about 300 yards downstream. Best time is early morning. The knife is sharp, so be careful. ~ Your Guards."

Stunned, he sat down. Tears came to his eyes, as he remembered what the tall man had said, "If you ask for help, the Lord will give it to you. But it will come in a way that you didn't expect." *Thank you, God. I'm grateful for this help.* He wiped his eyes and got up and built a fire. Then he spread butter in the pan and on the trout filets. After they were cooked, he set aside two filets for the next day.

He took a bite. *Umm*, he thought. *Best I've ever had.* He sat on the hearth and continued his reading in the Thomas Sowell book, by firelight.

*   *   *   *   *   *

On day fifty-five of his Course in Reality in the forest, some of Barry Block's green beans, new potatoes, and green onions were ready to pick and eat. On day fifty-six, some tomatoes were ripe enough to pick. He picked enough for four meals. He now had plenty of food to last him until day seventy. On day fifty-seven, he returned after his trek for firewood to find a bottle of beer, a shaker of salt, and some cut-up steak. And another note.

"Congratulations! Your gardening work is paying off. This meat, plus your vegetables, will make a great beef stew in your fry pan. Enjoy the beer. ~ your guards." Barry smiled, shook some salt on his palm and licked it. *Umm.*

*   *   *   *   *   *

On day seventy, Barry Block was fit, tanned, and self-reliant. He was healthy. He was forty pounds lighter and down to what his doctor would call his ideal body weight for his age.

His muscles were toned and he was sleeping like a baby, without alcohol. He woke up early, caught six trout, filleted them, and began frying all six with the remaining butter. He was just removing the first fillet when his five guards showed up, including the tall man.

"Gentlemen, you're just in time for a hot breakfast. Welcome, and sit down!"

The tall man smiled. "Why thank you, Judge. We brought coffee and biscuits." He held up a large thermos. Another man held up a bag from a fast food restaurant. They sat down and began to eat in fellowship.

After breakfast, one of the guards handed a small backpack to Barry. "Here's a change of clothes. There's some soap in there, in case you want to wash up at the creek. A towel, too."

Barry smiled and said, "Thanks." He hoisted the pack and went down to the creek. He returned refreshed and smelling better.

The tall man produced a small mirror. "Judge, did any of these squirrels tell you that you look like Abraham Lincoln now that you have a beard and are skinnier?"

Barry looked at himself in the mirror. "Just don't invite me to any theatre performances!" They all laughed.

Barry looked around at each of their faces. "Fellas? Unless you're in a hurry, I want to talk a while before we go. This time in the woods has changed me, perhaps more than you expected. Got a few minutes?" They all nodded, and sat back down on the logs around the fire pit.

Barry began, "First of all, I now know firsthand how hard it is to raise your own food . . . ." He talked for a long time about his experiences and what he had learned from his *Course in Reality*. He was a changed man; changed by living with his answers. Changed by living in a real world that he couldn't change with an abstract legal ruling.

On the drive back to San Francisco, Barry Block continued his conversation with the five men. "Guys, I know you can't trust me yet, but I want to become a member of the Constitutional Resistance Movement. I want to help roll back this governmental madness that I helped create."

The five men looked at one another and said nothing. "We'll see," said the tall man.

*   *   *   *   *   *

For more excerpts from this book, visit www.TheNoahOption.com
To visit ".ARK" go to www.TheNoahOption.com and click on .ARK

www.ingramcontent.com/pod-product-compliance
Lightning Source LLC
Chambersburg PA
CBHW072205170626
46813CB00003B/804